A Cry in the Dark

Books by Denise Grover Swank

Discover Denise's other books at
denisegroverswank.com

A Cry in the Dark

Carly Moore Book One

Denise Grover Swank

D^G_S

Chapter One

N o, no, no, no, NO!" I shouted, banging the heel of my hand on the steering wheel of my Honda.

"Dammit!"

This could not be happening again.

I popped the hood of my car, got out, and circled around the front. It took me three tries to get the hood propped on its stand, but I wasn't sure why I was even bothering. I hadn't learned anything about car engines since my last car had broken down in Southern Arkansas, where I'd met people who'd helped me, strangers who had become friends. That kind of luck didn't happen twice.

Leaning over the engine, I looked over all the hoses—intact—and the radiator—not steaming—which meant I had no idea what was wrong with it.

I was in a parking lot off Highway 25 at a scenic pull-off overlooking the Smoky Mountains and what I presumed was the Tennessee–North Carolina state border. It was an off-the-beaten-path road, which meant I was basically in the middle of nowhere. I'd crisscrossed the state lines a couple of times since I'd left Gatlinburg, but I was fairly sure I was currently in

Tennessee—only fairly sure because I'd lost cell service a couple of hours ago.

I was in big trouble.

Pissed, I swiped my hair out of my face and turned to face the view, suddenly overcome with rage. The fact that it was beautiful just made me madder. I'd pulled over to the lookout on a whim less than five minutes ago, wanting to get one last look at the Smokies. I'd spent a few minutes staring at them, soaking in the sight and trying to feel something, only to return to the car and find it wouldn't start.

I pulled the burner phone I was using out of my jeans pocket, not surprised to still see the no service symbol in the top left corner. Which meant I couldn't call a roadside service. Besides, where would I have them tow it? The last town I remembered passing through was in North Carolina, but that had been a good hour or so ago, minus this stop. The tow bill was going to be astronomical.

What in the hell was I going to do?

The hum of an approaching car caught my attention, and I wasn't sure whether to hide or try to flag the driver down. Ideally, I'd check out who was in the car before making the decision. A family with kids was a safe-enough bet. A solitary guy in a beat-up truck—maybe not. The problem was that the lookout was at the edge of a curve in the road, so I wouldn't have much opportunity to make the call.

The car breezed by, a small, older hatchback. I couldn't make out who was inside, but the way they zoomed past and kept on going, it was obvious they weren't going to stop.

Which meant I had no choice but to wait for the next car.

The next vehicle didn't show up for another twenty minutes. The 18-wheeler was struggling to handle the steep downgrade, its brakes announcing its appearance a good thirty seconds before it drove right on past, but I'd already decided I was okay with that. I'd heard too many stories about over-the-road truckers, although I suspected most had been embellished.

I briefly considered sitting inside the car. I was still standing outside, my butt leaning against the driver's door so I could get a good view of the approaching vehicles. The early November mountain air was chilly, probably in the 40s—cold enough the cold metal of the car cut right through my jeans. But I stayed put. I'd take the cold over the stench of smoke ingrained in the interior.

My plan, inasmuch as I had one, was to head to Wilmington and look for a job. It would be suitably far from the people who were looking for me, plus I'd always liked the ocean. But en route to the coast, the sign for Gatlinburg had grabbed at me. My mother's grandparents had taken her there when she was a kid and my mom had told me that story so many times that after all these years I still remembered their trip as if I'd been there myself. She'd been dead for over two decades, and they'd been gone for even longer, but I still missed her. Fiercely.

So I'd taken the exit to Gatlinburg hoping I'd feel closer to her if I did all the things she'd told me about. Hoping it might…inspire me in some way. But it turned out that Dollywood was closed the first week of November, and I didn't have the right shoes or clothes to hike in the Smoky Mountains National Park. So in the end, I'd mostly just lain in bed for four days and watched TV, with a splurge on The Pancake House for breakfast a couple of mornings, and rode the Smoky Mountain Wheel, getting a view of the mountains in one of the all-glass gondolas. My mother hadn't mentioned the gondola trip, but I'd felt the need to do *something*. When I finally felt ready to move on, having spent several hundred dollars I couldn't afford on a pity party that had somehow made me feel worse, the clerk had suggested I take the back roads to enjoy the last of the fall foliage.

Which had brought me here.

The sun would be setting in a few hours and I had some decisions to make. Did I continue to wait for someone to stop? Or did I start walking? I had no idea how far I'd have to hoof it, not to mention it would be suicidal to walk on the winding, narrow two-lane road at night.

I wished I'd taken that paper map the desk clerk had offered.

Leaving the car, I perched on a boulder at the edge of the lookout, tucking my knees under my chin and staring out into the scenery. Cold seeped into my butt through my jeans, but the view truly was beautiful. The bright shades of yellow, orange, and red that the mountain trees were known for had begun to fade and fall, but it was still breathtaking, making me feel a little less sorry I'd stopped to take it in.

Lost in thought, I didn't hear a vehicle approach, so I startled when a man said, "Having car trouble?"

Heart racing, I turned to face him. How could I have been so careless?

I jumped to my feet, taking a defensive stance, which was utterly ridiculous. I was on a ledge. All he had to do was give me a hard shove, and I'd tumble right over. He definitely looked strong enough to do it.

I scrambled over the rock onto the sidewalk, sizing him up as I prepared to face him.

I guessed he was in his early to mid-thirties, and he looked like he was used to manual labor. The beat-up red tow truck behind him helped confirm my presumption. He was handsome in a rugged sort of way, with overgrown brown hair and eyes to match, and had on a brown work jacket, dark T-shirt, dirty jeans, and work boots. Something about the way he carried himself—full of confidence and self-assurance—made me apprehensive.

Yet it also stirred something inside me, a feeling I hadn't experienced in a long, long time.

Not now, Carly.

It took me a second to realize I still hadn't answered him. "Yeah."

"Do you know what's wrong with it?" he asked, glancing down at the still-exposed engine.

"It won't start," I said, walking toward the car and trying to avoid eye contact. Hoping my previously dormant feelings would go back into hiding. "It makes a grinding noise when I turn the key."

"You got someone comin' for you?"

My breath caught. I didn't know anything about this man. For all I knew, he was seeking confirmation that there wouldn't be any witnesses to my abduction. Or perhaps he was a garden-variety psychopath, someone who preyed on women out on their own. Why had I left my gun in the car?

Careless. I wouldn't be making that mistake again. I needed to be even more guarded since I was apparently attracted to him. Just because a guy was good-looking didn't mean he was trustworthy. Indeed, the opposite was often true.

Sensing my apprehension, he held up his hands in surrender. "I only want to know if you need my help. If not, I'll be on my way." When I still didn't answer him, he said, "Would you like me to turn it over and see what I think? Maybe it's an easy fix." He gestured to his truck. "I know what I'm doing, and I won't charge you just to look."

"Yeah…okay." My heartbeat picked up again. My purse was on the passenger seat, and my gun was inside. What if he found my gun and used it against me?

He followed my gaze to the front seat, then took a step back. "All I want to do is check the engine, but if you'd prefer for me to call someone, I understand."

I'd been out here over an hour, and now that I'd gotten up from the rock, I realized how stiff and cold I'd gotten. He was the first person to stop, not to mention he was driving a tow truck, for heaven's sake. He was literally what I needed—a direct answer to the prayer I hadn't said.

"No," I finally said, running a hand through my hair. It had been short for a couple of weeks now, cut into an angled bob that wouldn't yield to a ponytail, and I still couldn't get used to the length. Or the auburn color. When I looked in the mirror, I sometimes had trouble recognizing myself.

I tried to cover my unease with a tight smile as I lowered my hand to my side. "Sorry. I'm just a little jumpy."

He held up his hands again. "Understandable." Taking several more steps backward, he nodded toward my car. "How about you get your purse out before I get in? All I need is the key."

Obviously I wasn't doing a great job of guarding my expression, but I didn't think he was playing me. Besides, once I had my purse and my gun, I'd feel a hell of a lot better about the whole situation. "I don't mean to insult you…"

"I'm not insulted," he said, taking two more steps backward. "You're smart to be wary. You get what you need, and then I'll check it out."

Keeping an eye on him as I opened the passenger door, I grabbed my purse and slung both straps over my right shoulder, clutching it to my side. "The key's still in the ignition."

He'd been watching me with guarded curiosity, but now his mouth tipped into a hint of a grin. "You left the keys in the ignition?"

I was acting so cautious—as though I feared he'd rob me blind—that I could see why he was amused. "It won't start, so it's not like someone could steal it." I shrugged. "Unless you have a magic touch."

His grin spread.

Blood rushed to my cheeks, stinging my windblown skin. "With cars."

Amusement filled his eyes. "I've been told that too."

Just when I thought my face might actually combust, he got into the car. The grinding sound followed a few seconds later. He climbed out and walked around to the engine for a few moments, then said, "When was the last time you had the oil changed?"

"I haven't," I admitted. "I just got this thing a couple of weeks ago."

His brow shot up. "You didn't ask for the maintenance record?"

My friends in Arkansas had given me the car, just like they'd arranged for the documents in my purse. I hadn't been in a position to haggle or ask for details. "No."

He scowled as though I'd committed a cardinal sin against car ownership, which I supposed I had. "I think the engine's seized."

My heart sank. "I take it that's not something you can fix?"

"I can…but not here," he said, but he didn't sound sure. He closed the hood. "I'd need to tow it to my garage."

Studying him, I worried my bottom lip between my teeth. "How much is that going to cost?"

"This far up the mountain?" He rubbed the back of his neck. "The tow will run you seventy-five. Then I can dig into it tomorrow and give you an estimate on the repair."

The towing charge wasn't as bad as I'd thought, but the rest of his statement gave me pause. "Tomorrow?"

"It's gonna take some time to tear it apart, and after I figure out what's wrong, I'll need to get parts. I suspect we're lookin' at a couple of days."

A couple of days? Which meant at least two more nights in a motel, plus meals, not to mention the cost of the repairs. "What do you think it's going to cost?"

"I won't know until I get in and look around."

This felt an awful lot like déjà vu. This is exactly what had happened to me in Arkansas, where I'd spent the last few months. In some ways, it felt like fate had brought me there, to the very people who could help me with my...unique situation. Rose Gardner and Neely Kate Rivers had found me by the side of the road. They'd offered me shelter and kindness, and eventually I had spilled my secrets to them. When it had come time for me to leave, they had known exactly how to help me. How to *hide* me. Except I'd made a mistake and landed myself back in the same situation. Borrowed car, seized engine. Dependent on the kindness of strangers. But this time the breakdown felt a lot more like carelessness than fate.

Why hadn't I thought to check the oil? It would likely cost more money to repair the car than I had in my shiny new bank account. My stomach twisted into a knot.

"I understand if you don't trust me to work on your car, what with you being a captive audience and all," he said. "If you prefer, I can tow it into Greeneville, but I can't do it until tomorrow."

"How much?" I blurted out.

He hesitated. "It's a haul down there," he said with a frown. "An hour from my shop. I'd have to make it worth my time, which would include the trip back."

"I understand," I said, then repeated, "How much?"

"Three hundred."

Shit. But he didn't seem like he was trying to screw me over, and I didn't see the point in having the car towed to a bigger city, where everything was likely to be more expensive.

"Or I could tow it to Ewing." He paused and rubbed his chin. "That would only be about an hour and a half round trip for me, so let's make it two hundred."

That wasn't much better.

"Maybe you'd rather call someone to come get you," he said. "You can use my radio since your phone probably doesn't work up here."

He could have been asking to make sure I was really alone, but I didn't think so. Although I certainly wouldn't call myself the best judge of people—I'd gotten myself into this situation by trusting the wrong people—I admired his sense of integrity. It made me want to trust him. Or maybe it was my desperation influencing me. "No. There's no one close enough to call."

He nodded. "I saw the Georgia plates, so I didn't think so, but didn't want to presume." He turned to look out at the view, soaking it in for a moment, and shifted his weight. "There's another option." He turned back to face me. "I can call a deputy sheriff to pick you up and take you to Ewing. Then you can figure out what to do about your car later." He gave me a lopsided grin. "That's your cheapest option at the moment. You'll still have to tow the car, but it will give you time to figure everything out."

My heart skipped a beat.

"No. No sheriff," I said a little too quickly. A deputy might ask for ID, and while I'd been assured my new identity was solid, I wasn't ready to test it quite yet.

Some of the warmth faded from his eyes, but he nodded. "Okay. That option's off the table. Do you need a minute to consider the others?"

"No," I said, feeling nauseated at the amount of money I was about to hemorrhage, but it wasn't like I had a choice. "Just tow it to your garage."

"I'll do my best to keep the cost of the repairs as low as possible."

Call me stupid, but I believed him.

Chapter Two

He gestured toward the car. "It's going to take me a few minutes to get it loaded. If you have anything you need to get out, you'd best do it now."

"Uh, yeah," I said, my nervousness returning. "I have a suitcase in the trunk."

He grabbed the keys out of the ignition, then walked around and opened the trunk, barely exerting himself to heave out my suitcase.

I'd lifted that bag. I knew how heavy it was, which meant his jacket was covering up some impressive biceps.

I shivered, partially from cold but also from the realization that this man could easily overpower me. I held my purse tighter. I had a gun, but could I bring myself to use it? It was one thing to shoot cans off fence posts, and a whole other thing to shoot a man. If I needed to pull it out, I hoped the threat would be enough to get my point across.

He must have seen something on my face—again—because he cast me a wary look as he walked to the truck, holding the nearly fifty-pound bag as though it were a roll of toilet paper.

Yep. He definitely worked out.

"It's a good thing we're getting you out of here now," he said, glancing up at the sky before lowering his gaze to mine. "They're saying it might snow."

"Snow?" I hadn't paid any attention to the weather. *Smart, Carly.* Way to drive into the mountains with the possibility of snow, though to be fair, if my car hadn't broken down, I suspected I wouldn't be in the mountains anymore.

"Yep." He opened the passenger door of the truck and tossed the bag into the cab, easily maneuvering it into the space behind the seat. When he stepped down, he held the door open. "Why don't you wait in the truck while I get this hooked up?"

I glanced inside, surprised by its tidiness. Based on the peeling paint and extensive rust spots, the truck had to be a couple of decades old, so I'd expected the interior to be in similar condition. While the black vinyl seat was ripped in multiple places, for the most part it was clean.

"Uh…" I said, glancing up at him. "I'm about to get into your truck, and I don't even know who you are."

"Wyatt Drummond, owner of Drummond Auto Repair and Towing." To my surprise, he held out his hand to shake.

His callused hand was grease-stained, but it looked clean. I shook it, surprised it felt so warm wrapped around my cold one. I wasn't prepared for the shiver that ran through my body at his touch, but I tried to convince myself it was because of the frigid temperature.

"Carly Moore," I said, proud that I'd remembered my new last name. I'd spent a week and a half practicing in front of a mirror while I waited for my documents to come through in Little Rock. I'd had little else to do, given I'd left my new friends behind in Henryetta.

17

His handshake was firm, but he quickly released it. "Now that you know who I am, get inside and I'll start the truck so you can warm up."

Without waiting to see if I'd listen, he walked around the front of the truck and climbed behind the wheel to start the engine.

I almost insisted I'd wait outside, but the wind had picked up, delivering a cold bite that stung my cheeks. I'd already agreed to let him tow my car into town. No sense being stubborn for the sake of it.

The cab heated up quickly, so I reached over and turned the heat down. A few minutes later, Wyatt climbed back inside and backed the truck up to the front of my car. Somehow he'd managed to back my car out of its space and get it angled correctly. It didn't take him long to get the car hooked up and hoisted onto the winch.

By the time he returned to the cab, the sky was turning a light pink with the approaching sunset. He didn't say anything, and for some reason I felt compelled to fill the silence.

"It gets dark early out here," I said as he pulled onto the road. Since the dashboard was old and didn't have a digital display, I took out my phone to check the time. It was nearly five. How long had I been out here?

"The mountains to the west make sundown come earlier, and the time change this weekend didn't help," Wyatt said, shifting gears.

"Where exactly are we going?" I said. "I just realized I never asked."

"Drum," he said. "It's about ten miles down the mountain. I figure I'll drop you off at the tavern and then haul your car to the shop. My brother Max owns the place and runs the motel across the street. He'll rent you a room for the night."

My guard hiked back up. Was this some kind of scam? Tow unsuspecting tourists into town for a small fee, then charge them inflated prices for motel rooms? I knew I was being paranoid, but I was on the run and had an alias. Was there such a thing as being too paranoid in this kind of situation?

I hugged my purse tighter to my side. "Should I call ahead and reserve a room?"

"Nah," he said, keeping his eyes on the curvy mountain road, downshifting to accommodate the grade. "You'll be fine."

"There's not much traffic," I said, realizing I hadn't seen another car for nearly an hour. "I figured there'd be more people driving the roads to see the changing leaves. Isn't the Smoky Mountains known for that?"

"There used to be more people in these parts about five years ago," Wyatt said. "But things changed when the state park system moved the entrance to the hiking trail up to Balder Mountain. This road used to take hikers to the entrance, so Drum sees a whole lot less traffic now. It was a tourist town until the move. Then business dried up, which is why I'm certain Max will have a room available."

"Oh," I said, "I'm sorry."

He gave her a wry grin. "Probably for the best."

I wasn't sure what to make of that.

"What were you doin' out this way?" he said. "If you don't mind me asking?" It was an innocent-enough question, but the friendly tone he'd had at first seemed to have dried up. Just like the look in his eyes had changed when I'd refused his suggestion to call in a deputy.

"I guess the same as most people," I said. "Taking in the scenery."

He shot a pointed gaze at my purse, as if he had laser vision that allowed him to see the gun, then shifted his attention back to the road. "Not everyone."

20

"Then what do *you* think I was doing out there?" I asked before I could stop myself.

"Who knows what people do?" he said, shooting me a smile that didn't quite reach his eyes. "I was just curious."

Maybe so, but it felt judgy in a way that made me wonder what, exactly, this man suspected me of doing.

We rode the rest of the way in an uncomfortable silence until we reached downtown Drum. I hadn't expected a bustling town, but it was even smaller than I'd imagined—just two short blocks with businesses on either side. About a third of them had "Going Out of Business" signs in the windows. Max's Tavern was halfway down the road. The front entrance boasted a small sign informing any passersby of its presence, but when we turned down the cross street, I saw a much bigger sign painted on the side of the building. There was a nearly empty gravel parking lot out back, and Wyatt parked lengthwise across it. As soon as he stopped, he hopped out of the truck and walked around to the passenger side. When I opened the door, he was already standing in front of me, waiting.

I'd had enough of his silent accusations.

"What?" I snapped as I climbed out.

He held his ground, searching my face as though he was trying to see through me—not under my clothes, but into my character.

Wait. Wasn't *I* supposed to be judging *him*?

For a moment I thought he was going to block me from getting out. Fear jolted through me. I started to reach into my purse, but his gaze followed my movements. Maybe he was seeing through me again, because he immediately backed off and offered me a hand. I ignored the gesture, turning in the seat to get my suitcase out of the back.

"You'll never get it," he said in an amused tone. "It's wedged in there."

The two seconds I spent tugging on the handle proved that to be true, but when he tried to nudge me to the side so he could take over, I turned my back to him and found the lever to fold the seat forward. It hit my knee hard enough that I was sure it would leave a bruise, but I felt vindicated when I pulled my suitcase free, even if it fell to the ground with an ungraceful thud.

"I'm impressed," he said, his arms crossed over his chest.

I gave him a long hard stare. "Don't ever tell me I can't do something."

Guarded amusement filled his eyes. "Point taken." Then, as though remembering himself, his face hardened. "Let me take you inside and introduce you to Max."

The last thing I needed was a babysitter, especially one who seemed to think I was up to no good.

"Are you going to get me a special rate or something?" I asked in a terse tone as I leaned over and grabbed the handle of my bag. "Because if not, I'm perfectly capable of renting my own hotel room."

He looked properly chastised. "Don't you need help with your bag?"

"No," I snapped. "I do *not*." I started to roll my suitcase over the packed earth, most of the gravel long gone, giving it a jerk when it got stuck on one of the few remaining stones. Of course.

"Want to give me your number?" he asked, his accusatory tone back.

I stopped and turned around to face him. *"Excuse me?"*

"For the car." He nudged his head toward the tow truck. "So I can give you the estimate."

This was what I got for being all sanctimonious. "Uh. Yeah."

He pulled out his phone and tapped the screen. "Okay. Go ahead."

21

The problem was I didn't remember my phone number. I'd decided to use the burner until I got a job. I'd get a real phone after saving up a few paychecks. "How about I just text it to you. What's *your* number?"

His face was a blank slate as he rattled off a number, which I entered into a text message and typed. I started to enter my real name, the one I needed to keep hidden, then deleted it and entered **Moore**. Damn, that was going to take some getting used to. I pushed send, only to get an error message. I still didn't have service.

"I don't have cell service in town," I said, holding it up as though to offer proof. "So my phone number won't be of much use."

"I'll just call you at the motel, then," he said, his gaze on my phone.

I stuffed it into my purse. It wasn't like it was going to do me much good here. Besides which, I had no one to call. "Do *you* have cell service?"

"Nope." Then he turned and headed for the cab of his truck.

If he didn't have cell service and neither did I, why was he asking for my number? At least his attitude had dampened my attraction to him. The last thing I needed in my life was to be distracted by a handsome man.

I decided not to waste any more time on it and resumed lugging my suitcase toward the tavern. It continued getting stuck on chunks of gravel, so I eventually picked it up and carried it to the front of the building. It kept banging my shins, likely hard enough to leave more bruises. I almost admonished myself for packing too much, but other than my car, all my worldly possessions were either in my purse or my suitcase. When I reached concrete, I tried to roll it, but one of the wheels was wobbly and the suitcase started going sideways.

I might as well have gotten my honeymoon luggage from Target instead of Neiman Marcus for as well as this bag was holding up.

Honeymoon luggage.

I'd bought this blasted suitcase for the three-week Hawaii vacation I'd planned with my fiancé, Jake. Back then, I'd thought I was happy, or happy enough. I'd thought I understood the world and my part in it. But it had all been a lie. I'd heard something after our rehearsal dinner that had opened my eyes to the truth. Instead of taking this bag on my honeymoon, I'd brought it in my getaway car—and, thanks to my last broken-down car, to Henryetta, Arkansas. To the people who'd given me a new life.

The thought of Henryetta and the friends I'd made there brought back a fresh wave of grief, but I took a deep breath and pushed it down. I could feel sorry for myself later. Now, I needed to get a room for the night…or more likely for the next several nights.

What was I going to do if I didn't have enough money to pay for the repairs? Because I needed to face the possibility that it might happen.

I'd deal with it when I got the estimate.

I opened the front door and walked inside. The décor was dark—wood, floors, and ceiling—but it felt homey rather than off-putting. A family sat in a booth to my right and ESPN was playing on the large screen TV mounted to the back wall.

A man with dishwater blond hair stood behind the bar, leaning his elbow on the counter as he watched me enter the establishment. He was young and good-looking, and the shit-eating grin that spread across his face when he saw my suitcase indicated he was pretty confident in his own skin. "I have a lot of people comin' into the tavern, but I've never had anyone want to camp out here."

He didn't look anything like Wyatt, but something about his grin reminded me of the man who had just dropped me off.

"You must be Max," I said as I fought my suitcase to follow me across the floor.

He laughed. "Should I be worried that you know who I am, but I don't remember you?"

So he was a player, not that I was surprised. He had that cocky confidence most players wore like a glove.

"We haven't met," I assured him. "Your brother told me about your bar and your motel."

His eyebrows shot up in surprise. "Wyatt?"

"Drives a tow truck?" When he nodded, I said, "He towed my car here." I gestured to the luggage. "Hence the suitcase."

"So you need a room for the night?" he asked.

"Probably several nights. He said it would take a few days."

"You must have done a number on it."

Standing across from him, I leaned into the counter. "I don't have much luck with vehicles."

"Know your strengths *and* your weaknesses," a woman said behind me with a country twang. "That's what I always say."

I turned to see a waitress who looked to be in her mid-thirties, carrying a platter topped with several plates of food. She was wearing jeans and a dark blue scoop neck T-shirt that read *Max's Tavern*. Her short blonde hair was pulled into two tiny pigtails at the back of her head, and she was pretty even with little make-up.

I shot her a grin and she grinned back.

"I like her, Max," she said. "Don't you scare her away."

Max laughed. "She's renting a room across the street."

The woman shifted her attention to the family in the booth as she set down the plates one by one. When she returned to us, she propped a hand on her hip. "Like I said, don't be runnin' her off."

I cringed. "That bad?"

"Are you really stayin' overnight?" She looked me up and down. "You're not the Alpine Inn's typical client."

Oh crap. What did that mean? Was it a rent-by-the-hour kind of place? "I'm scared to ask what the typical client is."

"Don't you listen to her," Max said, picking up a rag behind the counter and wiping down the bar top. "I'll put you on the end where there's not much action. It'll be quiet as a graveyard."

The waitress leveled her gaze on him.

"What?" Max said, holding his arms out from his sides. "For what it's worth, Ruth, I don't have any other guests tonight besides Big Joe and Jerry, so Ms...." He gave me an expectant look, waiting for me to offer my name.

"Carly," I said cautiously.

"So Ms. *Carly*," Max said with a grin, "will have plenty of quiet and privacy."

"Uh-huh," Ruth said. She turned to me with resignation in her eyes. "I'll have Franklin bring up a set of sheets when he meets me for my break."

"Hey now!" Max protested. "Don't go besmirching my establishment!"

"When was the last time you ordered new sheets for the dump you call a motel?" Ruth asked, both hands planted on her hips again.

His back straightened. "That's neither here nor there."

The woman turned to me with a tight grin. "And that's why I'm havin' my man bring you a set of sheets. Don't you worry. I replaced all my sheets a couple of months ago when we went to Costco down in Knoxville. Four-hundred-thread-count sheets and they feel as smoooooth as silk," she said, her drawl becoming more pronounced on the last few words. She shot Max a glare. "Damn cheapskate's too tight to buy good quality sheets."

"Ruth," Max said with a sigh, "you're gonna make her think my place isn't good enough for her."

"Maybe that's because it's not," she snapped back.

"I'm kind of stuck here," I admitted. "My car broke down, and Wyatt says the repair might take a few days." Then before I could chicken out, I added, "Say, if you know of anyone needing temporary help while I'm here, I'm available."

Ruth leaned her arm on the bar top and leveled her gaze with Max. "We're down a waitress what with Lula running off to Chattanooga with that trucker. You should hire Carly until she comes back."

"I ain't decided if I'm gonna let Lula come back this time," Max grumbled. "I'm tired of her taking off whenever she damn well feels like it then popping back in as if nothing happened."

"Who do you think you're foolin'?" Ruth said with a disgusted shake of her head. "This ain't the first time she's run off, and it surely won't be the last. You'll take her back, just like you always do."

I decided to jump in before they really started arguing. "I'm not looking for anything permanent, but I can definitely fill in until I leave or Lula comes back. I waitressed back when I was in—" I shut myself down before I could get out the word *college*. The old me had a master's degree in elementary education. Charlene Moore had barely graduated high school. The thought provoked another wave of unexpected grief. I loved teaching, but the credentials would have been too difficult to fake. The thought of going back to school for another five or six years to study something I already knew…

I could cry later. Right now I had to finish the statement I'd left hanging before my new acquaintances regarded me with the same suspicion I'd seen in Wyatt's eyes. Of course, it didn't matter much if they thought I was strange. In a few days, this place would be in my rearview mirror.

Make the best of it, Carly. You need the money.

"I used to waitress back when I was in Michigan, before I moved to Atlanta." *Too much backstory. It makes you look desperate.* "In any case," I said, sounding a little too chipper, even to my ears. "I can fill in until you take Lula back. *If* you take her back."

He groaned. "Ruth's right. I take that fool-headed girl back every time, but one of these days, enough will be enough."

"Well, it won't be anytime soon," Ruth said, then looked me up and down. "The jeans'll do, and I'll get you a T-shirt from the back. How soon can you start?"

"I can start right now," I said in shock. This had been way too easy.

"Then come on," she said, gesturing for me to follow her into the back. "Let's get you ready for the Monday night rush."

I followed her, tugging my worthless suitcase behind me. This place was empty. Monday night rush? It looked like they didn't need one employee, let alone two.

"Hey!" Max called after us. "I never said she was hired!"

"We all know who the real boss is around here," Ruth said over her shoulder. "So don't you worry your pretty little head about it." Then she snickered.

"I heard that slur against my manhood!" Max shouted at her.

"I meant you to!"

Once we were in the back, Ruth took my suitcase and wrangled it into a small office that barely had enough room for a desk. Several keys on plastic key chains hung from hooks on the wall behind it.

"Isn't Max the owner?" I asked, trying not to worry that he might fire me any second just to remind Ruth of her place.

She waved a hand in dismissal. "Max likes to be the face of the bar, the good-time guy, but everyone knows I run it. He pays me well, so I let him pretend he's the boss." She winked. "Most of the time."

"So you think he should fire Lula?"

She angled her head back and eyed me up and down. "Damn, girl. I thought you said this was temporary."

"What?" Then I realized what she thought I was getting at. "No. I mean, yes. It is. I'm out of here as soon as Wyatt fixes my car, which will hopefully be in a few days."

She laughed. "I was teasing you. Lula's just wild and unreliable. But she's sweet as sugar, so we all seem to tolerate the inconvenience." She led me into a back storeroom lined with wire racks weighed down by huge boxes. Along the back wall was a metal cabinet above a collection of smaller lockers. A couple of them were secured with padlocks, but the rest were unlocked. Several coat hooks jutted out from the wall. Only two were in use—a navy blue woman's coat hung from one and a man's work jacket hung from the other. It struck me that it looked much too large for Max.

She saw my gaze and laughed. "That belongs to Tiny, the cook. I'll introduce you in a minute."

"Oh." Of course there was a cook. There was likely more than one, but the size of that coat scared me. It had to be from a big-and-tall men's store, which meant Tiny was someone's idea of a cute nickname.

"Hang up your coat while I find you a shirt," Ruth said as she tugged a plastic bin off the bottom of one of the shelves.

"Yeah, sure." I shrugged my coat off one arm at a time so I didn't need to let go of my purse.

Ruth seemed to notice my reluctance to put down my bag, but she remained silent as she sorted through the small stack of shirts in the bin.

"It might be on the small side," she said, tossing one of them to me, "but it looks like you've got good tits, so show 'em off, honey. I suspect you need the money for that multi-day car repair, which means you're gonna need the tips. But it's your lucky day because tonight is Monday Night Football, sugar. Cute face, nice tits, and somethin' new and intriguin' for the boys? They'll tip you well as long as you're friendly."

"*How* friendly?" I asked, my voice tight.

She laughed. "Not as friendly as you're insinuating. Max won't tolerate that—from either side. So don't go promising some big reward after you finish your shift because he'll fire you lickety-split. On the flip side, he won't tolerate any man trying to grope you, so you be sure to tell one of us immediately if that happens. Got it?"

The fiery look in her eyes promised me she meant every word. I pushed out a sigh of relief. "No worries there."

With a sharp nod, she said, "Good." A smile spread across her face. "I think I'm gonna like workin' with you."

I smiled back. "I think I'm gonna like it too."

She laughed. "We'll see if you're saying the same thing at midnight."

Chapter Three

After I swapped my long-sleeved T-shirt for my snug Max's Tavern shirt, Ruth assigned me a locker and gave me a padlock and a key. I locked everything up and stuffed the key in the front pocket of my jeans.

"Don't you worry about anyone stealing anything," she said. "Max won't put up with that nonsense, and Tiny would make them regret it until their dyin' day, which would likely be sooner than they anticipated. But no one would dare try. For one thing, Tiny is slow to anger, but once he's pissed...look out. As for Max, this is the only bar in a thirty-mile radius, and too many men in these parts love to come in for Monday Night Football to risk pissin' him off." She grinned. "Like I said, if you're short on funds, you've picked a good night to show up. The Tennessee Titans are playin' tonight, so we'll be busier than ever. Truth be told, I'm thankful I won't be workin' it alone."

I was only partially relieved. All the Tiny references had me on edge.

Chuckling, Ruth tucked her hand around my right arm and pulled me to the door to the hall. "By the look on your face, something I said scared you, but don't you worry. Max and Tiny don't take no shit from anyone, and they definitely don't make us take shit from anyone either." She leaned closer. "I've waitressed a few places, and nobody takes care of his girls like Max does."

I wasn't sure how to respond to that. Takes care of his girls? I was hoping the antiquated description wasn't as misogynistic as it sounded.

Was it wrong that it made me feel safer?

"Let's go meet Tiny before the rush hits," she said, dragging me out of the storeroom and down a short hall into the kitchen.

A huge man with closely cropped red hair stood in front of the grill. "You stop right there," he said, waving a spatula at us. "What do you think you're doin', Ruthie?"

He had to be at least six-foot-five or six, and while he was wide and thick, he didn't have an ounce of fat on him. It was easy to see why Tiny was Max's enforcer, but the hairs on the back of my neck stood on end at the thought of Max needing someone like Tiny in the first place. We'd never needed an enforcer at Applebee's.

What kind of place was this?

"Don't you be worryin'," Tiny said to me with a warm smile. Then he shot a mock glare to the woman beside me. "It's Ruthie I blame. She knows the rules."

Ruth laughed. "Tiny doesn't allow anyone not workin' in the kitchen to step foot inside it." Then she said, "I only wanted you to meet Carly before the chaos hits."

"You keep the chaos out there." Tiny pointed to the rectangular window opening on the wall to my right. "I'll control it in here." He squinted at me. "New girl, huh? Max finally decided to replace Lula?"

"Oh, no," I said, lifting up a hand. "I'm just temporary help for a few days while my car's getting repaired."

He gave me a look that suggested he didn't believe me but didn't call me on it. "The menu's pretty simple, and the system's not complicated. Take the order on a notepad, then pin it on the line. We'll pull the ticket and put it with the plate when it's done."

"What if there's an appetizer?" I asked.

Tiny released a belly laugh, then said, "This ain't no hoity-toity res-taur-aunt." He tried to make the last word sound French but did a very poor job of it. "It all comes out at the same time."

"Got it," I said.

"Don't you worry," Tiny said. "If Lula can handle it, you won't have a lick of trouble."

"Thanks, Tiny," I said, feeling foolish for being frightened of him and also relieved by his reassurance. I hadn't waitressed in nearly a decade. I hoped it all came back.

***

An hour later, the tavern was half full—a big group of men had descended on us, scooting the tables and chairs around so they could get the best views of the big-screen TV. Ruth had been right about their interest in me, but their attention seemed good-natured and respectful.

"Gentlemen," Max said, walking over to the group and putting a hand on my shoulder. "I'm sure you've all met Carly by now. She's fillin' in for Lula. I expect you to treat her with the respect she deserves or you'll be answering to me or Tiny."

"That goes without sayin', Max," one man grumbled in the back. "The rules ain't changed since you took over the place."

"A little reminder never hurt anyone," Max said. "Be sure to tell your friends when they come in. Now, to celebrate our newest employee, how about a round of beers on the house?"

A round of cheers went up and my mouth dropped open in shock.

Max gave me a wink. "Come on over, and we'll start passin' 'em out."

"Why would you do that, Max?" I asked quietly as I followed him behind the bar.

He grabbed a mug and started filling it up with the beer on tap. "Had to get 'em all in a good mood," he said, then lowered his voice. "Some of 'em are partial to Lula. She's a pretty little thing and sweet as honey. They might not be too happy with you for fillin' in for her."

I was starting to understand why Max put up with Lula's antics.

"In any case, they're gettin' free drinks because you're here, which will make them happy," he said, handing me the first mug. "You'll get better tips now."

I stared at him in surprise. The cynical part of me might have accused him of wanting to maximize his own share of the tips, but Ruth had told me that he never took his share. He only asked that we share ten percent with Tiny and whoever was helping him—either a man named Samson or a woman named Bitty, a nickname Tiny had given her that had stuck. Ruth said she couldn't even remember her real name. Samson's name was supposedly legit, and while he was working tonight, I had yet to get a good look at him.

When I had a tray full of mugs, I carried them over and started handing them out. Ruth was busy with another table, but she shot me a wink and mouthed, *You've got this.*

I knew what she was up to. She was giving me a chance to butter up the crowd.

"How y'all doin' tonight?" I asked with a huge smile, letting my Texas drawl slip in.

"Doin' great, little miss," one of the men said, and while I wondered at his choice of words, he seemed innocent enough. He was old enough to be my grandfather and he had a friendly face. "Whereabouts you from?" he said as he took a full mug from me. "Because I know every pretty girl on this side of the mountain, and I ain't never seen you before."

"Georgia," I said, forcing a smile to remain plastered on my face while my heart hammered against my rib cage. The old me had been born and bred in Texas. The new me was from Michigan and had moved to Atlanta after high school.

"Georgia," his friend next to him spat in disgust.

But a man at the next table perked up at the mention, keeping his gaze on me.

I placed a mug of beer in front of the Georgia-hater and winked. "Obviously, I learned the error of my ways. I'm here in Tennessee now, aren't I?"

The table let out an uproarious wave of laughter. I glanced up at the bar and saw Max pulling the tap as he filled a mug, but the approval on his face let me know he was pleased. A happy boss was a good thing. I hoped I could keep it up.

I took the tray to the table with the man who'd perked up at the mention of me being from Georgia.

"Y'all from around here?" I asked.

Four men sat at the table and two of them snickered. "Honey, we're *all* from around here."

I cast a glance at the sandy-brown-haired guy. "You got family in Georgia, then?"

He stared up at me in surprise and confusion.

"I just noticed you took interest when I mentioned my home state is all. Was looking for a fellow Georgian."

The guys at the table turned to the man with perplexed expressions.

"You got kin down in Georgia, Dewey?" one of his friends asked. "How come this is the first I've heard of it?"

Dewey shot me a glance that suggested I was an imbecile. "Not me. Looks like Sweet Thing here is anglin' for more tips."

He was lying. He'd been interested, and his denial only made me nervous.

I cocked my head to the side and gave him a beaming smile. "Just tryin' to be friendly. It's not always easy bein' the new girl."

"We'll make you feel welcome, Carly," a man at the next table said.

I nodded in acknowledgement but kept Dewey in my sights. "Nice meetin' you, gentlemen. I'm sure I'll see plenty more of you before the night is through."

I passed out the rest of the free beers, meeting all thirty or so men. Most of them were friendly, although a few asked me when Lula would be back. I assured them I wasn't out to steal her job. One man sat by himself in the corner, refusing to make eye contact with anyone. He looked to be about sixty and was so rail-thin I suspected he'd blow away in a strong wind. I could tell that he'd gone a few rounds in life and hadn't ended up winning any of them. My heart went out to him, so I respected his space and left the beer in front of him.

Once I'd passed out the free drinks, Ruth pulled me over and gave me a beaming smile. "You're doin' great."

"Thanks." But how hard was it to give away free alcohol? The real test of whether my waitressing skills were still intact would come once I started taking food orders.

"I see you met Jerry."

I gave her a blank look.

"Jerry"—she nodded toward the door—"The odd duck in the corner. He rents one of Max's rooms across the street. He keeps mostly to himself, barely talkin' to anyone, but he likes to hang out here on Monday nights. Most of the guys leave 'im be, but every so often one of 'em gives him a hard time. Max doesn't tolerate that shit and will kick 'em out quicker than lickety-split, so if you see anyone botherin' him, you let us know."

I nodded, casting a glance at him. Jerry had a quarter in his hand that he tapped on the table while staring at his beer. His gray hair hung over his ears, though the length looked like less of a style choice and more of a lack of maintenance.

Ruth leaned in closer. "His wife died about five years ago. Her income paid the mortgage and Jerry lost his home. Max put him up in number one at the Alpine Inn. He says Jerry lives on social security, but it ain't a lot, so I don't think Max charges him much to stay there. We always slip him meals and tell him that Bitty or Samson screwed up an order in the kitchen, otherwise he won't take it. He's strange, but he's harmless."

If I was looking for proof Max, Ruth, and Tiny were good people, this was surely it. They reminded me of the friends I'd left behind in Arkansas, and I let my guard down a tiny bit. "I'll look out for him. I haven't seen him eat since he got here an hour ago. I'll make sure he gets something soon."

Ruth smiled. "I knew you had a good heart."

Her compliment made me smile. "Thanks."

I started taking food orders, and when I took them to the back, I told Tiny that Jerry was in my section.

He nodded and gave me a warm grin. "I'll have something up for him soon."

The median age of the Monday Night Football crowd was around fifty or sixty, which made sense given what Wyatt had told me. If the town had run on tourism and all the visitors had stopped coming, most of the younger guys had probably moved away to find jobs.

At a certain point in the evening, there was enough of a lull that Ruth and I retreated behind the counter with Max for a momentary break. I'd decided my waitressing skills were mostly still intact, but before I could say as much to Ruth, I heard a dull roar of engines outside.

She shot me a look with raised eyebrows. "Now the real action starts."

"What?"

She gave me a tight smile, then headed out to check on her section, asking if anyone needed refills. I was about to do the same, but Max grabbed my arm and held me in place.

"Wait."

I turned to him in surprise and my stomach churned when I saw the worry in his eyes.

The door burst open and a group of men walked through the door, younger and rougher than the early crowd. While the older men didn't have any women with them, some of the new guys did. They settled in at tables behind the first group and shot Ruth expectant looks as she walked over to greet them.

I glanced up at Max, but he shook his head. "Not yet."

Something about his tone made me nervous, but we both waited behind the counter until the last of the stragglers were seated. Max's eyes hardened as he pulled the remote from under the counter. "Follow me."

I followed like a dutiful puppy, stopping short just to his left.

A few of the new guys had already noticed me and were eyeing me like I was a grade A sirloin steak. Others looked downright hostile.

Max flicked a button on the remote and the sounds of the game immediately silenced. A loud groan of protest went through the crowd, but Max just stood there until the men quieted. Someone's eyes flicked to his right leg, and I swallowed a gasp. He had a huge hunting knife strapped there. Just how dangerous was this place?

"Gentlemen," he said just like he'd started his previous speech, but his earlier teasing tone had been replaced with an edge of warning. "This is Carly. She's filling in for Lula. I have no idea where Lula went, nor do I know when she'll be back. But until she returns, Carly's been kind enough to fill in. You will treat her like the lady she is, and if you don't, Tiny'll kick you so hard in the ass you'll be shitting out your ears, and that's after I get done with you. Any questions?"

A few men gave me an inquisitive look, but everyone remained silent.

"I'd also like to add," Max said, sounding more good-natured, "that Tiny's taken a shine to Carly, so he's bound to be extra contrary if you step out of line. Capisce?"

A few men muttered *capisce* but didn't ask any questions.

"Now, you newcomers are lucky. To celebrate Carly joinin' our team, she'll be passin' out a round of free beers for y'all."

"I don't want a damn beer," one of the men shouted. "I want a whiskey."

Max's hard gaze landed on him, and they had a momentary staring contest until Max said, "Then when Carly comes around with your beer, you'll give her a polite 'no, thank you,' and when she's finished passing out everyone else's drinks, you can order your whiskey."

"That's bullshit, Maxwell!" another man shouted.

"You're always free to walk your lazy ass up to the bar and order it from me," Max said with an ornery grin. "I don't smell as nice as Carly and I'm definitely not as good of company, but suit yourself." He shrugged, then spun around and headed to the bar, giving me a glance that suggested I should follow.

When we got behind the bar, I said sarcastically, "Thanks for the warning."

An apologetic look washed over his face as he started filling a mug. "I didn't want to scare you, and I had no idea what kind of mood they'd be in when they finally showed up."

"Why did they all come together in a pack?" I asked. "And why would their moods collectively change from night to night?"

"Most of them hang out together, and I'd heard they were havin' a meetin' earlier. They must have headed over here after it broke up." His tone suggested he knew what they'd been up to but didn't feel like elaborating.

I frowned, wondering if I'd just jumped into a hornet's nest. Did it matter since I'd be leaving in a few days? That brought up another good question. "Why are you spending all this money on me?" I asked, gesturing to the mugs. "I doubt I'll be here long enough to make it worth your while."

He winked. "My momma always told me to be sweet to pretty ladies. Just doin' like she taught."

"I know you're doin' it so they'll like me more, but still, Max. That's a lot of beer."

"I ain't fillin' 'em all that full," he said, putting a three-fourths-full mug on the tray as if to prove his point. "Besides, some of 'em don't like it when Lula takes off. They'll be inclined to like you more and not give me grief, which makes *my* job easier. Win-win."

I took it we were buttering up the first group of men to tip me well. The second group we were bribing to not stir up trouble, although some had visibly flinched at Max's casual suggestion that Tiny would cause them bodily injuries if they got out of line.

I carried the first tray over and started passing out the beer. It was obvious this group wasn't as chatty as the first lot, but a guy in his mid to late twenties shot me a curious gaze.

"What are you doin' in these parts?"

"Just stoppin' through for a few days," I said with a huge smile. "And helpin' Max out while Lula is gone."

"We're not used to strangers around here," he said. "How'd you find out about the job?"

It wasn't any of his business, but I figured he'd likely find out anyway since it was such a small town. Might as well look friendly and pretend I had nothing to hide. "My car broke down out at the overlook. I'm staying here while I'm waiting for it to get repaired."

"You were out at the overlook?" asked a guy with a handlebar mustache and a pockmarked face. "What were you doin' out there?"

"I guess I was doin' what most people do out there—takin' in the pretty view." My smile was starting to make my cheeks hurt. Why was this guy so suspicious of me?

"Ain't nobody go out there no mores," another guy said. He said something else, but it was drowned out by an eruption of loud cheering.

The Titans had made a touchdown.

I started to move on to the next table, but the guy who'd spoken last grabbed my wrist and pulled me back, making some of the beers slosh on the tray.

"Where's your car?" he asked. "Wyatt's garage?" He wore an AC/DC T-shirt so old and threadbare it looked like it had been worn nearly every day since its purchase at a concert when the band was in its heyday. Only, the guy was young enough that he must have gotten it at a thrift store or from his father's closet.

"One and the same," I said, careful to keep my cheerful tone intact as I made a show of extracting my arm. "He towed it down a few hours ago."

Thankfully, the guy didn't try to grab me again. "He didn't say nothin' about it when I saw 'im."

My smile started to slip, but I tightened my cheek muscles. "Well, I sure hope it was Wyatt Drummond that took off with my Honda hooked up to the back of his tow truck or I'm in a world of trouble."

That produced some laughter, and I moved on to the next table to pass out the remaining two beers on my tray.

I set a beer in front of a guy who was leaned back in his chair with his arms crossed over his chest, studying me like I was a crib sheet for his final exam in trigonometry. He had dark brown hair that hung over his ears and his collar, but not long enough to be pulled back into a man bun or ponytail.

"How long you plannin' on stayin'?" he asked in a dark tone. He adjusted his arms, and it struck me that he was powerfully built for a man who appeared to be in his forties.

I tried not to let him know he'd rattled me and gave him a flippant answer. "I guess as long as it takes for Wyatt to fix my car."

"And how long's that gonna be?"

I set the last beer in front of his companion, then put my hand on my hip and infused plenty of attitude into my stance. "Your guess is as good as mine. Maybe Wyatt will conference-call us both so we can find out together."

He sat up so quickly his chair legs slammed into the floor. "This here's my town and I ain't gotta put up with your shit."

I stared at him in disbelief, taking a half second to come up with an appropriate response. Ignore him or rip him a new one? It helped that I knew Max kept a baseball bat behind the bar.

But Max beat me to it.

"Hey!" he shouted, setting down the mug he'd been filling with a loud thud. Beer sloshed out over the sides and onto the counter. He placed his hand flat on the bar next to the mug, leaning forward with hard eyes. "This is your only warnin', Bingham."

Bingham's face was a mask of contempt as he slowly lifted his hands up next to his head, showing Max his flexed fingers and empty palms. "I didn't lay a hand on 'er."

But the look in his gray eyes told me he was a dangerous man. It was easy to see that he didn't like being issued orders—and liked following them even less. If the Drummonds were seen as some sort of authority in this town, it was little wonder he seemed challenging.

Max tilted his head ever so slightly, the small gesture banishing the good-natured, affable man I'd known for the past two hours. "I'm pretty damn sure I made myself clear just moments ago. Do I need to bring Tiny out to show you how to treat the staff? He's busy as shit, gettin' a mess of wings ready for y'all, but he'd be more than happy to oblige if you're being disrespectful to Carly."

Bingham held Max's gaze for several long seconds as he slowly dropped his hands, and I had a wild fancy that Bingham was about to whip out a six-shooter for an Old West shoot-out. Instead, he gave me a sarcastic grin. "Welcome to Drum, *new girl*."

"Thanks," I said, trying not to let him see my shaking hands. I gripped the tray so hard I was surprised it didn't break in half as I made my way back to the bar. I wasn't sure what had just happened, but it had scared the shit out of me.

Max had his eyes on Bingham as he filled a mug, while Bingham's gaze was still firmly on me. The beer overflowed onto Max's hand, and he flipped the tap shut and set the mug on a second, half-full tray. He snuck a glance at me and murmured, "You okay?"

No. I was stuck in a one-stop-sign town with a potential maniac who obviously detested me, with no way to escape for several days. Oh, and I was hiding from two people who should love me. I was far from okay, but I'd be damned if I'd admit it. "I'm fine."

"He's in your section, but I'll have Ruth cover his table," Max said, shooting me a guilty look. "I should have warned you. Bingham has his good days and his bad."

"I sure as hell hope this was a bad day," I muttered.

Max made a face, letting me know he could get a whole lot worse.

Even so, something refused to let me back down. I was sick to death of bullies.

"He doesn't scare me," I said.

Max's eyebrows shot up.

I lowered my voice. "Okay, he does a little, but I'm sure as hell not gonna let him know it." An ounce of fear would be like blood in shark-infested water. Rose, the woman I'd lived with back in Arkansas, had taught me a lot about dealing with rough men. She didn't let any of them run roughshod over her, and neither would I. Sometimes the only way to get respect was to demand it. No more kowtowing. Carly Moore would be fierce. "I can do this."

He nodded slowly, a grim look plastered on his face. "Okay. But don't antagonize him, and if you get into trouble, look my way. I'll jump in immediately, and Tiny is literally three seconds away. He may be big, but he can move fast."

"Thanks," I said, meaning it. I'd worked a lot of jobs in my thirty-one years and never had a boss back me up like this. It was obvious he truly cared about his staff. He thought of them as family. It warmed my heart to realize I was part of that group, if only for a few days.

I picked up the tray and steeled my resolve as I headed back to Bingham's table to finish handing out beers to the rest of the men.

An amused grin lit up Bingham's face as he held his hands out at his sides. "And she's back for more."

I gave him a sweet smile as I served the other men sitting with him. "I can't leave your friends thirsty just because you and I got off on the wrong foot."

He didn't say anything else and I moved on to the next table, but I could feel his eyes pinned to my back—or perhaps my ass—as I made the rounds to the twenty or so new guys.

I'd just handed out my last beer when the door opened again. Wyatt walked in, a cold breeze trailing in with him. A few flakes of snow clung to his dark brown hair and his brown jacket. His cheeks were tinged pink from the wind.

My breath caught at the sight of him. He scanned the room, and my heart skipped with anticipation…until his gaze landed on me. He stopped in his tracks, but it was clear he was anything but happy to see me—his expression hardened and he made his way to the bar as if on a mission.

"What's Wyatt doin' here?" I heard one of the men ask. "Can't remember the last time I saw him here."

"Dunno," a second guy said, but he flicked a glance in my direction.

Me? While I could see that I was the variable here, why would Wyatt give two shits about me other than worrying about me stiffing him on his bill?

Max walked down to the end of the bar to greet his brother, but from the looks on their faces, it wasn't a friendly reunion. So this was why he hadn't paid a visit in some time. The brothers clearly didn't get along.

I shot a glance to Ruth, who was watching with open interest. She gestured for me to join her by the food counter.

"Do you know what that's about?" Ruth asked.

Although they were much too far to have heard us, the Drummonds both turned to look at me before facing each other again, Wyatt's mouth pressing into a tight line.

"Holy shit, they're arguing over *you*." Her eyes lit up with excitement.

"I have no idea why they'd be doing that," I said, trying not to panic. "Wyatt and I didn't exactly hit it off, but I didn't do anything to elicit him coming in and chewing out his brother."

"Oh, I suspect you're not the cause of it," she said. "Just an excuse. They've been feuding since before Wyatt went to prison."

That sucked the air out of my lungs. "Prison?"

She made a face, her gaze still on the two brothers. "DUI. There were a couple of other charges, robbery and breaking and entering, but the robbery charges didn't stick because the only witness disappeared."

"Disappeared?"

There was a second-long delay before she acknowledged my question. Waving her hand in dismissal, she said, "Not like you're thinking. Everyone's of the mind the Drummonds paid her off to keep quiet and she left town."

That made me feel better. Sort of.

"The real question is why Wyatt Drummond gives two figs about you," she said, her gaze landing on me as she gave me a once-over with heightened interest.

"I can assure you that Wyatt Drummond isn't interested in me. Although I'm grateful he came along, he was downright rude to me on the drive down the mountain." But there was no denying he'd been friendly enough until I'd refused to involve the sheriff. He clearly thought I was up to no good.

She shrugged. "That's Wyatt. Ever since he came back from prison, he's been distant. Prison changed him."

I resisted the urge to shudder. "How long's he been back?"

Her mouth twisted to the side as she considered it. "About five years, I guess. He took over the service station and got himself a tow truck. I'm surprised he came back at all, considering."

"Because he went to prison?"

"Nah," she scoffed, looking amused. "Hell, a good third of the guys in this room have done time. It's because of his family." She leaned closer. "The Drummonds practically owned Drum once upon a time, and they didn't take to Wyatt besmirching their good name."

Bingham had called Drum *his* town, and the way he'd said it wasn't out of pride for his hometown. Had he taken over the ownership? "Because of his conviction?"

She laughed. "Hell, you really *aren't* from around here. No, because he denounced them. Rumor has it they cut him off, but that makes everyone question where he got the money to buy the station and the tow truck. The place he supposedly robbed? It was unclear what he tried to take in the first place. The owner took off soon after that and refused to discuss it. Dropped the robbery after the only witness left." She shrugged. "No one knows why Wyatt came back to town. He refuses to have anything to do with his family, Max included, and yet here he is…talking to his brother about you." She shook her head, beaming at me as if the gossip had fed her soul. "Color me intrigued."

"I can assure you that I have no idea why they'd be talking about me. My car broke down, Wyatt found me and towed my car down the mountain. He suggested I get a room in Max's motel and dropped me off here. End of story."

She grinned and cocked her head. "You're a bundle of surprises, Carly Moore. I'm gonna like havin' you around."

She better not get too used to my company. I planned to get the hell out of Drum as soon as my car was ready, even if I had to push it down the mountain.

Chapter
Four

After Wyatt and Max had said their piece, Wyatt surprised the hell out of everyone by getting a beer and taking a seat at a table with some of the rough crowd. Bingham didn't look too pleased to see Max's brother, but as far as I could tell, neither of them said a word to each other.

Bingham left me alone for the rest of the night, but he kept an eye on me—and about half the other men were watching me too. Wyatt was keeping an eye on me as well, although he was trying to be more subtle about it. He sat in Ruth's section, so I never had to deal with him.

The Titans won, which put everyone in a good mood, and the customers ordered several more rounds of drinks to celebrate. A good portion of the men left before eleven, with a few stragglers sticking around until Max shut the place down at midnight. Bingham had left with the first group. Wyatt had left soon after.

When Max shooed the last men out—a couple of old guys—he turned to face me with a huge grin. "Damn, Carly. You not only worked your ass off, but you won them boys over. How long you plannin' on stayin' again?"

I couldn't help wondering if he was asking because of his conversation with his brother. "I'll be leavin' as soon as my car is fixed and ready to go."

Given the fact that I'd earned nearly two hundred dollars in tips, I might actually be able to afford the repairs in the not-too-distant future.

"If you change your mind," Ruth said, "you've got a job. Max's right. Most of those boys loved you, and they don't usually take to newcomers." She turned her attention to Max. "What was Wyatt doin' here?"

Max's smile spread. "Just two brothers chattin' it up."

"I ain't never seen him in here since he came back to town, and he seemed mighty interested in Carly," Ruth countered.

"He asked me to give him Carly's paycheck to make sure she didn't stiff him with the tow bill and leave her car behind."

"He did *what?*" I demanded.

"Don't you worry," Max said in a genial tone. "It's *your* hard-earned money, not his. If he's got a beef with you, then that's between you two."

"He never once asked me for payment!" I said in outrage. "I would have been more than happy to pay for the tow and give him a deposit."

"That's just my fool brother," Max said as though that explained everything. He headed toward the back. "You girls go settle up with Tiny and Samson, then I'll walk Carly over to her room."

"Not without my sheets," Ruth called after him as we walked up to the serving window to the kitchen. Ruth's boyfriend, Franklin, had shown up around the third quarter of the game, and I'd covered Ruth's station so the two of them could sit at the bar for ten minutes.

Tiny was scrubbing the grill while Samson—a small, older guy so frail he looked like he'd snap like a twig if you bumped into him just right—put the last remaining dirty dishes through the dishwasher.

"You done good, girl," Tiny said, his voice warm and accepting.

"Thanks." I couldn't stop the broad smile spreading across my face. I'd left Rose and the others two weeks ago. It had been too long since I'd had a substantial interaction with anyone. I'd had no idea how much I missed this. Human contact. The feeling of a job well done. Acceptance. I only hoped I'd find it as readily once I reached Wilmington.

Ruth and I counted out their share of our tips, and then Tiny asked, "Do you want me to walk you across the street to your room?"

I stared up at him in surprise and gratitude.

"I've got it covered," Max said, stepping out of his office in a winter coat. He had my suitcase in hand, and the weight didn't seem to bother him any more than it had his brother. "If for no other reason than to wrestle her monster of a bag across the street."

"You don't have to do that," I protested.

"The wheels are busted and it's so heavy I have to wonder if you have a dead body inside."

It was a joke, but it felt too close to home. I had to force a smile. "Thanks, Max. I'll get my coat and purse."

Ruth and I grabbed our things out of our lockers, and she handed me the plastic bag. "You be sure to change those sheets, now. Otherwise, you'll show up for your shift tomorrow lookin' like you slept on sandpaper."

"Thanks so much, Ruth," I said as I took the bag. "You have no idea how much I appreciate you hirin' me." I grinned. "And yeah, I said *you*. I know I wouldn't have been here tonight if not for you."

"Ah," she said with a smile. "Max would have put it together if we'd given him a few more minutes. Can you come in a little before noon tomorrow? We open for lunch then, although I'll warn you that it's pretty slow. Not much business and the tips suck, but Lula was supposed to cover it and I have plans. Max'll let you read or do whatever while you're sitting around during the downtime."

"I'm happy to do it," I said. "And I can work a double if need be. I need the money, and I've got nothing else to do. I'd much prefer working to sitting around."

"Why don't you plan on it," she said as her smile spread. "I'm really gonna like workin' with you. Lula's sweet, but damn that girl's a slacker." She grabbed my coat off the hook and handed it to me. "I'll be in around five tomorrow, but Max and Bitty can help out if you feel overwhelmed."

"Thanks, Ruth."

I slipped my coat on as I walked into the dining area, finding Max standing at the shade-covered windows, peeking out through the closed blinds.

He turned when he heard me approach. "You got a warmer coat than that?"

The answer was no, but I didn't want him to feel obligated to get me something warmer. I glanced down at my heavy fleece jacket. "This should be enough to walk across the street."

"There's a dusting of snow on the ground, but the wind has kicked up. It looks cold."

"I'll be fine," I said as I reached him. "You don't have to carry my suitcase, Max."

"I don't mind," he said, opening the front door. "I'm walkin' over with you anyway."

I walked out, shivering from the blast of cold. He shut the door behind us and motioned to the L-shaped brick building across the street and catty-corner to the tavern. The street was covered with a fine layer of snow, with drifts several inches high along the front of what looked like a vacant motel office. A faded piece of paper with curling edges had been taped to the window, with *All inquiries go to Max's Tavern* handwritten in black Sharpie. The wind was blowing the snow off the street and into the first barrier it came across. I noticed there weren't any houses around, just businesses.

"You don't need to lock up?" I asked.

"Nah, I'm coming back." He nodded to the tavern. "I live upstairs. Comes in handy when we run on a bare-bones crew."

"I can't believe you kept up with all those drinks tonight," I said.

"Practice," he said with a laugh. "And as you noticed, most guys order beer. Those are easy enough to pour."

"I was surprised every single one of them paid cash."

"That's because they'd prefer to deal in cash since we don't have a bank up here except for the payday loan place, and it only cashes checks. I like 'em payin' in cash so I don't have to deal with the credit card fees. More profit."

That made sense, but most of the world dealt in electronic transfers of money. It was like they were fifty years behind the times. Then a new concern hit me. "Does Wyatt only take cash? I don't have that much on me."

"Last I heard, he takes cards, but like I said, most folks around here don't use 'em."

Since Ruth had said a good portion of the guys had done time, I had to wonder where the cash was coming from.

None of my concern.

"Ruth told me that you and your brother aren't very friendly," I said, worried I was about to cross a line. "I hope I didn't cause any more trouble between you two."

"You weren't the cause of our disagreement tonight," he said, steering me across the motel parking lot. A couple of cars were parked in front of the units closer to the street, one of them a rusted brown and white station wagon that had to be thirty or forty years old. Max headed toward the rooms at the opposite end. "He's had a beef with me for a while now, and him showin' up was a long time comin'." He paused, then said, "I don't think Wyatt was really after your paycheck. I think he was just lookin' for an excuse to come in and confront me, and you were as good an excuse as any."

I wasn't sure if that made me feel better or worse.

"For what it's worth," he added, leading me past the very old, beat-up cars, "I seriously doubt he would have taken your money if I'd let him. Like I said, he was lookin' for some kind of excuse."

"Thanks." There was no doubt that Wyatt didn't trust me, but I saw little point in saying so. "Ruth asked me to come in and cover Lula's lunch shift tomorrow," I said, intentionally changing the subject. "I told her I could work tomorrow night too."

"Sounds good," Max said as he reached into his jacket pocket and pulled out a key attached to a large plastic disk that bore the number 20 in faded blue ink. "I really appreciate you fillin' in, although I have to warn you that the rest of the week won't be nearly as lucrative as Monday nights."

I hoped to God I'd be gone by then. "I didn't expect it to be, and anything's better than nothing. It's a win-win for both of us." I gave him a wry smile. "Three of us if you include your brother and the money I'm going to owe him."

His eyes twinkled with amusement.

He stopped in front of the last door on the right. Two rusted house numbers—*2, 0*—had been nailed into the door. I watched as Max unlocked the door, opened it, and reached inside to flick on the light switch. Without entering the room, he set my bag down inside the doorway. "We open at noon tomorrow, but there's no need to come in much earlier than that. We don't get much of a lunch crowd on a Tuesday afternoon, so if you've got something to keep you busy during the downtime, feel free to bring it."

"Thanks, Max," I said gratefully, taking the key from him.

"See you tomorrow, Carly."

"See you tomorrow."

I walked in and closed the door behind me, locking it as I got my first look at the room.

Ruth had been right. It was bad. Really bad. Worn green shag carpet that looked so old and threadbare I could see the fiber-backing in a few patches. The walls were covered with thin wood paneling riddled with scratches and dents, particularly behind the wooden headboard for the full-size bed. I cringed as I thought about what had made those marks while staring at the polyester bedspread covered in faded yellow and orange flowers. The furniture must have come from the 1970s—heavy dark pieces that looked like they'd been cheap in their time and hadn't been treated well. Half the drawers in the dresser were catawampus, and one of the nightstands was missing a drawer completely. A TV sat on top of the dresser, but it was a large monstrosity that had to be at least twenty years old, and I had to wonder if it worked. I grabbed a remote from in front of it and flicked it on to check. To my surprise it turned on.

Ruth had suggested that Max needed to buy new sheets, but I would have suggested a total gut job. Belatedly, I realized I hadn't asked for the rates. My only reassurance that Max wouldn't try to gouge me was the fact he'd gone out of his way to ease me in with his customers tonight. Someone that nice wouldn't try to overcharge me for a disgusting motel room, would he? I'd ask him tomorrow, because there wasn't anything I could do about it now. I literally had nowhere else to go.

I made quick work of stripping the bed, trying to ignore the stains on the mattress. After I got the new sheets on—unfortunately Franklin hadn't brought a blanket and the one in here smelled like mothballs—I went into the dated bathroom and took a shower, relieved there was hot water.

The tension of the day hit me hard as the water cascaded over my body, and I soon found myself crying, a luxury I hadn't allowed myself for several days. Wallowing wouldn't help me in the long run—I needed to accept my fate and move on. Today had been hard, but I knew I'd been lucky too. I added Max and Ruth and Tiny to my list of blessings. I'd had plenty of blessings since my ordeal had begun a little over two months ago. I just needed to dwell on the good things instead of the bad.

After I dried off and put on my pajamas, I cranked up the heat and crawled under the sheets and the blanket I'd decided to use out of desperation. I considered turning on the TV for white noise, but the silence outside my room calmed my anxious soul. To my surprise, I soon fell asleep.

***

I bolted upright disoriented, my heart pounding. I'd been dreaming about my rehearsal dinner. Only this time it happened differently—Jake caught me listening in on his conversation with my father and pulled a gun to shoot me.

At first, I thought my own cry had awoken me, but then I realized I'd heard something outside of my room.

I jumped out of bed and reached into my purse, pulling out the gun and checking to make sure the chamber was loaded. Lightheaded with fear, I crept to the window and lifted a slat of the blinds to look outside.

Two men were dragging someone from one of the motel rooms. They tossed him to the ground and then stood on either side of him, only about twenty feet outside of my room.

The accosted person scrambled to his feet, but one of the men pushed him to his knees on the snow-dusted asphalt. The lighting was poor, so I had trouble making out any of the men's distinguishing features, but I could see that the kneeling man wasn't wearing a coat. And that one of the men standing over him was pointing a handgun at him.

Panic had me reeling and dark spots flashed before my eyes.

"What are you doin' here, boy?" one of the men asked. He sounded familiar. "And on a school night, no less."

"Nothin'."

"*Nothin'?*" the other man asked in exaggerated disbelief. I didn't recognize the voice.

"I was just out havin' a good time. You know."

"Actually," the second guy said, "I *don't* know. I always shot the shit with my friends. You got any friends with you?"

"No, sir," the boy said, and from the way his voice cracked, I realized he was a teenager. "I don't."

"Then let me repeat my original question, son," the first guy said in an icy tone. "What. Are. You. *Doin'*. Here?"

What was *I* doing here? I was witnessing a crime and I was just gawking at it. I rushed toward the phone to call 911, only to realize there wasn't a dial tone. The phone didn't work. I scrambled to dig my cell phone out of my purse. No service. I carried it around the room, moving carefully, quietly—if I could hear them, they might be able to hear me—hoping to find a bar of service. Nothing.

"Did you find it, boy?" the second man asked.

"Find what?" the boy said, and then I heard a grunt.

"Don't you back-talk me, son," the second man said. "You know damn good and well what I'm talkin' about."

I moved carefully back to the window and peeked out of the blinds again. The kid was still hunched over in the parking lot.

What should I do? Rush out there with my gun to stop the men? I suspected they'd kill us both.

"Find anything?" the first guy called over his shoulder. A third man approached him from the motel room several doors down, his features shrouded in shadow.

"It's all gone. Every last bit of it, but you'll be interested in what we *did* find." He held something in his hand that I couldn't make out.

"What is it?" the first guy asked.

"One of them digital video cameras. The kid stole our shit, then set up a camera to record us when we showed up to get it."

"That true?" the first guy asked the boy. He backhanded him in the face before he could answer. "Where'd you hide it, boy?"

"Nowhere," the boy said. "I didn't have nothing to do with any of that!"

"Bullshit," the second man snarled, then hit him again.

"Check the other rooms," the first guy said. "All of them. They were stashin' it in a room. Maybe we got the wrong one."

"How do you explain the kid bein' in there?" the third guy asked. "And the damn camera?"

"I dunno," the first guy drawled out disdainfully. "Why don't we ask 'im?"

"Why're you here, kid?" the second guy asked.

The boy remained silent.

"Start kickin' the doors in," the first guy said. "It's supposed to be in a bag on the dresser." He motioned to the guy next to him. "Go with him."

The second and third guys moved to the unit a couple of doors down from mine, and the sound of splintering wood filled my ears. A couple of seconds later, I heard one of their muffled voices. "Nothin'."

"If you don't tell me right now," the second guy said, whipping out a gun as he strode from the unit and pointing it at the boy's forehead. "I'm gonna blow yer brains out."

"I don't know!" the boy cried out. "I didn't take it!"

"Keep searchin'," the first guy said.

My hand tightened on the gun in my own hand. Unless they found what they were looking for, they would eventually bust into my room, and from the look of it, it would be sooner rather than later. Would I shoot them? *Could* I shoot them?

I felt like a coward hiding in my room, leaving that boy defenseless.

I had to do something. Something that might save us both.

What if I created a distraction?

I had a spare key fob in my purse. I could press the panic button on my keychain and hope I was close enough to Wyatt's garage it would set off the car alarm. But if I did it, they'd likely know I was the person who'd set it off. They would know I'd seen something.

I had to take the chance.

My hands were shaking, so it took me a couple of seconds longer than usual to grab the key out of my bag and press the button. Sweet relief rushed through me when the horn started blaring.

"Fuck!" the second man said. "What the hell is *that?*"

"Car alarm," I heard the third guy say.

"We gotta get out of here," the first guy said.

"We haven't found it yet!" the third guy protested, then kicked in the door to the room next to mine.

"Where the fuck is the stash, boy?" the second guy demanded, his tightly controlled voice more alarming than if he'd sounded mad.

"Go to hell," the boy spat out.

"How about you go first, you little pissant!"

The unmistakable sound of muffled gunfire rang out twice and the boy fell onto his back.

I covered my mouth to stifle a scream.

"What the fuck did you do that for?" the third guy said in disgust. "Now we'll *never* find it."

"It wasn't in any of the rooms we checked or the one where he was hidin'. He moved it and planted that camera to implicate us," the first man said. "I suggest we keep lookin'."

The second guy turned directly toward my unit, but a streetlamp was behind him, and a dark shadow crossed over his face.

"Goddammit!" he cursed, then stomped across the street toward a red truck parked on the opposite side of the road. A long scratch ran along the back panel. I could see a figure sitting behind the steering wheel. The second guy climbed into the passenger side as the other two followed, jumping into the pickup bed before the truck drove away.

I stared after them in shock. I'd tried to save that boy and all I'd done was hasten his assassination.

Bolting for the door, I fumbled for the latch. Once I got it open, I clicked the button to turn off the car alarm as I ran to the boy, only second-guessing my decision when it occurred to me that he was still alive and might be armed himself.

"Help," he said. Between the dark and the bruising and swelling, it was hard to make out his features, but he looked young. Barely driving age.

I fell to my knees next to him, dropping the gun and the key fob onto the concrete as I searched for his wounds. The parking lot lights didn't illuminate much, but it wasn't hard to see the spreading stains on the shirt over his chest.

"Oh, God…" I briefly considered running into my room to get a towel but didn't want to leave him. In desperation, I stripped off my long-sleeved thermal shirt, leaving me in a cami in the cold, but I barely noticed. My focus was on pressing the shirt to his chest to stop the bleeding.

He whimpered in pain.

"You're her, ain't you? Are you gonna finish me off?" he asked in a reedy voice, his eyes wide with fear.

Why would he think that?

"No, I most definitely am *not*. I'm here to help you," I said, trying not to panic. "I need to go call 911."

I started to get up, but he grabbed my arm. I could have easily broken free from his weak grip, but I stopped.

"You have kind eyes," he said with a soft smile. "My momma always said you could tell a lot about a person by lookin' 'em square in the eyes."

I wasn't sure how to respond to that, so I asked, "Will you let me help you now?"

"I need you to give my granddad a message." When I didn't answer, the fear in his eyes increased. "*Please.*"

My throat tightened. "Okay. Then I need to call 911."

"Tell him I had to do it." His jaw trembled. "Tell him I'm sorry I hurt him. That I tried."

Not trusting myself to speak past the lump in my throat, I nodded.

"Tell him I have the evidence to put them away. The code's on my hand." He turned his left hand palm up, and I took a quick look at the numbers—5346823—that were slightly smeared in blue ink.

Those guys had found the camera, but maybe he had already gotten what he needed from it—maybe the footage was stored elsewhere. I knew nanny cams sent the footage to a website. The code must be an access code.

The shirt under my hand was becoming soaked with his blood. "Okay. I'll tell the police."

"No!" he shouted, then began to cough.

Blood splattered on my arm and my shirt and I tried not to recoil in horror.

"Don't tell the sheriff," he said, his words barely audible. "Some of 'em are part of this. It was one of their deputies that shot me."

The chill that shot down my back had nothing to do with the cold night air.

I needed to call for help, but he was quickly bleeding to death, and I was scared to leave him alone. Besides, the room phone didn't even work. So I did the next best thing.

"Help!" I shouted. "*Help!*"

The kid gave me a sad smile. "I ain't gonna make it. You're wasting your breath."

I shook my head. "*No.*" Then I leaned back my head and screamed at the top of my lungs.

Lights flicked on in the second floor of the tavern as well as in one of the motel rooms.

Knowing help was on the way, I turned my attention to the boy. "What's your name?"

"Seth."

"I'm gonna stay with you, Seth."

Tears welled in his eyes. "Thank you, ma'am."

Still pressing on his chest with my left hand, I reached for his hand and held on tight.

"You're gonna tell my grandfather, right?" he whispered. "You look like a nice lady. You'll keep your promise?"

I nodded, trying not to sob. "I promise, Seth. I'll tell him."

"And not the sheriff."

That one was harder to promise, but if he didn't want the sheriff to know, I wasn't sure I wanted to be the one to tell them he had something on them. Besides, if a deputy had really shot him, who could I trust? "I'll only tell your grandfather. No one else."

His grandfather could figure out what to do with the information.

"Thank you," he whispered with a little cough.

"Carly?" I heard Max shout in panic as he sprinted across the street in jeans, barefooted and bare-chested. "What happened? I heard you scream!"

"I'm okay," I said as he approached. "We need an ambulance." But Seth's hand had become limp and his chest wasn't rising and falling under my hand. His eyes were wide open, staring blankly up at me.

"You're covered in blood," Max said, his voice tight with worry. "What happened?"

"Seth was shot," I said, feeling numb.

Oh, God. He was dead. He'd died holding my hand as I'd soaked up his blood in a shirt I'd only worn for a few hours. It all felt surreal.

Max tried to pull me to my feet, but I resisted. "No! We need to give him CPR."

Kneeling on one knee next to me, Max gently pulled my hand from Seth's chest, and lifted the teen's shirt to survey the oozing wounds on either side of his chest. Cursing under his breath, he lowered the shirt. "CPR won't do any good, Carly. He's lost too much blood."

"We have to at least try!"

He gave me a sad look. "No. You need to let him go."

I stared at Seth in shock. I'd just witnessed a murder and I couldn't trust the sheriff's department.

My complicated life had just become exponentially more difficult.

Chapter
Five

In a daze, I let Max pull me to my feet. I was only vaguely aware when he began leading me across the street toward the bar.

"You're not wearing shoes," I said, feeling like I was watching the scene from afar.

"Neither are you," he said, wrapping an arm around my upper back and tugging me to his side. "Let's get you inside and warmed up."

"We need to call 911." I pulled away from him. "I have to stay with Seth."

"Seth's already gone. No point in you freezin' with him." He ushered me through the front door to the tavern, and as soon as he was through, he shut the door and dropped his hold on me. The room was pitch black except for a faint glow of light toward the kitchen. Terror shot through me, but I resisted the urge to reach out and hold on to Max for dear life.

"I'm gonna turn on the lights," he said, his voice already sounding farther away. Seconds later, the darkness burst into light and I blinked with a start.

I spun around and separated the slats of the blinds, staring at Seth's body, which still lay at the edge of the parking lot, alone.

Tears stung my eyes. I couldn't just stand in the warm bar and leave him alone like that. I'd told him I would stay with him. I had to do *something*.

When I moved to the door and reached for the doorknob, Max said behind me, "Where do you think you're goin'?"

"He's all alone out there," I said, my voice breaking as I turned around to face him. He was wearing a long-sleeved T shirt. "He needs someone."

Shaking his head, he walked straight for me. I noticed the look of devastation in his eyes first, the shirt he was trying to hand me second. "Carly, you'll catch your death of cold, and there's not a damn thing you can do for him now. Sit down and put this on while I go call the sheriff."

"You haven't called him already?" I asked in dismay.

"No, I was more worried about you." He reached for me and guided me toward a table. Once I sat, he thrust the shirt into my hand. "Come on, now. Put this on and sit before you pass out. You're as white as a sheet. I'll call the sheriff and start a pot of coffee to warm you up."

He waited for a second to make sure I started to put on the shirt, then took off for the back, leaving me alone again.

My hands had begun to shake, and it took me several attempts to put on the shirt. It was a thermal shirt, much like the one I'd left on Seth's body, only much larger. The sleeves engulfed my hands. But as I pulled up the fabric, I saw the deep red staining my fingers.

My vision turned spotty again, and I lowered myself into the chair, nearly missing it as panic engulfed me.

I'd just witnessed a murder. I'd seen the men who did it. I'd seen their getaway vehicle. And the dying boy had told me not to tell the sheriff what I knew.

What was I going to do?

I needed to get the hell out of Drum.

"Thanks, Marco," Max said, his voice carrying from the back. "See you when you get here." He appeared around the corner, studying me with worry in his eyes. "Would you rather have some tea or hot soup instead of coffee?"

I stared at him as though he'd spoken in Mandarin.

"I need to talk to Wyatt."

Max's eyes widened in shock and he took a step toward me. "What? Why?"

"I have to get out of here."

He hurried across the room and squatted in front of me, taking my wrists in his hands. "Carly. It's gonna be okay."

I slowly shook my head, my unshed tears making his face blurry.

"You're in shock is all. I already called Ruth. She's much better at handlin' crises."

I started to cry. "I have to go home."

It was an empty sentiment, and I knew it—I could never go back to Dallas. My friends in Arkansas might have some advice, but I could only call them from my burner phone and I didn't get cell service up here. I was good and truly stuck.

Max gave me a warm smile. "You're safe. I won't let anything happen to you, okay?"

I appreciated the sentiment, so I nodded, but I didn't feel safe. I wasn't sure I'd ever feel safe again.

"Why don't you tell me what happened?" he said in a soft, quiet voice.

I opened my mouth to tell him—then stopped. If I told Max the entire truth, there was a good chance he'd tell the sheriff. Even if he agreed to keep it quiet, what if the murderers found out either of us knew something? I was certain at least

65

one of those guys had been in the bar earlier. Would they kill Max? I had no doubt they would kill *me*.

His brow furrowed. "Carly. I promise you're safe."

"I heard a noise outside and found Seth lying on the ground. Bleeding."

He frowned. "How'd you know his name? I didn't see him in the bar last night."

I took a shaky breath and let it out. "He told me."

His eyes went wide. "He was alive when you found him? Did he tell you who did it?"

I shook my head, a little too fast and insistent, and hoped Max didn't realize I was lying. "No." Then a new thought hit me. Drum was a very small town. "Did you know him?"

He sank back on his heels, still holding my hand, and for the first time, his face fell. "He was a good kid." His voice broke and he cleared his throat. "I coached him in football and baseball a few years back before his momma died last year." He paused. "His granddad's gonna take it hard."

I needed to see his grandfather, but now didn't seem like a good time to bring that up. "I'm so sorry."

Surprise filled his eyes. "Why are *you* sorry? You held his hand as he died, and you tried to save him. There was nothin' else you could have done."

"Someone beat him up," I said, my panic rising again. "They beat him up and shot him. Why?"

He shook his head, his lips pressed into a thin line. "I don't know, but if the sheriff doesn't take this seriously, I know a few guys who will be more than happy to look into it. Everyone loved Seth."

Well, apparently not *everyone*.

"Do you remember anything else he said?" Max asked.

Could I trust Max? I sure hoped so, but Seth had made it clear he only wanted me to talk to one person. His grandfather could decide whether he wanted to share what little Seth had told me. I'd be long gone by the time Max found out I'd lied—*if* he found out—but it still hurt my heart to be dishonest to someone who'd been so kind.

I shook my head. "I asked him what his name was and told him I'd get him help." Tears were flowing down my cheeks again. "I lied to him, because I didn't get him help at all. I lied to a dying boy."

He gave me a soft smile and squeezed the back of my hand. "You didn't lie. You tried to get him help, but the closest medical facility is half an hour away, and it's not even a trauma center. He was shot in the chest. Twice. There was no savin' him, Carly." His voice cracked and he looked down, his cheeks flushing. He swiped his face and got to his feet. "I'm gonna check on that pot of coffee."

I nodded, not trusting myself to speak, not that he stuck around to hear anything I might have said. Max's shoulders shook a little as he rounded the corner. The realization that Seth was dead had to be hitting him full force.

I glanced down at my hands, feeling the urge to wash them. I wasn't sure if the sheriff's department would want to see them as part of their investigation. Which was when I realized there was something else that would interest them.

My gun.

I jumped out of the seat and ran for the front door, but just as I got it open, I saw flashing lights in the distance.

The sheriff was just down the street.

Oh crap. Oh crap. Oh crap.

My gun was on the ground next to Seth, but there was no way I'd be able to run over there and retrieve it and run back. The sheriff's deputy would see me.

I was screwed.

"Carly!" Max called out behind me.

"The sheriff is here," I said, my hand trembling on the doorknob.

"Come back inside and shut the door," he said. "You don't have any shoes. The deputy will come over here to talk to you."

I turned back to look at him, realizing he'd put on his own shoes and donned his jacket. "Are you going out there?"

"I'm gonna go talk to the deputy. Ruth's on her way, so stay put until she gets here."

The deputy's small SUV pulled to a stop on the tavern side of the street, but the deputy remained inside…parked between me and my secrets.

The door to my motel room was still standing wide open, a big gaping chasm to my precarious new life. What would they do when they found the gun? It wasn't registered to me. I had no idea if it was registered at all, and it definitely had my fingerprints all over it. I wasn't in any criminal databases, but I'd been fingerprinted in a couple of states as part of the background checks required for my teacher certification. Could they link my old identity to the gun with those?

Even if they didn't, their search might alert the people who were looking for me.

My stomach churned and my mouth turned sour.

Max started to move past me, but something in my face stopped him. He grabbed my upper arms as he searched my face. "It's gonna be all right, Carly. The deputy will come in and ask you a few questions and that will be that, okay?"

I opened my mouth, just barely stopping myself from telling him about the gun. What would he do if I told him I'd had one? Would he assume I'd shot Seth? Would he turn me in? Or would he help me? But if he did help me, he'd be breaking the law…

His brow furrowed as he watched me work through my dilemma. My mother had always told me I had a terrible poker face, that every emotion that floated through my head was plain as day. I'd worked on that over the years, but I was tired and scared, and I was sure he knew I was hiding something.

I decided to take a leap of faith.

"I had a gun."

He blinked. Then his brows shot up and his mouth parted. "What?"

"I have a gun and I took it out when I heard him moaning outside my room. I didn't know if the people who'd hurt him were still out there, and I was scared. But then I saw how badly he was hurt, and I dropped it on the ground so I could put pressure on his wound. I completely forgot about it," I said in a breathless rush. "It's not registered to me and if the deputy finds—"

His grip on my arms tightened and his eyes hardened. "Shh. Don't you worry about it. I'll take care of it."

I gasped. "What? How?"

"I know you didn't do this, and you were smart to carry a weapon with you. Now stay inside and trust me to deal with it, okay?" He dropped his hold and left the bar, the night air whooshing in as the door closed behind him, and I watched him jog across the street as a deputy started to get out of his car, his flashing lights bouncing off the red brick motel building.

Torn between bolting to the bathroom to vomit or staying to watch, I chose to stay and witness the end of life as I knew it.

Because when the deputy picked up that gun, it would start a chain of events that would reveal my true name. And if Carly Moore was unmasked, I was as good as dead.

"Carly?" Ruth called out in a panic behind me. I nearly jumped out of my skin.

I spun around to see her coming toward me across the dining room. She had on a pair of pink fuzzy pajama bottoms covered in tiny rubber duckies, and a dark puffy coat that hit just below her butt. Her fake Uggs were darker where they'd gotten wet from the light snow cover.

"What are you doin' in front of that open door, honey? You'll catch your death of cold."

I stared at her, frozen and unable to answer her.

She reached me and wrapped her arm around my back, gently tugging me away from the open doorway. I turned back to see Max standing to the side of Seth's body, his hands propped on his hips as both he and the deputy stared down at the boy.

Tears filled my eyes, and I reminded myself that a boy had died here tonight. His heartless murder was more important than my own worries.

Ruth shut the door and led me to the back of the restaurant and then into the kitchen.

"Tiny won't like us bein' back here," I said, resisting her tug to cross over the invisible line.

"Tiny won't give a single shit," she said, pulling me in and shoving me onto a high-backed metal barstool Tiny likely used for breaks. As I took a seat, she headed straight for the coffee brewer and poured steaming liquid into two ceramic mugs. "Cream or sugar?"

"Uh…both." Seth was dead. His murderers had driven off as casually as if they'd just finished a shopping trip at Walmart. I knew secrets that might help find them, but I couldn't trust the sheriff. My gun was lying on the ground next to Seth's body, a possible homing device for the people who were searching for me. All of this, and Ruth was asking if I took cream or sugar in my coffee.

I started to laugh.

Ruth squinted over at me as she poured coffee into both cups. Once she was done doctoring them, she set down the creamer carton with a decisive thud and reached into a cabinet, pulling out a small flask of whiskey. She poured a generous helping into each cup, then handed one to me. "Drink."

It was a direct order, and I found myself taking a big enough gulp to burn both my tongue and the roof of my mouth.

She must have caught a glimpse of my hands, because after taking a sip from her own mug, she grabbed a fresh dishrag and held it under the water from the faucet. When she returned, she swiped at my face, removing blood splatters I hadn't felt or noticed. She washed out the rag and returned, picking up one of my hands as she began to gently swipe at the stains, much like I used to clean up the preschoolers I'd watched at a daycare during my early education courses in college.

"I don't think you're supposed to do that," I said, my tears back. "The sheriff's deputy might need to—"

"Bullshit," she said, continuing to wipe. "If you're suggesting he might need this for evidence, then he'll just have to go without it. You're in shock and staring at his blood on your hands isn't gonna do anyone a lick of good, least of all Seth Chalmers, God rest his soul." Her eyes turned glassy and her hands began to shake.

"Did you know him?" I asked.

"Everyone knew him, especially after his momma died last year," she said as she continued to wipe off my hands.

I knew I should stop her, but her touch was comforting and grounding, and I felt myself calming down. "What happened to her?"

She shook her head and clucked. "Drugs. That's what happens to a good portion of the people in this godforsaken town. Meth. Like to have killed Hank, especially with his history and the stand he's always taken against hard drugs. His wife had just died of breast cancer and then he lost his daughter. Seth was all he had left."

My heart broke a little more. I couldn't bring Seth back, but maybe the information I had would help his grandfather seek justice. "Does Hank live close?"

"He lives over in White Rabbit Holler, out by me, but he ain't there." She shook her head again. "Hank Chalmers is in the hospital down in Greeneville." She made a face. "Got his leg amputated. Was supposed to come home in a day or two, and Seth was gonna take care of him." She pushed out a huge sigh. "Guess somebody should've been lookin' out for that boy."

"Someone shot him, Ruth," I said. "Do you have any idea who would do that?"

Her hand paused for a fraction of a second before she looked up at me. "Everybody loved that boy. His momma raised him with manners before she got addicted and passed, and he never forgot 'em. He helped Hank around the house as best he could, but you can't make a turnip bleed money, ya know? Still, he took care of the house and went shopping since Hank has mostly been housebound the last six months or so." She sighed again. "This is gonna kill him."

"I tried to save him," I said, close to breaking down again. "I tried to stop the bleeding."

"Honey," she said, "ain't nobody gonna blame you. You obviously tried to help him. Max said you heard him moaning and ran out to see if you could help. That's courageous in anyone's book."

"But I didn't save him."

"That's not on you. It's on the person who did this to the poor boy." She swiped at a tear rolling down her cheek with the back of her hand.

Throwing caution to the wind, I said, "Do you think any of the men in the bar last night could have done it?"

She went still, then looked up at me again, her eyes fierce. "We don't hurt our own."

We don't hurt our own.

If that was true, had the killer decided Seth wasn't one of their own? I definitely wasn't one of theirs, which meant I needed to mind my own business until I could get the hell out of here.

Chapter Six

By the time Ruth had gotten me cleaned up and forced me to down the entire cup of coffee mixed with whiskey, my anxious edge had softened a bit. But my heartbeat picked back up when Max appeared in the kitchen doorway with a middle-aged man in a dress shirt and jeans behind him.

"Carly, this here's Detective Daniels with the Hensen County Sheriff's Department," Max said, stepping into the room, which gave me a good look at the deputy. "He's investigating Seth's murder."

He was shorter than Max by a couple of inches and definitely at least fifty pounds heavier. I guessed him to be ten to fifteen years older too. His jacket hung open and the buttons on his shirt stretched the cloth to help contain his abdomen. The dark circles under his eyes indicated he'd been in bed when he'd received the call. Hopefully that meant he wasn't one of the "bad" deputies Seth had mentioned.

"Carly Moore?" he asked as he approached me.

Ruth was sitting next to me and reached over to squeeze my hand.

He didn't look all that scary, but I needed to watch myself, especially if he'd found my gun. "That's me." Then I added so hopefully it wouldn't be an issue later, "My real name's Charlene Moore, but I go by Carly."

"I understand you found the victim."

I nodded. "Yeah."

He slipped a small notebook and pen out of his coat pocket. "I know you've been through an ordeal, and it was obvious you tried to help Seth. That's what I'm trying to do now. I know I can't bring him back, but I can do the next best thing and find his killer. It will really help if you give me a brief statement telling me what happened."

His spiel about helping Seth seemed odd, like he was trying to convince me to do the right thing. Did he suspect Seth had given me some secret to keep from the sheriff's department? Or maybe he thought I'd accidentally shot Seth then tried to cover it up?

I glanced over at Max. He gave me a reassuring nod. Did that mean he'd taken care of my gun?

"Ruth," Max said in his congenial tone. "Before they get started, why don't we get Detective Daniels a cup of coffee to warm him up? He's been outside for a bit and that wind is brutal tonight."

She hopped off her stool and headed to the coffee brewer. "Do you take cream or sugar, Detective Daniels?"

His face lit up at the mention of coffee. "Black."

"I suspect this interview might be easier if both of you are sittin' down," Max said, reaching for me. "I'll take Carly out to the dining room and help get her settled." Before the detective could respond, he started leading me out the door.

He leaned in close and whispered, "He never saw the gun. You're covered."

I nearly stumbled as I pushed out a sigh of relief. "Max, you shouldn't have risked yourself like that."

"Don't you worry about it. Just get through your statement, then we'll deal with the rest later."

Deal with the rest? I started to ask him what he was talking about, but the detective was coming out of the kitchen with a cup of coffee in hand.

We settled at a four-person table—the detective and I sitting opposite each other. Max and Ruth took seats at the bar—still within earshot, I noticed, but it provided the illusion of privacy.

"Ms. Moore," the detective said as he opened his notebook again. "How did you know the victim?"

I blinked in surprise. "I *didn't* know him."

"Had you ever seen him before?"

"No."

He cocked an eyebrow. "You're certain?"

I shot a glance at Max and Ruth, but their expressions were stoic. Unreadable. "I'm very certain," I said with a tight smile. "I just got into Drum yesterday and worked here at the tavern last night. Seth never entered the establishment. Not that I saw anyway."

"Huh," he said, writing something in his notebook. "Tell me what happened. Be sure to start at the beginnin'."

I started with being woken up, then repeated the story of hearing a moan outside my room. Of running outside to check on Seth. I started to cry when I got to the part about trying to stop Seth's bleeding and the earsplitting scream I'd let out when no one had heard my cries for help.

"But he died just as Max reached us," I finished, not hiding my tears.

The deputy was writing in his pad, but he looked up when he asked, "And you didn't see who shot him?"

I paused. The detective seemed like he genuinely wanted to solve Seth's murder, and my silence could potentially let the murderer go free. Except Seth had warned me about trusting the sheriff's department. No, I'd let Seth's grandfather decide how to proceed, although it struck me that I could be in big trouble for giving the deputy false information. Something I was trying not to do. Withholding information was still a lie of omission, of course, but maybe I'd be in less trouble if I stuck close to the truth. "I didn't see anyone when I went out to check on him."

"No car driving away?" he asked. "You never heard a gunshot?"

"I woke up to his cry of distress," I said. "And when I went out to check on him, he was alone. No other car or trucks in sight." All technically true.

He jotted down a few lines and closed his notebook. "Max says you're not from around here, but you're sticking around for a few days."

So he knew I was new to town but still seemed to think I might have met Seth. Did he suspect I'd murdered the boy? Did he think I'd beaten him too? But he was waiting for an answer, so I pulled myself together.

"My car broke down," I said. "It's at the auto repair shop here in town."

"Where are you from?"

I swallowed, trying to hide my nervousness. "Atlanta."

He narrowed his eyes as he angled his head to one side. "How'd you end up in Drum? It's not usually a place people just drop in on. Got family around?"

"No. Just supreme bad luck." Silence hung between us, making it obvious he expected me to fill in more information. "I was driving through while on vacation."

"Through Drum?" He didn't try to hide his incredulousness.

The hairs on the back of my neck stood on end. "There's an overlook that gives you a good view."

"Oh, I know the place," he said. "It's just that no one uses it much since the state moved the road up to Balder Mountain a few years back."

Why was he questioning my story? Did he really suspect me of something, or was he just covering his bases? "When I checked out of my motel in Gatlinburg yesterday morning, the motel clerk suggested this route. She said it was a more scenic way to Interstate 40."

"You got to Drum on your way to the interstate coming *from Gatlinburg?*"

"My GPS didn't work, detective," I said with a bit more attitude than I'd intended. "I wandered around for a bit, then broke down at the overlook. I guarantee you that I'm now wishing I hadn't taken that scenic route."

He studied me for a long moment, then nodded. "We'll want to take a more formal statement later today, so we'll be in touch. There'll be some follow-up questions too. I'd prefer you don't leave town until we make sure we've gotten everything we need from you." He handed me a business card. "Since most cell phone carriers don't work out here, Max says the best way to reach you is here at the tavern."

I shot a glance to Max, who gave me a reassuring smile.

"Yeah," I said, facing the detective. "I'll be working all day today, but I'm not sure about my hours on Wednesday."

"We'll make sure you can reach her," Max said. "No worries there."

"Sounds good," the deputy said as he got to his feet and started for the door. He stopped and turned back to Max. "How's your father?"

Max's back straightened a fraction of an inch. "He's good."

"And your momma?"

"She's feelin' mighty fine after her last round of chemo," he said congenially. "Thanks for askin'."

The detective nodded. "Glad to hear it. Rumor has it that Bart's got somethin' in the works to get Drum back on the map."

"So I hear," Max said, shoving his hands in the back pockets of his jeans. "He likes to surprise his kids as much as he likes to surprise the town."

The detective cocked his head to the side. "Rumor also has it that Wyatt's still out of your parents' good graces."

"Oh, you know how the rumor mill works," Max said with a slow drawl and a cocky grin. "A whole lot of hearsay and such."

"So he's not on the outs?"

"Seems like you should be talkin' to Wyatt and my parents about their relationship, not me."

The detective studied Max for a moment before nodding. "All righty then. Maybe I will."

Then he headed out the door without a backward glance.

We were silent for a moment before Ruth jumped off her stool, her fists clenched at her sides like she was spoiling for a fight. "What the Sam Hill was that about?"

Max pushed out an exaggerated sigh and then turned around to face her. "You know Hensen County deputies. They ain't happy until they've harassed the residents of Drum and gotten in a good kick or two."

"Why was he askin' you about Wyatt?" Ruth asked. "Does he think Wyatt shot that poor boy?"

"I doubt it," Max said, walking behind the bar. He grabbed three glasses and set them on the counter. "He's fishin', but not for poor Seth's murderer. He's bound and determined to take the Drummonds down, and he's gonna use this excuse to rev up the chainsaw."

"He needs to let it go," Ruth said. "The past is in the past."

"What happened?" I asked, walking over to the counter, directly in front of Max. "Why the bad blood?" Technically, it was none of my business, but I was in the middle of this now. I needed to get my bearings, and it was obvious whatever was up with Detective Daniels had something to do with the Drummonds.

Max reached for a bottle of whiskey from the shelf behind him, then filled each glass with a generous pour. "My family's past is littered with plenty of not-so-legal ventures, but that ended in my grandparents' time. Moonshinin' and such. If we were mixed up with illegal ventures now, I sure as hell wouldn't be workin' seven days a week in this hellhole." After handing out the glasses of whiskey, he lifted his tumbler in a toast. "May the Hensen County Sheriff's Department's justice be swift and harsh for the perpetrator of Seth's death, and when they're through, may they clear out and leave the rest of us the hell alone."

He lifted his tumbler even higher and downed the amber liquid.

I gulped mine just as quickly. I could definitely drink to that.

"Should we be worried?" Ruth asked with a frown, only part of her whiskey gone.

"Why would we be worried?" Max asked. "We didn't do anything wrong. What do we have to hide?"

"What about Wyatt?" she asked. "The deputy seemed mighty interested in him."

Max frowned, pouring another generous amount into his glass. He picked it up, his lips still pressed together in thought. Finally, he said, "Wyatt's family, whether he wants to be or not. We'll bring him back into the fold eventually. Family sticks together."

What did that mean?

"Do you think Wyatt killed that boy?" I asked, my hand shaking.

Max snorted. "No. Wyatt's a lot of things, but he's no murderer."

"That's not what the rumor mill says," Ruth said, her brows raised.

"The rumor mill is a bunch of gossipy old hens and roosters with nothin' better to do than stir up shit," Max said in disgust. "That girl left town, plain and simple, and my parents were several thousand dollars lighter after helping speed along her departure." He winked at me. "But that's inside information, so I'd appreciate it if you didn't go spreadin' it around."

This entire conversation was putting me on edge. Why would Max share information with me that he didn't want the rest of the town to know? Then again, I'd shared a secret with him, so maybe he figured that made us even. Which reminded me that I had questions too... "About that thing I left next to Seth..."

Max finished his drink and poured more for himself and for me. "It wasn't there."

This time he slammed the whiskey down even faster.

Whatever was going on had Max on edge, but I had more immediate worries.

My hand tightened around my ridged glass. "Say again?" I was hoping I'd misheard or misunderstood.

His lips pulled back, exposing his teeth as he spun around and grabbed a clear, unlabeled bottle from the shelf behind the bar.

"*Max*," I said more insistently.

Ruth glanced between the two of us. "What are all y'all talkin' about?"

Max gave me a look that suggested it was my call.

Did I want to share this with Ruth? I barely knew her, but I felt like I could trust her. I had to trust *someone*. Besides, I suspected most people around here would think nothing of carrying a gun for protection.

Pushing out a sigh, I leaned my elbow on the counter and rested my forehead on my hand. "I knew something was wrong, so I brought a gun outside with me. I set it down when I was trying to help Seth, then I forgot all about it until right before the deputy showed up. I told Max, and he said he'd take care of it, now he says it was gone."

"It just up and vanished?" she asked him incredulously.

"Hell if I know," Max said with a shrug. "But I know it wasn't there when I distracted Detective Hard-on-for-the-Drummonds to go get it."

"Did another deputy get to it first?" Ruth asked, worry on her face.

"I don't see how," Max said, pouring himself another drink. "I came upon Marco as he got out of his car. Then we walked together to the body. It wasn't there. Marco was the first on the scene. There's no way the Hensen County Sheriff's Department has it."

"So who does?" I asked, my stomach falling to my feet.

"Now *that* is a mighty fine question," Max said, pointing a finger at me as he lifted his glass, now half full of a clear liquid. Had he moved on to vodka?

"Did you see anything else?" I asked him.

He squinted. "Like what?"

"I don't know...clues? Evidence?"

"There was nothin' on the ground next to him. Trust me. I checked."

"Who would take my gun?" I asked, trying not to panic. *And my key fob.*

I decided not to mention it. If I admitted to setting off the alarm, they'd wonder if I'd seen more than I was saying.

"Somebody who was watchin'," Ruth said solemnly.

I turned my head to face her. "Someone who saw the murder?"

"Maybe."

"Or someone who heard you scream bloody murder," Max said, taking a generous sip of his drink, then grimacing as it went down.

"You're gettin' sauced," Ruth said with a frown. "That deputy got you worried about your daddy?"

"My father ain't got nothin' for him to find," Max said, topping off his glass.

Ruth didn't look like she believed him, but she didn't press. "Max, it's three in the mornin', so you need to go back to bed. And so does Carly."

"She can't go back over to the motel," Max said. "The deputies have her room roped off for their investigation, not to mention the whole rest of the motel since whoever did this kicked in some doors."

"They can't go into my room, can they?" I asked in a panic. "Wouldn't they need a warrant?"

Max's eyes narrowed. "You got somethin' in there to hide?"

He laughed like he'd made a joke. But I didn't want the police to look too hard at my identification paperwork. My cell phone. Of course, the gun—the only thing that could really incriminate me—was gone.

The gun just didn't vanish into thin air, though. Someone had taken it, along with my key fob…the real question was what they planned to do with them.

Chapter Seven

Ruth offered to take me to her place, but first she insisted on leading Max upstairs and making sure he got to bed. I decided to clean up while I waited, but first I picked up the clear bottle and removed the lid to get a whiff. The smell of pure alcohol made my nose burn, and I made a face as I set it down.

"You're besmirchin' what's supposed to be the finest moonshine in all of Eastern Tennessee," Wyatt said from the door to the back room. He was leaning his shoulder into the doorframe as though he didn't have a care in the world.

Startled, I jumped a good couple of inches, and my heart started to race. I wasn't sure if it was because he'd scared me or because of his effect on my hormones, but I chose to believe it was the former. "What in the hell are you doing here? I thought you and Max were at odds."

"You've already been drawn into the Drummond family secrets, huh?" he asked, sounding bored. "That didn't take long."

"If you came to see Max, he's—"

He slowly began to advance toward me. "It wasn't Max I came to see."

"If it's Ruth, she'll be—"

"I didn't come to see Ruth either."

I swallowed hard. "What do you want?"

He laughed, but he didn't sound amused as he walked behind the bar and picked up the bottle. Although he supposedly didn't spend much time at the bar, he seemed comfortable enough as he reached under the counter and retrieved a glass. He poured himself a small amount of moonshine, then downed it.

"Same damn garbage it always was," he said, setting the glass and the bottle on the counter, his gaze fixed on me.

He was close enough to make me uncomfortable, and while I had plenty of space to back up and put some distance between us, I didn't want to give him the satisfaction of letting him know I was intimidated. Max had said he didn't think Wyatt capable of murder, but was he capable of hurting a woman? Plenty of men were.

"What do you want?" I repeated, but with a lot more attitude than before.

A hard look filled his bloodshot, slightly puffy eyes. He'd either been crying or drinking, but the moonshine on his breath made it difficult for me to tell the difference. "I'm gonna give you one more chance to tell me what you're doin' here."

What did he think I'd done? It struck me that he might have been at the garage at the time of the murder. The car alarm would certainly have given him a jolt. If he'd run over to the motel, he might have witnessed something.

Had he seen me next to Seth's body?

Was he the one who'd taken my gun and key fob?

I propped a hand on my hip and glared up at him. "Or what? What are you gonna do to me, Wyatt? Kill me?"

As the words fell out of my mouth, I wanted to reel them back in. If he actually *did* want to kill me, was it a good idea to so blatantly accuse him of it?

I blamed the whiskey and my nerves.

But his reaction was more startled than intimidating—his eyes flew wide and he took a step back. "*What?*"

"What's goin' on here?" Ruth asked in a hard voice as she came around the front of the counter, holding a handgun of her own. When she saw who was with me, she relaxed a little but didn't put down her gun. Wyatt's look of surprise might have been comical if I'd been in a laughing mood.

"What are you doin' here?" she asked him.

Frustration tightened his face. "I came to talk to Carly. No need for a weapon."

"We're all a little jumpy what with poor Seth lyin' out there in the parking lot, surrounded by a chalk line."

"If you think I'm gonna hurt either one of you, then you really don't know me at all, do you?"

"And whose fault is that?" she asked, still pointing her gun at him. When he didn't answer, she gave him a sharp nod. "Little early in the day to be givin' her that car repair estimate."

"That's not why I'm here."

"Well, she's about to head home with me, so you can talk to her tomorrow during business hours." She motioned toward the back door with her weapon. "Now get along."

He turned to look at me as though searching my face for something, but I had no idea what. Maybe he really *did* think I'd killed Seth.

Finally, he pushed out a breath of frustration and took another step backward. "I'll be back to talk to you after the lunch rush."

"I'm hopin' you'll have an estimate for me by then so I can get the hell out of here," I snapped back, even though I knew I wasn't going anywhere.

Unless I ran for it.

Could I? The thought filled me with equal parts relief and fear.

Even with a new identity, I wasn't sure it was a good idea, yet I was terrified I'd landed in a mess big enough to attract the exact wrong kind of attention. What if someone from the sheriff's office *had* found my gun and key fob and considered me a suspect? I really needed advice from my friends back in Arkansas, but first I had to find someplace in this godforsaken town that had cell service.

Wyatt continued backing up until he reached the end of the counter. With one final look I struggled to define, he turned around and strode out the back. As soon as we heard the thud of the heavy metal back door, Ruth said, "What the hell was that about?"

"I have no idea," I said, resting my forearms on the counter and leaning forward. This night was going from bad to worse. I nearly confided everything to Ruth, but something told me that would be a mistake. She wasn't Rose, and this town was clearly messed up. I decided to change the subject to one that wasn't much more pleasant. "Who's gonna tell Seth's grandfather?"

Based on the way she flinched, I'd caught her off guard. "I guess a sheriff's deputy. I hadn't really thought about it."

"I'd like to see him." That surprised her even more, so to avoid suspicion, I said, "Seth was still alive when I found him. I just think his grandfather might want to know about his last moments." I paused, then pushed past the lump in my throat. "I know I would."

Her face crumpled and tears filled her eyes. "I would too. How about I take you down there before you start your lunch shift? I was planning to go to Greeneville anyway. I just planned to do it later in the day."

"I don't want to put you out, Ruth."

"No worries," she said with a wave of her hand. "Like I said, I'm goin' anyway. I'll just go earlier than I'd planned."

I didn't have a coat, but I assured Ruth I didn't need one. Max must have told her I didn't have shoes, because she'd brought me a pair of open-back slippers in case my feet were bigger than hers. (I was a half size smaller.) I followed her out to the parking lot, light snow crunching under our feet, and Ruth led me toward an old sedan that was as big as a tank. I walked around to the passenger side. I'd never seen a car this big in person.

"The door sticks," she said as I reached for the handle.

She was right. It took me three tries and finally a hard yank to get it open. The door sagged and it took me several more attempts to get it closed.

"I keep nagging Franklin to fix it, but he claims there's nothin' to be done."

"It's not a problem," I said, wrapping my arms around myself as I shivered.

"You're a terrible liar," she said with a laugh, inserting a huge key into the ignition and turning the engine over. "It's a beast of a car, but the engine gets hot fast in the winter." She glanced over at me with a huge grin. "And I can tell all my friends I drive a Cadillac…even if it's from 1973."

"At least it runs," I said with a chuckle. "It's more than *I've* got."

She laughed again. "True enough."

After she let the engine idle for a few seconds, she backed up and pulled out of the parking lot.

"Ruth, you have no idea how much I appreciate you coming in after Max called you," I said. "And bringing me home on top of that?" I shook my head. "I don't know how to thank you."

Ruth shook her head. "You've already done plenty. You saved my ass tonight with the Monday Night Football crowd, and you're fun to boot. Givin' you a place to crash is nothin'." She cast a glance my way. "Tell me you were usin' my sheets before you were woke up."

"I was," I said, leaning my head back into the velour seat back. "They were heavenly."

"Don't you worry. I have 'em on my guest bed too. You'll be able to sleep like a baby."

I wasn't sure how much I'd sleep, but at least I'd be lying on soft sheets.

We were quiet for the rest of the fifteen-minute drive. It was dark, so I couldn't make out much other than we were surrounded by trees. She turned from the two-lane road onto a narrow paved road and took another turn onto a gravel road about five minutes later, pulling up to a clear patch of earth with a mobile home that looked only slightly newer than her car. A newer dark green pickup truck was parked in front of it.

"At least Franklin's home," she said, sounding relieved.

"Does he work the night shift?" I asked.

"No, he was hanging out at his friend's house after he left Max's. He wasn't home yet when Max called."

I focused my attention on the trailer ahead of us.

"I know it ain't much," Ruth said, sounding embarrassed.

"It's the heart of the home that counts," I said, "not the contents."

She pulled to a stop next to the truck and shifted the large gear shift into park before turning to face me. Her face brightened. "You know what? You're exactly right."

"My mom used to tell me that," I said, still hearing her murmur the words into my ear as she held me on her lap. I'd

89

been too old to be cradled like that—around eight or nine—but she and my father had just had a knock-down, drag-out argument that had scared me. It was the first time they'd ever fought so brutally, and I'd hidden in the closet so they wouldn't be able to find me. Only my mother had come looking. "Oh, Carly," she'd said, pulling me to her, "don't you worry. We'll always have each other. You and me, we're the heart of this home."

If only it had been true.

"She sounds like a wise woman," Ruth said, letting the engine idle. "Do you want to call her? I've got a workin' landline."

My mouth lifted into a tight smile. "Thanks for the offer, but she died when I was a kid." That didn't fit Charlene Moore's purchased narrative, but my heart was too raw to pretend the mother whose death had destroyed me could be reached by a simple phone call. And I didn't want to lie to Ruth any more than necessary.

"I'm sorry," she said.

I shrugged. "Water under the bridge."

"I lost my mother a couple of years ago," she said, then made a face. "Drugs. She'd lived her entire life clean, so nobody would have guessed she'd surrender herself to meth in her late forties. Men and alcohol had been her vices of choice."

"I'm so sorry, Ruth."

She bit her lower lip and studied the metal trailer in front of us. A soft light glowed through the curtain-covered front windows. "Just like you said, water under the bridge."

She turned off the ignition and opened the car door. Something about the way she did it suggested the water under her bridge hadn't traveled very far downstream.

I put my all into opening my own door, pleased when it unlatched on the first try. After I shut it, I followed Ruth up the rickety stairs to the front door.

She opened the it without using a key and stepped to the side so I could walk in.

The interior furnishings were in better shape than the outside. The tan sofa looked worn but clean, and while the dark brown faux leather recliner was covered in cracks, the afghan draped over it made it look homey.

"It ain't much," she said as she shut the door and set her purse on a small oak kitchen table with white legs.

"I haven't felt so at home in weeks," I confessed before I thought better of it.

She gave me a look of surprise.

"I'm in the middle of moving," I said. "All my stuff's in storage until I figure out where I'm going to end up." Only then did I remember I'd told the deputy I was on vacation. Crap.

"You're movin' and you don't know where you're goin'?" she asked in surprise, slipping off her coat.

"No," I said. "I just decided I needed a change, and I'm figuring out where to land."

A huge smile spread across her face. "Maybe you'll stick around Drum." The horror on my face must have shown, because she laughed. "I'm teasing. No one willingly sticks around Drum except for the Drummonds themselves. Seems like the rest of us are stuck here." She wrapped her arms across her chest. "Well, on that happy note, let me show you to your room."

She led me down the hall to the first room on the right, a small bedroom with a full-sized bed and a wrought iron headboard. A silver metal lamp sat on the blue-painted nightstand. "This is your room. The bathroom's across the hall.

Franklin's gotta go to work early, so you might hear him clomping around at six or so. I apologize in advance."

"No need. I'm just grateful to be here."

"If we're gonna get to Greeneville for you to see Mr. Hank and back in time to get you to your lunch shift, we should probably leave here around eight."

"Sounds good." She left the room and shut the door behind her, leaving me alone with my memories and my fear.

Since I was still in my pajamas, I just climbed under the covers and pulled them up to my chin. I lay there for a long time, staring up at the dark ceiling and wondering if my life would ever be normal again.

Chapter
Eight

I woke up to the sound of running water, and it took me a few seconds to orient myself.

Seth.

A spike of pain stabbed my heart as I remembered holding his hand and soaking up his blood with my shirt while I watched him die. No one should die like that, but especially not a seventeen-year-old kid. Had I gotten him killed by setting off my car alarm? There was no way of knowing, and the guilt was excruciating. I jerked upright in bed, trying to dislodge the claws that had sunk into my back.

I hoped Hank Chalmers would help me decide what to do about the sheriff's department. Perhaps go above their heads? I could always go to the state police if the sheriff's department was corrupt. And even if the deputy who'd reported to the scene last night wasn't involved, someone clearly was—Seth had been adamant that a sheriff's deputy had shot him.

I tried to turn over and get more sleep, but the smell of coffee eventually lured me out of my room.

When I walked into the kitchen, Franklin was making a sandwich at the counter. Thankfully, he didn't look too surprised to see me. I could understand why Ruth was attracted to him. Franklin was a solid man—good-looking but not enough to get him into trouble. Tanned skin from working outside and a toned body to go with it. He looked to be a couple of years shy of forty, even though he had crow's-feet around his eyes, also likely from working outside.

"We didn't get properly introduced last night," I said. "I'm Carly Moore."

He gave me a warm smile. "Franklin Tate. Ruth calls me Franklin, but just about everyone else calls me Tater."

I fought a grin. "So you want me to call you Tater?"

He shrugged, still grinning, "Sure. Why not?"

"I guess Ruth filled you in on what happened," I said, still standing in the entrance to the kitchen.

He shook his head as he slapped a generous helping of deli turkey from a hard-plastic container onto a slice of white bread. "Ain't right that a boy was murdered like that, and it definitely ain't right that you had to see 'im." He turned his gaze to me as he picked up a mustard bottle from the counter. "But Ruth said you stayed with him until the end." He gave a sharp nod, his eyes glassy. "That was good of you."

"No one should die alone," I said, overwhelmed with an onslaught of sorrow.

He nodded again, then turned back to his lunch, squirting a generous amount of mustard on his turkey. "Ruth also said you needed a place to stay."

"I hope this was okay. I suspect they'll let me back into my room in the motel tonight, and if not, I'll ask Max to give me another one."

"Don't you worry about that," he said, slapping a piece of bread on the mess and slipping the sandwich into a plastic baggie. "You stay as long as you need to. Everyone knows that motel ain't fit for flea-bitten dogs, which was why I was more than happy to bring the sheets."

"Thank you," I said. "That's really kind of you and Ruth to take in a stranger."

"Ruth says you're good people," Franklin said, tossing his sandwich, a huge bag of chips, and a prepackaged cupcake into a hard-sided lunch bag. "That's good enough for me."

"Thanks, Frank—I mean, Tater. If I can help out in any way, you and Ruth let me know."

He grinned. "I'm just happy she's got some help at the tavern. You can call me Franklin if you'd like. Help yourself to coffee and a shower or whatever else you need. Ruth put some clothes out for you in the bathroom in case you woke up before she did."

"Thanks," I said again as he headed for the door. "Have a good day."

He grabbed a ball cap off a hook on the wall by the door, tugged it on his head, then tipped the brim to me. "You too."

I poured myself a cup of coffee after he left—finding a flavored creamer in the fridge—then took it into the bathroom with me. A snapshot of Seth's face appeared in my head and I shuddered as I tried to expel it.

I stripped off Max's overshirt, startled when I saw the splotches of blood on my cami from when Seth had coughed on me. Ruth had washed the blood off my hands and face, but the overshirt had hidden the remaining evidence of my involvement in Seth's death.

Horrified, I snatched it over my head and tossed it onto the floor, then sat on the toilet and began to cry, trying to muffle my sobs so I didn't wake Ruth.

I couldn't do this. I couldn't face this. I needed to get the hell out of Drum. And not after Wyatt fixed my car—I needed to leave *today*.

When Ruth took me to Greeneville to see Mr. Chalmers, I'd find a bus schedule and plan a way out of town. But first I needed to get my things out of the motel room. At the very least, I needed my money and brand-new ID. At the moment, I literally only had my pajama bottoms and a bloody cami.

I showered off the grime and remaining blood that had dried to my skin, washing my hair too. I let myself cry through most of it, but as I shut off the water, I steeled my spine and pulled myself together. Either I could flounder in despair or do something to get myself out of this mess. Self-pity could come later.

When I got out, I found the clothes Ruth had set out for me on one of the storage shelves. Underwear and a white lacy bra, jeans, and a pale blue button-down shirt. The bra was one size too big, and the jeans were a little snug in the hips, but I didn't look like I was wearing someone's hand-me-downs. Ruth hadn't just tossed me an extra pair of clothes. She'd put some thought into it.

I didn't have any makeup to conceal the dark circles under my eyes, but there was nothing to be done about that. I towel-dried my short hair, then headed into the kitchen.

Ruth was sitting at the kitchen table in her pajamas, nursing a cup of coffee and reading a paperback romance. Her face tilted up and she smiled. "Feel better?"

"It's amazing what a shower can do."

"A good cry too," she said sympathetically.

I grimaced. "Sorry. I tried not to disturb you."

"Don't you dare apologize," she said, setting down her book as she got to her feet. "You experienced a major trauma last night. Frankly, I'd be leery of you if you *hadn't* cried at some point."

"It's just…" Seth's face popped into view again, and a lump clogged my throat.

Ruth gave me a hug, then pulled back. "No apologies. I'm gonna take a shower, then I thought we'd head into town and grab breakfast from the café. I want to check on Max, and I'm hopin' we can get your things out of your room. Franklin and I want you to stay with us until your car gets sorted out."

"Thanks, Ruth. You have no idea how much I appreciate your generosity."

"Don't you think a thing about it." She squeezed my arm, then disappeared into the bathroom. Twenty-five minutes later, she emerged in jeans and a bulky black sweater that looked great with her complexion. She'd taken the time to blow-dry her hair and had put on a little eyeshadow and mascara. "We have to get you a coat of some kind."

"I'll be fine until I get the jacket from my room," I said.

"I should have given you a sweater too."

I waved her off. "I'm fine."

"Everything fits?"

I laughed. "You have bigger boobs than I do, but the push-up cups are doin' wonders."

She laughed too, but the humor soon slipped from her face and she reached out and squeezed my upper arms. "I'm here for you, girl. Okay?"

My tears were back, dammit. I nodded. "Thank you."

"Let's go get some food and some coffee that isn't thick enough to double as motor oil. Damn. I love that man, but Franklin needs to learn how to make a decent pot of coffee."

***

I paid more attention as we made the drive to town. I realized we weren't that far from Drum as the crow flies, but the narrow, torn-up paved road switchbacked left and right as it descended toward the town, making the journey seem deceptively longer. The snow that had dusted the sides of the roads the night before had mostly disappeared.

"Hank Chalmers' property is back that way," Ruth said, pointing to a gravel driveway on my side of the road. Hank, as in Seth's grandfather. A house stood about seventy feet back from the road, and I could see a couple of deputy cars out front.

"What are they doin' there?" I asked, my heart in my throat. What if they'd found whatever evidence Seth had hidden?

Her mouth pursed. "Likely lookin' for drugs or whatever reason he was killed." She turned to look at me. "He didn't say nothin'?"

Guilt consumed me, and I had to glance away before I answered her. "He was a scared kid who wanted to make sure his grandfather knew he loved him."

"So he *did* say something to you besides askin' you not to leave?" she asked in surprise. "That's not what you told that deputy."

Oh. Shit. I gave her a sheepish look. "I don't know about you, but a boy's goodbye to his grandfather seems like a private thing. If I'd told that deputy, he would have put it into the report. If Mr. Chalmers wants me to tell the deputy, then I'll do it, but not without his blessing."

Her mouth formed an O and she was so busy staring at me she nearly drove off the road. She righted the course with a sharp jerk of the wheel. "*That's* why you want to see Hank. You've got a message for him."

"Please don't tell anyone," I pleaded. "For one thing, I could get in trouble with the sheriff, and like I said, it feels private. If I gave my grandmother a farewell while I was dying, I don't think I'd want the whole world to hear it."

"I guess," she said with a slight shrug, holding the wheel with both hands as she studied the road. "You're special people, Carly. Most folks wouldn't go out of their way to deliver a message."

I squirmed slightly. "Maybe they would if they'd promised a dying boy."

"Maybe." She didn't seem so certain.

"Do you have any family around here?" I asked to change the subject.

"Not much anymore. I had a few cousins who got lucky and up and moved to Knoxville. I stuck around to help my momma with the rent, but she started stealing my money for drugs roundabout the time I turned thirty. She had men in and out of her life, but I have no idea who my father is. She had me at fifteen and never said. If he's anything like the others, that suits me just fine."

I took it she didn't have kids. If she did, they could have been living with their father, but there was something fierce and protective about Ruth, and I was fairly certain she'd never willingly give up her kids to someone else.

"I don't have any kids," she said, as though reading my mind. "After livin' with my momma, there wasn't any way on earth I'd put them through something like that."

"I highly doubt you'd be like your mother," I said.

She shook her head. "I wouldn't lose myself to drugs, that's for damn sure, but I still live in a hellhole. I don't want to be raising kids in this mess."

She didn't want to have kids if she couldn't provide for them. I respected that, but I hoped that she'd find a way to have kids if she really wanted them.

The narrow road ended on a two-lane county road, and Ruth turned right. The land was flat on her side, but a cliff butted up to the road on my side. The rock had clearly been cut away for the road.

About ten minutes later, the town came into view and I paid more attention this time than I had when I'd driven in with Wyatt. The first block included a Laundromat and a café on the right side, along with some barren storefronts with worn *For Rent* signs on their grimy windows. Drum City Hall and a small library hunkered on the left. Next to them were a beauty salon and an insurance office.

Ruth stopped at the four-lane intersection. The tavern was on the right. A small vacant building sat opposite it, next to the motel, surrounded by crime scene tape. I could see a church halfway down the road to the left, followed by several houses.

Ruth turned right and pulled into the parking lot behind the tavern, clucking when she saw all the cars already parked there.

"I should have known," she said. "The looky-loos are already here, and the tavern has the best view in town of the crime scene. They'll be hanging out inside, hopin' to get a front seat to the action. Max won't have the good sense to turn them away."

"Maybe he's still in bed," I said as I opened the door and climbed out. "He *did* have a lot to drink last night."

"Let's hope," she said as she slammed her door shut. "I've never seen him shaken up like that. Not even after Wyatt shunned the family."

I slammed my door too, thrilled when it actually shut, and hurried after her. She'd lent me a pair of her athletic shoes. My toes slipped forward, leaving a slight gap at my heels.

She glanced back at the car, then grinned at me.

"Good job. It usually takes people a half dozen times to get the hang of it." She shoved her shoulder into mine as we kept walking.

I grinned, knowing it was stupid to feel proud of something so trivial, but I'd take what I could get. "It's a special skill set."

She laughed as she unlocked the back door, holding it open for me to enter first.

I heard voices when I walked in, and Ruth and I exchanged a look and headed straight for the dining room. Max was standing behind the bar, nursing a cup of what I hoped was coffee, while a group of older men and women were gathered around the front window.

Ruth didn't waste any time making a beeline to Max, leaving me to follow.

"What the hell, Max?" she snarled in an undertone when she reached him.

He stared at her with hooded eyes underscored with dark circles. "Good morning to you too, sunshine."

"Why are all these people in the bar?"

He waved a hand toward them in a broad sweep. "What's it look like?"

"It looks like a bunch of bullshit," she said, stomping past me and over to the group. "All right now. Show's over."

One of the women turned toward her with a haughty glare. "Max said we could be here."

"Well, Max may own the place, but I'm the manager. And seein' as how we're servin' neither food nor drink yet and you haven't purchased a damn thing, you need to head on out."

"But—"

"You're more than welcome to come back at noon if you feel so inclined, but only if you're paying customers."

"We're not hurtin' anything," another woman objected.

"Actually," Ruth said, with plenty of attitude, "Max has a raging headache and he's in dire need of peace and quiet. He'll be ready to face the lunch crowd in about four hours." She walked over to the front door and held it open. "So y'all head on out and we'll see you in a bit. Don't forget that chicken-fried steak is the Tuesday lunch special!"

The small crowd shuffled out, although several people shot Ruth belligerent looks on their way out. When the last of them left, she shut the door behind them and locked it. "No one comes through that door until we open for lunch."

I knew she wasn't talking to me, so I snuck a glance at Max, who looked like he was about to barf up last night's dinner.

Ruth marched back over to him and snatched the mug from his hand and took a whiff. With a look of disgust, she dumped it into the sink.

"Hey!" he protested.

"The hair of the dog won't help you, Maxwell Lincoln Drummond. You need breakfast."

He gave her a surly glare.

"Don't you be giving me that look, young man," she snorted, and I nearly laughed because she couldn't be more than a couple of years older than him. "You need a generous helpin' of grease."

He narrowed his eyes at me. "Why aren't you sick as a dog?"

"Because you were the only fool drinking himself into a stupor," Ruth responded.

"If we go to Watson's Café, everyone's gonna be grilling me, wanting to know what happened," he said, digging in his heels. "I don't want to deal with the questions."

"Then why the hell did you let those fools in?"

"It seemed like the best way to get the banging on the door to stop."

The front door started to open, and Ruth stared at it with a look of disbelief. "How the hell...?"

A man walked in wearing a cowboy hat, brown leather jacket, and jeans. Ruth had definitely locked the door, which meant he had a key. He removed his hat, revealing thick dark hair, as he shut the door behind him.

"That didn't take long," Ruth muttered under her breath.

At the sound of her voice, he looked up and did a double take when he saw the two of us standing side by side. The slightly wary look in his eyes told me he'd hoped to find Max alone, but our presence mustn't have bothered him, because he strode into the bar. He didn't give off a threatening vibe, so I relaxed, especially since neither Ruth nor Max seemed intent on kicking him out.

Max groaned. "I wondered how long it would take for you to show up, Carson."

"Don't go shootin' the messenger, Max," Carson said with a little chuckle as he lifted his hands in surrender. "Just doin' as I'm instructed."

Max leaned into the counter and waved his free hand in a circle. "Go on, then."

Carson's warm eyes filled with sympathy. "As you can imagine, your father wasn't pleased to hear there was a murder on his property."

"Yeah, well I'm none too pleased myself," Max said, staring down at his coffee cup, his face drawn. "And not because my father's upset." He looked up and met Carson's eyes. "Seth was a good kid."

"Your father plans to personally extend his sympathy to Hank." Carson started to say something else but shut his mouth as his gaze shifted to me. "Perhaps we should discuss this in private."

"Yeah," Max said with a huge sigh. Then he gave Ruth an expectant look.

"Carly needs to get her things," she said. "We'll go on over and see about gettin' 'em, then come back to get you before we go to breakfast."

Max grunted his acknowledgment as he waited for us to walk out the front door.

"Who was that?" I asked once we were outside.

"Carson Purdy. Bart Drummond's faithful lackey." She paused for a beat before adding, "He runs the Drummond property and does a host of other 'jobs.'" She said the last word with air quotes.

Did Bart have an interest in the bar? Otherwise, why did Carson have a key?

I shot her a look of surprise. "He's here about Seth's murder? Does he have an interest in him or his family?"

"Bart Drummond has an interest in absolutely everything that happens in Drum." She gave me a sideways grimace. "I suspect Carson's not only quizzing Max about Seth but about you too."

"*Me?*"

"Nothin' gets by Bart Drummond. If you stick around, you'd best not forget that."

That sounded ominous, but not as ominous as the scene before me.

Most of the motel parking lot was surrounded by yellow crime scene tape, even the two cars that had been parked in the lot the night before. Little yellow plastic evidence markers with numbers were spread around the asphalt. Thankfully, Seth's body had been removed and replaced with a chalk outline. A large dark stain spread outside the line.

I stopped in my tracks, my heart racing as I remembered holding his hand. Looking into his battered face. His terrified eyes.

"Carly," Ruth said, standing in front of me to block the view. "You don't have to do this. Why don't you go on ahead to Watson's Café and wait for me?"

That would be the easy way out, but it would be a chicken thing to do.

"No," I said, taking a deep breath and stiffening my back. "I need to get my own stuff, but I want you with me, if that's okay."

She wrapped an arm around my back. "Of course it's okay."

Several deputies were milling about, and we caught the attention of one of them, who then headed over to us.

I froze in fear. A deputy had killed Seth, and for all I knew, he was here at the scene, cleaning up his evidence.

This deputy appeared to be in his late thirties to early forties, and the grumpy look on his face suggested he didn't appreciate his current assignment. Was that because he'd played a role in the crime? "This is a crime scene, so y'all need to head on out."

His voice wasn't familiar, and I felt a tiny bit of the tension between my shoulder blades ease. I wasn't sure what I would have done if I'd come face to face with the murderer.

Ruth gave him a smile. "This here's Carly, the woman who found the murdered boy. And that right there"—she pointed to the open door to my room—"is Carly's room with all her worldly possessions. We just want to get her things, then we'll get out of your hair."

"We're not supposed to let anyone in," he said, looking Ruth up and down, his gaze lingering on her chest even though it was covered by her bulky sweater.

Ruth put both hands on her hips and gave him a sassy stare. "We won't touch a thing other than her suitcase and her purse."

"I suppose if I go in with you…"

"That's okay with us," she said enthusiastically.

He glanced around and then lifted the tape, motioning for us to duck underneath it. Ruth went under first, and I caught his gaze landing on her butt as she scooted under.

I wanted to call him out on it, but I needed my things, so I bit my tongue and followed.

He gestured toward the room and we walked over, catching the attention of the other officers working the scene.

"She's just getting her belongings," the deputy told them. "I'll keep a close eye on 'em."

I walked into the room and stopped in my tracks when I saw my suitcase on the floor. My personal items were strewn everywhere.

Ruth walked into my back, making me stumble. She pushed around me. "Tell me you didn't leave your clothes like that."

"The suitcase was on the dresser, and while it wasn't zipped up, I'm fairly certain I closed it."

Ruth turned to the deputy and lifted her brows. "What the hell happened to her shit?"

His cheeks flushed. "They searched it, ma'am."

"Searched it?" she shouted. "Why in the hell would they search her things? She was the only person to actually try to *help* that poor boy, and you reward her by throwing her shit all around? Are you fucking *kidding me?*"

He went from bewildered to pissed in a matter of seconds, and I worried he was going to kick us out, so I squatted by the suitcase and started tossing my things back in. "It's fine."

"The fucking hell it is!" she shouted. "Is this how we treat heroes in Hensen County? By destroying their shit?"

"Now settle down, ma'am," the deputy said in a patronizing tone. "She's a person of interest, so we've got *every* right."

My heart stuttered at his pronouncement. I was a person of interest? I needed to get the hell out of Drum. After I talked to Seth's grandfather, I'd catch the first bus from Greeneville to anywhere.

"Why in the Sam Hill would she be a person of interest?" Ruth shouted, her fists balled at her sides. "Any fool could see that there's no way she did this."

"It's okay, Ruth," I said, jamming the rest of my clothes into the bag. I started zipping the side.

"Is there a problem here?" I heard a familiar voice ask, but thankfully, it didn't belong to one of the murderers.

I glanced up at Detective Daniels.

"It's nothing," I said, getting to my feet and tugging my suitcase upright as I stood. "I'm just getting my things."

"Plannin' on goin' somewhere?" he asked in a dry tone.

"No, I'm staying with Ruth and her boyfriend, but I still need clothes."

"I see," he said, but it was obvious he didn't trust me. He seemed even more sour this morning than he had last night. "Don't forget you can't be leavin' town."

"I'm takin' her down to Greeneville," Ruth said, her chin issuing a challenge.

He cocked his head to the side, his eyes lighting up. "Is that so?"

"I'm not *leaving* leaving," I insisted. "I'm just riding down with Ruth to pick up some additional things since I hadn't planned on staying here."

"Is that so?" he repeated. It made the hairs on my arms stand on end.

Ruth looped her arm through mine. "That's right. There's nothin' in this town other than the Dollar General, so we're heading to Greeneville to get her supplies. We need to be back by noon so Carly can work the lunch shift, so the longer you keep us here, the longer it will take for her to get back to Drum."

He narrowed his eyes, glancing back and forth between us. "You're Ruth Bristol, aren't you? You work at Max's Tavern. That's why you were there last night."

I didn't remember him asking for her name the night before, so the fact that he knew it set my nerves on edge.

"So?" she asked, looking unconcerned.

"If you take her out of the county and she doesn't return, I will hold you *personally* responsible and arrest you for aiding and abetting her escape."

My throat constricted. Could he do that? Now I was truly stuck in this nightmare.

Chapter
Nine

F ine," Ruth said with a head toss. "You'll look like a fool when I have her back for her lunch shift. So can we go now? We don't want to be late gettin' back."

He stepped out of the doorway. "Safe travels."

I snatched my purse and coat off the dresser, then grabbed the handle of my suitcase. I rolled it past him as I left the room, fighting the broken wheel while Ruth followed.

We hurried across the parking lot. Max must have already finished his conversation with Carson, because he was waiting just outside the crime scene tape, chatting with one of the deputies. They stopped talking as we approached, and the young deputy lifted the crime scene tape so Ruth and I could duck under it.

"See ya, Marco," Max said as he took charge of my bag and rolled it across the street toward the front door of the tavern. I nearly told him to put it in Ruth's car, but there was no way I could leave and risk Detective Daniels arresting Ruth. Which meant I'd be returning to Drum.

I fought the urge to cry.

"I called in an order to Watson's," Max said, casting a glance to Ruth. "But *you* have to go pick it up."

She narrowed her eyes. "Why are you avoidin' that place? I know it's more than dealin' with gossip." When he cringed, she let out a groan. "Who did you screw now?"

He made a face. "Greta."

She gave him a dark look. "Greta? Really, Max? Ain't you ever heard of the saying 'Don't shit where you eat?'"

"How was I supposed to know she'd get a job at Watson's?" he asked in dismay.

"How about you treat a woman like a lady and quit goin' through 'em like tissues," Ruth snapped. "Drum's only so damn big, you know."

He rolled his eyes then groaned. "Don't be a drama queen, Ruth. I don't go through that many women, and I can't help it if they want to get serious after I've made it clear that I don't."

"Greta must not have lasted long if I never heard of it."

His cheeks flushed. "Greta was a mistake born of moonshine and a sexy red dress."

She shook her head in disgust. "Well, we have more serious issues to deal with. Carly's a suspect."

"No," he said with a frown. "Marco told me a bit about what's going on. She's a person of interest. There's a difference."

"Doesn't feel like much of a difference to me," I said.

"That's the most ridiculous thing I've ever heard," Ruth protested. "Why on earth would she kill Seth? She didn't even know him."

"Marco says they're lookin' for the easy pickin's," Max said. "It'd be a whole lot better for everyone involved if an outsider killed him, and they caught wind that someone from Atlanta was makin' a drug drop here in Drum last night. So what with Carly bein' from Atlanta and all…"

A drug drop from Atlanta? Was that why several of those guys had given me funny looks last night? My mind jumped to the guy who'd showed interest in my connection to Atlanta—and then hotly denied it. Was that what those three guys had been looking for? Drugs?

"Wait," I said, holding up my hand. "When you say for *everyone* involved, are you talkin' about your father?" He likely hadn't sent Carson just to get the scuttle on gossip.

Max's cheeks tinged. "Don't you worry about that. I told Carson in no uncertain terms that you had nothin' to do with it. And my father has a lot of sway with the sheriff's department. He gives them a large donation every year."

"Why, just last year he bought the department six new SUVs," Ruth added.

I wasn't sure that made me feel any better. His pull could just as easily be used against me as for me.

He shot me an apologetic look. "Between my father's influence and the lack of evidence, they'll drop their interest in you soon enough and figure out they're barkin' up the wrong tree. Marco told me they found a couple of bullet casings close to the street, so hopefully it will help them find the real murderer."

While that sounded great, the murderer hadn't shot Seth close to the street. He'd been shot about ten feet from my door. So where had the bullet casings come from? Were bullet casings randomly lying around the streets of Drum?

What if the murderers had come back and dropped spent shells from my gun, setting me up for murder?

My skin felt clammy.

"Max is right," Ruth said cheerfully. "They'll figure out they're barkin' up the wrong tree soon enough. In the meantime, the trip to Greeneville might take your mind off things." Then, as though remembering the purpose of my trip to Greeneville, her smile fell.

"Greeneville?" Max asked in surprise. "What the hell are you goin' down there for? Carly's workin' the lunch shift."

"I've gotta run some errands and I'm takin' her with me so people'll leave her alone," Ruth said.

The look on Max's face suggested he didn't buy her excuse, but he didn't call her out on it. I had to wonder why she hadn't told him the real reason I wanted to go to Greeneville, but maybe she knew he'd ask questions that I didn't want to answer.

"I'm going to grab our breakfast," Ruth said, then gave me a once-over. "Why don't you stay here with Max while I pick it up?"

"You worried about the gossipers?" I asked in a sly tone.

"No sense jumpin' into shark-infested waters," she said. "They'll start circlin' soon enough."

I suspected she was right.

Max gestured to the front door of the tavern. "You want to wait inside?"

I shook my head as I faced the crime scene. If someone was trying to pin this on me, it might be a good idea to ask some questions of my own.

"Those two cars," I said, gesturing to the station wagon and a rusted compact car. "Who do they belong to?"

Max's brow shot up. "Uh...the guys who live in units one and two."

"Jerry and...?" I'd forgotten the other guy's name.

Max's eyes narrowed. "Big Joe. How'd you know he lived there?"

"Ruth," I said. "Remember when you were discussing where to put me?"

He closed his eyes and pushed out a long breath before giving me an apologetic grimace. "Yeah."

"Do you think they might have seen something?"

Max hesitated. "I don't know. I haven't talked to them."

"Did your friend Marco say anything?"

When he gave me a suspicious look, I said, "While I'd love nothing more than for the police to come to the obvious conclusion that I'm innocent, forgive me if I don't feel like sitting back and waiting for everything to fall into place."

"You *do* realize you can get in trouble if they think you're interfering in their investigation?" he asked.

I gave him a sassy grin. "There's nothin' wrong with a neighbor checking on and commiserating with her neighbors, is there?"

He gave me a look that suggested he was seeing me in a new light. "I suppose not," he said, smiling back at me. "As your mutual landlord, let me introduce you."

We walked across the street and Max knocked on unit one's door. One of the deputies cast a glance at us. He looked like he was about to head over, but Max lifted his hand and waved. "Checkin' on my tenants."

He knocked again, and the door to unit two opened.

An elderly man popped his head out of a foot-wide crack. "Jerry's gone."

"Gone?" Max asked in surprise. "Gone where?"

"Dunno. He left and hasn't come back."

"But his car is still here," Max said. "Did someone pick him up?"

"Dunno," the man said. "He beat it out of here after the sheriff's deputies started showin' up in the middle of the night."

I stepped forward. "Hi. I'm Carly, and I was in room twenty." I gestured toward my room. "I was wondering if you happened to see or hear anything."

"I heard you screamin' bloody murder," Big Joe said with a look of outrage. "Woke me out of a good dream."

"You do realize that Seth Chalmers was murdered here last night?" Max asked, his words drenched in disgust. "A boy died."

"Ain't my concern," Big Joe said and started to close the door.

Max moved faster than I would have thought possible for a person with a hangover, shoving the door back open with the palm of his hand and his foot. "You have two days to vacate the premises."

The older man's eyes bulged, and it took him a second to respond. "What?" he finally asked.

"If you don't give a shit about the murder of a teenage boy—a good kid at that—then I want you the hell out of my motel."

"*Your* motel?" Big Joe asked with a sneer. "You mean your *daddy's* motel."

Max's face reddened. "My father may own it, but *I* run it. So if I say you're gone, you're gone. If you want to protest, you can take it up with Bart Drummond personally."

Fear filled Big Joe's eyes. "No. That's okay." Then the reality of his situation seemed to hit him. "I've rented from you for three years, Max. Never been late with my rent. I ain't got nowhere else to go," he whined.

"Did you see anything or not?" Max asked in the same tone he'd used on Bingham the night before.

"No!" Big Joe protested. "I done told you I didn't! I only heard her screaming, but I ignored it, thinking it was just a ho pissed she hadn't gotten her twenty bucks. Didn't think much about it until I heard the sirens."

"Nothin' else?" Max asked, his face tight.

"Nothin'. So can I stay?"

Max turned to me. "Carly, you satisfied?"

My mouth dropped open. "Uh…yeah."

Max turned to Big Joe. "You can stay, but you better make an appearance at the funeral, and I expect you to make a donation to the funeral fund. There'll be a jar on the counter in the bar, but you can hand it to me personally."

Big Joe nodded emphatically. "Yeah. Can do."

"Then you can stay."

Detective Daniels was giving us an assessing look I didn't much like. I averted my gaze toward the street and spotted Ruth approaching us from the café. "I think we should go now. Ruth's back."

Max shot a pointed look at his elderly tenant. "I'll be lookin' for that donation," he said.

Big Joe bobbed his agreement, then quickly shut his door.

"Do you believe him?" I asked as we started across the street. "Do you think he didn't see anything?"

He grimaced. "Yeah, Big Joe's one of the laziest men I know. I'm surprised he got up to answer the door. He must have been worried we were cops."

"What about Jerry? Do you think he's okay?"

He paused, then said, "When Jerry gets scared, he wanders off sometimes. He'll be okay."

"Do you think he saw something that scared him?" I asked.

"I don't know," Max said with a worried look. "I guess we'll ask him when he turns up."

Ruth had almost reached us when I asked, "Would you have really kicked Big Joe out?"

"Yep." He turned his gaze to me. "That place might not be much, but I still control who lives there. And if he doesn't have more concern for a good kid than that, then I don't want him."

"But you let him stay."

He started to answer, but Ruth held up a drink carrier with three coffees and two bags as if they were sacred offerings. "The front bag's yours, Maxwell. I can't guarantee that Greta didn't spit on it."

He let out a long-suffering sigh.

She gave him a pointed gaze, which then drifted to me before landing back on him. "I hope you learned a valuable lesson, Maxwell. You don't shit where you eat."

"Point taken," he grumbled.

"Good."

He pointed at Ruth. "You better have Carly back by noon. You know it's bound to be as busy as shit with the nosy people comin' in. I'm gonna need her and then some." The pleading look on his face made it clear he was asking her to volunteer to work too.

"No freakin' way," she said. "I deserve a day off, Max, and you damn well know it, and I'm not even getting that. Just the lunch shift."

"Fine," he grunted, then reached for a coffee cup in the tray and pulled it free. "But just remember it's Carly you're leavin' hangin'."

Ruth's lips pursed. "I guess I'll just take that chance."

She headed around the building toward the back parking lot, leaving me to follow.

"Y'all be careful," Max called after her. "The bridges might still be icy."

Ruth lifted her hand in the air in a half wave. "It's warmin' up and you damn well know it. Love you too."

We were silent while we walked to her car. As we headed out of town, the opposite way that I'd come in with Wyatt, she tossed me the bag.

"Put two of those flavored creamers in my coffee and hand it over, would you?" she said. "I'm needin' a caffeine fix."

"How long have you worked for Max?" I asked, stirring her creamer into her coffee and replacing the lid.

"That's a good question," she said, taking the cup without shifting her gaze from the windshield. "Max has owned the place about eight years. He took it over from Wyatt right after his arrest."

I blinked in surprise. "What?"

She cast me a confused look. "I already told you that Wyatt went to prison."

"Not that part. The part about Wyatt owning the tavern."

She released a bitter laugh. "Wyatt never owned it. He ran it for his parents. Max was at college and had to come home to take over the business. Bart was too busy runnin' Drum to run it himself." She took a sip of her coffee and cursed. "Why do they have to make it so damn hot it scalds your tongue?"

"Good question," I said as I started doctoring my own. "But Max owns the tavern now?"

"Yep. Bart signed it over to him when Max came back. Max said he wouldn't run it unless it was good and truly his."

"Did that piss Wyatt off?"

"You would think so," she said, risking another sip. She had to be really desperate for caffeine. "But Wyatt had turned his back on 'em all, even Max, while he was waiting for his trial, then totally snubbed his family when he came home."

"So Max quit college to come home and run the tavern? What was his major?"

She shrugged. "I forget. Something to do with business, but Bart told Max he'd teach him everything he needed to know about business. Maybe that's true, maybe it's not, but Max never went back."

"How old was he?" I asked, wondering what kind of relationship Max had with his father. I knew what it was like to have a manipulative father, one who bent and twisted you to suit his own wishes. Did he regret coming back all those years ago?

117

She released a small chuckle. "Just turned twenty-one. Barely legal to drink in his own establishment. But this happened before they moved the entrance to Balder Mountain. Back when we put up and fed a bunch of the tourists. Max made good money before the big move. Drum's a whole lot quieter now."

Last night had been nothing but locals, which made me wonder who had been staying in the other motel units besides Jerry and Big Joe. Maybe it really was a by-the-hour kind of place. The elderly man had mentioned a prostitute, after all. Then a new thought hit me. "Did you work for Wyatt?"

She hesitated. "Yep."

"How long?"

"A couple of years before his arrest. Max took over before the case went to trial."

Something about the way she was acting made me ask, "Did you and Wyatt used to date?"

She hesitated again. "Yeah, but not for long, and only while he was on a break from Heather."

"Was Heather the woman his family paid to leave town?"

"That's the one. Bart and Emily never approved of Heather, and they were glad to help speed her way along."

I had more questions, but I felt weird asking them, especially since I felt a twinge of something that felt a lot like jealousy.

What the hell was that about?

Sure, Wyatt had been nice and respectful up at the lookout, but that had changed before we hit the town limits. I had never been a woman foolish or masochistic enough to fall for a man who wasn't crazy about me.

That's not true, a little voice said in my head. *You believed Jake.*

Jake didn't count. He had lied through his teeth, weaving together a story about the life we'd led together, the partnership

we'd build. I'd believed him, but all along he'd been courting my
father, not me.

Chapter Ten

Thankfully, Ruth didn't pick up on my thoughts. We ate our breakfast sandwiches and drank our coffee as she told me about her life in Drum.

Although I tried to keep the conversation on her as much as possible, she asked me plenty of questions too. Which meant I had to lie. I told her I'd grown up in Michigan and followed a man to Atlanta. I'd worked retail and some waitressing in the beginning between my own men to help with rent. I hated to consider how Ruth would feel if she ever found out the truth, but if she did, hopefully she'd know I'd lied out of necessity. Each lie about my past not only killed part of my soul but killed off the person I'd been piece by piece.

She drove into Greeneville and headed straight for the hospital. As soon as it came into view, I started to regret eating that breakfast sandwich. Ruth had kept me busy talking, which had kept me from thinking too much about the reason I'd come to Greeneville—I was here to see Hank Chalmers and shatter what was left of his heart.

"You okay?" she asked, worry in her eyes.

I swallowed. "No, but that won't stop me."

She gave me a warm smile. "I guessed that about you." She turned into the parking lot. "Do you want me to come in to help?"

The thought of doing this alone terrified me, but I didn't want anyone else to hear what I had to say, and it would have been rude to invite her in only to ask her to leave. "I'll manage."

"You got cell service here?" she asked, pulling up to the circle drive in front of the entrance.

How had I forgotten about that? I snatched up my purse and dug out my cell phone, my heart jumping when I saw four bars of service. "Yes!"

She chuckled. "Bet you've taken cell phone service for granted up to now, huh?"

"You have no idea."

"Take my number so you can call or text when you're done," she said. "I have some errands to run, but I'll come get you as soon as I can."

"No worries," I said. "I can wait for you in the cafeteria or the lobby. I'm grateful you went out of your way to bring me."

"Don't think a thing about it."

She told me her phone number, and I sent her a text to make sure I'd gotten it right.

"Got it!" she said, then turned somber. "I feel it's only fair to warn you that Hank is known for being a cranky bastard."

Great. I could only imagine how well he'd take this news. But I'd made a promise and I intended to see it through. "Thanks for the warning."

"Tell him that Franklin and I are so sorry about Seth, and that we'll do anything we can to help."

A lump formed in my throat and I nodded, croaking out a "yeah" as I climbed out of the car.

Ruth drove off as I approached the information desk in the lobby, trying to pull myself together. It struck me that I'd been so worried about getting here, I hadn't thought enough about how Mr. Chalmers would react. Would he want to talk to me? Would he be upset that I'd withheld information from the sheriff?

There was only one way to find out.

The elderly woman at the front desk looked up Hank Chalmers' room number, then told me how to get there. Stalling, I considered getting flowers or something from the gift shop, but it felt wrong. There was something disrespectful about handing him a smiley face mug with daisies and then saying, "Oh, by the way, I saw the men who shot your grandson and held his hand while he died."

No. The only thing I could give him was the truth about what had really happened to Seth. I suspected it was the only thing that really mattered.

I got on the elevator and pushed the button to his floor. When it opened, a brown-haired man in a dress shirt and jeans bumped into me. I nearly called him out for his rudeness, but his hard brown eyes stopped me. He looked to be in his mid-thirties—definitely old enough to have manners—but I didn't feel like saying so. At the moment, I didn't have enough gumption to hold my own if he put up an argument.

I headed down the hall, and when I reached Hank's room, I stood outside his door and took slow, deep breaths to calm down. I was scared to death and second-guessing every decision I'd made in the past twenty-four hours, but I was here. There was no backing down now.

Before I could change my mind, I knocked on the door. "Hello?" I called through the partially open doorway. "Mr. Chalmers?"

"I told you I ain't got nothin' to say," a man called out.

I pushed it open anyway and walked in. An elderly man sat in the bed, the back upright. He was hooked up to several machines with wires attached to his chest and tubes in his arms, and a hospital tray was placed across his bed as well as a tray of barely touched food.

He waved his hand in dismissal and turned from me. "I'm not feelin' up to physical therapy today. Just talk to Nurse Patty. She said it was okay."

"Mr. Chalmers…" My voice sounded croaky, so I cleared my throat and tried again. "I'm not here to take you to physical therapy. My name is Carly, and I'm here about Seth."

He turned his head to face me. "What about 'im?" he asked belligerently. "I already told you people he wasn't mixed up in drugs."

I swallowed, feeling lightheaded. "I'm not with the sheriff either." I took a breath. "I was with Seth when he died."

His eyes slowly widened, and his mouth formed an O. "You're the one who found him."

I nodded, tears filling my eyes. "Yes, sir."

"And you came to see me?" he asked in surprise.

I moved closer to the side of his bed, grasping the handrail to keep myself upright. "Yes, sir. I hope that's all right."

Tears filled his eyes and he reached his wrinkled, age-spot-covered hand toward me.

I grasped it and held it tight, his grief breaking my heart.

"He loved you," I forced past the lump in my throat, and tears leaked out the corners of my eyes.

"He was alive when you found him?" he asked, his hand beginning to shake.

I nodded. "He was. I'm so sorry. I tried to stop the bleeding, but he'd been shot twice at a close range."

His chin quivered, and then he said, "The deputy said they didn't know what happened. He said you didn't see nothing."

I hesitated, wondering how to broach this, then decided to tell him everything from the beginning. "I was asleep in my room when I heard a cry. I jumped out of bed and peeked through the blinds. That's when I saw two men dragging Seth out of a motel room. They threw him down to the ground."

"What was he doin' at the Alpine Inn?" he asked. "And in a room?"

"I don't know, sir," I said. "Maybe the rest will help you figure it out."

"Go on, then," he said in a gruff voice.

"Seth was on his knees while the two men faced him. One man was pointing a gun at him. He asked Seth where the stash was. Seth told him he didn't know what he was talking about. A third man came from Seth's motel room, saying he'd found a camera but that the stash was still missing, and Seth kept claiming he didn't know anything. They started kicking in doors trying to find it, but when they got close to mine, I set off my car alarm, hoping they'd run off and leave Seth alone." A lump clogged my throat, and I had to force out, "Instead they shot him." I started to cry.

Mr. Chalmers sat still in his bed, watching me with his bloodshot eyes. "Go on when you're ready."

I nodded and grabbed a tissue off his nightstand. After I dabbed my eyes and took a breath, I said, "As soon as they took off, I ran out to Seth. He was still alive. I wanted to get help— I'd already tried calling 911, but the phone in my room didn't work and I didn't have any cell reception." I released a tiny sob. "He begged me not to leave him, and there was so much blood..." I paused. "He asked me to give you a message."

Mr. Chalmers put his hand over mine, then nodded, giving me permission to continue.

"He said to tell you that he had to try. He knew how much it would hurt, and he was sorry."

His shoulders shook with a suppressed sob, and I considered stopping, but I decided it would be better for both of us if I let it all out, like ripping off a Band-Aid.

"He also said that he had evidence, but when I told him I'd call the sheriff, he panicked. Said the man who'd shot him was a deputy, and some of the other cops are also involved."

The older man nodded but didn't say anything.

"He had some numbers written on his hand. He showed them to me, but I have no idea what they mean. I figured it might have something do with the camera. Does that mean anything to you?"

He shook his head and my heart sank.

"He was getting weaker, and I'd called out for help, but no one was coming, so I screamed and Max came running out of the tavern. By the time he reached us, Seth was dead." I broke down, starting to sob. "I'm so, so sorry, Mr. Chalmers."

Mr. Chalmers patted the back of my hand with his free one, tears streaming down his cheeks. "This wasn't your doin'. This wasn't your fault."

"I set off that alarm. I made them shoot him."

"No, girl. Don't you take that blame upon yourself. It was those men's doin', not yours."

"If I'd gone out there..." I lifted my gaze to his. "I should have tried to stop them. I had a gun."

"If you'd threatened them, you'd be dead too and I wouldn't know the truth of it. You couldn't take on three men with a gun." His eyes turned watery. "You done him a good deed. If they'd taken him, they would have beaten and tortured him until he finally confessed." A tear slipped down his cheek. "And that boy was stubborn, boy howdy, was that boy stubborn."

I covered my mouth with my hand to contain my sobs. "If I'd only..."

"If you'd only what?" he asked in a hard tone. "Seth brought this on 'imself, and I *guarantee* that he wouldn't want you to be takin' on the blame. He knew what he was doin', even if I begged him not to do it." He shook his head, then held my gaze with his watery eyes. "Once my grandson was shot in the chest, there was no savin' him. Not that far up the mountain." He took a deep breath and his shoulders shook again. "But knowin' he didn't die alone…thank you."

My chest heaved as I tried to control my tears.

We sat there in silence for a moment, both of us crying. He mourned the grandson he'd obviously deeply loved while I ached over a boy's death and his grandfather's deep loss. After several long minutes, Mr. Chalmers said, "You told the sheriff he was dead when you reached him."

I cringed. "Not exactly. This morning, I told the detective that Seth had asked me to tell you his goodbyes, but they don't know that I saw him getting shot or that I saw the killers hightailing it in a red truck driven by a fourth man."

"You kept that from them to protect yourself?" he asked.

I hesitated. "I'd be lying if I said I hadn't considered that, but I wanted to talk to you before I told them anything else. After what Seth said about the shooter, I didn't think the deputies would have justice in mind." I squeezed his hand. "I was hoping you could tell me what I should do."

His eyes widened in surprise, but sorrow quickly engulfed it. "Only you can decide that, girl."

"Do you know what evidence he had? I think it involved drugs."

"I'm *sure* it was drugs," he said in disgust.

"Maybe we could tell the state police."

Mr. Chalmers shook his head. "I don't have any idea what evidence he was talkin' about. I only know he was trying to implicate the person who sold his mother the drugs that killed her."

"Your daughter?" I asked.

He nodded. "My Barb. She was a user back when she was a teen, but she got clean and stayed that way until a couple of years ago. Got mixed up with a man who started her usin' again." He shook his head. "Stopped takin' care of her boy, so I moved him in with me. She lived there too, but she wasn't around much since I didn't allow her drugs in my home. Seth always thought his mother would come around, but she died of an overdose. The toxicology report said it was poisoning from some unusual drug. Nothin' from around Drum. Folks say it was a new poison outta Atlanta, Seth was tryin' to find out who sold it to her."

"Do you think he found his proof?" I asked.

"Sounds like it if they shot him." He was quiet for a moment. "If you ain't tellin' the sheriff, then you can't tell no one, you hear? That deputy didn't act alone, which means two other somebodies in that town took part in murdering my grandson. Three if you count the driver. If they figure out you know something, they'll show up wantin' to kill you too."

A tingle of fear shot up my spine. "The sheriff's department considers me a person of interest."

His mouth parted. "Why?"

"I'm from Atlanta, and the sheriff's department heard someone from Atlanta was doing a drug drop last night."

His eyes narrowed. "Whatcha doin' in Drum if you're from Georgia?"

I explained the breakdown and the fact that Wyatt had towed me into town. I told him about Max and the temporary job at the tavern.

"You're sure they're lookin' into you?" he asked.

"The detective told me not to leave town. Max was the one who told me about the Atlanta person."

He nodded again, his lips pressed together. "They're keepin' a close watch on you."

"To find out if my story changes? To find out what I know?"

"To find out if you can implicate them."

If they'd killed a boy they knew, a local boy, just to keep their secrets, what was to stop them from killing me? Based on the story I'd told everyone, I was the kind of person who wouldn't be missed.

I felt like I was going to be sick. "So the sheriff's department *is* corrupt. Not just one deputy?"

"Not all of the deputies, but enough of them that you can't trust *any* of 'em."

"You're right," I whispered. "They mean to kill me."

Mr. Chalmers squeezed my hand again, and I noticed the unshed tears lining his lower eyelids. "No. You keep tellin' 'em that you saw *nothin'* and Seth only lived long enough to give you a message for me that he loved me. Nothin' else."

"If I don't tell anyone else what I know, they'll get away with murder," I said. "The man who killed your grandson in cold blood deserves to pay." The need to make them pay burned through my blood. My mother had been buried years ago, and no one would ever be able to prove her accident had been anything but. But Seth had staked his life on making his mother's killer's pay, and according to him, he had found the evidence he needed.

Maybe I could find justice for him.

Maybe it would give me a taste of the peace that eluded me.

He leaned his head back on the bed. "Oh, to be young and idealistic." He closed his eyes and tears streamed down his cheeks. "This is the way of the world, girl. The evil rule the earth and profit from abusing it."

My mind shifted to my father. To Jake. To the plans I'd heard them make on the eve of my wedding. "It's not right."

"Spoken like a dreamer," he said, a wry smile cracking his lips. "Sometimes you have to know when to give in. What's one more poor mountain boy who likely would have lived and died in Drum? That's exactly what happened to him, only he had fifty years of misery and bondage chopped off his life sentence."

I might have believed his speech if not for the tears tracking down his cheeks.

I sat in the chair next to him, holding his hand. Hank Chalmers might be willing to accept his grandson's death as another cruel hand dealt by fate, but I wasn't.

I would dig up whatever evidence Seth had found and hand it over to the state police myself.

I only had to survive long enough to find it.

Chapter Eleven

Hank? You doin' okay?" a woman asked from the doorway. When he didn't answer, she walked the rest of the way into the room, revealing herself. She was a dark-haired woman in scrubs, her hair pulled back into a ponytail. "Oh, you have company."

"Patty," Mr. Chalmers said, "this is my new friend Carly."

"Friend?" she asked with suspicion. Then she gave me a dark look. "You a reporter here for a story?"

"No," I said in surprise, dropping Mr. Chalmers' hand and getting to my feet. "It would be highly unethical to sneak into a bereaved man's room and try to get a quote about his deceased grandson."

Her brows rose. "So you know his grandson was murdered? The sheriff's department swore me to secrecy, claimin' they haven't released any names yet. I ain't never seen you here before, so you mustn't be too close to Hank. If you're not a reporter, who the hell are you?"

I stared at her in shock.

"Patty," Hank barked, "she's the one who found Seth."

Her face fell. "What?"

"She came to tell me about his last moments." His voice caught. "She brought me a blessin'."

All her fire had guttered out, and she looked close to tears. "Sorry for the misunderstandin'."

"I'm glad you were looking out for Mr. Chalmers," I said. "Especially if there are unscrupulous people who would stoop to such lengths."

She cleared her throat and turned her attention to Mr. Chalmers. "Speaking of lookin' out for you…" She grimaced. "Now that your grandson won't be able to take you home tomorrow, I think we should make arrangements for you to be transferred to Sunny Dale."

"The rehab place?" Mr. Chalmers shouted. "There's no way in hell I'm goin' there."

"Your drain tube is coming out today, which means you're ready to be discharged, Hank. Medicare says it's time to go. One way or the other, you're out of here." She pushed out a sigh. "I don't make the daggum rules, but unfortunately, I've gotta enforce 'em."

I remembered Ruth telling me that Mr. Chalmers had come to Greeneville for a leg amputation. My gaze shot to the lower end of his bed, and for the first time I realized the lump for his left leg was longer than his right.

"You know I can check myself out at any time," he snapped at her.

"That's true, but you gotta have someone pick you up," she countered with plenty of sass. "There ain't a taxi or Uber in town that'll haul you up that mountain."

"I'll pick him up," I said before I could think it through. I didn't have a car, but maybe Ruth would let me borrow hers. Or maybe Wyatt would be finished with mine, although I highly doubted it.

"He doesn't just need a *ride*," Patty said in a condescending tone. "He needs someone to take *care* of him. He needs his dressing changed and help getting in and out of bed and onto the toilet. Are you gonna provide that kind of help for him?"

I glanced back at Mr. Chalmers. "Do you have someone to help you with that?"

He lifted his chin. "I've got a home health nurse comin' at the end of the week. I can make do at home until she gets there."

My time in Arkansas came flooding back. I'd spent the last month taking care of Rose's dying sister, Violet. Surely that medical experience could be of use.

"I'll do it," I told her, then glanced back at him. "Max was putting me up at his motel, but frankly, I'd rather not stay there again. So I'd rather work out a barter. I can stay with you and help with the home health stuff in exchange for room and board." I'd still need to work at Max's for the money, but this would give me a chance to look for whatever evidence Seth had found...presuming the sheriff's deputies hadn't found it first.

"I don't want no charity," Mr. Chalmers said with a hard look in his eyes.

"I don't want it either," I countered. "And right now, I'm set to stay with Ruth Bristol and her boyfriend free of charge. If I stay with you, at least I'll be earning my keep."

"You can't just up and decide to be a home health nurse," Patty said in disgust. "It takes *trainin'*, and frankly, it takes a strong stomach. Hank just had his leg amputated. You ready to deal with *that*?"

I swallowed the bile that rose in my throat. I wasn't sure I was, but I'd figure out a way. "I just spent the last month takin' care of a dying woman. I learned how to give her injections, change her IV lines, help her in and out of bed and into the bathroom. I can handle it."

Patty's face softened.

"I'm goin' home tomorrow," Mr. Chalmers announced. "And that's that." He glanced up at me. "What time are you pickin' me up?"

"Uh…" I had no idea when Max would need me tomorrow, if he'd need me, but surely he'd give me the afternoon off so I could bring Hank Chalmers home. "In the morning, by eight. So we have plenty of time to get you settled at home."

"And plenty of time to get you up to speed on how to take care of Hank," Patty said with a look that suggested she still wasn't convinced I was capable. "I'll go let the doctor know."

Then she sashayed out of the room, leaving the two of us alone.

"Thank you, Mr. Chalmers," I said, turning back to him.

"Enough with the Mr. Chalmers shit," he said. "Call me Hank."

I grinned. "Okay, Hank."

His mouth pressed into a firm line. "I gotta warn you, my house ain't fancy. I reckon you're used to nicer places."

"I was staying at the Alpine Inn. I don't need fancy," I said. "I'm just grateful for a place to stay."

"And where's that?" a familiar male voice said. My stomach dropped when I turned and saw Wyatt's large frame filling the doorway.

Dressed in jeans and his brown jacket, he was more handsome than he had any right to be. His dark hair looked windblown and his dark eyes were narrowed in suspicion at me. It wasn't fair that my heart leapt at the sight of him when he had nothing but contempt for me.

"Wyatt," Hank said in surprise.

Wyatt shot me a glare as he walked into the room. "I wanted to check on you. How are you holdin' up, Hank?"

Hank's eyes welled with tears again, but he didn't answer.

"I'm sure you're not up to company," Wyatt said in a gruff tone. "I'll walk Ms. Moore out."

Hank held up his hand and shook his head. "No need for that. She's helpin' me move home tomorrow."

Wyatt's jaw hardened, and his gaze darted between Hank and me. "And how'd that arrangement come about?"

"She stopped by to talk about Seth, and seeing as how Seth was supposed to take me home tomorrow, Carly volunteered to help in exchange for a place to stay."

"The Alpine Inn's not good enough for you now?" Wyatt asked me in a cold tone.

"It's either Carly takes me home or I go to the shithole rehab center," Hank snapped. "So get off your damn high horse."

"You don't even know her," Wyatt protested. "And now you're inviting her to stay at *your house*?"

"She tried to help my grandson," Hank said in a gruff tone. "Nobody else saw fit to help him, and she didn't even know him." His eyes hardened with challenge. "That's enough for me."

I could tell Wyatt wanted to say more, that he was practically gnawing on his tongue to hold it back.

What the hell was his problem? While I understood why he'd be suspicious of me, the circumstances were unusual, to say the least, I was sick and tired of dealing with his attitude.

"Let's just get this out in the open," I said in a direct tone, the kind I would use on the third-grade class I used to teach when the kids got unruly and I needed to regain control. "I didn't kill Seth. I had nothing to do with his death other than that I held his hand as he took his last breath. I'm sorry you don't trust me—I suppose you've got no reason to—but I'm not out to hurt Hank. I need a place to stay, and Hank needs someone to take him home and stay with him until his home health nurse shows up at the end of the week. It's that simple."

"How do you plan on bringin' him home when you don't have a car?" Wyatt asked, obviously unmoved by my speech.

"I can—"

"She can use my car," Hank said.

"You haven't driven that thing in *years*," Wyatt said. "I'm not sure it'll even start, let alone make the trip to Greeneville and back."

"Then she can use Seth's," Hank said, his voice cracking.

"The sheriff's department found it off Highway 25," Wyatt said. "It's impounded while they look for evidence."

I was about to say I'd planned to ask Ruth for help, when Hank said, "Then *you* can drive 'er. You've admitted you don't have enough work at that garage of yours. You can spare a couple of hours to bring her down to pick me up."

"*I'll* come get you," Wyatt said, shoving his hands in his back pockets, "but I'm not bringin' her with me."

"Fine," Hank snorted. "You can learn how to change the dressin's on my stump and learn how to check my blood sugar levels."

Wyatt's mouth opened, and then he turned back to me with a suspicious gaze. "You plan on learnin' how to be his nursemaid?"

I sent him a haughty glare. "Considering a nursemaid typically changes diapers, no, I do *not*. But I *do* plan on learning how to provide home healthcare assistance."

"And what makes you qualified for that?" he demanded.

"I have previous experience caring for a very sick woman," I said. "That's all you need to know."

"Quit your yapping and just deal with it, Wyatt Drummond," Hank snapped. "You want to do somethin' for me? You either bring her down tomorrow or find a way for her to come get me, because I don't wanna spend a minute longer in this godforsaken place than I have to."

"I'll bring her," Wyatt grunted. "And I'll help get you inside the house too."

"Fine by me," Hank said. "Because I'm still too weak to hobble around on those damn crutches yet."

Wyatt shot me a piercing glare that softened when he turned back to Hank. "I need to speak to you. Alone."

Hank started to protest, but something in Wyatt's gaze must have moved him because he gave me a sharp nod. "I'll see you tomorrow."

"I'll be here as early as Wyatt gets me here," I said with a tight smile.

Tears filled his eyes again, and he glanced away. "See you then."

I headed out in the hall, making my way toward the main entrance, my stomach in knots over my interaction with Wyatt. Sure, I was supposedly from Atlanta, but that didn't explain the extent of his suspicion. Besides, he hadn't reacted much to my Georgia plates at the outlook—he'd started acting weird after that, after I shut down the idea of calling the sheriff.

Something else stuck out at me.

Had Wyatt heard about the drug dealer from Atlanta? Did he think I was somehow connected to them?

Surely Wyatt wouldn't have heard anything about that— Max had only heard about it this morning, from his deputy friend. Yet I couldn't ignore the fact that Wyatt had sat with Bingham's crowd last night. If Wyatt *did* know about that dealer, it was simple enough to figure out how he'd have known.

A shiver of apprehension had me stopping in my tracks. Why was Wyatt here? Surely a surly man who had friends like Bingham didn't pay friendly visits to grieving old men in hospitals. I didn't want to put words to the whirl of thoughts in my head. Surely there was nothing to fear, leaving Hank alone in the room with Wyatt. But what if there was?

My heart was racing, and I felt a pull to return to Hank's room like a hook on the back of my neck. I nearly ran back, but something stopped me. Hank was a tough man, but his eyes had softened at the sight of Wyatt.

Hank trusted him.

So I went down to the lobby instead. I tried to call Ruth, but it went straight to voicemail. I left her a message and then sent a text for good measure, saying I was done and would wait for her in the hospital lobby.

I started to call my friends in Arkansas, but then hung up before it could ring. Every time I made contact with them, I put us all in danger. Not to mention, Rose and Neely Kate would be worried sick if they thought I was in trouble. They'd want to do something, and there was nothing to be done. They had enough troubles—they didn't need to step between me and my ruthless father. Besides, while I couldn't leave Drum, I hadn't been arrested. It was a stalemate. No use putting them through unnecessary worry.

All that was left to do was wait. I was about to take a seat when I realized I hadn't checked my bank account balance since leaving Gatlinburg. I'd remembered seeing an ATM by the elevator, so I walked over to it and fed it my debit card, then followed the prompts to check my balance. I wanted to weep when I saw $1363.27 on the screen. I'd thought there would be at least three or four hundred more.

"What are you up to?" I heard Wyatt ask behind me.

I pressed cancel on the screen, then grabbed my debit card when it popped out. "This is an ATM machine, which is commonly used to get cash." I turned around to face him. "Or do they not have ATM machines in Drum? Want me to show you how to use it?"

It was a bitchy thing to say, but I was tired of defending myself to him.

"Got enough money to pay for those car repairs?" he asked in a dry tone.

I propped a hand on my hip. "I'd be able to tell you if I had an estimate, which I'm guessing is hard to come up with if you're an hour away from my car."

"Ever consider the fact that I might have another mechanic workin' on it back in Drum?"

Why *hadn't* I considered that?

"Care to tell me why you decided to show up in Hank Chalmers' hospital room?" he asked.

"I thought we'd both made it pretty clear," I said. "Seth wanted me to give Hank a message." While I would have loved nothing more than to talk flippantly about this to piss Wyatt off, I couldn't do it. I was talking about the senseless death of a teenage boy. "After my mother died, I wanted to know every detail. Was someone with her? Was she scared? I couldn't save Seth, but at least I could tell Hank that his grandson didn't die alone."

His gaze hardened. "You were with him when he died? I thought he was dead when you got to him."

My eyes burned with tears. For some reason, it mattered that he didn't seem to like me, although I didn't want it to. Now I'd gone and given him personal information, *my* personal information. Charlene Moore's mother was supposed to be alive and well in Grand Rapids. And, fool that I was, I was more upset that he'd responded with scorn than that I'd opened my mouth in the first place.

My phone buzzed in my pocket and I pulled it out, scanning the screen. It was a text from Ruth: **So sorry! Running one hour late. Tell Max you'll be late for lunch.**

I turned away from Wyatt and started walking back into the main part of the lobby, trying to figure out what to do. I suspected Ruth was right about the tavern drawing a big crowd, and I didn't see how Max could handle it on his own. I told myself that it wasn't my concern. Twenty-four hours ago, I hadn't known *any* of these people.

Twenty-four hours ago, I'd been completely alone.

I sat in a chair, racking my brain for a solution that would get me back to Drum on time. I could rent a car, but then I'd have to bring it back because I was fairly certain there wasn't a car rental return center in Drum. Not to mention it was an expense I couldn't afford.

"How'd you get down here to Greeneville?" Wyatt asked, standing in front of me.

"It's not your concern, Wyatt," I said, refusing to look up at him.

He squatted in front of me, his expression softer. "Carly. How'd you get down here?"

I glanced away from him, fighting the urge to cry. "Ruth."

"Is she comin' to pick you up?"

"Not for at least another hour."

"I heard you were working the lunch shift at Max's."

A fire lit in my gut. "Checking out my schedule now?" I snapped.

Was he really that worried that I wouldn't be able to pay him?

To my surprise, he didn't erupt at my hateful tone. Instead, a wry smile twitched at the corners of his lips. "It's a small town. Sometimes you find out things whether you want to know them or not."

I believed that.

"I'm headed back to Drum. I'll give you a ride."

I shot him a glare. "You think I'm going to get in your truck with you after you just insulted me?"

"You're gonna get in it tomorrow, so why not today?" His mouth twisted into a grin, his eyes warming. "Or maybe you plan on sittin' here until tomorrow."

"Ruth will be here in an hour," I reminded him.

"Fine, suit yourself," he said, but he didn't sound insulted and he'd still made no attempt to stand. "But I promise not to insult you durin' the drive if you change your mind."

I looked him square in the eyes. "How do I know I can trust you, Wyatt Drummond?"

"How do I know I can trust *you?*" he countered. But his words didn't hold the contempt he'd recently shown me.

"Maybe I haven't earned your trust enough to give me your debit card pin or whatever, but I've given you absolutely no reason to *distrust* me," I said, my attitude returning.

"That's not how trust works around these parts," he said, his tone a little firmer. "You have to *earn* trust. It's not just handed out, carte blanche."

I could understand the concept, especially given everything that had happened in the last twenty-four hours. While I could make the argument that I hardly looked like a drug dealer, my connection to Atlanta notwithstanding, maybe I was wrong. Maybe my impression of what a drug dealer looked like had been influenced by Hollywood.

"I'm too tired and upset to fight with you, Wyatt," I said, looking away so he couldn't see I was close to tears again.

"So don't fight with me," he said softly. "Just let me give you a ride back to Drum. We don't even have to talk."

I had absolutely no reason to tell him, not other than my pride and the potential awkwardness of being cooped up with him for the hour-long car ride. I wasn't worried about my safety.

If he'd planned to hurt me, he'd had plenty of opportunity to do so by now. "Fine."

I expected him to respond to my terse agreement, but he simply stood and waited for me to get up.

"I'm parked out front," he said, gesturing toward the lobby doors.

We walked toward them, side by side, and I got confused when I didn't see his tow truck. Instead, he headed toward a beat-up, red pickup truck.

I stopped in my tracks, my heart racing.

Wyatt realized I was no longer walking with him and turned back to face me.

"What's wrong?" he asked immediately.

Was my fear so obvious?

I took a step back, fighting to catch my breath. While pickup trucks were popular in this part of the state—I'd seen several of this make and model on the road—how likely was it there'd be two red ones within the city limits of Drum? If Wyatt was somehow involved with Seth's murder, it would explain why he'd been so pissed to see me in Hank's hospital room. Maybe he was worried I'd rat him out.

My mind tried to work through the possibility that Wyatt had played some role in last night's tragedy, but certain pieces didn't fit. If he'd had something to do with it, why had he shown up at the tavern this morning to verbally accost me? Was it because he'd found my gun and key fob? If so, why hadn't he confronted me?

"Carly?" Wyatt walked toward me, worry in his eyes. When he reached for my upper arm, I involuntarily recoiled. He lifted his hands up next to his head, fingers splayed as he took a step back. "I'm not gonna touch you."

To my horror, I started to cry.

His hands dropped to his sides, and he took a step toward me, then stopped.

"Are you afraid of me?" he asked, sounding incredulous.

How did I answer that? Lie and say no? Tell him yes, and possibly risk my life?

He took another step back, taking my nonanswer as answer enough. "Okay, that's fair. I've been an ass, and now I'm about to take you on remote mountain roads while there's a murderer out in Drum. You don't know me from Adam, and I haven't really gone out of my way to earn *your* trust."

I took another look at his truck and realized it didn't have the long scratch the killers' truck had sported, and now I felt like a fool.

"I don't want to go back up there," I confessed, wiping tears from my cheeks. "Part of me wants to jump on the next bus out of town, no matter where it goes, just to get the hell out of this nightmare."

He watched me for a moment, mulling over my words, and then finally said, "So why don't you?"

I expected to hear sarcasm, but he sounded genuinely curious. "What about my car?"

"Look," he said with a sigh, "we both know it's likely gonna cost more than it's worth to fix it. You'd be better off puttin' the money on a vehicle that actually works."

But it wasn't that easy. First, if I left, there'd be a warrant out for my arrest. The last thing I wanted was for my picture to get circulated with the name Charlene Moore attached to it. And what about Ruth? Detective Daniels had said he'd hold her accountable if I didn't return to Drum. But I couldn't tell Wyatt any of that. Whether he thought I had something to do with Seth's death, or if he thought—or feared—I might have seen more than I'd admitted to before Seth died, no need to hand him another log to add to the fire.

Then there was Hank Chalmers. True, I barely knew him, but he'd just lost his grandson, and he needed help. For some reason, I felt compelled to give it to him. Perhaps it was guilt for not saving Seth. Or perhaps it was that I'd liked caring for Violet during her last month, offering the quiet support to help her die with dignity. Hank wasn't dying, but he deserved to convalesce with dignity too. Besides, surely he needed to get home to plan his grandson's funeral.

In the end, one point mattered more than the rest. Those men had shot down Seth in cold blood and casually left him to die. There were other wrongs I wasn't strong enough to right, but I wanted to make Seth's killers pay.

Still, could I really get in a truck with someone who might be involved in the murder? Part of me wanted to trust Wyatt, but Jake, my lifelong best friend had snowed me. I'd known Wyatt less than twenty-four hours.

I stopped crying and faced him with reluctant resolve. "No," I finally said. "I have to go back to Drum."

"Why?" he asked, taking a step closer. To my surprise, his eyes were still warm. Compassionate. He sure didn't look like a murderer. Maybe I was a fool, but I decided I'd accept the ride. Whatever he might know, I didn't think he'd hurt Seth. I didn't think he had it in him. "Maybe I can help you."

I inhaled deeply. "I don't need any help other than the ride, but thank you for the offer."

Sorrow and defeat washed over his face, but he just turned and walked toward his truck, leaving me to follow.

There was no way I could risk telling him anything.

Wyatt was right. He didn't have my trust, and he was a long way from earning it. I knew the cost of trusting the wrong man.

Chapter Twelve

About fifteen minutes into the drive, Wyatt must have gotten tired of the silence that hung between us, taut as a wire, because he turned on the radio and country music filled the cab. After about ten minutes, he seemed to forget himself and softly sang the refrain of one of the songs, tapping his finger on the steering wheel of the truck. I couldn't help smiling, but I turned to look out the side window, a mistake given the incline and all of the curves. My stomach started roiling.

At the top of the eleven o'clock hour, a newscaster came on and announced the national news. An update about Congress and something the president had done that had people all up in arms. I'd tuned most of it out until I heard the announcer mention my name. Caroline Blakely, not Carly Moore.

I sucked in a breath and turned to face the radio, hoping I hadn't missed most of the report.

"...has been missing since August. Caroline was last seen the night before her wedding to Jake Wood, son of Roger Wood, CEO of Wood Technologies. Police have had few leads on the case, and the oil magnate and Caroline's fiancé have held a press conference announcing a reward for her safe return."

The audio switched over to a feed from the news conference. "Caroline, if you're out there," my father said in a strong, clear voice, "I will do anything and everything in my power to bring you home. I *will* find you. God help the persons who get in my way."

Hearing his voice was like a punch in the gut. My heart hammered in my chest and I clutched my hands to hide their shaking. Most people would have taken his words as a loving father who was out of his mind with worry over his missing daughter. I heard a man who had issued a *very* clear threat.

In the back of my mind, I could hear my father telling Jake, "You don't have to be married long. We can arrange an accident just like her mother's."

I'd tried to snuff the memories out, to contain them, because they had the capacity to break me. Helplessness clawed at my throat. I knew what he'd done, but there was nothing I could do to make him pay. He had every resource imaginable at his fingertips and I was just a third-grade teacher on the run.

"Whoever took my bride…" Jake said, his voice breaking, "we just want her back. Please."

It almost sounded like he meant it. I would have believed him if I hadn't heard him beg my father for "what he'd promised."

"We're offering a five-hundred-thousand-dollar reward," my father said. "Send any and all leads to bringcarolinehome.com or this number." He called out a number, but I sat stiff in my seat, trying not to freak out and clue Wyatt in that something was wrong.

The announcer's voice returned. "Caroline is thirty-one years old and is described as being 5'4", one hundred and twenty-five pounds. She has long blonde hair, blue eyes, and a one-inch red birthmark on her lower left abdomen. There's a photo of her on our website, along with the tip line number."

"I don't know about you," a female host said, "but I could sure use that half million dollars. With Blakely Oil, you know Randall Blakely is good for it."

"I hear you, Jane," the male announcer said. "I may go look for her myself."

The announcers shifted to a discussion of an upcoming Christmas tree lighting ceremony in Johnson City, but I was still trapped in my freak out. Would my friends in Arkansas be safe? I hadn't disguised my looks while living in Henryetta, and I'd left for fear my father was hot on my trail. What about Austin, my friend in Dallas who had hidden me those first two nights? He'd gone as far as to give me his mother's old car for my escape. Last time I'd checked in with him, he hadn't even been contacted by my father's people, but what if Dear Old Dad had started digging deeper into my circle of friends? Based on what I'd learned the night of my rehearsal dinner, he had the resources— not just money but a circle of criminals who'd been breaking the law and getting away with it since before I was born.

What would my father do to him?

I needed to call Austin.

Instinctively, I pulled my phone out of my pocket and checked the screen. No service. I'd sent Ruth a text saying I'd caught a ride back to Drum, but it occurred to me I wouldn't even see her reply, if she'd replied, until I returned to Greeneville in the morning.

"Do *you* have service out here?" I asked Wyatt.

"Nope. You thinkin' about callin' in a tip?"

So he *had* been listening. I was totally blowing this. He was probably wondering why I seemed so interested in the news segment. "Maybe," I hedged. "I think I might have seen her in Gatlinburg."

"Gatlinburg, huh?" he asked, shifting slightly in his seat but keeping his gaze on the road. "I thought you came from Georgia."

Had I told him that? I couldn't remember, but maybe he'd made the connection because of my Georgia plates. Still, I was telling too many stories to people, and I was having trouble keeping track of my lies. "I *live* in Atlanta, but I spent a few days in Gatlinburg."

"And you think you saw this Caroline Blakely there?" he asked, sounding unconvinced.

"Hey," I said, "why not? Stranger things have happened."

"You were there by yourself?" he asked.

Great, we were back to twenty questions.

"What does that have to do with whether I saw her or not?"

"If you were with someone else, they might want a share of the reward money," he said in a lazy drawl.

"You seemed pretty skeptical it could have been her," I said.

He shot me a grin, then parroted back, "Stranger things have happened."

We were silent for a moment before I said, "I've heard *some* people get cell phone service in Drum. Do you know what service they're using?"

"Thinkin' about switchin' cell phone plans?" he asked dryly.

"I don't know. Maybe."

His lips twisted and he turned to look at me for a second before turning back to the road. "There's a smaller service that recently put up a cell phone tower. Most people think it was due to the influence of my father, Bart Drummond." His hands shifted on the wheel. "I would guess you've heard of him by this point."

"His name has come up," I conceded.

"The cell phone company is Allegon."

"Never heard of it," I said.

"Like I said, it's small, but my father convinced them to put up a tower so the community could have cell service. Only most people can't afford a monthly plan, and Allegon doesn't offer pay-as-you-go plans."

"Is there an office in Drum?" I asked.

Wyatt sat up straighter. "Why would you be interested in getting a cell service that likely won't be of any use when you get to…" His eyes narrowed. "Where is it you were headed?"

I nearly told him it was none of his business but decided I didn't feel like fighting. "Wilmington."

"And what waits for you there?"

I shrugged, deciding to tell him a partial truth. "I'm between jobs. I was on my way to Wilmington to search for a new one…and I figured I'd take a vacation while doing it."

He didn't say anything, and we fell back into silence. I couldn't help but stew about Austin. I needed to find a way to contact him, but I couldn't risk calling him from a landline. I'd gotten a VPN account with my new identity, which would prevent anyone from tracing the source of any emails I sent, I just needed to find a computer to use.

"Does the library have computers?" I asked.

Wyatt's brow lifted. "Uh…yeah. But good luck gettin' access to one. The library's only got three computers, and seein' as how it's the only internet most people have access to around Drum, there's usually a waiting list to get on them."

"But I can sign up to use one?"

He turned to study me as though trying to figure out whether he should tell me something. Finally, he said, "I have a computer at my shop," he said. "I use it to search for parts, but you can use it if you don't want to wait on the library."

I tried to hold my suspicion at bay. "Why would you help me?"

He grinned. "If anyone at the library figures out you're tryin' to turn in a tip about Caroline Blakely, they'll try to horn in on it to get a portion of your reward."

"But you won't?" I asked, cocking my head.

"What would I do with a quarter of a million dollars?" he asked. "I've got everything I could ever want or need in Drum."

He was full of shit, but I refrained from telling him so.

"Is that why you came back?" I asked before I thought better of it.

"You mean from prison?" he asked without shame. "You heard, huh?"

My cheeks flushed. "Yeah."

"I figured," he said. "I came back because, for better or worse, Drum is my home. I've got nowhere else to go."

I had never felt that way about anywhere, not since my mother had died. I wasn't sure I ever would again. It made me feel like a coward, but my only plan, currently, was to live my life on the run. A small voice inside my head begged me to stop my father, to destroy him, but I had no evidence against him, and he had resources beyond my comprehension.

When we drove into Drum, Wyatt turned into the parking lot of the garage and pulled to a halt. It was a two-bay garage with a waiting area to the left of the building. It looked like it had once been a service station, but the pumps had been removed. Wyatt's tow truck was parked on the side of the building, and a dark sedan was parked out front. The garage brought back memories of Henryetta, Arkansas. Neely Kate's boyfriend, Jed, had worked on my borrowed car. But although he was now a mechanic, he had a background in the criminal underworld, and he was the one who'd secured my new identity a couple of weeks ago.

A new wave of grief hit me, but I quickly shoved it down. If I wanted to survive, I didn't have the luxury of grieving.

Wyatt reached for his door handle. "If we're lucky, Junior will have figured out an estimate for your car."

I followed Wyatt into the small waiting room area, which was really two folding chairs under the windows overlooking the parking lot, facing a tall counter. As I got closer, I realized it was a two-tiered counter—a higher counter for the customers and a lower desk area, which held a desktop computer and keyboard, along with a mess of papers.

Wyatt walked around and booted up the computer, then opened the browser tab. "Have at it," he said. "I'm goin' to check with Junior to see how he's makin' out on your car."

I sat down on the stool and dug into my purse, pulling out a small notebook that held my VPN login information as well as Charlene's social media logins. I logged into the VPN site, which assigned me a VPN in California, then signed into Facebook. The number of unrecognizable people in my feed caught me off guard, but I told myself it didn't matter. I was looking for Austin.

He wasn't Charlene's friend, but I found his profile easily enough. He hadn't made his email address public, though, and he hadn't posted in a while. I had better luck on Instagram— he'd posted a foodie pic at a restaurant the day before. Relief flooded me. Yesterday, Austin had been alive and well. That was a good sign.

Maybe the best way to keep him safe was to not contact him at all.

Maybe I could ask my friends in Arkansas to do it instead.

I signed into the email account that Jed had set up for me, unsure how to get my message across without just coming out and saying what I meant. I needed to be cryptic in case my father ever linked me to this account, but I couldn't be too cryptic or they wouldn't understand.

Hello, my darlings,

I hope you are well. I've gotten myself into a pickle, but I have no doubt that things will work out, so try not to worry.

It has come to my attention that my past is rearing its head again, and this time it has teeth. Can you let my friend in Texas know that dangers lurk, and he needs to protect himself? I worry for you as well. I'm sorry for any trouble I've brought you.

C

My heart panged with loneliness. I'd lived with Rose and her sister for two months, and Neely Kate had been around so much it felt like I'd lived with her too. I owed Jed more than I could ever repay. They were true friends, close friends, and there was every likelihood I'd never see them again. My father's Dallas crime syndicate was moving into their small Arkansas county. Someone in his organization had discovered I was hiding there, and I'd been forced to flee. I'd already spent two weeks grieving the loss and knew I needed to find a way to move on, but at the moment, it all felt so hopeless.

"You upset because you found out you're not gettin' the reward?" Wyatt asked in the doorway.

I jumped, pressing a hand to my chest. "Do you always sneak up on people like that?"

"It is *my* office."

I pressed send on the email and shut down the page, then made sure I'd signed out of Charlene's social media accounts.

"Just having a moment," I said, signing out of the VPN and closing that page too. "It's been a rough twenty-four hours." I closed my notebook and returned it to my purse.

He watched me for a second, as though scrutinizing my answer, but I didn't owe him anything…other than what it cost to fix my car.

"Do you have an estimate yet?"

He leaned into the doorframe. "Not entirely. It looks like the oil pan was rusted out and something punctured it. The hole was small enough that it wouldn't have leaked out all at once. If you'd been driving for a few hours, the puncture could have happened during the drive and the oil might have finished leaking out at the overlook." He paused. "You could have checked the oil in the morning before you took off and your dipstick would have read fine, so it's not a matter of you lettin' the oil run too low."

I gave a small nod. "Thank you for that. Believe it or not, it makes me feel better." I grimaced. "So how much will it cost?"

"Well, we found some other things too. Your timing belt needs to be changed and your brakes are about shot. Did you notice any problems on the hills?"

I grimaced. I had.

He must have taken my expression as my answer. "If you don't change the timing belt, it could make it to Wilmington, but I'm hesitant to let you go without fixing the brakes. It definitely won't pass any state inspection if you end up movin' to North Carolina."

My heart sank.

"I've gotta search around for parts," he said, "but since it's a Honda, it's gonna cost you more."

"Of course," I said in a dry tone. When he looked insulted, I said, "That wasn't an insinuation that I thought you were cheating me. Just that I know some car parts run higher than others. Give me a ballpark estimate."

He hesitated. "Twenty-five hundred." Then he added, "I'll throw in the tow for free and cut as many costs as I can on the brakes. Like I said, I don't feel good about letting you drive down the mountain as they are now."

Holding on to the counter, I closed my eyes, took a deep breath, then opened them. "I don't have that kind of money."

"I might be able to find some used parts to lower the cost."

"By how much?"

"Maybe a few hundred."

The now-familiar burning in my eyes was back, but crying wasn't going to help a damn thing.

"I'll be upfront," he said. "A good portion of that is labor, but Junior…he's got a wife and kids. I'd give you a discount on labor, but he needs the money."

I shook my head. "No. I'd never ask you for a discount on labor. If you do the work, you deserve to be paid for it, and of course I'd never expect Junior or his family to go without."

"I'll get you a revised estimate," he said, his voice softening.

I slid off the stool. "Thank you. Well, I'd better go. I'm pulling a double today."

I started for the door, but he said, "There's one more thing."

When I stopped and turned back to him, he looked uncomfortable. "I want to assure you that we'll take care of this part ourselves."

I narrowed my eyes. "What are you talking about?"

He grimaced. "Junior discovered that your car was broken into last night."

My mouth dropped open.

"Did you have anything of value in it? If so, my insurance should cover it. The expense to fix the trunk as well."

"The trunk?"

"They pried it open."

I sagged into the desk.

"You okay?" he asked, sounding concerned.

"I don't know," I said, putting a hand to my forehead. "Do you have security cameras?"

He snorted. "It's Drum."

I shook my head, my irritation growing. "From what little experience I've had in Drum, they seem warranted."

"There weren't any cameras," he said.

I found myself thinking of Seth, and of the video footage he had likely taken. Without knowing where to look for the footage, I was at a severe disadvantage—even though I hadn't looked yet, I was pretty sure there were dozens, if not hundreds of camera companies with online storage—but I was hoping there might be some clue at Hank's house.

"Carly?" Wyatt asked, his voice rising with expectation, and I realized I'd missed whatever he'd said.

"I'm sorry. What?"

"I said, do you want me to call the sheriff and file a report or do you want to do it yourself?"

If I reported the break-in, would it absolve me in the eyes of the sheriff's department, or would it only add to their suspicions? "Um…I need to think about it."

"You don't want to file a report?"

"I don't know." When he gave me a curious look, I added, "I'm not sure it's worth the hassle. I didn't have much in there, and the thought of dealing with the insurance company…" I waved my hand in a vague gesture.

"My insurance should cover it all."

But he'd have to report it to the authorities. "I still haven't decided if I want to move forward with the repairs. If I end up trashing the car, there's no sense fixing it."

"True, but you can take the check and apply it to the new one."

"But that could take weeks," I said, "and I need a car sooner than that." I shook my head. "Don't do anything for now. I wouldn't want your premiums to go up for no reason. I'll give it more thought."

He didn't respond, just watched me with an emotionless expression. "Okay. I'll work on gettin' that estimate to you, but it might not be until tomorrow."

Nodding, I bolted out the door.

Chapter
Thirteen

The smart thing to do would be to junk the car. Move forward with my plan to go somewhere with good public transportation. But not Wilmington. Even if it did have a good bus system, I'd already told Wyatt and Ruth about my original plan.

When I walked into the tavern, Max was behind the bar, dumping a container of ice into the bin. He glanced past me to the open doorway. "Where's Ruth?"

Had he been hoping she'd change her mind about working the lunch shift? "She had to stay longer in Greeneville, so I caught a ride back from someone else."

He leaned a forearm on the counter. "Who the hell did you get a ride back with?"

Would Max be pissed that I'd come back to town with his estranged brother? But it seemed there was little point in equivocating. There was a good chance someone had seen me either in Wyatt's truck or walking from his shop. "Wyatt."

It took him a full second to respond. "*Wyatt?*" His shoulders flexed. "What the hell was he doin' down in Greeneville, and how in the hell did he *find* you?"

"Ruth and I weren't completely truthful with you earlier. I went to Greeneville with her so I could see Hank Chalmers."

He stared at me for several seconds, still in shock. "What on earth for?"

"I had to tell him about Seth's last moments." I gave him a weak smile. "I thought he'd want to know."

He looked perplexed that I'd do such a thing. "It could have waited, Carly. You could have told him when he got back home."

"That's just it, Max. He wouldn't be coming home if I hadn't gone to see him. Seth was supposed to pick him up tomorrow. And since he had no one to bring him home, they were going to put him in rehab."

His eyes narrowed. "Why are you sayin' all that in the past tense?"

"Because I'm gonna bring him home tomorrow instead."

"You're gonna do what, now?" he asked, wide-eyed. "How are you gonna do that when you don't even have a working car?"

"I planned on borrowing one," I said. "But it turns out I don't need to. Your brother showed up at the hospital, and he offered to give me a ride to the hospital and back in the morning. Still, I'm going to need tomorrow morning off and likely part of the afternoon so I can get Hank settled in at home."

"Who's going to take care of him after you get him settled?" Max asked.

I hesitated, unsure how he was going to take this. "I'm going to stay with him."

He stared at me like I'd told him I was becoming a Hare Krishna. "Let me get this straight. *You're* going to stay at Hank Chalmers' house? And take care of him?"

"Only for a few days," I said. "Until his home health nurse shows up at the end of the week."

157

"Who's gonna watch him while you're workin'?" Panic spread across his face. "You're not quittin', are you? I'm not ashamed to say we'd like you to stay around longer. You caught on faster than any other new hire I've had."

"No," I hastily said. "At least not yet. I need the money to fix my car, plus everything else. I'll figure something out." I said the last part with unintended desperation.

Max's face softened, and he gave me a warm smile. "You're a good person, Carly. And Hank needs our help. We'll make it work."

"Thanks, Max." I liked that he said *we*, like he wanted to be part of it.

"Go get you a new shirt in the back," he said, glancing down at my borrowed button-down. "In fact, take a few with you. I have no idea what kind of laundry situation Hank's got goin' on out there."

I headed to the back. Tiny was working the kitchen again with Bitty, an average-sized older woman who didn't seem as friendly as the rest of the staff. I suspected she'd heard that I was a person of interest.

She wasn't the only one.

When we opened at noon, there was a crowd lined up to come in and plenty of them gave me suspicious looks. Most them treated me like I had the plague, but they weren't turning me away as their waitress. They'd come to gawk at me, after all, and there was no one else to wait on them. A few people tried to broach the subject of the murder, but I ignored their questions or deflected by saying I needed to get to the kitchen to check on their order.

I was relieved when Jerry showed up close to the end of the lunch rush, choosing a seat at the bar. Part of me had worried something might have happened to him.

"Hey, Jerry," I said when I got a chance to check on him. "I'm happy to see you."

Keeping his gaze on the counter, he asked for water and a hamburger. I added a side of fries before passing the order on to the kitchen. When I served him his food, I pretended it had been a mistake.

"I can take them back if you like," I said with a warm smile, "but we'll just have to throw them away." I lowered my voice, pretending I didn't want Max to hear me. "You'd be doin' me a huge favor if you keep them. I really need this job right now, and I'm afraid Max and Tiny will think I'm inept."

He studied me with a serious expression. "I'll take them," he said slowly.

"Thanks," I said with a warm smile. "Are you doin' okay after what happened at the motel?"

He blinked at me. "What are you talkin' about?"

My brow shot up in confusion. "Seth Chalmers' murder?" When he didn't respond, I asked, "Did you see or hear anything?"

He picked up a fry and kept his gaze fixed on his food. "I woke up when the deputy knocked on my door. I didn't see nothin'."

I hesitated, wondering if I should press him further. "Big Joe said you took off for a while."

"My place was too noisy." He reached for the ketchup bottle. "I like the quiet."

"I like the quiet too," I said, knowing I'd been dismissed. "You let me know if you need anything. Okay, Jerry?"

Despite my chilly reception from the other customers, I was friendly to everyone and offered lots of smiles. By the time the crowd thinned out a few hours later, I'd made about thirty dollars in tips—not as much as I should have earned if they'd tipped 20% (not that I'd gotten 20% the night before with a friendlier crowd)—but more than I'd expected, considering. Max told me it was one of his biggest lunch crowds in ages. He still looked dog-tired, despite having drunk a vat of coffee, but he seemed pleased by the increase in revenue.

When Detective Daniels walked in, the only customer we had left was Jerry, who was nursing his water while he watched *Judge Judy*. The detective's beady eyes scanned the room, pausing on Jerry briefly before landing on me.

My heart stopped. Was he here to arrest me?

Jerry had looked like he was in no hurry to leave, but he quickly put some money on the counter and bolted out the door.

I was standing behind the counter with Max. "Why did Jerry leave so quickly?"

"Don't know. He's always had anxiety issues, but he became extra skittish after someone beat him up about a year ago."

I wanted to press Max for more information, but the detective started walking toward me.

"Ms. Moore," he said, resting his hand on the counter.

"Detective Daniels," I said with forced cheerfulness. "As you can see, I'm back in Drum, safe and sound."

"So I see. I'd like to get your formal statement now." He shot Max a questioning glance. "Is this a good time?"

Max turned to me, giving me a look that suggested it was my call.

"Yeah," I said with a tight smile. "Now's good."

"Is there somewhere private we can go?" he asked.

Max looked around the empty room. "This won't take long, right? There's no one else here at the moment, so how about I put up the closed sign?"

A smug look covered Detective Daniels's face. "The amount of time it takes is entirely dependent on Ms. Moore."

160

Without giving me time to respond, he walked toward the same table we'd used in the middle of the night and pulled some papers out of his bag.

I cast another glance at Max, and he reached out and squeezed my hand. Although it didn't really reassure me, I was grateful for his support. I squeezed back, then headed around the counter and took a seat across from the detective. Daniels handed me some official paperwork and told me to fill out my statement from the night before, adding in anything else I might have remembered.

Max headed to the back and told us to let him know when we were finished.

It made me nervous to handwrite my statement. It meant they'd have a copy of my handwriting to analyze. Even if I tried to mask it, there were experts who could detect such things. It would be one more piece of evidence tying me to Caroline Blakely.

I didn't waste any time writing down my very brief account. I said that Seth had asked me to tell his grandfather that he loved him and he was sorry, and left it at that. At least I'd have an explanation if Detective Daniels figured out that I'd gone to see Hank.

When I finished, he read it over, then looked up at me. "You're sure you don't remember anything else?"

I gave him an innocent look and slowly shook my head. "No. That's it."

He stared at me for several long seconds before I asked, "Is there a problem, Deputy?"

"Detective," he said in a short tone. "And no. If that's all, I guess we're done." But he remained in his seat.

"I need to get ready for the evening crowd," I said, getting to my feet.

"Just one more thing," he said, finally standing up. He took a step toward me and invaded my personal space. "Where did you say your car was?"

"At Wyatt Drummond's garage."

"Uh-huh."

I started to head to the back, but he called after me. "Have you had any trouble with it since it's been there?"

Did he know about the break-in? I'd asked Wyatt to keep quiet about it, but had he told the sheriff anyway?

Turning back to face him, I said, "Seeing as how it's still broken down, I'd guess I'm having all sorts of trouble with it."

A hint of a smile lifted his lips. "True enough. But no other trouble that you know of?"

"I haven't seen my car since Wyatt dropped me off at Max's Tavern's parking lot yesterday early evening, but I'll be sure to let you know if he doesn't repair it to my satisfaction."

He only made it a couple of steps toward the door before he turned around to face me. "Oh," he said, "one more thing. You say you're from Atlanta, but you don't have much of an accent."

Shit. Was he suspicious about my past?

I tried to look more friendly with this one. "That's because I moved to Atlanta from Michigan, Detective. My accent is a strange hybrid of both."

More accurately a hybrid of my East Coast schooling and my Texas roots.

He nodded. "We truly are a meltin' pot, are we not?"

"Greatest country in the world."

He nodded again. "God bless the U.S. of A."

I gave him a little wave. "You have a good day, Detective." With that, I headed to the back before he had a chance to "one more thing" me again.

Chapter Fourteen

After I pulled myself together, I found Max sitting at the desk in his office and told him the detective had left.

He swiveled his chair to face me in the doorway. "How'd it go?"

"Fine, I guess. He seems a little suspicious of me, although I have no idea why." Which wasn't precisely true. People in Drum didn't seem too keen on outsiders, and no one here really knew me. Easier to suspect a stranger than a neighbor.

Max grimaced. "I called Marco while you were giving your statement. He said they're trying to work up a case against you."

My throat tightened. "Do they have any evidence?"

In my mind, I saw my gun and my key fob. Those casings that may have been deliberately left behind. They didn't even need to pin it on me. All they needed to do was attract the wrong kind of attention.

"No. It's all circumstantial. I've given my own statement about walkin' you to your room after you got off work last night. I made it very clear they're barkin' up the wrong tree."

"I had nothing to do with Seth's death other than finding him, Max," I said. "I swear it."

He gave me a reassuring smile. "Shit, Carly, I know that. Even a blind man could see that you're incapable of such a thing. Don't you worry. I have an ace up my sleeve to help."

"What is it?" I asked.

He leaned forward. "You'll find out later." He checked the clock on the wall. "It's nearly three. Why don't you go have Tiny fix you something for lunch. Then I'll open back up in about a half hour."

"You don't have to keep the bar closed on my account, Max," I said. I hated that he was potentially losing money because of me.

"We're usually dead anyway, and this will give you a chance to take a break."

Tears stung my eyes. "Thanks, Max."

"Hey," he said good-naturedly. "I'm protectin' my own self-interest here. You've already proven yourself indispensable." He made a shooing motion. "You run along now. Have Tiny make you his grilled cheese and tomato soup. Perfect comfort food."

Tiny must have known I'd met with the detective, because he welcomed me into the kitchen and fed me soup and a warm sandwich and regaled me with tales about cranky customers. Bitty just gave me a long look and walked out the back door. When I finished, Max had reopened the tavern. He sat at the bar, writing in a ledger, and the place was empty except for Jerry, who had returned and was sitting in a booth close to the TV.

"We're good here," Max assured me. "Why don't you sort out the afternoon sales so you can start fresh when Ruth gets in."

I sat in a corner booth, combing through the tickets and cash to figure out what I owed to Tiny and Bitty from the afternoon's tips. Just as I finished up, Ruth strolled in through the back and sat opposite me in the booth.

"I am so sorry I abandoned you like that," she said with a grimace. "I wanted to check out the brand-new Hobby Lobby, and I got lost." She put her hand on the table and leaned forward, lowering her voice. "Did you know they have damn near anything you could ever want in that store?"

"Don't worry about it," I said. "Like I told you in my text, I found a ride."

"Yeah," she said suspiciously, "but you never answered my text asking who you had caught it with."

"In fairness," I said, bracing myself, "I never saw your text. We must have lost cell service before it came through."

"That doesn't tell me who you caught a ride with, now does it?"

"Oh, for Christ's sake," Max said in disgust from behind the bar. "Wyatt drove her home."

Her eyes flew wide. "*Wyatt?* You got into a vehicle with him after he stormed in here at three in the morning, demanding to know what you had to do with Seth's murder?"

"Whoa!" Max said as he walked around the bar and over to our table. "Wyatt showed up at three a.m.? Who let him in?"

"He must have walked in through the back door," Ruth said. "Because that's the way he left."

Max's face hardened. "Wyatt still has a key?"

"You didn't change the locks after he left?" Ruth asked, giving him an incredulous look.

"Why the hell would I waste money changing the locks?" he asked. "He was in prison."

"He's been back for five years, Maxwell!" Ruth retorted.

"He walked out on the place," Max said. "He walked away from everything that had anything to do with the Drummonds. Why would I be concerned that he might want to use his keys?"

"He could have robbed you blind!" Ruth said.

"Wyatt Drummond's not a thief," Jerry said in a shaky voice, turning to point his finger at us. Ruth and Max hadn't bothered to make sure the place was completely empty before starting their fight, although I got the sense a lot of people forgot about Jerry being around. He seemed to prefer it that way. "He's got more integrity in his pinkie finger than your father and grandfather put together, Maxwell Drummond."

Ruth's mouth dropped open in shock, and she murmured to me, "I ain't never heard that man stand up for anything, let alone for a person."

Max took a few steps toward him. For a moment I thought he might blast into Jerry for disrespecting two Drummonds to compliment a third, but instead he said, "Yeah, you're right. Wyatt's no thief."

I couldn't help wondering if he meant he was right about all of it, but mostly I wondered why he was defending his brother when there was obviously bad blood between them. And when Wyatt had supposedly gone to jail *because* he was a thief.

"You still need to change the damn locks, Max," Ruth insisted.

"I will," Max said with a sigh. "First thing tomorrow."

A few customers walked through the door and sat at a table in my section from the previous night.

"We keeping the same sections as before?" I asked Ruth as I started to slide out of the booth.

Her brow furrowed. "I've got a lot more questions for you, missy, so don't think you got off the hook." But she didn't sound mad, just a little grumpy and a lot curious.

"Got it. So same sections?"

She shrugged. "Sure, why not."

Now that it was after five, more people wandered in for dinner. The dining room was packed by six, and Ruth and I were hopping to keep up while Tiny and Bitty cooked like a well-oiled machine in the kitchen.

A few of the dinner customers were braver than the lunch patrons, asking me questions about the prior night. Was it true that I'd found Seth? Had he told me who'd shot him? A couple of them even asked if I'd been the one to pull the trigger.

The dinner crowd cleared out by seven thirty and the drinkin' crowd came in. Tonight it was just a few couples hanging out together and some older guys at the bar.

Carson walked in around eight. I expected him to approach the bar to talk to Max, but to my surprise he took a seat in my section.

He greeted me enthusiastically when I walked up to his table. "We didn't have the chance to be properly introduced earlier," he said with a smile. "I'm Carson Purdy. I work for the Drummonds." He released a chuckle. "The *elder* Drummonds."

I smiled back, grateful for a friendly face after being pummeled by frowns all evening—even if the elder Drummonds *had* sent him here on some kind of fact-finding mission. "I'm Carly Moore."

He shook my hand. "Nice to meet you, Carly Moore. Max speaks highly of you. Says you're from Georgia."

Was he fishing for information? The warm look on his face suggested he was just trying to be friendly, but I didn't know enough about him to judge. "That's right. I take it you were born and raised around here?"

He laughed. "I'm from Ohio, believe it or not. I know how hard it can be to break into this town, so if you ever want to chat—outsider to outsider—you let me know."

He pulled a business card out of his shirt's front pocket. Did he have a stack of them in there, or had he carried this one around just for me?

"Thanks, Carson, but I'm not staying. Just passing through."

"Offer still stands."

I glanced at the card. He'd likely approached me with hopes of getting some information, and yet it occurred to me that I could do the same. He likely knew a lot about the town…and the Drummonds. "Have you worked for the Drummonds long?"

"Since Max and Wyatt were boys. I was practically a kid myself."

"So you saw this town when it was in its prime." Taking a risk, I added, "When the town and the Drummonds were thriving."

He hesitated, obviously suspicious of my comments. "You interested in the history of Drum or just the Drummonds?"

I forced a chuckle. "From what I've come to understand, it's one and the same."

Shifting in his seat, he picked up the saltshaker and twirled it between his fingers. "The Drummonds have run this town for nearly two hundred years, but times are hard."

"Max said his father had something secret in the works to help the town."

A grin lifted his lips, but it didn't reach his eyes. "Max is speakin' out of turn. Bart Drummond doesn't like people discussin' his personal business. If you want to stick around, you'd do best to remember that."

"I suppose you'll be sure to report my nosiness," I said before I thought better of it.

"Not me," he said, his smile returning. "You're still learnin' the way of the place, and like I said, us outsiders need to stick together." He pointed to the card in my hand. "I meant what I said. We should have a chat sometime."

He seemed sincere, but I wasn't sure what to think of him. Maybe it was a bad idea to trust anyone in Drum. "I take it you don't need a few minutes to consider the drink menu?"

He chuckled and asked for a Coke, which Max took over to him personally. The two of them chatted for several minutes, their heads bent together, and Carson left soon afterward. He'd left a pile of cash on the table, with a bigger tip than I'd gotten all night.

About ten minutes later, Ruth approached me while I was standing by the kitchen window, taking a breather, but the look on her face told me my short moment of respite was over. I decided to head off the questions I knew were coming.

"Does Carson Purdy come in here often?"

She made a face. "Seein' as how it's one of the few places to eat in town, yeah. He's here often enough."

"What's he do for the Drummonds, anyway?"

"He takes care of their land, runs errands, typical assistant stuff."

"And checks in with Max about the motel?"

"Sometimes."

Was Carson Purdy Max's ace in the hole? If so, I wasn't sure how I felt about it. I wasn't sure I wanted any help from the elder Drummonds—even if they were so inclined.

Ruth gave me a questioning look, but when I didn't offer any information, she changed the subject for me. "How is it that you caught a ride with Wyatt?" she asked in a hushed tone. "What in the world was he doin' in Greeneville?"

"Same as me," I said. "Visiting Hank."

I expected her to show more surprise, but she simply pressed her lips together.

"Is Wyatt a family friend?" I asked.

"You could say," she said. "Wyatt was kind of a mentor to the boy, and he helped out around the place. Hank's been pretty much homebound for a while, so Wyatt ran the boy down to Greeneville and Ewing for things they couldn't get in Drum."

Hearing that did something to me, as if a handful of rocks had been sent ricocheting through my empty places. Wyatt must have been devastated to hear the news. No wonder he'd shown up at the bar in such a state.

"Did he hear you tell Mr. Hank about Seth's last words?" Ruth asked.

"No," I said. "He showed up after I told the nurse I'd bring Hank home tomorrow morning."

She propped her hands on her hips and jutted her body to one side. "You did what, now?"

I was having déjà vu of my conversation with Max. "The nurse told Hank that he'd have to go to a rehab center if no one showed up to get him. So I offered to do it."

"You must be out of your ever-lovin' mind," she said. "That man just had his leg amputated. Who's gonna take care of him?"

"I am," I said "I'm gonna stay with him until his home health service kicks in at the end of the week." Then I quickly added, "But I'm still gonna work here at the tavern."

"Who's gonna watch him while you're workin'?" Ruth asked.

"I will," a firm male voice said from the doorway to the back. Wyatt stood in the opening, his confident air demanding my attention. To my frustration, my reaction to him seemed to intensify every time I saw him. But the look on his face made it clear he wasn't here for a friendly chat.

"What the hell are you doin' back here, Wyatt?" Ruth demanded, fury in her eyes. "Wasn't busting in here last night enough for you?"

"Max told me Carly was back here."

The veins in her neck popped out. "Max let you back here? We'll just see about that."

Giving herself a wide berth around him, she marched off toward the bar.

"I take it you two aren't fast friends," I said, gesturing to Ruth. Maybe their short romance hadn't ended well.

Standing in front of me, he turned to cast her a long glance, his face expressionless. "You could say that."

But he didn't elaborate, and it was none of my concern. "Did I hear you correctly that you'll stay with Hank while I'm working?"

He shrugged, trying to look nonchalant but failing miserably. "He won't stand for a full-time babysitter, whether it's you, me, or a nurse. He'll want us to check on him and get out."

"That'll be hard to do if I'm living with him."

"About that…" He held my gaze. "That's a bad idea."

"Why?" I asked, telling myself to listen to him before I jumped to any judgments. I'd just met Hank this morning and he'd been stricken by shock and grief. Maybe he was the devil incarnate and Wyatt was about to warn me. But I doubted it. Sure, Hank had been on the cantankerous side a few times, but I'd seen the sorrow in his eyes. He'd loved that boy with his entire being, and a man who loved that fiercely wasn't evil.

"Do you really want me to spell it out for you?" he asked, his face hardening.

I crossed my arms over my chest and gave him a saucy glare. "Apparently I do."

His jaw tightened and he took a step closer, looming over me. "He's a harmless old man. Leave him alone."

That wasn't the response I'd been expecting. Especially after he'd been so kind to me earlier. I'd thought we'd come to an understanding, and it hurt more than it should to find out I was wrong.

"What exactly do you think I'm going to do to him?" I asked, my temper flaring. "We went over this already. I didn't kill that poor boy. I may be a stranger in town, but that's no reason to assume I'd kill a child in cold blood."

He hesitated and said, "No. I know it wasn't you."

That fanned the flames of my suspicion. "How do you know it wasn't me?"

"Because I saw you after he died. You were too upset for it to have been you."

"You didn't just show up here at three in the morning for nothing. What exactly do you think I did? What exactly are you accusing me of?" Another question lingered on my lips, unsaid: *Did you find my gun?*

"I don't know, Carly," he said in exasperation. "Don't you think it's mighty coincidental that your car was broken into the same night Seth Chalmers was shot in front of your motel room?"

I did. We both knew it likely *wasn't* a coincidence, but he thought I'd done something wrong. He didn't know my only crime was seeing something I shouldn't have.

"Sometimes there are coincidences, Wyatt, and apparently this is one of them."

"I'm going to go pick up Hank tomorrow morning," he said in a grim tone. "I'll bring him home and get him settled. Then I'll schedule some of the women in town to drop in on him every few hours to make sure he's okay. You don't need to concern yourself with him. I'll stay over at his house until he gets his service set up." When he saw my gaping expression, he said, "You're an outsider, Carly. You don't belong here, and you definitely don't need to be stayin' in his house, stirrin' up trouble."

While I was logical enough to realize he wasn't completely off-base, I wasn't about to back down. I'd made a promise to Hank, and my arrangement was with him, not Wyatt. Besides, I wanted to look for the evidence Seth had mentioned.

But before I could say anything, Wyatt turned around and strode past a shocked Ruth, who'd returned in time to overhear every ugly word. From the look of him, he thought he'd just laid down the law and there was no reason for rebuttal.

Fuck that.

"I'm going to pick him up, Wyatt Drummond!" I shouted after him. "And I'll be staying with him too, so you might as well climb off your tiny high horse and deal with it!"

The customers' chatter came to a dead halt.

Wyatt stopped at the front door and turned back to face me, giving me an expressionless glance, then walked out.

"Ruth," I said, still staring after him. "I'm gonna need to borrow your car tomorrow morning."

She was watching him too, and while I'd worked up my temper, Ruth's glare was full of hate. "I'll make sure it has a full tank of gas."

Chapter Fifteen

I had no idea what time Wyatt planned on picking Hank up, but I was up by six and left at the same time Franklin did. Ruth assured me she'd catch a ride to work. I suspected Max himself would pick her up.

Ruth had given me directions, which I'd written down since I didn't have a GPS to guide me. I'd taken a travel mug of Franklin's coffee out of desperation but could only force about half of it down. When I walked into Hank's room, he was sitting upright in bed. His face lit up the moment he saw me, and he sent a smug look to Wyatt, who was sitting in the chair next to the bed, his chin in his hand, his elbow propped on the chair's arm. He must have beaten me by a few minutes. Had he hoped to check Hank out before I arrived?

"Good morning, Hank," I said, approaching his bed. "Are you ready to go home today?"

"I can't get out of here fast enough." He pressed the nurse's call button multiple times.

"I told you I'd give you a ride," Wyatt said insolently, dropping his arm and sitting up straighter.

"And I told *you* that Carly was comin' and I'd wait for *her*." He pressed the nurse's button a few more times.

"Yes, Mr. Chalmers?" a nurse asked over the intercom.

"My ride's here and I want to get the hell out."

"As I told the equally impatient man in your room, we just had a shift change. You'll have to wait for us to finish your discharge paperwork."

"I want to eat lunch in my chair in my own home, so hurry it up," Hank said.

The nurse didn't respond.

"I told you I was comin' to get him," Wyatt said in a cold tone, directed at me.

"And I promised Hank that *I* would do it," I said. "I made a promise, and I don't break them, Mr. Drummond."

He raised his eyebrows. "So you're callin' me Mr. Drummond now?"

"If you're going to accuse me of things I haven't done, then I think formality is appropriate."

Hank glanced from Wyatt to me and back again. "Did you accuse her of something?" When Wyatt didn't answer, Hank said, "What do you think she's gonna do? Rob me?"

"I don't know," Wyatt said, his voice a growl of frustration. "And that right there is the problem. None of us really know her."

Hank's gaze found mine and he gave me a sad smile. "Oh, but I do, boy."

Tears filled my eyes, and I reached for his hand and squeezed it. Wyatt was right. Hank barely knew me, and vice versa, but we shared a secret that drew us together in a way that went beyond normal relationships.

Hank dropped my hand and turned to Wyatt. "Carly's stayin' with me whether you like it or not, so deal with it or get the hell out."

Wyatt gave him a defiant glare, yet there was something deferential about it, which caught me by surprise. I'd seen him tell off his brother and stare down hard men at the tavern. But Wyatt was kowtowing to Hank, and I wanted to know why.

A nurse came in a few minutes later, looking exasperated. "I know you're in a hurry to go home, but we had to get all your paperwork in order, Mr. Chalmers."

She turned to me and Wyatt. "Which one of you is Mr. Chalmers goin' home with?"

"That would be me," I said.

"Me," Wyatt said, getting to his feet.

She chuckled. "We got a custody battle goin' on?"

"We'll both be takin' care of him," Wyatt said. "At his place."

She glanced between us again, shaking her head a little in amusement. In all likelihood, most older patients didn't have a line of people wanting to take care of them. "Whatever y'all do is your own business. I just need to know who to teach about carin' for his wounds. Someone will also need to make sure he's checkin' his insulin."

"Both of us," Wyatt said. "We'll be workin' in shifts."

I expected Hank to protest, but he sat in silence, his previous amusement gone.

The nurse pulled back his covers and exposed the bandaged stump of his right leg. "We took the drain out yesterday, which is why he's ready to go home today, so you don't have to take care of that part, but you *do* need to watch the incision for any signs of infection or cellulitis." She glanced up at us. "A fancy way of saying the tissue is dyin'."

My stomach churned.

For the next fifteen minutes she showed us how to care for Hank's stump. She made both of us take turns unwrapping and rewrapping it, and to my surprise, Wyatt didn't flinch. Once

Hank's leg was rewrapped, the nurse gave us a list of supplies and prescriptions for the various medications—pain, antibiotics, injectable insulin, and a pill to help manage his diabetes—we'd need to pick up before taking Hank home. She reminded Hank that he needed to check his blood sugar more regularly.

"Yeah," he grumped. "I know."

"Do you want me to show your caregivers how to check your sugar and give you insulin injections?"

"I've been managing my own damn diabetes for over fifteen years," he groused. "I had a leg amputated, not my brain."

I couldn't help wondering what I'd gotten myself into. Taking care of Violet had been relatively straightforward compared to the whole business of changing bandages and monitoring medications. I was sure I was going to screw up. Part of me couldn't help but wonder if Wyatt was right. Maybe I was overstepping. But Hank needed help, and I needed a place to stay where I felt like I was earning my keep. And this gave me an opportunity to look for Seth's evidence. Sometimes you had to listen to fate.

Next, the nurse helped Hank get dressed. I offered to step out of the room, but she told me I should stay—dressing him would be part of the job. He put on a faded and stained blue and white button-down shirt and a pair of jeans, the right leg of which had been cut off. The nurse carefully pulled the pant leg over his stump, telling us it was important not to tug too hard and possibly disturb the sutures. Finally, she brought in the wheelchair and helped Hank out of bed, making him use his crutches to walk to the chair and sit down.

"He'll need help at first," she said. "At least until he builds up his upper body strength. Going to the bathroom will likely be the hardest. Toilets are often shorter than chairs. I suggest you get one of those raised seats to make it more comfortable."

Hank hung his head, refusing to look at us. I understood his embarrassment. The nurse was talking about him like he was a child.

The nurse wheeled Hank to the lobby and told us to pull our car up to the front doors so she could help us load him in.

Wyatt and I stared at each other, something in his gaze telling me I wasn't the only one who realized we'd signed up for a monumental undertaking.

"I take it you drove Ruth's car," Wyatt said. When I nodded, he turned to the nurse. "I've got a 1985 Ford pickup truck, and Carly has an old Cadi. High or low—which do you think would be better?"

I couldn't believe Wyatt was considering letting me drive Hank home. Maybe he'd decided what I had: the more help, the better.

"I suppose high," she said. "He'll need help gettin' in, but he'll be able to slide out once you get him home—assisted, of course."

Wyatt nodded, then turned to me. "How about I take Hank to his house and you can get his prescriptions and medical supplies. They'll need to be filled here in Greeneville."

Prescriptions could be expensive. This was going to wipe out my money, but I couldn't very well tell him no. "Do you have insurance, Hank?"

"Medicare," he said, still refusing to look me in the eye. He pointed to his knapsack. "My card's in there. In my wallet."

He handed me the bag. I felt like I was violating his privacy by digging inside, so I quickly found the wallet and started to hand it to him.

He turned away. "You get the card out. Take my cash too."

Reluctantly, I opened his wallet and found his Medicare card and checked for cash, finding forty-three dollars.

"Just keep the whole thing," Hank said, his cheeks tinged with pink. "I ain't got a need for it right now."

I glanced over at Wyatt, sure he was going to accuse me of trying to steal Hank's money and run. But to my surprise, he told the nurse he was going to get the truck. Turning to me, he said, "Carly, will you walk out with me?"

My chest tightened, but his voice didn't have the Asshole Wyatt tone. "I'll see you back at your house, Hank," I said cheerfully, then followed Wyatt out into the parking lot.

"Do you know how to drive a stick?" he asked as we followed the sidewalk of the circular drive.

"Yeah," I said in confusion. "But Ruth's car is an automatic."

He reached for my hand and pressed his keys into my palm. "You take the truck and drive Hank back to Drum. I'll get the supplies and the medication."

My temper flared. "You're really that worried I'm going to run off with Hank's money?" I demanded. "I didn't even see a credit card or debit card in his wallet, and forty-three dollars won't get me very far."

"Exactly," he said matter-of-factly. "Forty-three dollars likely won't pay for his medication either, let alone all of the supplies on that list." He pushed the keys into my hand again. "So you drive Hank home in my truck, and I'll pick up the supplies and meet you at his house."

"I probably have enough to pay for it," I said, unsure whether to be grateful or insulted.

"I hope to God you do or I'll have to impound your car for years," he said with a grin that quickly turned somber. "Seriously, Carly. I doubt Hank'll be able to pay you back before you leave, if ever. Let me deal with it. I'm not goin' anywhere."

I looked at him, seeing a glimpse of the man I'd met at the overlook—the kind of guy who stopped to help a stranger.

"Thanks," I finally said, deciding simple was better. I saw no reason to argue with him. Instead, I dug out the keys to the Cadillac and traded with him. "Ruth said she had a ride to the tavern for the lunch shift, but I'll need to bring it back this evening."

"Not a problem," he said. "I plan to be back long before then."

I wanted to say something else, to assure him that he and Hank could trust me, but I was worried I'd say something to piss him off, so I just walked over to his truck and started the engine. I sure hoped driving a manual would come back to me.

Hank was surprised when I pulled up instead of Wyatt, but he didn't question me, simply urged the nurse to help get him up into the truck.

It took the two of us, but we got him in and belted up, and then we were on our way.

"Before we head out of town," Hank said, "how about stopping at Popeyes and getting me some fried chicken and a biscuit?"

I narrowed my eyes at him. "Are you supposed to be eating that when you're diabetic?"

"So?" he said. "I'd rather be dead than give up my fried chicken and biscuits. You still got my wallet?"

"No," I said. "I thought you were supposed to check your insulin before you ate."

"And we did, remember? I gave myself a damn injection. I'm good to go."

I wasn't sure if this was the right thing to do, but he wasn't a child and my job was to help him with his amputation not manage his diabetes. "Biscuits sound good to me, but I doubt Popeyes is open. It's barely ten o'clock, and I'm not sure it's a good idea to hang around waiting." I shot him an apologetic look. "How about McDonald's? They have biscuits. We can go through the drive-thru. My treat."

"It's not the same, but I guess it'll work," he said dejectedly. He gave me directions as I struggled to shift the gears.

"Turn right there!" he shouted at the last moment, pointing out the window.

I hit the brakes and nearly stalled the truck as I downshifted and took the turn. A black pickup truck almost slammed into me, but I made it around the corner without getting hit. I glanced over in panic to make sure Hank hadn't been jostled too badly. "You okay?"

He scowled. "I'm fine, just hungry for biscuits."

"Promise me you won't tell Wyatt I almost got rear-ended," I said, trying to catch my breath. "I'll never hear the end of it."

"If you get me McDonald's, I'll take your secrets to my grave," he said.

Considering the reason I was with him, it seemed like an alarming analogy. We went through the drive-thru in record time and were soon on our way, me with my sausage biscuit and coffee, and Hank with his breakfast burritos, sausage and cheese biscuit, hash browns, Egg McMuffin, and an orange juice.

I had serious doubts that he could eat it all, but bearing in mind that there weren't any fast food restaurants in Drum, I got him everything he requested without comment.

Before I pulled out of the parking lot, I got out my paper with the directions to Drum. When Hank figured out what I was looking at, he snorted. "You don't need damn directions. I know where to go."

He gave me instructions—often too close to the actual turn—but it didn't take me long to realize we weren't following Ruth's route. "Where are you taking me, Hank?"

"Don't you worry. It's only a couple minutes longer than the way you likely came, but it'll bring us through Ewing."

I shot him a frown. "Why do you want to go to Ewing?"

He glanced out the window, refusing to look at me, and his voice trembled when he spoke. "I want to see my grandson."

Why hadn't I thought of that? Hank had been stuck in the hospital and hadn't had a chance to identify his body or possibly even make arrangements.

"Do you need to identify him?" I asked quietly.

"Nah," he said. "Wyatt already gave the official ID. The sheriff's deputy said Max did it unofficially. But I want to see him anyway."

Wyatt had officially IDed him? That fit with Ruth's story about him taking Seth under his wing. "Do you know where they took his body?"

He was silent for a second. "He's at the funeral home. I need to talk to them about the funeral too."

"Of course," I said. "I'll be more than happy to take you."

Once I got on to Highway 107, the lull of the truck and Hank's medication had him dozing. He'd told me that 107 ran right into Ewing, and sure enough, forty-five minutes later, Ewing came into view.

"Hank," I said softly. When he roused, I said, "We're here. Now what?"

He sat up, his eyes sleepy and his gray hair smooshed on one side, and glanced around to get his bearings. "Go a couple of miles and we'll turn left."

After a moment of silence, I asked, "How are you doing? Are you in any pain?"

"Nah, they jacked me up on aspirin before they let me go. I'll be okay until this afternoon."

Aspirin? That's all they were giving him? But the nurse had said he had a prescription for pain medication…

When I pulled into the parking lot, I began to worry about getting him out of the truck and inside on his crutches.

I said as much, and he waved a hand at the doors. "Just park in front. Then go inside and tell Mobley I need a wheelchair."

"Okay…" I did as he said and walked through the front doors, glancing down the hall for someone to help. I heard a faint doorbell chime in the back.

"Can I help you?" a middle-aged man asked, walking out a door down the hall. He wore a dark gray suit and a pale blue tie. His dress shoes were shiny black. His hair was black too, for the most part, with a sprinkling of gray. His eyes were warm and kind.

"Hi," I said, taking a step closer. "I'm with Hank Chalmers. He's here to see his grandson."

"I've been expecting him," the man stated, holding out his hand as he approached. "I'm Pete Mobley, the director."

I shook his hand. "Carly Bla—" I cut myself off and said, "I'm Carly and I'll be taking care of Hank for a few days."

"Nice to meet you, Carly," he said as he released my hand. "Hank said you'd be comin' by too."

He sure hadn't let any grass grow under him.

"Mr. Chalmers is in the truck. He's going to need assistance to get out and see his grandson. He said you'd have a wheelchair?"

"One of my employees has one ready for him. I'll send him out to collect Hank. I'd stay with you, but I'm dealin' with a difficult situation that needs my attention. I'll meet you both when you're inside."

"Not a problem, Mr. Mobley. Thank you."

"No need for the mister," he said with a friendly smile. "Everyone just calls me Mobley."

"Well, thank you, Mobley."

"Anything I can do to help you and Hank through this difficult time. Death is tragic, but it's even more so when a boy is gunned down in cold blooded murder." He stood there quietly for a moment, as if giving that thought the consideration it deserved, then smiled at me one last time before heading back down the hall. "Dwight," he called out, "can you bring the wheelchair up to meet Mr. Chalmers?"

"Sure thing," a man called out as Mobley walked back through the door he'd come through.

I heard the squeaky wheels of the chair before I saw it appear in the hall, being pushed by a man with shaggy blond hair and a scruffy beard. He slowly ambled toward me, wearing dress pants and a button-down shirt that looked like hand-me-downs. A leering grin spread across his face the moment he saw me.

"Well, ain't this a surprise?" he said.

It was the guy from Monday Night Football at the tavern, the one who'd acted weird about my supposed history in Georgia, only his buddies had called him Dewey.

"I sure didn't expect to see *you* here," he said, soft enough that his boss wouldn't be able to hear him. "Who knew the old coot had it in him?"

I wanted to give him a piece of my mind, but for all I knew, he'd take it out on Hank.

"Mobley said you'd help me get Hank inside," I said, trying to keep my tone calm.

He gestured to the glass doors. "If you'd kindly hold it open." As I moved toward the door, he said, "I heard you were stayin' with him, and since you didn't deny it, it must be true."

My hackles rose. "How'd you hear I'd be stayin' with Mr. Chalmers?"

Then I realized I'd announced it to the whole damn town when I'd shouted at Wyatt last night.

"Drum's a small town," he said. "It don't take long for word to get round." He leaned closer, his eyes glittering. "You know half the town thinks you did it, and you're only stayin' with Hank to find the fortune."

There was no containing the bark or laughter. "What fortune?"

His grin spread and he nodded. "Good call. Play stupid. I like it."

Whatever people were saying in town, I highly doubted Hank had any money, let alone a fortune. Still, there was no point in engaging a man like this in conversation. I was here for a grieving grandfather. I went out the door and stood to the side as I held it open.

"I'm sure Hank will appreciate havin' a fine young thing givin' 'im sponge baths," Dwight said as he stopped next to me, looking me up and down. He had the audacity to give me a leering wink.

I held his gaze and tried to rein in my temper. "I highly doubt that Mr. Chalmers will be thinking about *sponge baths* while mourning the death of his beloved grandson."

He shrugged with a grin. "He may be in mournin', but he ain't dead."

"I'm here to help Mr. Chalmers see his dead grandson," I said in a voice that should have frosted the glass door I was still holding. "If you can't help me with that while treating us both with respect, I'll be happy to have a chat with your boss."

He held up his hands in self-defense. "Whoa. Down there, girl. No need to get your panties in a bunch."

I was about to jerk the wheelchair from his grasp, but he pushed ahead of me and guided it down the ramp, toward the truck. He did a double take and asked, "Is this Wyatt Drummond's truck?"

Should I be worried that this lowlife was familiar enough with Wyatt to recognize it?

"That's none of your concern," I snapped.

He shot me a grin, then opened the passenger door of the truck, calling out good-naturedly, "Hey there, Hank. I'm Dwight and I'm gonna be helpin' you inside." His respectful tone caught me by surprise. "The whole damn town's upset about Seth."

"Dwight…" Hank said faintly. "You Ben Henderson's son?"

"Yes, sir," Dwight said as he helped Hank turn sideways in his seat. "One of 'em."

Hank nodded but didn't say anything.

Dwight slung Hank's arm over his shoulder and helped him down. He got him settled in the chair and started pushing it toward a side door.

"I thought you were workin' at the dog food plant down in Greeneville," Hank said as Dwight pushed the chair across the parking lot.

"I was, sir," Dwight said, still sounding respectful. "But my pa took sick, so I found something closer to home. I was lucky enough to get hired on by Mobley a couple of months ago."

Hank nodded with an absent look in his eyes. "That's good. Family's important."

"If you could get the door?" Dwight said to me. His tone was civil, but his snide grin told a different story.

I walked ahead of them and opened the single door, hoping the wheelchair would fit. Once I reached it, I turned around to see Dwight's gaze on my denim-covered ass.

He pushed the chair past me and licked his lower lip.

It took everything in me not to throat-punch him.

"Hank," I heard Mobley call out in a soft voice. When I followed Dwight and Hank inside, I saw the funeral director coming down the hall to greet us. "I am so sorry to hear about your loss. And after the loss of your poor daughter last year and Mary a year or so before that…" He shook his head. "I'm just so sorry."

Hank's eyes welled up and he hung his head. "I can't believe he's gone. That's why I'm here. To see it for myself."

"When I heard you were wanting to see him today, I explained the situation to the medical examiner's office in Johnson City. They let us pick him up early this morning, but I've got to warn you, Ol' Jimmy hasn't had a chance to work his magic yet."

"That's okay." Hank's voice shook, and his face had lost color.

"Maybe this is all too much, Hank," I said, pushing past Dwight and squatting next to the chair. He'd just been released from the hospital. He likely shouldn't even be making this trip. "We can come back tomorrow or come early for the visitation."

"No," he said, sitting up straighter. The adjustment made him look even frailer, but there was nothing weak about his voice. "I want to see my grandson."

"Then we'll do it together," I said with a reassuring smile.

Hank nodded, his eyes glassy and his chin trembling.

I wanted to get this over with and get him home and settled.

"Let's all head on back," Mobley said as he spun around and started walking.

I stayed next to Hank and studied him. If I saw any sign that he couldn't handle what was happening, I'd find a way to get him out of here.

We headed down a long hall into what looked like a hospital room—or a morgue—with a stainless steel table in the center of the room. A body covered with a sheet lay on top of it, the head to my right.

Hank released a strangled sound.

Dwight guided the chair into the room and parked it a few feet from the table. I stopped next to Hank and reached down to pick up his hand. He glanced up at me with vacant eyes and squeezed.

Dwight shuffled to the head of the table and started to uncover Seth's head, but Hank blurted out, "Wait! I wanna be standin' when I see him."

My stomach was in knots. I really didn't want to see Seth again, not like this, but Hank needed to see his grandson and he needed support. I sure didn't want to leave him with Dwight.

"You can't stand," Dwight scoffed. "Your leg's cut off."

"Dwight," Mobley snapped. "Treat Mr. Chalmers with respect."

Dwight looked pissed and he stepped to the other end of the table as though saying he wasn't having any part of this.

I locked the wheels of the chair and squatted in front of Hank. "I'm gonna help you stand, then we'll move up to the table."

I regretted not bringing his crutches in with us, but I figured I could support him for a minute or so. When I'd helped lift him into the truck with the nurse less than an hour ago, I'd realized he didn't weigh all that much.

He nodded, but he didn't look happy about it. I could understand that. He wasn't the kind of man who liked accepting help, although he was smart enough to know when he needed it.

"Mobley," a woman called out from the hallway. "There's a phone call for you."

"It's gonna have to wait, Verna," Mobley said with an edge of irritation. "I'm busy."

"It's important," she said, sounding nervous. "That client from before's not very happy."

The client was clearly someone important—more important than poor Seth Chalmers—because Mobley's smile wavered, and he gave us a slight nod. "If you'll excuse me, I need to take this." And he hurried out the door.

I considered asking Dwight for help getting Hank out of the chair, but his foul expression suggested he wouldn't be gentle. Giving Hank a soft smile, I said, "Okay. Let's do this."

It took some maneuvering, but I got him balanced on his remaining foot. He wrapped his right arm around my shoulder, and we took a couple of awkward steps toward the table. When we got close enough, Hank grabbed the table with his left hand to help him stay balanced.

Since Dwight didn't seem inclined to help us any further, I slowly reached for the sheet and pulled it down to Seth's collar bone, exposing his bruised and battered face. His left eye was swollen, and his lip had a cut. A deep bruise discolored his right cheek.

I felt lightheaded, but a guttural sound from Hank snapped me out of it. His knee buckled, and I shifted my position to brace his weight.

"Do you want to sit down?" I asked quietly, fighting the urge to cry.

He shook his head, opening his mouth to speak and then shutting it.

Dwight released a yawn.

I jerked my gaze to him, barely holding back my temper. "Can you show a little respect here?"

Dwight just leered at me.

Was Dwight just an asshole or had he played a part in Seth's murder? Would he be so blatantly cavalier if he were involved? I studied his irritated demeanor. He struck me as the kind of guy who thought he could do whatever he wanted, damn the consequences.

Hank ignored him, his chin trembling as he stared down at the boy.

I hadn't paid much attention to Seth's features in the dimly lit parking lot, but I got a better look at him now. He had a sprinkling of freckles across his nose and cheeks, and even with the bruising and swelling I could see that he'd been an attractive boy. Had he left behind a grieving girlfriend? How were his best friends handling this? I couldn't help thinking about the empty seat in his classes. On Monday, this boy had probably been at school, worried about homework and football games, and now he was dead on a stainless steel slab.

My resolve steeled—whoever did this had to pay.

Hank slid his arm from around my neck, so I tightened my hold around his waist to keep him upright. He reached for Seth's cheek, cupping it slightly at an awkward angle.

"What did you do, boy?" Hank whispered, tears streaming down his face. One dropped onto the white sheet.

"They say he pissed off the wrong people," Dwight said as he gave me a point-blank stare.

Was he talking about me?

I started to defend myself, but this creep wasn't worth my effort. At least not for me. But I'd be damned if I'd let him talk to Hank like that. "Mr. Chalmers is grieving. Could you please keep your hurtful comments to yourself?"

Dwight shrugged, leaning a hand against the table and taking a leisurely pose.

Now I was good and pissed. "You need to leave and give Hank a few minutes to pay his respects in privacy."

"No can do," he said with a laugh.

I released my hold on Hank, making sure he was supporting himself against the table, and took a step toward Dwight. "Then we'll be taking Seth's body elsewhere, and I'm sure your boss won't be too happy you're the reason, what with you needing this job and all."

Dwight stood upright and towered over me, his jaw working as his face flushed.

"Do as she says," Hank said in a surprisingly firm voice. "Leave us be or I'll move him to Valley Funeral Home."

Dwight released a string of curses, but he headed for the door. Before he left, he turned around in the doorway and said, "You have five minutes or until Mobley comes back."

I shut the door behind him and locked it, the clacking sound of the lock catching bounced off the hard-surfaced room.

Once Dwight was gone, Hank hunched over the table, his shoulders shaking with silent sobs.

I tried to hold back my own tears, but the sight of the broken man was too much. I moved next to him and placed a hand over his. "I'm so very sorry, Hank."

Although Hank had absolved me of any responsibility, I hadn't absolved myself. I still questioned whether that car alarm had led to his death. I probably always would.

He nodded, his head still hanging as he stared at his grandson's face. After a half minute or so, he sucked in a deep breath and rose up. His hand fumbled with the sheet to pull it down further.

I reached past him and grabbed the edge. "Are you sure?"

He pushed my hand away and jerked down the sheet himself, exposing Seth's naked chest. A brutal Y-shaped cut marred his pale skin, along with two angry red holes on either side of it.

Hank's body stiffened and he placed his hand flat on the table, his body now shaking with anger instead of grief. "I told that boy to leave it alone. I told him it would get him killed."

I didn't respond, just leaned my arm gently against his, silently offering what support I could.

He tugged at the sheet again. At first I thought he was trying to expose Seth's entire body, but instead, he freed Seth's left hand and fumbled to hold it.

I picked up Seth's cold hand, expecting his arm to be stiff, but it bent enough for me to move his hand into Hank's reach. My fingers brushed against something rough. Turning Seth's hand over, I gasped at the blackened wound in the center of his palm.

"That wasn't there when I saw him," I whispered.

Hank's gaze jerked to mine. "Are you sure?"

I nodded. "That's where the numbers were written." I repeated them in my head—5346823.

His eyes widened. Then he whispered, "Shh."

My heart hammering, I nodded.

Hank picked up Seth's hand and stared down at the rough-edged rectangular wound.

"I want to take pictures of it," I whispered. "If this is part of a coverup, we need to prove this was here."

"Yeah," he said, sounding weary, and I realized his leg was trembling.

Grabbing my phone out of my pocket, I snapped photos from several angles, hoping they were good enough. The camera on my burner phone wasn't very high quality, and the photos were slightly grainy. Still, it was better than nothing. Just as I slipped my phone back into my pocket, the doorknob jiggled, and I jumped.

"Dwight?" Mobley called from the hall. "What's goin' on in there?" The door rattled as he tried to open it again.

Hank leaned forward as he lifted Seth's hand, kissing the back of it. "Rest in peace, boy. You done good."

The door shook with Mobley's attempts to get in.

Hank pushed out a sigh. "Help me into that chair, girl, and take me home."

Keys rattled in the hall and I knew we only had seconds.

"Yes, sir." I returned Seth's hand like we'd found it and tugged the sheet up to his chin. After I unlocked the wheels on the wheelchair, I rolled it right up to Hank. I was helping ease him into the chair when the door flew open.

Hank landed on the seat with a hard thud, and he grimaced with pain.

"What's goin' on in here?" Mobley asked, his eyes wide. "Why is the door locked? Where's Dwight?"

I grabbed the handles of the wheelchair and turned Hank to face the funeral home director, who was standing in the middle of the doorway. Was he part of this? Because sometime between Seth's death and this moment, someone had burned off the numbers on Seth's hand. Had it been Dwight?

Mobley took a look at my face. "What's wrong?"

"We kicked your hired man out," Hank said. "He was bein' rude and disrespectful." Hank reached up and patted my hand on the wheelchair handle. "I wanted to see my grandson in peace. When he shut the door behind him, he must've locked it."

Mobley frowned. "I'm sorry. Dwight's a new hire, and we've had a few other reports of poor customer service. I assure you, he *will* be dealt with."

"Thank you," Hank said, his shoulders slumping with exhaustion. "I appreciate you lettin' me see my grandson, Mobley."

"Of course," Mobley said kindly, squatting in front of Hank and taking his hand. "And don't worry about runnin' into Dwight when you're dealin' with the funeral and such. He won't be around."

Was Mobley going to fire him on our account?

"I still need to pick out Seth's coffin," Hank said, his voice breaking.

"Didn't I tell you?" Mobley said with a soft smile. "Wyatt Drummond took care of it." He grimaced. "Of course, you're welcome to change anything, but after Barb and the money issue…"

My mouth dropped open in shock. Wyatt had paid for Seth's funeral? That wasn't something people just did.

Hank just stared up at him for a moment, struck silent by the news. Finally, he seemed to collect himself and said, "No. Thank you."

"Wyatt said you'd want to have the service at Drum Methodist Church, then have him buried in the Drum Cemetery. Just like we did with Barb."

Red-eyed, Hank nodded, and said in a rough voice, "Yeah."

"We're planning the service for Friday with the visitation tomorrow night."

Hank's eyes turned watery. "I gotta wait two days to bury my grandson?" He shook his head. "No. Let's do it tomorrow."

"Wyatt thought you'd want a couple of days to get your feet back under you." Mobley darted a glance at the place were Hank's right leg should have been and his face turned red. "Uh…it's too soon to plan the visitation for tonight."

"I don't want a visitation. All them people paradin' by the deceased like they're a circus freak show," he said in disgust. "I lived through it with Mary and Barb." He gave the funeral director a hard glare. "I ain't livin' through it with Seth."

"I understand, Hank. No visitation, but there's no way we can do the funeral tomorrow. We're already booked. We'll have to stick to Friday."

Hank gave a sharp nod, his eyes hard. "Fine. Funeral only. Friday afternoon."

"We can set the funeral at three and let people file by and pay their respects startin' at two," Mobley said.

"No," Hank said, his jaw set. "We'll have an open casket so people can see it's him and stop any wild, fanciful tales that might spring up that I buried an empty casket." He shook his head in disgust, and I wondered if that had happened to him before. "But they can pay their respects from their damn seats."

Mobley started to protest, but I cut in. "Thank you for seeing to all the arrangements. I'm sure Hank feels better knowing everything is in your capable hands. Now that he's made his wishes clear, I should be getting him back home."

Mobley's mouth pressed into a thin line. "Of course." Then he leaned over in front of Hank and patted his hand. "Don't you worry, Hank. We'll take care of everything."

"Thank you," Hank said, sounding broken, and as soon as Mobley stood, I wheeled Hank out of the room and got him the hell out of there.

Chapter Sixteen

After I got Hank settled into the truck (not an easy feat since he was beyond exhausted), I took the wheelchair back inside and left it in the foyer. I was worried Dwight might be lurking about, but I made it back to the truck without seeing anyone.

"Tell me how to get back to Drum," I said, my hands shaking as I gripped the steering wheel.

He gave me directions to a county road that would take us there, and neither one of us said anything until we were well out of Ewing.

"Who do you think burned Seth's hand?" I finally asked, keeping my gaze on the road. I had one goal in mind—get Hank home and hope that Wyatt showed up soon afterward. Which was a strange thought. Up until this morning, Wyatt had seemed like my enemy, yet he clearly cared about Hank, and I felt confident he'd help protect him.

Hank closed his eyes and leaned his head back on the seat. "I don't know."

"Seems like Dwight might be a suspect. Do you know much about him?"

"He's a bad seed. He gets into trouble all the time."

"Is that the real reason you didn't want a visitation?" I asked. "So no one would pat his hand and find it?"

He cast me a dark look. "I knew you were a smart girl within the first ten minutes of meeting you."

"You're okay with waiting until Friday?" I asked.

"Whether that boy gets buried Friday or three years from now, it don't mean a damn thing. Dead is dead and that boy ain't comin' back." His voice broke off, choking up at the end. His face was pale, and I was sure he'd overdone it. I needed to get him home and to bed.

"How much do you trust Wyatt?" I paused for half a second, then added, "You must trust him if you let him identify Seth."

He didn't answer.

"I'm not sure we can do this on our own," I said. "The question is if we can trust Wyatt to help."

"He's more trustworthy than his brother."

"Max?" I asked in surprise.

He chuckled, but it wasn't an amused sound. "Max wouldn't hurt a fly, but I wouldn't necessarily trust him to keep a secret. When he gets drunk, he talks."

After what I'd seen yesterday morning, I wasn't surprised by his assessment.

"You'd be worried about it getting back to their father?" I asked. "Bart?"

"Bart Drummond likes everyone to think he's their savior, swoopin' in to save the day, but the truth of the matter is Bart Drummond would sell Drum down the river if it lined his pockets, and he'd spin it so that whole damn town would thank him for it."

"Do you think Seth's murder has something to do with Bart Drummond?"

"Seems like everything that happens in Drum ties back to Bart Drummond, but in this instance, I don't see how. Seth was after the dealer who sold his momma drugs, and Bart wouldn't dirty his hands with something like that."

"Do you know who would?" I asked.

"Todd Bingham," he said as he stared straight ahead, his body stiff. "He runs the drug business in Drum."

Bingham, the man who'd gone out of his way to intimidate me on Monday night. I'd already suspected he was involved in the drug trade in Drum. I figured if anyone in this town had a foot in its criminal underworld, it would be that creep, but I knew he wasn't one of the three. The man who'd killed Seth scared me enough that I wouldn't be forgetting his voice anytime soon. Technically speaking, Bingham could have been the driver, but I doubted he'd ever take such a backseat role. "Do you think Bingham had anything to do with Seth's death?"

"If it involves drugs, then he's got his hand in it." He turned to face me. "You need to stay far away from Todd Bingham. *Very* far away."

My stomach cramped as I shot him a long look and then returned my gaze to the road. "Why doesn't the sheriff's department arrest him?"

"'Cause he's got the sheriff's department in his pocket."

Which fit with what Seth had said about his murderer being a deputy. ""You know that dealer I mentioned from Atlanta . . . how they were supposed to have made a delivery? Do you think Wyatt could have anything to do with the drug deal?"

"*Wyatt?*" he asked in surprise, then shook his head. "Hell, no. He can't stand drugs. He dropped by often enough to see Seth, and I heard 'em discussin' it."

"Do you want to involve Wyatt in this, then? Tell him what we know?" I was in over my head, and if Wyatt could be trusted, I wasn't opposed to involving him.

Hank didn't answer for a few seconds. "I need to think on it." He paused for several seconds, then said, "We can trust him not to harm us. I just can't be 100% certain he won't run to his daddy with anything we tell him. While he and his family give the appearance that he has nothing to do with them, he's barely makin' enough to pay Junior, so how'd he come up with the money to pay for Seth's funeral?" He frowned. "I need to ask him more questions."

I slowly nodded. Getting more answers sounded like a good call.

"If Barb died over a year ago, why was Seth goin' after the dealer now?" I asked.

"I didn't want him to get messed up in any of this, so I told him Barb's boyfriend had purposely overdosed her. Figured that would put an end to it, since George was gone too," Hank said. "About a month ago, Seth found out that wasn't true."

"Oh dear."

"The night of Barb's overdose, George went berserk in downtown Drum. Breakin' windows and shoutin' nonsense. Someone called the sheriff and a deputy shot and killed him." When my mouth dropped open in shock, he said, "Whatever he and Barb took made 'em batshit crazy. Witnesses said the deputy told George to put down the bat he was holding, but instead he lunged for the sheriff. That's when he got shot."

"How did Seth find out the truth?" I asked.

"There's plenty of drugs here in town, but nothing like what they were on. Things have been pretty quiet since they passed, but a month ago, someone had the damn same reaction. Then another. Those people didn't die and they never caught the attention of the sheriff's department, but Seth put it together with his momma's death and started digging around until he found the truth."

"Sounds like he was a smart boy," I said.

He swallowed thickly, his Adam's apple bobbing, and looked close to breaking down. "He was. He was gonna go to college. He was gonna get the hell out of here and make something of himself."

I nearly told Hank how sorry I was again, but all the apologies in the world weren't going to bring Seth back. The best way to help him was to find out who'd killed his grandson.

"I think I recognized the voice of one of the killers," I said, taking a quick glance at Hank.

His eyes widened slightly. "You know him?"

"That's just it…I know I've heard his voice before, but I don't know him. He was at Max's for Monday Night Football, but there were so many guys there that night and everyone was new to me…" I cringed. "I can't remember who it was, but I'm sure he came in with Bingham's group."

"He'll likely be back next week," Hank said with a nod. "You need to play dumb. You can't let him know you suspect anything or you'll be next."

"I can't just let this go, Hank."

"That's exactly what you'll do. We're both gonna let this go. End of story."

I wasn't sure he meant it, but he was tired, and I suspected he thought we were both in over our heads. Although he was likely right, I'd picked this battle and meant to stick with it. Still, it had already been a long, excruciating day for him, and I didn't want to push him. "I'm set to work every night this week and weekend, but Wyatt says he'll help keep an eye on you."

"I don't need anyone to take care of me," he grunted. "I'm too damn old for a babysitter."

"No one is babysitting you, Hank. We're just making sure you have what you need until you regain your strength."

"What I need is my grandson, and ain't nobody can give me that," he said, his weariness obvious.

There was no arguing that point.

We drove in silence again, mostly because Hank was falling asleep again. The county road was curvy, and we were climbing fast.

Before I reached the road that led to either Drum or Greeneville, I noticed a sign that announced the entrance to Balder Mountain trail and realized it was the infamous trailhead that had ruined the town. If I had the lay of the land right, the trailhead was now closer to Ewing. I couldn't think of a reason why anyone would continue up the mountain unless it was their destination. No wonder the town was drying up.

About ten minutes past Drum, when I turned onto the narrow county road leading to Hank's house, I noticed a shiny black pickup truck make the turn with us.

That truck made me nervous, and it took me a few seconds to figure out it was more than just paranoia—a shiny black pickup just like it had almost rear-ended us in Greeneville. There were thousands of pickup trucks in the Tennessee mountains; it was unlikely it was the same one, but I was still on edge.

I knew the turnoff for Hank's property—I'd purposely sought it out this morning after leaving Ruth's house—but I didn't know the road well enough to anticipate our distance from it. If the truck followed us onto the property, I'd have a hard time losing it.

I would have sold my right kidney to be able to call Wyatt, but I didn't even bother wasting my time to check my phone. The only time I'd had service today was in Ewing and down in Greeneville.

We continued for a couple more miles, the truck still behind us but at a distance of several car lengths, and I began to hope the color and make of the truck were a coincidence.

But as I noticed Hank's drive up ahead, the truck began gaining on us.

Oh shit.

I considered speeding up and going past the turnoff, but then I caught sight of Ruth's monstrous Cadillac parked in front of Hank's house. I turned onto the gravel driveway, taking it faster than I normally would, sending a spray of gravel onto the road and pelting the truck.

Hank jerked awake as his side slammed into the door.

"What happened?" he asked, looking around wildly.

The truck continued on past the driveway and I felt like an idiot.

"Nothing," I said, my pulse pounding in my head. "False alarm."

Wyatt came bursting out of the house, and the look on his face made me tense defensively.

"What the hell?" he shouted as I opened the driver's door. "What about that road made you think it was a racetrack? This isn't *Dukes of Hazard*!"

"I'm sorry," I said, embarrassment washing through me and making my cheeks hot. "I thought someone was following us."

"Where are they now?" Wyatt asked, still angry as he opened Hank's door.

"They drove on past," I said sheepishly. "But it looked a lot like the truck that almost rear-ended us in Greeneville."

"You almost wrecked my truck?" he asked in dismay.

"Now, hold on there, boy," Hank admonished. "It wasn't her fault, so lighten up."

Wyatt pursed his lips and started to slip his arm under Hank's legs to carry him inside.

"You stop right there," Hank snapped. "I ain't gettin' carried into my house like a damn baby." He glanced behind the seat. "Where's my crutches?"

Wyatt grabbed them out of the truck bed and handed them to Hank. "What took y'all so long?"

"We had to make a couple of stops," Hank said, swinging his legs around the side of the seat and slowly sliding down.

"A couple of stops?" Wyatt demanded as he held Hank upright once his foot hit the ground. "Where the hell did you go?"

"I made Carly stop for breakfast," Hank said, gingerly tucking the crutches under his armpits. "And then I made her take me to see Seth."

"You went to *Johnson City?*"

"No," Hank said, taking a wobbly step. "Mobley had Seth moved to his funeral home early this morning."

"How'd he make that happen?" Wyatt asked. "They don't usually release bodies that quickly."

I wasn't sure I wanted to know how Wyatt knew that piece of information. "Maybe they figured it was a cut-and-dried case," I said. "Gunshot wounds to the chest. No questions about cause of death."

Wyatt sent me a scowl.

"I cancelled the visitation tomorrow," Hank said. "Funeral's on Friday. I was hopin' you could say a word or two."

Wyatt's eyes widened slightly, but he swallowed and nodded. "Yeah," he said, his demeanor now subdued. "I'd be honored, Hank."

"Good. That's settled." He cast a glance at the road as we heard a vehicle approach from the left. "There's that truck again." He nodded to road. "It *is* the same truck that nearly hit us in Greeneville."

The truck had turned around and was now slowly passing Hank's property, continuing down the hill without stopping.

"How can you be sure?" Wyatt asked, his voice tight.

"Because it had the same sticker on the tailgate," Hank said. "The kangaroo."

"How would you know that if it nearly rear-ended you?"

Hank shot him a look of annoyance. "I wondered why it hadn't honked at her, so I turned around and looked at the back end after Carly turned. Didn't honk at her now either, when she turned into my drive and showered them with gravel."

Wyatt's face hardened and he rushed toward me, holding out his hand. "Keys."

"What are you going to do?" I asked, feeling the terror of that night, of the cry in the dark, all over again.

"I'm gonna go chase it down. Now give me my keys!"

"No! You're gonna get yourself killed!" I shouted.

He stared down at me, fury in his eyes. "If those are the guys who killed Seth, then I've got to find out who they are. Give me the fucking keys!"

I shook my head and stood my ground. "The man who killed Seth didn't drive that truck, Wyatt, so let it go!"

"Are they still in the ignition?" Wyatt took my silence as confirmation and bolted for the driver's door, not even bothering to close the passenger door. He jerked the truck into reverse, making a three-point turn, and the passenger door slammed shut as he whipped the vehicle toward the road.

"He's going to get himself shot," I said, trying not to freak out.

"Wyatt Drummond's no fool," Hank said. "He'll be fine. Now help me inside before my leg gives out."

I considered going after Wyatt, but what good would that do? I'd only get in the way. So I helped Hank inside and got him settled. Wyatt had left the prescriptions and supplies on the kitchen table. A raised toilet seat was on the floor.

The house was filthy, but it looked like someone had started to clean the toilet. Wyatt? I finished the job, then set the new seat on top so it would be ready when Hank needed it.

When I emerged from the bathroom, I glanced at a clock on the living room wall. "How long do you think Wyatt's been gone?" I asked.

"He'll be fine," Hank said.

But anxiety churned in the pit of my stomach. How long *had* Wyatt been gone? Twenty minutes? A half hour? What if something happened to him?

What would he do if the men in that truck confronted him?

Heading back into the kitchen, I took a closer look at the three prescription bottles in the bag, thinking it was likely time to give Hank another pain pill. I found an antibiotic to be taken twice a day, pain meds to be taken every four hours, and a pill that Hank was to take daily with his evening meal. Plus lots of bandages and wraps, along with a thermometer and ibuprofen.

I moved to the doorway to the living room. "Hank, I think it's time to take a pain pill."

"I ain't takin' a pain pill," he grunted, his eyes on the television. To my surprise, he was watching a soap opera.

"You *have* to take a pain pill. You need to keep the pain under control. You heard the nurse."

"Drugs is what got my Barbara killed," he said, turning his head to look at me. "She started by takin' her momma's pills. I ain't havin' 'em in the house. Get rid of 'em."

"But—"

"Just get me some aspirin. That'll be enough."

Frowning, I got two ibuprofen pills and filled a glass of ice water, shocked at how little food was in the fridge and freezer.

When he saw the glass of water, he gave me a indignant look. "I ain't drinkin' that shit. Where's the Coke? The Dollar General had a special a couple of weeks ago. Seth stocked up."

"There wasn't any in there. I opened the fridge lookin' for a water pitcher."

"That damn boy must have drank it all while I was gone."

"You know," I said carefully. "I suspect you shouldn't be drinking Coke with your diabetes."

"My diabetes can go straight to hell," he spat. "I want a damn Coke." But to my relief, he swallowed the pills and set the glass on an end table with a hard thunk.

I pushed out a sigh, suddenly worried my new landlord was going to be more difficult than I'd expected.

"You're out of most of your groceries," I said. "How about I go get some before I head to my shift at Max's?" I wasn't exaggerating. The only items in his fridge were bottles of ketchup and mustard and a nearly empty jar of strawberry preserves, but I also had an ulterior motive for leaving.

He rattled off a list of junk food that he wanted me to pick up.

I started to protest, but I knew how he'd respond. He'd tell me it was none of my business, and in a sense he'd be right. At the same time, I couldn't help but think it had become my business the moment I'd accepted this role.

"Wyatt's not back yet," I said, my anxiety increasing. "Do you think he has the keys to Ruth's car with him?"

"Nah. Around here nobody takes the keys out of the ignition when they're at home," he said. "The keys'll be in there."

Why did everyone think this town was so damn safe when everything I'd encountered proved it was anything but?

"Where do people go grocery shopping around here?"

"At the Dollar General in town. It's a block north of Max's Tavern."

"Okay, then," I said. "I'll be back as soon as I can."

The moment I grabbed my jacket and walked out the door, it struck me that my purse was in the truck and Wyatt hadn't returned yet.

Maybe he hadn't planned on coming back. Maybe he'd just gone to the shop after chasing the truck down. Or maybe he was lying on the side of the road with a bullet in his forehead.

One way or the other, I was finding Wyatt.

Of course, that had been my plan all along.

Chapter
Seventeen

Caroline, the rule follower, was horrified to be driving without a license, but Carly had realized that following the rules sometimes wasn't an option. So I started Ruth's car and took off down the mountain, driving slowly while on the lookout for Wyatt's truck. I hoped that I'd find him at his garage, oblivious to the way he'd made me worry. But before I could start formulating a speech about his rudeness, I saw something that made my stomach plummet: a flash of red on the right, down a sharp incline.

I pulled as close to the edge as I could get and threw the car in park, leaving the engine running as I ran over to the side of the road.

Wyatt's truck was about twenty feet down a fifty-foot hill, the left side smashed nose-first into a tree.

My mother had died in a car accident. She'd run off the road and hit a tree. Her body had been thrown from the car. I hadn't seen the accident—either in person or in photos—but panic coursed through my veins, and I started to cry. *"Wyatt!"*

"Carly?" he called back.

I pressed a hand to my chest and slumped over my knees as relief swamped my head, making me dizzy.

"Are you okay?" I asked, realizing it was a stupid question. His truck had crashed into a tree, which had uprooted on impact and was starting to fall over from the weight of the truck.

"I'm fine" was his muffled response. "My truck door won't open, and I can't get my seatbelt undone. If I can cut the seatbelt, I can get out the other side."

"Give me a second." I stared at the embankment, wondering if I'd be able to get back up if I crawled down. The snow from the day before had melted, but it looked wet and muddy in places. There were a bunch of scrub trees—although a six- or seven-foot-wide path had been cleared out by Wyatt's truck—but we could use the small trees on the sides to pull ourselves back up. Assuming he was fit enough to make the climb. What if he'd just told me he was fine so I didn't freak out?

I popped Ruth's trunk and searched around until I found a tire iron along with some yellow nylon rope, but there weren't any blades or sharp objects. Nothing I could use to cut his seatbelt. Then I remembered my purse was inside the cab of his truck. I had a small pair of scissors inside it. Having a rescue plan and the tools I needed to carry it out helped subdue the worst of my terror.

The truck released a metallic groan.

"Wyatt?" I yelled in panic.

"What the hell's takin' you so long?" he shouted up at me.

"What do you expect me to do?" I called back even as I was tying the rope to a tree about six feet to the right side of his path.

"Go for help!"

"You expect me to run to town and just leave you here?" I pulled hard on the rope to test the knots. It held. "It would be a good twenty minutes before anyone showed up to help!"

"I was alone before you showed up," he said, sounding pissed, but I suspected he wasn't mad at me. He was pissed to be in this situation.

"Yeah, and look how well that's working for you."

Holding the tire iron in my left hand, I tossed the end of the rope down the hill and then scooted down on my butt, grunting when a stump poked me in the leg, my jeans getting muddy in the process.

When I reached the truck, I balanced precariously on the hill as I reached for the passenger door. The front end of the truck was about six feet above the ground, which put the door handle around the height of my head given the grade of the incline. I unlatched the handle and opened the door enough to get my shoulder wedged into the opening, then pushed it open even more.

The truck groaned and shifted closer to me.

"Carly, back up!" Wyatt shouted, sounding panicked. "What the hell are you doin' down here?" He had a cut on his forehead and blood had trickled down the side of his cheek. His mouth quirked as he took in the sight of the tire iron. "Here to finish me off?"

"Shut up. I'm rescuing you," I said, scanning the floor for my purse. "I can see how it might be confusing to you, what with your caveman attitude and all."

"Who said I had a caveman attitude?"

He had a point. Acting like an ass and offering to carry my suitcase didn't exactly qualify him for caveman status. "My apologies. I shouldn't have made the presumption."

"Stop talkin' nonsense and get away from this truck. If you try to climb inside, it could fall and smash you or take you with me."

I glanced down and realized there was plenty more hill for the truck to fall down, with a bed of large rocks and boulders at the bottom of the thirty-foot deep ravine. I briefly wondered if I should go for help after all, but then the truck groaned again and slid a couple of inches down the length of the tree, which was bowing dangerously close to uprooting completely or snapping off from the weight of the truck.

I jumped back, losing my balance and nearly tumbling down the slick hill.

My panic began to resurface, but I took a deep breath to center myself. I could do this. I *had* to do this.

"Carly. Get out of here," he pleaded, and I was surprised that he sounded genuinely concerned.

"Look," I said, trying to think this through. "My purse is in the truck and I have a pair of scissors in there. If I can reach them, then you can cut yourself out."

He thought about it for a moment. "Fine," he said. "*I* can try it, but if the truck starts to move, then you get the hell away from it and go get help."

"Okay," I agreed. "Do you see my purse?"

"It's at my feet," he said, "but I can't reach it. I already tried once before you got here."

"Maybe you can grab the purse with the tire iron. You can loop the handle with the end."

He was silent for a moment. "Yeah. It's worth a shot, but you're going to have to throw it to me. Don't touch the truck."

I considered tossing the crowbar to him from where I stood, but I didn't have the best aim, and I was worried my adrenaline would make me heave it too hard and smash him in the face. So I sidled closer to the open door. At least the floorboard was lower now, the seats about shoulder-level to me.

"You're too close, Carly," he said, looking anxious. "Get back."

"I'm not sure I'll get it to you if I'm this far away, and I only have one shot."

He held up a hand. "Just be careful. It's not worth me gettin' out of here if the truck smashes you in the process."

I shot him a grin, but it was wobbly. "Ah, see I knew you liked me after all."

Guilt filled his eyes. "Carly…"

"Let's discuss it when I get you out of here." I lifted the tire iron. "You ready?"

"When you toss it, back the hell up in case this thing comes crashin' down."

"Okay."

Whispering a quick prayer, I heaved the crowbar toward him. As soon as it was free from my grasp, I scrambled backward, watching to make sure he caught it. But just as his hand wrapped around it, I promptly lost my footing and hit a patch of mud. With nothing to hold on to, I started sliding down the hill.

"Carly!" Wyatt shouted.

I'd only descended about five feet before I grabbed a scrub tree. The trunk bent but held my weight. I took a deep breath, then called out, "I'm fine!"

"Can you get back up?"

"Yeah. I didn't slide very far." I took another deep breath to slow my racing heart. "Did you get my purse?"

"I'm not moving a muscle until I'm certain you're out of the way. I'm not going to risk taking you with me if the truck falls."

I took a moment to reassure myself I was fine, then started pulling myself up the hill, one tree at a time, until I was even with the truck. Sure enough, Wyatt was pretty much in the same position he'd been in when I'd fallen down.

"Shit, Carly," he said. "What're you doin'? Get up to the road!"

"Let's get something clear, Wyatt Drummond. I don't take kindly to orders."

He gave me a cockeyed grin. "Hell, I figured that out the night I met you."

"Then you know I'm not going up that hill until you do, right?"

"What if I add a please?"

"I'm going to stay right over here and watch your progress."

He looked like he wanted to argue, but I was out of harm's way, so instead he slowly lowered the tire iron and started reaching it toward the floorboard and fishing around. After several attempts, he lifted the metal rod and dragged my purse up with it.

Once he had the purse next to him, he tossed the tire iron through the passenger door opening. It landed on the ground in front of me.

After Wyatt found the scissors, he zipped the bag back up and tossed it out to me too. I scooped it up and heaved it up the hill. It landed in a patch of mud, but at least the important contents would be safe enough.

He started cutting through the thick strap over his chest. "Why are you carryin' around a pair of sharp scissors in your bag, anyway?" he asked.

"You really want to know?"

"I didn't ask to make conversation."

"Protection."

He didn't respond, instead finishing his hack job. As soon as he made the final cut through the thick fabric, his body fell forward into the steering wheel and dashboard, but he stretched out his arms and braced himself.

The truck groaned and dipped forward several more inches.

"Wyatt!" I screamed in terror. I couldn't watch him die. I *refused* to watch him die. I was getting him out of that truck.

"I'm okay," he said in a soothing voice, and I found it odd that he was reassuring me even though he was the one in danger. "It's the next part that's tricky." He lifted his feet against the dashboard, then scooted across the cab until he reached the passenger door. "Carly, climb up a little higher."

I grabbed the rope I'd tied to the tree up above and pulled myself up several feet, figuring it was faster than using the trees. "What's your plan?"

"I'm gonna jump." He made a move to dive out, but just as he started to leap from the truck, it creaked and then pitched hard toward the passenger side.

I screamed, but Wyatt somehow managed to remain inside the truck as it slid down the hill again, barely missing me, and fell another fifteen feet. The passenger side smashed into two pine trees with a terrifying crunch.

Panic hit me full force. "*Wyatt!*"

"I'm okay," he called back, his voice muffled. The smashed-in driver's door was angled up toward me, the window still up and intact. "Are you okay?"

"I'm fine." I wanted to take a minute to recover, but I needed to get him out of there. Grabbing the rope, I let gravity pull me down the hill, the rope burning my palms as I pulled myself to a halt to grab the tire iron. "I'm coming!"

"Stay where you are!" he shouted, his voice dampened inside the closed-up cab. "If you get near this thing, it might fall again."

I took a good look at the position of the truck, and I judged that it likely wasn't going anywhere. At least not yet. "I told you I don't take orders, Wyatt."

"Dammit, Carly!"

Thankfully, the rope extended all the way down to the truck, so I continued my descent, trying to come up with a plan as I went. The driver's side window was too high for me to reach, and even if I smashed it he would have to climb up, something that could jar the truck too much. I could only think of one way to get him out—climb into the truck bed and smash in the back window. It seemed safest to keep all the weight in the truck balanced in the middle, so instead of crawling in by the bumper, I climbed up the back tire and hiked my leg over the side into the truck bed.

"What the hell do you think you're doin'?" he shouted through the intact back window.

"Getting you out of there." I lifted my other leg over the side and spread my feet apart to keep my balance on the sloping bed. Holding the tire iron like a bat, I said, "Cover your head."

He stared at me in disbelief but scooted to the passenger side, which wasn't hard, since the truck was listing that way. At least the trees had managed to close the door.

"Hit it on the driver's side," he said.

I nodded as he pulled his jacket over his head, and then I swung hard. The impact reverberated up my arm into my shoulder, but I'd only cracked the glass, so I swung again, shattering it this time. The pieces on the driver's side exploded into the cab, but half the window remained in place, a spiderweb of cracks spread throughout.

Wyatt sat up and lowered his jacket.

"Back up," he said, scooting to the middle of the seat.

I did as he said, giving him about three feet. He lifted his elbow and smashed out the rest of the window, then slipped off his coat and laid it over the bottom edge. Diving headfirst out of the window, he landed in a heap in front of me.

One of the trees began to crack. The truck pitched a few feet to the passenger side.

I started to fall over toward the trees, but Wyatt grabbed my arm as he got to his feet, pulling me to the other side, the one closer to the road above us. He pushed me up and onto the edge. "Jump!"

I looked down at the ground, which was about six feet below the nearly sideways truck.

The tree cracked again, and the truck jerked, tilting to the side even more. We didn't have long.

Terrified out of my mind, I let him launch us off the truck toward the ground.

The tree trunk made a loud snapping sound.

Wyatt rolled me over midair so that his back hit the ground with a hard thud and I landed on top of him.

The truck let out a loud, yawing groan, then fell tail-bed-first, rolling end over end several times until it landed on its now smashed-in roof on top of the rock bed.

I stared down at it in shock. "You could have been in there," I gasped.

He lifted his head to stare down at the crash. "And you could have been trapped underneath," he said, his voice tight. "What were you thinkin'?"

"I was thinking that you could be in that truck right now," I answered, my temper rising.

Wyatt rested his head back on the ground and stared up at the sky.

We'd almost died.

Lightheaded, I laid my cheek on his chest, waiting for the dizziness to pass as I listened to his wildly beating heart. At least he was shaken up too.

After a few seconds, he shifted slightly, and I realized I was lying on top of Wyatt Drummond, his arm draped across my back. I found far too much comfort in his embrace, yet I couldn't seem to find the gumption to move out of it.

"Are you okay?" he asked softly.

"You're the one who wrecked his truck."

"I didn't wreck it," he grunted. "I was run off the road."

"By the black truck?"

"Yep."

"Do you know who was in it?"

"No."

"Did you get a license plate number?"

"Nope."

I wasn't sure I believed him, but I could tell from the way he was holding me that most of his suspicions had withered away. Which meant he was likely trying to protect me. I lifted up to look him in the eyes. "Are you hurt?"

He made a face. "Mostly my pride."

The cut on his forehead suggested otherwise.

I knew I should move off him, but my arms and legs started shaking and there was no way I'd make it up that hill.

He sat up and shifted me so that I was sitting on his lap, my legs draped to one side. His arm tightened around me, pulling me to his chest. "Your adrenaline is crashing. Give it a minute and it'll pass."

I rested my head on his shoulder, trying to pull myself together, but I had a perfect view of the truck crashed at the bottom of the ravine.

"They tried to kill you," I said. "Why?"

"They didn't want me to know who they are?" he said. "They're worried I know something and tried to permanently shut me up? They don't like Drummonds? Or maybe they were just good ol' boys who were pissed I was riding their ass. The possibilities are endless."

He had a point, but the fact that they had been following me since Greeneville ruled out his last suggestion. Had they been following Hank because they thought he knew where the stash was hidden? Or maybe they'd suspected I knew more than I was letting on? But I couldn't ignore that we'd been in Wyatt's truck. What if they'd thought they were following *him*?

"Why'd you do it?" he asked quietly.

"Do what?" I asked defensively. What was he accusing me of now?

"Risk your life to help me."

How could he ask me that? But at least this question had an easy answer—one I could give him without any lies or equivocation. The muscles in my back relaxed. "Because it was the right thing to do."

"You could have been killed, Carly," he said emphatically.

"And you could have too. You were lucky you only lost your coat."

"Don't forget my pride," he said in a teasing tone.

We were silent, lost in our own thoughts. I knew I needed to get off his lap, but for some reason I felt less scared down on the side of the hill with Wyatt. Which was ridiculous given we were looking down at his totaled truck. "I have to get to the Dollar General before I go to work."

His brow shot up. "What?"

"Hank doesn't have any food, and he said the only place to shop in Drum is the Dollar General."

"Why are you helpin' him?" he asked with narrowed eyes. "I know for a fact there's no money in his house. Do you know differently?"

I groaned. "Are we back to that? Is that the rumor in town? That Hank has a buried treasure somewhere and I'm out to get it? I've already been accused of being after his 'fortune' once today. I don't need it from you after saving your life."

I started to get up, but he pulled me back down. "Carly. Wait."

"What do you want to hear, Wyatt? That I'm out to rob him blind?"

"You say you're helpin' him because of Seth, but you have to understand that this is above and beyond what a normal person would do. The whole town's gonna be talkin' about it."

"Ruth and Franklin let me stay with them. Are you worried about them too?"

"That's different. People know Ruth and Tater can take care of themselves, but some of them are gonna think you're out to scam Hank and that you killed Seth to make it happen."

"And the others will think I killed Seth over drugs?" I asked with raised eyebrows. "I can't help what people think. Plus, I won't be here much longer. Let 'em talk. It likely means more customers for Max."

He frowned. "But I suspect not more tips for you."

I flashed him a smile. "I'm hopin' to win them over with my charming personality."

He gave me a soft smile, and I realized I didn't want Wyatt to think I was a bad person. Maybe it was foolish of me, but I wanted him to understand my motivations.

"I'm helping Hank for the reason I told you. He can't be alone right now, and I need a place to stay." I turned my head to face him. "Sometimes people can just be nice for the sake of being nice."

He looked deep into my eyes. "No. I think there's more to it, but your reasons aren't sinister." A sad look washed over his face. "You saw more of Seth's murder than you're lettin' on. You saw the getaway vehicle."

My heart skipped a beat. "I didn't see anything."

"That may be what you told the sheriff, but when I started to go after that truck, you told me it wasn't the truck the murderer had escaped in."

"Maybe I was only saying that to protect you," I said, my voice shaky. "Maybe I was scared of what would happen to you if you chased after them." I motioned to his truck. "See? I was right."

"You saw the murder," he said quietly, and when I didn't protest, he added, "Hidin' what you know was smart."

My mouth parted. "What?"

"You're right not to trust the sheriff's department," he said. "Some of them are dirtier than a pig in a mud bath."

"Can I trust *you?*" I asked, and it was his turn to look surprised.

"I guess I haven't given you much reason to," he said, "but I was protective of that kid and his grandfather, and I thought you were a drug dealer from Atlanta come to town for a drug drop."

I scooted off his lap onto the ground. "I figured."

He stared at me in disbelief. "Excuse me? You knew about it?"

"You're not the first person to mention it. Max told me the sheriff knew about a drug runner from Atlanta. But surely the fact that I'm from Georgia isn't enough to convict me. Plus, you knew my plates were from Georgia the minute you pulled up. You were nice to me at first."

"Where I found you—the only people who go up there are locals who want to make out or screw. Or do drug deals. Strangers definitely don't go up there anymore. Then you got skittish as hell when I mentioned calling the sheriff, *and* you had a gun in your purse."

He knew I had a gun in my purse? I started to get to my feet, but his arm tightened around me. "Carly. Stop. I'm not your enemy."

"But you're Bart Drummond's son."

He hesitated, then said, "What do you know about my father?"

"Not a whole lot, but I've heard enough to be worried about that fact."

"What you've heard about my father depends on who did the tellin'. Some people love him. Some people hate him. Some people do both simultaneously."

"And which camp do you fall into?"

He held my gaze. "I'm not loyal to my father, Carly."

I wasn't sure what to think. He could have gone anywhere after his prison sentence, but he'd chosen to come back here. Although he'd made it sound like he'd had no choice—that Drum had a hold on him—I struggled to believe that hold was sentimentality. "I've been told you're not entirely trustworthy."

"Because of my father?"

"Yes."

He inhaled slowly, gazing down at what was left of his truck. "If I'd died in that heap, my father wouldn't have given two shits."

So maybe Wyatt and I had more in common than I thought.

"Most people try to argue with me on that point," he said.

I gave him a wry smile. "Most people don't have a father like I do."

"I suppose not," he said. Then he dropped a bombshell I hadn't seen coming. "Then again, most people don't have Randall Blakely for a father."

Oh shit.

Chapter Eighteen

Shock reverberated through me, fueling my panic. I broke free of his hold and scrambled several feet away from him, trying to figure out how to handle this.

Carefully, he got to his feet and I got the impression he wasn't moving slowly for his safety so much as he was trying not to spook me. Too late.

He held up his hands with an earnest expression. "Careful or you'll fall down the hill and land on my truck."

"Worried you won't get the reward money if I'm a little bruised or battered?" I sneered. "Don't worry. I don't think it'll be a problem."

"Caroline," he said, his hands still raised and staying in place. "I'm not gonna hurt you."

I hadn't been called Caroline for months, and it felt like he was talking to someone else. "No, you're just gonna turn me in for the reward money."

"If I was going to turn you in for the reward money, I would have done it last night before I came to see you at the tavern."

He had a point, but that didn't mean he still wouldn't do it. For all I knew, he'd already made the call and was waiting for my father's cleanup crew to take care of the dirty business. "It didn't take you long to put it together."

He released a short laugh. "You weren't exactly hiding your reaction to that news report. Then you used a VPN on my computer. Most people wouldn't do that."

I shook my head in horror as I berated myself for my stupidity. But I could still make a break for it. If I beat him up the hill to the car, I could…

Could what? Leave? Steal Ruth's car and abandon Hank? Flee the sheriff's department and put myself in even more danger?

Denial. I needed to deny the hell out of this.

"You're crazy," I snapped, facing him as I took a backward step up the hill, not an easy feat given that the ground was slippery.

"Am I?" he asked as he took a step up the hill after me.

Tears stung my eyes, but I held them wide, not wanting him to see. "So let's say I was this Caroline Blakely…why would I be here on the side of a ravine with you?" I asked, swiping an arm wide for emphasis. "Why wouldn't I be in Dallas with that fiancé who sounded so heartbroken she was gone?"

"I don't know. I haven't figured that part out yet."

"Why are you tellin' me this? You want me to confess so you can get some of the Blakely money? In case you haven't noticed, I don't have any."

He laughed again, but it was humorless. "Hell, I figured that out within ten minutes of meeting you."

"Then what do you want? You keepin' me busy until Randall Blakely's goons show up? Or maybe you're feeling guilty for turning me in because I just saved your life. Won't you feel bad when you realize I'm not even her and the reward money doesn't come."

He gave me a sad smile. "I didn't turn you in, Caroline."

There it was again. Caroline felt like someone else entirely.

"I'm not Caroline." Not anymore. It was startling to realize it was true. I'd chosen Carly because it was a nickname my mother had used for me. But she was the only one who'd ever used it, and before my stint in Arkansas, no one had called me that for two decades. And yet, it didn't matter—I felt more like Carly than I did Caroline.

"Okay," he said, still holding up his hands and bending forward slightly as he took a step toward me. "*Carly*. I didn't turn you in."

"Don't take another step closer." I moved a few feet up the hill toward my purse, not that it would do me much good. My gun was gone, and my scissors were in the truck at the bottom of the hill, but at least I had my shiny new ID. It was all the protection I had left.

"I'm not gonna hurt you, Carly. I swear."

"Forgive me if I have a hard time trusting you right now." I bent over and scooped up the bag, slinging the straps over my shoulder and continuing my climb.

"At first I wondered what in the hell the heiress of Blakely Oil would be doing in Drum, Tennessee," he said behind me, sounding a little breathless. He was following me. "And I confess that I found the coincidence of your appearance in town and Seth's death to be too much to accept."

"No shit," I said over my shoulder. "You made that *very* clear."

"But then I did some investigatin' of my own, and when I put two and two together, I realized you were on the run, hiding, not here as part of some big scheme."

Ignoring him, I continued my climb, my progress less graceful in my haste.

"I started to put it together when I saw the panic on your face while listenin' to the news report. Carly, will you please slow down?"

I reached the side of the road, sore and out of breath. I wanted to take a second to rest, but Wyatt was literally just feet behind me. I ran around the still-running car, about to open the driver's door, but Wyatt had reached me. He put his hand on the door to keep it shut, then gently touched my shoulders and turned me around to face him. Slow and steady movements so he wouldn't frighten me any more than he already had by seeing me. By knowing me.

He rested his hands on the car on either side of me, but instead of feeling trapped, I felt comforted. Like there was safety here between Wyatt's arms.

That feeling was dangerous.

I knew better than to think I could be safe anywhere.

"I know you're runnin' from him," he said softly, pleading with me to listen, "and you're scared he's gonna find you, but no one here will put it together."

I lifted my chin and gave him a defiant stare. "I don't know what you're talking about."

"No one here pays much attention to what's goin' on in the outside world, and they sure as hell don't give a shit about an oil heiress, but even if they did, they'd never figure out it was you." He lifted his hand to my hair, touching a few of the stubborn strands that had fallen forward. "You cut your hair and dyed it dark. You changed your name and you don't look like you came from money, but you're her."

I started to protest but stopped. There was no point. All I could do now was wait him out and make my escape.

Slowly, he pushed my jacket to the side and lifted the hem of the long-sleeved T-shirt I was wearing to reveal the skin above the waistband of my jeans. I didn't need to look down to know that he saw the irregular birthmark over my left hip bone.

His gaze lifted to mine, but instead of the gloating triumph I'd expected, I only saw concern and compassion. "Even without that birthmark, I'd know it was you."

"And how's that?" I asked. I'd meant it to sound belligerent, but instead it came out breathless.

"Those soulful blue eyes."

Which meant he'd seen other pictures of me. "You Googled me?"

"I wanted to be sure."

I pressed my back into the side of the car and whispered, "What do you want?"

"Nothin'," he said gently. "I want to help you."

"Why?" I countered, not trusting this turnabout.

"Because sometimes people do the right thing just for the sake of it." His arms dropped to his sides and he took a step back. "Can you drop me off at the garage? I need to check in and grab the tow truck so I can come back out to Hank's later."

Was he really just going to let this go?

"Why don't you want the reward money?"

"I already told you," he said, slowly reaching around me to open the car door. "I don't need a half million dollars."

"Because you have your own daddy's money," I said.

"I don't want my father's blood money," he said, his eyes darkening.

"But I know you paid for Seth's funeral, or at least took care of the arrangements, and those things you got for Hank must have cost a couple hundred dollars."

"And you're planning to buy Hank food with money you need to be spending on a car, yet I doubt you'd turn me in for reward money if our roles were reversed."

I lifted a brow. "Don't be so sure about that."

"Let me help you."

I turned serious. "There's nothing to be done."

"Then don't do it alone, Carly. Trust me, I know all about goin' it alone."

I didn't answer him, mostly because I didn't know what to say. Instead, I tossed my purse into the back and got into the car. I waited for him to walk around to the passenger side and get in.

I cast a sideways glance at him, then shifted the car into drive. I felt like I was sitting next to a total stranger, not the man I'd met two days before. I wasn't sure where we stood.

I wasn't sure where I wanted us to stand.

"Why does your father want you?" he asked after I'd driven for a few seconds.

I pushed out a breath and laughed. "He wants me to marry Jake."

"Why?"

I shook my head. It would be too dangerous to tell him why.

"Was Jake collateral damage when you fled?"

I laughed again, this time more bitter. "Uh…no. Jake was very much a part of my father's scheme."

"He betrayed you?"

I shot him a glare. "You know the truth about who I am. Can we just leave it at that?"

"Maybe I can help you, Caroline."

I held up my hand. "It's Carly. Caroline Blakely died the night of her rehearsal dinner. I've learned to accept it, and calling me Caroline dredges up old pain. It also puts me at risk of being found out. I'm Charlene Moore now, and you'd best remember it."

"Okay, then," he said. "Tell me what you saw the night Seth was killed."

I shook my head. I wasn't ready to tell him that either. Not until Hank gave me the green light. Although Wyatt had certainly implied he wasn't close to his father, he hadn't given me a straight answer.

"Carly…"

"I didn't see anything. I heard a cry in the parking lot. I ran out and found Seth and held his hand as he died. End of story."

He didn't ask me anything else until I pulled into the parking lot of the garage. "Do you know where the Dollar General is?"

"I think so."

"Drum's pretty small, so you shouldn't have trouble findin' it," he said, but he made no move to get out of the car.

I lifted my eyebrows and gave him a pointed stare.

"I'm not gonna tell your secrets, Carly."

I cocked a brow and asked sarcastically, "What secrets?"

"Point taken." He started to open the door, then stopped. "You don't have a ride to Hank's after you get off work, so I'll pick you up."

"I'm sure Ruth can drop me off since it's on her way."

Determination filled his eyes. "The guys who ran me off the road could really be after *you*. They wouldn't dare touch you at Max's, but they might try once you leave. You lost your weapons, so I feel like I need to do my part to keep you safe."

I hoped they weren't after me. I hoped they'd only run him off because he'd aggravated him, but something more pressing grabbed my attention. How had he figured out my gun had been stolen? Had he taken it after all?

"You know that I lost my weapons?"

"Your scissors?" he said, but Wyatt was an observant man. He knew I was talking about something else, and no doubt he'd noticed my gun wasn't in my purse.

"Yeah. My scissors."

"But I didn't see your gun, and I know it's not on you. Where is it?"

"I never said I had a gun." He went stone-faced and silent, his expression completely unreadable. Switching tactics, I decided to change the subject and try to gather more information, I asked, "What do you know about Barb's death?"

"Hank's daughter? Why are you askin' about *her*?"

"Because Hank mentioned it," I said. "I thought it might be good to know what happened."

He frowned.

"He already told me that she and her boyfriend died the same night. She overdosed, and he was shot by a sheriff's deputy after causing some chaos while he was high."

"That's the general story."

"Hank says they both took some drug from Atlanta."

"I've heard that too."

"That can't be a coincidence. Seth must have found out and somehow caught the attention of those guys."

He studied me. "Uh-huh."

"Do you have anything to add to that?"

"Nope."

"Seriously?"

He shifted in his seat and groaned. "Leave it alone, Carly. Ride this out until the sheriff clears you, and then I'll get you a car so you can get on your way."

"Yeah," I said, "because I get the feeling you're going to let the whole getting-run-off-the-road thing go. Shouldn't we be worried that someone just tried to kill you?"

"No," he said with a serious expression, looking me square in the eyes. "It was a couple of hotheads who thought I was followin' them too close. I'm lettin' it go."

"Well, good for you. You're a bigger person than me. How are you going to get your truck out of that ravine?"

"I'll have to hire someone in Ewing to help. My rig won't be able to cut it." He reached for the door handle. "I'll go sit with Hank tonight, then pick you up when your shift is over." He paused. "I know Ruth can drop you off, but until they arrest Seth's murderer, it might be a good idea if I'm with you at night."

"Why would you care?" I asked.

"Why'd you help me out of my truck?" He smiled, although there was a tinge of sadness to it. "Same reason."

Chapter
Nineteen

I hadn't been in many Dollar General stores before, but I didn't remember many of them having mini grocery stores inside. This one did. I got the items Hank had requested and looked around for some fresh fruits and vegetables. I knew Hank would likely pitch a fit, but I'd hoped to find a way to convince him. I didn't know much about diabetes, but I knew his diet of mostly processed foods couldn't be good for him. So I made do with the few options they had—some small, bruised apples, almost too ripe bananas, some yellow onions, and a bag of baby carrots. Hank had asked for Coke, but I also got him some milk and orange juice, as well as some real cheese, but I stopped at picking up wheat bread instead of white. I was already about to send him over the edge. I also got some hamburger and frozen chicken breasts and some other ingredients to make several real meals. It cost me over 10% of what was in my bank account, but I couldn't really complain. He was giving me a place to stay. Providing him with groceries was the least I could do.

When I got back to his house, I made quick work of bringing in the bags and putting the food away before I found my spare pair of jeans and put my dirty ones in the laundry room.

"Did you get my Coke?" he called out from his chair.

"Yes."

"Did you find Wyatt?"

I was thankful he was in the other room because I stopped what I was doing and tried to figure out what to tell him. Less was best, I decided. "Yep. I found him."

"Did he get a license plate number?"

"He says he didn't."

I heard him push out a sigh. "Probably for the best."

I scrubbed the rest of the bathroom, then helped Hank in to use the toilet.

"Why'd you go and clean it all up?" he asked in bewilderment. "It's just gonna get messy again."

"Not if I have anything to do with it."

I needed to be at the tavern by five, so I made an early dinner consisting of spaghetti and a homemade sauce I threw together with some hamburger, crushed tomatoes, garlic powder, and some of the yellow onion and basil and oregano. I made a list of more spices to get the next time I was at the store. Hank seemed pretty content in his chair, so I had him check his blood sugar and brought his bottle of insulin from the fridge.

"Doesn't that hurt?" I asked, watching him inject his stomach.

"Not anymore," he said, handing me the syringe. "Don't throw that away. I'll reuse it."

My eyes about popped out of my head. "Excuse me? Isn't that how people get HIV and Hep C?"

"I ain't gonna give a disease to myself," he grumped, lowering his shirt over his stomach. "Just put it on the counter and I'll take care of it later. Now where's my food?"

"Aren't you supposed to wait fifteen minutes?"

"Are you Nurse Patty now?" he asked with a frown.

"No, I'm Chef Carly, and since I control the food, I say you'll wait." I cast a glance to the clock on the wall and took note of the time. 4:13. At 4:18, I handed him his plate. He was in a foul mood when I handed it to him, but it quickly changed after a couple of bites.

Still, I couldn't help thinking this meal probably wasn't good for him either. I'd figure out a way to learn more about a proper diet for diabetics at the library tomorrow. Among other things.

"I'll put the leftovers in the fridge in case you get hungry later," I said after he finished. I'd been cleaning the kitchen in between taking bites of my own food. "Wyatt said he'd come check on you after he gets done at the garage, so he can fix you a plate." Then I added, "There's enough for him to have some too."

"It's so damn good he'll eat it all," he complained.

I laughed. "Then I'll make you more."

I'd barely had a chance to do any sleuthing in Seth's room, let alone the hours I needed to clean it up to make it habitable. Wyatt had carried my suitcase in earlier and set it inside the door, where it now lay on the floor. Although the clothes inside were a bit askew from my quick search for jeans, it was still the neatest part of the room.

Maybe I'd just sleep on the sofa tonight. It might be better to sleep closer to Hank anyway.

I gave Hank another dose of ibuprofen and left Wyatt a note on the kitchen table telling him I couldn't convince Hank to take his pain medication but maybe he could. Then I grabbed my jacket and told Hank I'd be back after midnight.

It was getting dark when I drove into town and I was paranoid, constantly looking in my rearview mirror for any sign of the black truck. Those people had almost killed Wyatt. Whatever they wanted, they weren't playing.

When I walked into the tavern, Tiny gave me a warm greeting and Ruth looked happy to see me. "I thought for sure you'd quit. Takin' care of Hank has to be a full-time job."

"Wyatt is going to stay with him tonight. He says he's going to help share the responsibility."

She gave me a look that suggested she thought my insistence was cute. "If you say so."

"Your car is parked out back with a full tank of gas." Which had cleaned out another sixty bucks from my bank account. Ruth's car was a gas guzzler and had a massive tank. And of course, gas cost more up here.

"Say," I said. "Seth's funeral is Friday, and I don't know how long it's going to last. Do you think Max will be pissed if I'm late Friday afternoon? I'm sure it gets busy on the weekend."

"Don't you worry about Max. He'll likely be there himself. We all will."

"Do you know where I could get something appropriate to wear to the funeral?" I asked, my cheeks flushing with embarrassment. "I don't have a black dress or anything." I wasn't sure I'd even be welcome at the funeral, but I suspected Hank could use the support, and I knew I needed closure, or as much closure as I could get until I found out who'd killed him.

"Yeah," she said, bright-eyed. "I've got a black dress you can wear. And shoes too. They might be a little big, but we can stuff tissues in the toes or something. I can bring them to you tomorrow. You still workin' the night shift with me?"

I gave her a grateful smile. "Yeah. Thanks, Ruth."

"Don't think a thing about it, but we better tell Max. I know *he* doesn't know about the funeral yet."

Ruth told him, and within minutes, Max had declared that the tavern would be closed from two thirty until six on Friday so the town could attend the funeral and pay their respects. Afterward, the mourners would be welcomed back at the bar for a post-funeral celebration of life. He tasked Ruth and me with spreading the word to the customers, knowing it would shoot through the town like wildfire. He also told us to be sure to bring around the jar he'd put on the counter to collect funds to help cover Seth's funeral expenses. I almost told him that Wyatt had covered it, but the last thing I wanted to do was stand between the two brothers. Still, I felt awkward.

The dinner shift was busy again tonight but less so than the night before. While the patrons weren't overly friendly, they weren't as openly hostile as they'd been.

Jerry came in early—within minutes of my arrival at the tavern. He sat in my section and ordered the Wednesday special and a coffee. I also brought him out two tiny pieces of pie, telling him they had been cut too small to serve to anyone else, when in truth, Tiny had cut a piece in half.

Jerry mumbled his thanks, refusing to meet my gaze, and I couldn't help thinking that he was scared of me. Did he think I'd killed Seth? For some reason, that bothered me more than when I'd wondered if Max and Wyatt might suspect me.

By nine, I'd already made more tip money than the night before, and I was about to take a break when I saw Dwight stroll into the bar with a small group of friends.

"You know him?" I asked Max while standing behind the bar.

"Dwight Henderson," Max said, keeping his gaze on the man. "Known as Dewey to his friends. He's bad news walkin'."

"He's working at Mobley Funeral Home. He told Hank his daddy's fallen ill and he got a job closer to home to take care of him."

"You don't say." He turned to look at me with an amused grin. "How do you know more about this town than I do?"

I flashed him a tight smile. "Friends in low places."

He turned serious. "You took Hank by to see Seth at the funeral home."

"That too." I paused, then said, "Dwight was crude with me and acted disgusting to both of us. I kicked him out of the room while Hank was paying his respects to Seth, and I *may* have threatened his job. His boss told Hank that he didn't have to worry about seeing Dwight again, and now I'm worried we got him fired." I paused. "Does he come in here very often?"

Max's jaw hardened. "Before Monday night, I hadn't seen that man step foot in here in over a year. So *no*, I don't think the fact he's here tonight is a coincidence."

We both watched as he and his two friends, who looked just as seedy, sat at a table in my section.

"I'll get Ruth to cover their table for you," he said.

"She's on her break." Franklin had brought her dinner, and they were sitting in his truck out back.

Max tossed the towel on the counter and started walking to the end of the counter. "Carly, cover the bar."

I grabbed his arm and tried to stop him. "Max. Don't."

He gave me a hard look. "No one comes in here and treats my staff disrespectfully."

"He hasn't even said anything to me yet."

"And I aim to keep it that way," he said, pulling free.

"Max!" I whisper-hissed, but he ignored me and sauntered over to the table.

"I'm here to see your new waitress, Drummond," Dwight said, leaning back in his chair. "Where is she?"

"Takin' a break. What can I get you gentlemen?"

"What you can *get me*," Dwight said in a loud voice, "is your smart-mouthed new waitress. I want to give *her* my order."

He sounded drunk and we hadn't even served him a drink yet.

"Well," Max drawled, propping his hands on his hips in a nonchalant pose. "Ruth's definitely got a smart mouth on 'er, but I wouldn't exactly call her new. And like I said, she's takin' a break, so lucky you gets me and my handsome mug instead."

A dark smile spread across Dwight's face. "I ain't talkin' about Ruth, and I ain't talkin' about Lula either." He turned his gaze on me. "I'll just wait here for your new girl to be done with her break."

Tiny appeared in the doorway to the back. "Carly. I need you in the kitchen."

I walked out from behind the counter, intending to go to Tiny, but something told me it would be a mistake. If I didn't deal with him now, I'd have to deal with him later. Better to face him here, where Max and Tiny had my back, than to risk him showing up at Hank's later.

I gave Tiny what I hoped was a reassuring look, then moved toward Dwight's table, stopping next to Max. "What can I help you with, Dwight?"

He placed a hand on the table and leaned forward with pure evil in his eyes. "You cost me my job, and I aim to take yours."

"Sorry," Max said. He sounded lighthearted, but his body was humming with tension. "But I'm not currently hiring."

"Well, there you have it," I said, thankful my tension hadn't leaked into my voice. "Max isn't hiring."

Dwight started to lunge over the table, but Max whipped out a ten-inch hunting knife from the sheath on the side of his leg and slammed it into the top of the wooden table between two of Dwight's fingers.

"What the fuck!" Dwight shouted, jerking backward. "You could have cut my fingers off!"

"Only if I'd intended to," Max said. "Trust me, I know what I'm doin'. Now state your business. Then you and your crew get the hell out of my bar."

"Her!" Dwight shouted, pointing a finger at me. "I want her! She got me fired! I need that job or I'll have hell to pay! I'm gonna let her pay it for me!"

What did that mean? Did he plan to hurt me? Kill me?

I swallowed my fear and said, "Seems to me your less-than-charming disposition got you fired. Mobley told Hank that today was just a long list of problems he's had with you."

His brow arched. "Hank? He had something to do with this too?"

Tiny was now standing behind me and Max, but Dwight didn't seem to care.

"Seems to me," Max said in his slow drawl, "that mortuary work is better suited for the meek and mild, Henderson. Perhaps it wasn't a good fit for you."

"It was a perfect fit for me, and now it's gone." His crazed eyes swung between the two of us. I wondered if I'd been wrong about him being drunk. Now I suspected he was high. "But I'll tell you what's not a good fit," Dwight shouted. "That bitch isn't a good fit for this town, and she needs to go! Everyone knows she got Seth Chalmers killed, and now she's using her siren ways to rob Hank blind, only he's too grief-stricken to realize it. It's up to us to protect 'im."

Tiny brushed me to the side and grabbed Dwight's arm, then began dragging him to the door. "Rule number one in Max's Tavern is you treat the help with respect, and I've listened to your nonsense long enough. *You* are no longer welcome here."

He opened the front door and gave Dwight a hard shove.

Dwight, the fool, tried to shove his way back in. Tiny pulled back his arm and punched him in the nose with one smooth movement.

Dwight let out a howl and covered his face. "You broke my fucking nose!"

"You were warned," Tiny said, then turned his hard gaze on Dwight's two friends. "Gentlemen."

They hurried past Tiny like rats scurrying from a fire, and Tiny slammed the door on their protesting faces.

Max called out, "A round of beers on the house!"

A cheer broke out and several men complimented Max and Tiny on their intimidation tactics. Another told Max he hadn't seen his knife skills on display since a bar brawl a couple of years prior. Max promised to give another demonstration soon, and not on a belligerent customer.

Tiny stopped next to me on his way back to the kitchen. "You okay?" he asked in a quiet voice.

I nodded, unable to speak.

"Chin up, Little Bit," he said. "You could have taken 'em."

I laughed, still in shock. "Thank you."

"You bet. I haven't had to break anyone's nose in a few months." He grinned from ear to ear. "Felt good. Thanks."

I followed Max behind the bar. He turned his back to the customers. His face was red, and he was shaking.

"Max, I'm so sorry," I said, scared to death he was going to fire me on the spot.

He swung his gaze to face me, his eyes wide with surprise. "What the hell are you sayin' *you're* sorry about?"

"It's my fault he came in here. I should have gone in the back with Tiny, but I figured if he didn't say his piece now, he'd find me later, and then I might be alone."

Concern filled his eyes and he put his hands on my shoulders. "Carly. I'm not mad at you. God, no. This wasn't your fault. Do you hear me?"

I nodded.

He dropped his arms and pressed his back into the counter again, fisting his hands in front of him. "I hate fuckers like him.

You have no idea how much I wanted to stab that knife into his hand."

His anger caught me by surprise. I started to say I would have cleaned up the mess, but Ruth came rushing through the back door, Franklin with her.

"What the hell just happened?" she asked as she approached us. "I saw Dwight Henderson storming to his truck, covering his face and dripping blood all over the parking lot. He was cursing Tiny and Carly up a blue streak."

Max took off toward the back, so I gave them a quick recap of events.

"Why do I always miss the good stuff?" she asked in a huff.

"It's likely for the best," Franklin said with a chuckle. "You tend to stir up enough trouble on your own." He leaned over and gave her a peck on the lips. "If you feel unsafe when you get off, call me at the house and I'll pick you up." He gave me a warm smile. "You too, Carly."

"Thanks, Franklin," I said.

He gave us both a wave as he walked out the back door.

"You've got a good man there, Ruth," I said as I followed her behind the counter.

"Don't I know it," she said. "We better start handing out those free beers Max promised."

"Why don't you fill the mugs, and I'll pass them out?" I suggested. It would give me a chance to make the rounds through her section and maybe pick up on some loose talk about Seth's murder. I hadn't heard anything in my section, and I was wondering if I should start asking questions because eavesdropping wasn't cutting it.

"Okay," she said with a bright smile, then grabbed a mug and started filling it. We worked silently for a few moments before she said, "We're in good shape now, but Franklin and I have had our share of rough patches."

"Everyone does," I said, taking the beer from her and putting it on a tray. "It's all about how you handle those patches, and if you're in a better place when you get to the other side of them."

"True. I've been through my share of men, but unlike my momma, I never let 'em beat me. The minute they laid a hand on me, they were out of my life. But Franklin, he ain't never laid a hand on me." She leaned closer and winked. "Not that I didn't want, anyway."

I chuckled.

"What about you? I take it you don't have a man in your life right now."

"No," I said softly. "I haven't had much luck with men."

"It's the way of the world, honey," she said, handing me another mug. "Did they beat you?"

"No," I said. "I've been lucky in that regard, but there are plenty of other ways for a man to hurt a woman."

"Did a man send you runnin'?"

I studied her out of the corner of my eye. She was obviously fishing for information, but was it friendly questioning or something else?

I hated that I distrusted nearly everyone, even Ruth, who'd been nothing but kind to me.

"No," I said truthfully. "I had that nasty breakup a few months ago, and I decided it was time to shake things up. Hence my decision to go on an extended vacation and look for somewhere else to live."

"Have you ever lived in a house?" she asked wistfully. When I gave her a curious look, she said, "Can you keep a secret?"

"I'm a vault with secrets."

She gave me a strange look, but it quickly faded, and a smile lit up her face. "Last weekend Franklin told me that he's been savin' up money. He nearly has enough for a down payment on a house."

I gave her a huge grin. "That's great!"

"I've always wanted a house of my own." She shook her head, her smile fading. "I've lived all my life in trailers. Is it wrong to want something that can't be carted away by a tractor trailer?"

"No, Ruth," I said softly. "You deserve it."

"Are you any good at decoratin'?" she asked as she returned to filling mugs.

"Yeah," I said, "I like to decorate."

"That's what took me so long at Hobby Lobby the other day," she said, beaming. "I was lookin' at all their home décor stuff. There was so much of it." Ruth was this badass woman who didn't take shit from anyone, yet talking about her future home seemed to take years off her. It made me want to go out and buy her a succulent.

"Decorating a new house is fun," I said, thinking about the condo I'd bought when I'd moved back to Dallas from the East Coast. "You should start a Pinterest board for decorating ideas." I cringed. "Sorry. I keep forgetting how hard it is to get internet here." I was never going to take internet or cell service for granted again.

"Yeah," she said. "I'm gonna make sure my house can get internet. They have it on the Ewing side of the mountain."

"Good idea."

"Ruth!" an elderly man in her section shouted across the room. "I need a refill!"

"You're gettin' a free drink, Oscar, so keep your pants on!" she called back. "Why don't you start handing out the beers?" She winked. "But don't give one to Oscar yet. We'll make him wait."

I cast a glance at the back room, realizing that Max hadn't come out yet. "Is Max okay?" I asked. "Should we be worried he hasn't come out yet?"

"He almost killed a man about eight years ago," Ruth said, "not long after he took over the bar. Some guys got too rowdy, and someone punched Max when he was tryin' to break it up. He kind of lost it on 'im." From the way she shuddered, I was pretty sure she'd seen it. "The Drummonds got him off, but he swore he'd keep his temper under control. Sounds like he lost a bit of control tonight and it's freakin' him out."

"It's all my fault." Guilt surfaced inside me, although truthfully it hadn't been very far down. Seemed like I kept letting people down lately.

"It wasn't just you, so don't flatter yourself," she said with a half-hearted grin. "Max hates guys like Dwight Henderson, so while you might have been a catalyst, he was pumped and primed to go. Now go pass out those drinks."

I carried out the first tray and started with the corner opposite Oscar. Two guys sat close to the door in the darkest corner of the bar...in Ruth's section. Coincidence? As I approached them, I realized I'd seen them on Monday night. They had been with Bingham's group.

Could one or both of them have been Seth's attackers?

There was one way to find out.

"Good evening, gentlemen," I said with a bright smile as I stopped next to their table. "I hope you both are doing well."

"Yeah," said the guy with the bushy beard. "Dandy."

Not him. I wasn't sure whether to be relieved or disappointed. I placed a mug in front of him.

"And what about you?" I asked the other guy as I handed him a beer. "How's Wednesday treating you?"

He gave me a cold hard stare and didn't answer.

"Well, all righty then," I said. "Let us know if you need anything else."

I finished passing out the drinks on my tray, and when I went back to the bar, I asked Ruth, "Do you know anything about those two guys in the corner?"

"Flint and Cecil? They're Bingham's guys."

"Do you think they could have had something to do with Seth's murder?"

Ruth's eyes flew wide. "What?" She lowered her voice and moved her head closer to mine. "Did you see something that night, Carly?"

"What?" I asked, taking an unconscious step back. "No. I just wondered." *Shit.* "They just don't seem too friendly is all, and *someone* killed him." I shivered. "I guess I'm imagining a killer around every corner now."

She made a face. "Yeah. I know what you mean. Especially after Dwight's meltdown."

I spent the next ten minutes thinking about what Dwight had said. What had I ruined for him? Was it his dream to work in a mortuary? Doubtful. Whatever his reason for wanting that job, he was clearly pissed he'd lost it, and I worried he might take it out on Hank.

Max kept a phone on a shelf under the counter—his emergency phone in case he ever needed to quickly call the sheriff—and since Max was still holed up in his office and likely didn't want to be disturbed, I figured this qualified as a semi-emergency. I dialed the number for Hank's landline, which I'd saved in my cell phone contacts list.

Wyatt answered after a couple of rings.

"Wyatt, it's Carly."

"Is everything okay?"

I ran my hand over my head. "Um...I'm worried about Hank."

"He's good. I convinced him to take half a pain pill, and it knocked him right out."

"I'm glad to hear it," I said, casting a glance at the two guys in the corner. They were both watching me with an unnatural intensity. "But that's not what I'm worried about. There was an incident at the funeral home today."

"Why are you just now telling me this?"

"I don't know," I said defensively. "Maybe because I was too busy trying to get you out of your truck."

"Okay," he said, his abrasiveness gone. "Tell me now."

I gave him an abbreviated version of the events, explaining what Dwight had said and done, although I glossed over the way he'd leered at me and how I had reacted. Then I filled him in on the confrontation at the bar.

He was silent for a moment after I finished. "Do you feel safe?"

"I'm worried about Hank."

"I realize that, Carly, but I'm askin' anyway," he said, sounding exasperated. "Do you feel safe?"

"Yeah," I said with a soft smile. "I feel safe."

"Call me back if anything changes."

To my surprise, I realized I would.

Chapter Twenty

Max stayed in his office for another hour and was subdued when he emerged. He and Ruth spoke quietly behind the bar for a few minutes, and then she gave him a hug and walked over to me.

"Tonight's pretty slow, so Max wants me to go home. I told him that I'm your ride, but he offered to take you home instead."

"Oh," I said, realizing I hadn't told her that Wyatt was picking me up, but now that I thought about it, I didn't like the idea of Wyatt leaving Hank alone. "Yeah. You go."

"Are you sure?" she asked with worry in her eyes. "Aren't you freakin' out about stayin' with Hank?" I thought she was talking about the worry of Dwight or someone showing up at the house, a legitimate concern, but she cringed and then added, "You know, about taking care of his leg?"

I tried not to cringe myself. "A little. I learned how this morning, and I'm not gonna lie…it's rough, but then I told myself it's a million times worse for poor Hank."

"Yeah, I guess you're right." Her mouth twisted to the side. "I'd tell you to call me for moral support when you're changing his bandages, but I don't think I could stomach it, Carly."

I gave her a warm smile. "Don't worry. I'm gonna make Wyatt help."

"I still can't believe he's gonna do that."

I shrugged. "He rewrapped his leg this morning. You should have seen him. I think he picked it up faster and handled it better than I did."

"Well," she said, taking a step toward the back door. "Call me if you need me for anything other than bandage changing."

"Thanks, Ruth. I will."

She'd been keeping track of her tips during the slow times, so she quickly settled up with Tiny and put the rest of the money and receipts in Max's office.

Max was sitting behind the bar, reading his book.

"Ruth says you offered to take me home."

He looked up and smiled. "Yeah. I hope that's okay with you. I guess we should have included you in that conversation."

"Please. I'm at the mercy of people offering me rides. Far be it from me to raise a fuss. But..." I lowered my voice and leaned in closer. "Wyatt offered to pick me up and take me to Hank's."

The smile on his face slowly fell. "Oh. So you and he...?"

I shook my head. "There's nothing between us, if that's what you're thinking. He's keeping an eye on Hank tonight, and he made the offer because he knew I didn't have a ride." I wasn't about to tell Max his brother had been run off the road. Wyatt hadn't asked me to keep it to myself, but he also hadn't reported it to the sheriff. Although it was plenty possible it was a deputy who'd tried to kill him, I suspected there was another explanation. "And after Seth's murder, I guess he's concerned about me being out late by myself or with just Ruth."

A shadow crossed his face. "Damn. He's right. I should have thought of it sooner."

"Why should you have?" I said in dismay. "I'm only telling you because I still want you to bring me home, if you don't mind. After Dwight showed up tonight, well, I'm worried he might take out his frustrations on Hank."

"I agree," he said. "That's a possibility, but I'm far more worried about *you*. Dwight moved to Greeneville for a spell because he beat his girlfriend, and her daddy ran him out of town. He's far more likely to take his frustrations out on you. I'd feel better driving you, which is one of the reasons I sent Ruth home."

"So I don't put her in danger."

His eyes hardened. "You're not puttin' her in danger, Carly. The asshole who killed Seth is. And Dwight." He lowered his voice. "It occurred to me that Dwight could have killed Seth. What if he thinks you saw something and part of the reason he's on the warpath against you is to keep you quiet?"

"Maybe…" But I didn't think so. For one thing, I'd heard the voices of all three of Seth's attackers. Dwight wasn't a match, although he could be the driver.

"You know you don't have to stay at Hank's," he said carefully. "I have a spare bed upstairs. You could stay with me tonight. Dwight wouldn't dare try anything with me here."

I considered it. I didn't think this was a thinly veiled attempt to put the moves on me, and Max wouldn't have to make a thirty-minute round trip if I stayed. But I needed to relieve Wyatt from his watch duty, and I didn't have any of my things with me. Not to mention I would need to get back to Hank's early in the morning to change his dressing. "Max, I really appreciate the offer, and if it weren't for Hank I'd do it, especially since I hate putting you out … Does Tiny live out that way? I can see if I can get a ride with him."

"Carly, don't you worry about the drive," he said with a good-natured smile. "I'll just take you out to Hank's. It's no big deal."

"Thanks, Max. I'm going to call Wyatt and let him know."

"Sounds good. You can use the phone in the office, if you like."

Wyatt answered on the first ring.

"Everything okay?" he asked when he answered the phone.

"How'd you know it was me?" I asked. I'd seen the rotary phone. Hank didn't have caller ID.

"Who else would be callin' Hank at eleven o'clock at night?"

Good point. "Max has offered to drive me out to Hank's so you don't have to leave him alone."

He hesitated, then asked, "Are you okay with that?"

"Yeah. I mean, I feel just as guilty about him doing it as you, but until I have a working vehicle, I'm stuck."

"If you change your mind, I can get Junior or someone to stay with Hank while I come get you."

"Thanks, but I think I'll be okay. I'd hate to inconvenience anyone else."

"If you feel unsafe, let me know. I'll come get you."

His insinuations were making me nervous. "Should I be worried about letting Max drive me home?"

"No," he said.

I waited for him to elaborate, but he remained silent.

"Okay, then," I said. "I'll be there as soon as I can."

The next hour dragged. We only had three patrons in the bar and none of them were drinking much, so I worked on tallying up my tips. I gave Tiny his portion, telling him I'd settle up the rest after my remaining customers left.

"No worries, Carly," he said in his deep timbre. "You can settle up with me tomorrow."

Tiny left, and Max ended up kicking the three stragglers out ten minutes early, telling them their last, unfinished, drinks were on the house.

"I'll pay for their drinks, Max," I said.

"The hell you will," he said, locking the front door behind them. "They'll be back, so there's no harm in the rest of us gettin' out ten minutes early. You got your things?"

"Not yet. I need to finish settling up the money."

"I'll meet you at the back door."

I put my tickets and cash on Max's desk, then headed to the storage room to get my jacket and purse. Max wasn't at the back door when I got there, but the door opened a few seconds later, and he beckoned me outside.

"My truck's warming up," he said as he locked the back door, then led me to the blue and white pickup that was usually parked in the corner of the lot. The engine was running, and white smoke streamed from the exhaust.

I headed to the passenger side while Max got into the driver's side.

"Do you know where Hank lives?" I asked.

"I know he lives out in White Rabbit Holler, near Ruth, but you'll have to point out which house is his."

"No problem."

He backed out of the parking space and headed toward the road. Once he was on the highway, he cast a glance at me. "Other than tonight with Dwight Henderson, how do you like workin' at the tavern?"

"I like it." I was surprised it was partially true. While I'd loved taking care of Violet, I was an extrovert. I needed to be with people, and it had been just me and Violet at Rose's house most of the time, and Vi had done a lot of sleeping at the end. If he'd asked me the night before, my answer wouldn't have been as enthusiastic, but people seemed to be coming around tonight. "You have no idea how much I appreciate you giving me a job."

"We're thrilled to have you. In fact, Ruth and I were talkin'… I know you're only stickin' around until your car gets fixed, but you've got a job as long as you want it. And if you decide to stick around longer, we'd love it even more."

"What about Lula?"

"Well…we have no idea when she'll come back, *if* she comes back, but if she does, Ruth wants to do some reevaluatin'." It looked like it pained him to admit it.

"I have no intention of takin' Lula's job," I insisted. "This job works for both of us because it fills a mutual need."

"If you're still workin' for us when she comes back, we'll figure it out then."

I wasn't sure what there was to figure out. There weren't enough customers to cover three full-time waitresses, but they could probably use a part-time waitress. Maybe they could move me to that, although I suspected it would entail working the slower and lower-paying lunch shift. But if I had any luck at all, I'd be gone long before it became an issue.

He was quiet for a moment. Then he said, "I can't help feeling responsible for what happened."

"You mean with Seth?"

"That too." He paused, looking uncomfortable. "I can't help but think…" His voice trailed off. "I almost put you in one of the units that got busted into because I know the phone doesn't work in twenty. But I figured it would be safer and quieter at the end, and anyway, who were you likely to call?" His hand tightened around the wheel.

The thought that he'd almost put me in one of those units freaked me out, and it took a second for my brain to sort through all the what-ifs.

"Did you try to call 911?" he asked.

His question shook me out of my thoughts. "What?"

"Did you try to use the phone?"

I pressed my palm to the side of my face. "Uh…" I turned to see him intently watching me. "Yeah, but it didn't work."

"Did you call when you woke up? Or when you saw him?" His hands were shaking on the steering wheel.

"Max," I said. "It's okay. I'm fine."

"But Seth isn't. If you'd been able to call 911 when you realized something was wrong, he might still be alive."

"No," I said, "because by then it would have been too late."

"You're sure?" he asked, turning to face me with tears in his eyes. "You're sure there wasn't a gap in between when you woke up and when you went outside?"

"Are you asking me if I lied to the sheriff?" I asked in a near-whisper.

"No! Fuck!" he protested, turning back to face the road. His face looked anguished, anxious, and he'd starting wringing his hands over the steering wheel. "I'm asking if you need to be protected."

"Protected from who?"

He gave a slow shake of his head, rolling his top teeth over his bottom lip. "Carly, if someone thinks you saw something, you might be in trouble. The official report says you didn't see anything. I'm just making sure you're sticking to that story."

"I don't understand."

"Bingham's men were in the bar tonight, and their eyes were firmly on you." He turned to face me. "I don't care what you saw or didn't see. I just need to know if you told anyone."

My chest tightened at the mention of Bingham.

"No," I lied, certain that Hank would keep my secret.

He pushed out a sigh of relief.

"That's why you wanted me to stay with you tonight," I said.

"I was already nervous when they showed up, but Dwight Henderson gave me the perfect excuse."

"Thank you."

He nodded. "We're a close-knit group at Max's Tavern, and you've helped us out of a bind. We take care of our own, Carly." He shot me a quick glance before facing the road. "You understand?"

Three months ago, I would have said, *No, I don't get it at all,* but then again, I'd closed myself off from other people after my mother was taken from me. Something had changed in Arkansas. When my car had broken down, Rose and her friends had invited me into their lives. They'd made my problems their own. They'd helped me realize that for all the world's evils, plenty of people were good. That family could be created out of circumstance, not just blood. "Like you and Tiny standing up to Dwight tonight."

"We'll always have your back, Carly."

Tears burned my eyes. It felt good to feel like I belonged somewhere. That I meant something to someone.

"So Wyatt...?" he said slowly.

He'd already asked this question, so what was he getting at? "Wyatt's helping Hank. I'm helping Hank. We have a common cause."

"I get Wyatt's interest in Seth, but why are *you* helping Hank?" he asked. "You know that people's tongues are gonna be wagging." He leaned toward me and cast me a teasing grin that did little to ease the worry lines around his eyes. "They say he's got a fortune buried behind his house."

"So I've heard," I said. "Dwight accused me of trying to steal it."

"It's all a bunch of nonsense," he said. "Some people say Hank's father left him the fortune and Hank himself buried it back there. Others think it's what's left from his past career." He shot me a knowing look.

What past career?

"And I've heard a few people say that his daughter, Barb," he continued, "stole it from Bingham."

"If everyone knows Bingham's bad news, why do you let him into the tavern?" I asked.

"Keep your friends close and your enemies closer." He shot me a rueful look. "It pays to be on Bingham's good side."

"Literally?" I asked, thinking of what Wyatt had told me about the police.

"No!" he protested. "I don't tolerate any kind of drugs in my place. And I don't show up at his place peddlin' the Drummond moonshine. We respect each other's boundaries."

"But the difference is he's dealing in illegal goods, Max," I said. "You're on the up-and-up." I narrowed my eyes. "Aren't you?"

"You've worked for me for three days," he said, clearly offended. "Have you even gotten a whiff of anything illegal?"

"Other than you almost stabbing Dwight's hand?" I said. "No."

"If I'd wanted to stab his hand, I would have," he said. "The people in this town lead miserable lives, and they drown out their misery either through alcohol or drugs. I just so happened to have a corner on the legal market, which left the illegal one to Bingham." He took a breath. "Look, if people wanna do drugs, they're gonna find a dealer. At least Bingham's is homegrown and he's not selling poison."

"Like the drugs that killed Barbara," I said.

He cast me a questioning glance. "Yeah. But you don't need to know any details and neither do I. We need to just live and let live."

I could read between the lines. Although I doubted he agreed with his own pronouncement, he was trying to get me to leave Bingham alone. I suspected Wyatt had done the same thing earlier, when he'd insisted he wasn't going to pursue the truck that ran him off the road. In their own way, they were both trying to protect me. Which also meant Max wouldn't answer any more questions that might help me understand Bingham and the Atlanta connection.

Max pulled onto the narrow road that took us up the mountain, taking the turns and switchbacks slow since his high beams didn't seem to reveal much in the pitch-black night.

"You got a replacement for the gun you lost?" he asked quietly.

I hesitated. "No."

He nodded. "I know Hank's got a few, but he might be asleep and who knows if Dwight plans to show up tonight. Open the glove compartment."

I did, fumbling for the latch in the glow of the dashboard lights. When it popped open, a dim light illuminated the interior and revealed a small bundle wrapped in a faded red shop rag.

"I want you to keep that with you. Not on you while you're working at the tavern, mind you," he hastily added. "I've got a strict no-weapons policy in Max's Tavern, but when Tiny and I aren't with you..." He turned to face me. "I think you need some kind of protection."

I carefully pulled the bundle out of the compartment and set it on my lower thighs.

"The safety's on, so go ahead and unwrap it."

I unwrapped the cloth carefully, slowly, as though I was scared I was about to get bitten by a snake.

"It's a Beretta," he said. "It's lightweight, so it shouldn't add much weight to your purse. It's loaded, and I have another box of ammunition in the glove compartment."

I pulled out the box, setting it on the seat next to me.

"I take it you're familiar with guns since you had one," he said.

I picked up the weapon and turned it over to examine it in the dull light, making sure it pointed out the passenger window. "I've had some training."

"And target practice?"

"That too," I murmured. I quickly checked the clip to verify that it was loaded, then held it up, pointing it at an imaginary target outside the window so my hands could get used to the weight and feel of it.

"Who are you, Carly Moore?" he asked with a grin. "You look totally badass right now."

His statement caught me off guard. I was supposed to be a twenty-nine-year-old woman who'd worked most of her life in retail—my resume said my last job had been as an assistant manager at the Gap.

I set the gun down on the rag and wrapped it back up.

"My father was a hunter. He taught me about guns." I said, suppressing a laugh. The closest my father had gotten to hunting was looking for me.

Thankfully, Max changed the subject. "How's Hank doin'?" Max asked. "Really?"

"He's got a lot going on—dealing with his amputation as well as the grief from losing Seth. He has his moments of sadness, but he's also strong."

"Losin' Barb was hard on him. Seth was all he had left."

"No brothers or sisters? Cousins?"

"All gone."

I was afraid to ask him where they'd gone.

I pointed ahead. "The turnoff is to the left up here."

Max slowed down and I slipped the gun and ammunition into my purse. As Max turned onto Hank's property, Wyatt's tow truck came into view, parked to the side of the house. Light glowed from the windows of Hank's home, and Wyatt had even turned on a dim porch light, though it barely illuminated the area in front of the door.

When Max pulled in, Wyatt emerged from the front door. He'd changed into jeans and a long-sleeved Henley. I'd expected he'd wait for us on the front porch, but he descended the steps and walked toward the driver's side of Max's truck.

Max had already opened his door, and he got out and met him at the front of the truck. I did the same, although I stopped far enough back to give them space.

"What happened with Henderson?" Wyatt asked, his voice hard.

To my surprise, Max told him, using more detail than I had.

Wyatt cast a glance at me, the first time he'd acknowledged my presence since he'd walked out the door, and the look of deep concern and relief he gave me took my breath away.

Why would Wyatt give a shit about me?

He turned back to Max. "I appreciate you bringin' her home. I didn't want to leave Hank."

Max nodded. "Of course. Carly's part of our family now. Family takes care of its own."

I didn't miss the hint of warning.

Wyatt didn't respond.

Max cast a quick glance at the tow truck. "You on call tonight?"

"Yeah" was Wyatt's response.

"Then maybe I should be the one to stay," Max said.

"We'll be fine."

"Wait," I said, taking a step closer. "What are you talking about?"

Max swung his head to face me. "I presumed he was stayin' to watch over you and Hank."

"I am," Wyatt quickly asserted.

Max nodded. "Who's bringin' her in to work tomorrow?"

"I'll make sure she gets there," Wyatt said.

I nearly protested that they were discussing this as though I didn't have a say in any of it. I opened my mouth to say as much, only I realized I *didn't* have a say in any of it. I was completely at their mercy, and I fucking hated it.

"Thanks for the ride, Max," I said, heading for the porch. "I'll see you tomorrow."

"Good night, Carly," he called after me.

I went inside and took off my jacket, which was still smeared with mud from my escapade on the ravine, then hung it up on the coat rack. I was surprised Ruth hadn't mentioned it. Nothing seemed to escape her eagle eyes.

A lamp on an end table was turned on, and to my surprise, Hank was asleep in the recliner, his light snores drowning out the low volume of the late-night talk show on the TV. Wyatt had put a blanket over him. I noticed someone had set a pillow and a folded blanket down at one end of the sofa. Was that where Wyatt planned to sleep?

I headed into Seth's bedroom, ready to strip the bed since Wyatt had claimed the sofa, and pulled up to a dead halt just steps inside.

"I changed the bedding," Wyatt whispered behind me. "I didn't want you to have to deal with it after workin' all night."

It was such a little thing, but it caught me off guard. "Wyatt...thanks," I said, setting my purse next to my suitcase.

"Yeah," he said, his voice gruff. "No problem."

"I saw Hank in the recliner."

"He has an easier time gettin' up and down from it. I figured we'd let him have his way the first couple of nights. Then we can encourage him to sleep in his bed."

I glanced back at him in surprise. He really *was* planning to be part of this for the long haul. "His diet is terrible. He planned to live off TV dinners and Pop-Tarts."

Wyatt grimaced. "An old man who doesn't cook livin' with a teenage boy…I suspect he'd been living like that for a while." He smiled at me. "Thanks for cookin' him dinner. He raved about it when I showed up. I had a plate, and he was right."

I felt my cheeks flush. "Maybe so, but I'm not sure he should be eating pasta. Turns out I don't know anything about the proper diet for a diabetic. I plan on going to the library to look it up, then I'll figure out a way to sneak it in. Make it so he's eating healthy but not realizing it."

His expression turned guarded. "You're getting attached to him."

"Well, of course I am," I said, insulted and hurt. "After all of this, you *still* think I'm here to hurt him?"

"No, Carly, I'm past that."

I crossed my arms over my chest and glared up at him.

"It's just that wanting to cook the right food for him goes beyond exchanging care for room and board." He shrugged. "Although judging from the groceries in the fridge and cabinets, you're providing the board too."

"He *has* to eat," I said in defense. "And he only had forty-three dollars in his wallet." Which I didn't even have, but I didn't see the point of reminding him of my financial situation.

"Most people around here qualify for food stamps," he said. "And processed food is cheapest, not to mention there's not a lot of fresh food and vegetables available in the winter."

"Oh."

He watched me for a second, then lowered his voice. "I wish you'd told me about Dwight Henderson sooner." He lifted a hand before I had a chance to protest. "I understand why you didn't, but I want you to trust me, Carly. I plan to earn your trust."

"I shouldn't be here long enough for that to be necessary." It was true, so why did I feel like a bitch for saying it?

Some emotion passed over his face, something that looked a lot like hurt. He opened his mouth to say something, but instead he nodded. "I'll be on the sofa if you need me."

Then he walked out of the bedroom, shutting the door behind him.

Wyatt had shoved the clutter that had previously been strewn all over the floor to one side. I knew the sheriff's department must have come here to search Seth's things, but for all I knew, the deputy who'd murdered him had shown up and searched under the guise of doing his job. I took a moment to scan the room.

The walls were covered in pencil drawings on loose-leaf notebook paper, which I supposed was more readily available in Drum than sketch paper. The drawings were mostly of wildlife, but a few were of people. Several of Hank, a few of a woman, and one of Wyatt.

Presuming these were Seth's, they were very, very good. He obviously had been uber talented, and it made me sick to think he'd never be able to explore it. To attend art school, or learn how to paint.

I moved closer to the drawing of Wyatt. While Seth had been better with animals, he'd had a way of drawing eyes that made them feel like windows to the soul. The woman's eyes were mostly confused and cloudy. Hank's were stoic and strong. But Wyatt's…it took me a moment to decide what emotions they conveyed. Gentleness and strength. What was Wyatt's role in the boy's life? Did he know more about what had happened to Seth than he was letting on? Would he help me find justice for him?

I started searching through Seth's bedside table and his dresser, looking for anything that could help me figure out what Seth had found and where he'd hidden it. My biggest dilemma was that I had no idea what I was looking for, and I couldn't help wondering how much of the mess was Seth's and how much was from the sheriff's deputies.

I sat on the floor and started to sift through the stuff I'd had to carefully step over just to make my way into the room. There were quite a few dirty clothes, and I searched pockets until I found a folded piece of paper tucked in the deep corner of an old pair of jeans. I pulled it out and carefully opened it, revealing a handwritten website address: eyecam.com

My heart started racing. Was this the site Seth had used to store the camera footage?

This felt huge, but I had no idea what to do with it. Even if I'd found the access code, I still didn't have the login information. My best bet was to keep searching his things for any clues.

I spent the next half hour going through the piles on the floor, folding the clothes and sorting the other items into smaller piles. A search of the closet didn't reveal anything else, and the walls in the closet seemed secure, so I doubted Seth had hidden a stash of drugs or a paper with his login info in some hidden hidey-hole.

Frustrated and exhausted, I changed into pajamas and lay down in bed, planning what to do next. I could check outside tomorrow. Maybe I'd find something in the detached garage. Feeling better that I had a plan even though I knew it was likely a long shot, I turned off the light hoping I fell asleep quickly. I needed my rest.

I had a lot of investigating to do tomorrow.

Chapter
Twenty-One

I woke to the sound of breaking glass.

At first the sound insinuated itself into my dream—Jake started smashing the crystal we'd gotten for wedding gifts with a golf club. But a grunt shook me free of sleep. I sat up in bed abruptly. The room was completely dark except for the moonlight streaming through the partially obscured window.

Partially obscured because someone was climbing through it.

By the time I was awake enough to react, the intruder had already climbed inside.

Running purely on instinct and adrenaline, I grabbed the table lamp and smashed it on the intruder's head.

He seemed momentarily dazed, so I lunged toward the end of the bed where I'd left my purse next to my suitcase.

I didn't make it. The intruder leapt for me, knocking me onto the floor and landing on top of me.

"Wyatt!" I screamed. "*Wyatt!*"

The intruder rolled me over onto my back and straddled my chest as he hit my cheek with an open hand. A flash of pain followed, but I realized that he'd held back. I took small comfort in the fact that he wore a ski mask. Maybe he didn't plan on killing me after all. The fact that he hadn't tried to knock me out meant he needed me coherent.

He slapped a hand over my mouth and nose and pressed hard. "Shut up or I'll smother you to death."

I recognized the voice. This was one of the men who had killed Seth.

Terror snaked through my head and I saw spots. Instinct told me to fight, but he was sitting on my prone body, in the few feet between the bed and the wall. Even if I tried to throw him off, there was nowhere to throw him off to.

I went totally still, and the masked man said, "Good girl. Follow my instructions and I'll let you live. If you scream, I'll make it painful for you. Do you understand?"

I slowly nodded, desperate to take in a breath. My pulse pounded in my head.

My purse was only about a foot to the left of my head, next to the wall. If I could reach the gun…

He removed his hand, and I gulped in air but remained silent.

"Good." He lifted his weight off me and grabbed my arm, pulling me to my knees as he stood. "Now you're gonna bring me to the stash."

"I don't know where it is."

He reached into his back pocket and pulled out a gun, pointing it at my forehead. "That's not good enough. I know you took it."

I fought the urge to sob, telling myself I needed to keep my shit together to get out of this.

Where the hell was Wyatt?

Could he still be asleep?

I needed to get this guy out of the bedroom and into the living room in hopes that Wyatt could take care of him—and do what I could to make sure Hank didn't get hurt in the process.

"It's in the kitchen," I said in a shaky voice. "Hidden under the refrigerator." Then, for good measure, I added, "With Hank's fortune."

"I *knew* that fortune was real," he said in triumph. He jerked me to my feet. "Let's go, but don't try anything funny or I'll shoot you. Don't think I won't. I've killed men before, but then you know that already."

I didn't answer. I didn't think it was necessary, but a couple of things went through my mind. One, he suspected I knew more than I'd let on, and two, he wasn't the guy who'd pulled the trigger on Seth, but I had no doubt that he'd killed before.

He pulled me toward the bedroom door. "Open it."

Terror clutched at me as I turned the knob. Was I about to get Wyatt and Hank killed?

I opened the door and stepped out into the living room, hardly able to breathe. Then a quick scan of the room revealed that both the sofa and the recliner were empty.

I was torn between relief and terror. Wyatt had been my backup plan. What was this guy going to do when he realized I'd lied to him?

"How'd you know I had it?" I asked, biding my time.

"We've been watchin' you. The way you've been stickin' close to Hank. It wasn't hard to figure out you'd found the stash here on Hank's land."

Shit. I had no idea where it was—or if Seth had even taken it—but I'd told this guy it was here and now I was stuck. Maybe there'd be something I could use against him in the kitchen. A cast-iron skillet or a pan, maybe. Only I'd put away all the dishes, hadn't I?

With a viselike grip on my arm, he dragged me across the living room toward the kitchen, careful about bumping into things and making noise.

"Aren't you afraid of waking anyone else up?"

"Drummond's not here and the old man's only got one leg. What's he gonna do?" he sneered in contempt.

Wyatt wasn't here? Max had asked Wyatt if he was on call. Had they arranged for him to be called out for a tow truck run? Although, that didn't explain where Hank had gone. Had Wyatt moved him to his bed?

It struck me that my chances would be better if I got him outside. I'd have a chance to run, maybe, and I'd also get him away from Hank.

"I lied," I said, realizing I was risking his wrath. "It's not in the kitchen."

I wasn't surprised when he hit me, but I wasn't prepared for the gut punch that stole my breath. I doubled over, panic seizing me when I couldn't breathe. I knew I just needed a few seconds to recover, but he was already dragging me to the front door. "You stupid fucking bitch."

He hauled me across the porch and shoved me down the steps to the ground. "I ain't playin'. *Where the fuck is it?*" He was losing his control, which made him dangerous.

"I'll show you," I gasped out, tears streaming down my face.

"Get up!" he shouted.

Climbing to my hands and knees, I tried to get up, but my body was shaking, and I couldn't get my legs to support my body.

"Get. *Up.*" He stood over me and gave me a vicious kick in my ass, sprawling me flat on my face in the cold, wet grass.

"Seems to me that's not the way to get her up," Hank said from the front door, his voice tight with fury.

I glanced up and saw him leaning his shoulder against the doorway. He had a shotgun in his hands, the barrel pointed at the intruder.

"Look at you, old man," the guy sneered. "Hoppin' along with one leg. Let's see how you do when I kick that leg out from underneath you."

He started back up the porch steps and a loud boom filled the night air, quickly followed by another one.

The intruder flew backward and landed in the yard on his back, within kicking distance of my feet.

His eyes were wide with shock, but the holes in his gut confirmed what I already knew.

He was dead.

"Carly," Hank called out. "You okay?"

I started to violently shake. "We need to call someone."

Would Hank be in trouble? Would he get away with self-defense?

Propping his hand on the side of the house, he hopped out the door toward a metal chair on the porch. "I already called for help." He motioned for me to join him. "Come away from that piece of trash, girl."

Still shaking, I got to my feet and nearly fell.

I felt the urge to sob, but if I gave myself permission, I knew I'd completely fall apart.

"Come 'ere," he said more gently. "It's gonna be okay."

"But the sheriff…" I said. "How can we trust them?"

"We're not." He sat down with a hard plop. "I need you to pull yourself together and go get my other shotgun out of my bedroom. Can you do that?"

"Who's comin', Hank?" I asked, feeling my grasp of control slowly strengthen.

"Just get the shotgun, girl. Do as I say, now," he ordered with a tone so gentle it felt like an endearment.

Nodding, I walked up the steps, feeling like I was having an out-of-body experience.

"The gun's on the bed," he said in an even voice. "Be sure to get your coat before you come back out, but don't dawdle. I suspect we don't have much time."

"Okay," I said, wiping my wet cheeks and heading to his room. Sure enough, the gun was on his bed, so I picked it up and carried it out to the front porch, lifting my coat off the coat hook on the way.

"Grab a chair and sit next to me."

His kind voice felt grounding, and I found myself doing as he instructed.

He shot me a glance. "Put on your coat. You're in shock. You need to keep warm."

Leaning forward, I set the shotgun down on the wooden porch and put on my coat.

"He was one of 'em, wasn't he?" he asked.

I nodded. "Yeah."

"I figured. I heard 'im talking. I heard him hit you too. I don't take to woman beaters."

"Who did you call, Hank?"

"Someone who wants Seth's murderers as much as we do."

I went lightheaded. "Bingham."

"I knew you were a smart girl," he said with pride. "We can't trust the sheriff, but I ain't up to cleanin' up a body. We need someone to take care of it, and I ain't puttin' Wyatt in that position. Bingham wants information about who's tryin' to gain a foothold in his territory, and the identity of that piece of trash will help 'im." He waved the muzzle of his gun at the body in the front yard.

"If he's helping us, then why are we sitting here with shotguns, Hank?"

"He thinks you know more than you're lettin' on." He turned to face me. "So this is to keep him from tryin' to get it."

"You don't want to tell him?"

His eyes narrowed. "It's never a good idea to play your hand too early."

Fear crept up my spine to the base of my neck. "This is a dangerous game, Hank."

"I know, girl, and I would send you inside and try to shield you from it, but you don't seem the type. Do you want to go inside?"

I stared into his deep-set, bright eyes. He looked totally sane and not high on pain pills, and he knew this town far better than I did. I suspected part of the reason he'd called Bingham was to protect me, and I wasn't letting him fight this battle alone. "No. I'm not hiding from this."

He gave a slow nod as we heard the rumble of vehicles approaching from down the mountain. Two trucks turned onto Hank's property and flicked off their headlights as they pulled up in front of the house.

"Let me take the lead on this," he said.

I didn't answer, just gripped the shotgun with my sweat-slicked hands, wishing I had time to wipe them on my pajama bottoms.

The two trucks came to a halt, and I noticed that one was a black truck with a crunched front end.

I gasped. "That's the truck that ran Wyatt off the road."

"It did what, now?" Hank asked.

"The truck that followed us to Greeneville. When Wyatt chased after it, it ran him off the road."

"You let me take care of this," he said, sitting up straighter and gripping his gun with a tighter grasp.

If Bingham thought I had more information, and perhaps a connection to his competition in Atlanta, I wasn't surprised he'd been following me, but why would he have tried to kill Wyatt?

The truck doors opened, and four men piled out and walked toward us.

"That's close enough," Hank called out when they were about twenty feet away.

A man laughed, but it was humorless. "*You* called *me*, old man."

It was Bingham. I resisted the urge to shiver.

Hank wasn't intimidated. "We need to work out a deal before I give you what you came for."

My gaze darted to the body on the ground then back to Bingham.

"What sort of deal?" he asked.

"First of all, you got a question, you come to me and ask me to my face. You don't send a goon after me and my own. I thought that arrangement had already been set in stone."

Bingham held his hands out to his sides. "Seems to me you're fresh out of kin, Chalmers."

"You know damn good and well I claimed Wyatt Drummond as mine. So why is your man runnin' 'im off the road?"

Bingham didn't say anything for a moment, and when he spoke again, there was a little less arrogance in his voice. "That was a misunderstandin'."

"A misunderstandin' that nearly got the boy killed."

I hadn't told Hank that part, but I supposed that getting run off the road in these parts could be considered attempted murder.

"He should have left my man alone," Bingham said.

"And your man shouldn't have been following me and Carly. He was protectin' his kin, Bingham. You of all people should understand that."

Bingham turned his attention to me and took a step forward.

Hank shifted in his seat and lifted the barrel of his shotgun, pointing it at Bingham's chest. Bingham's men all pointed their weapons at Hank, but he seemed unfazed. "You take one step closer, and I'll blow a hole in ya just like I did to that guy lyin' on the ground."

"And my men will kill *you*," Bingham said evenly. "*And* her."

"I'm trustin' in your sense of self-preservation to keep that from happenin'."

The air hung heavy with tension for a couple of heartbeats before Bingham patted his hand downward. His men lowered their weapons.

"So what's the deal, old man?" Bingham asked. "You claim you shot *one* of the men who killed your grandson. But how can I be certain this man was involved, and what's to say there was more than one?" He turned his attention to me. "Unless Ms. Moore knows more than she's let on up to this point."

"You can believe me or not," Hank said, his own gun still raised. "But ask yourself why else this man would be breakin' into my grandson's room in the middle of the night."

Bingham jutted a foot in front of him and shifted his balance. "I suppose you have a point. But what makes you think he wasn't the only one?"

"Because he mentioned that he and his buddies were lookin' for a stash. They thought Seth had brought it here."

"And did he?" Bingham asked.

"Hell if I know," Hank told him, "but if he had, I sure as hell wouldn't be tellin' *you*." His back stiffened. "We had an agreement, Bingham, and you broke it. And I'm not talkin' about running Wyatt off the road. I'm talkin' about my grandson."

"Hey now," Bingham said, raising up his hands. "I did no such thing."

"That's not what your man said when he paid me a visit the day Seth died." When Bingham remained silent, Hank said, "What? Cat got your tongue?"

"That doesn't count, Hank," Bingham said. "The boy came to *me*."

"And *I* told *you* that if I conceded my business to you, you would leave me and my kin alone. That was the deal." Hank's voice was tight, and he sounded so mad I wondered if he was about to shoot Bingham, consequences be damned.

Bingham was silent for a moment. "Okay, I can see your point. I should've come to you."

"Yeah," Hank said, his voice breaking. "He'd still be alive if you had."

Bingham took a step closer, his hands out at his sides again, pleading, "That boy was bound and determined to find out who'd supplied his mother with those drugs. There was no way in hell I could have stopped 'im, and you sure wouldn't have been able to stand in his way. Hell, you were laid up in the hospital."

Hank didn't answer.

"I didn't kill your grandson, Chalmers," Bingham said, more insistent this time. "You and I want the same thing. We both want to know who *did*."

"And I told you that I've got one of them. I'm willin' to make a trade."

"What is it you want to trade for a dead man?" Bingham asked.

"You get the identity of one of the interlopers, and in exchange, you leave Carly the hell alone."

I refrained from gasping, but Bingham didn't hide his surprise. "Why?"

"You don't need to know why. You just need to agree to the terms."

Bingham shifted his weight, looking like a wildcat preparing to leap. "Here's the thing, old man. None of that makes sense. If she doesn't know anything, then why are you so protective of her? And if she knows who killed the boy, why would you hide it?"

Hank didn't answer.

"Why would you stick your neck out for some woman you don't even know?" Bingham asked more insistently.

"This woman held Seth's hand as he died," Hank said. "This woman has stepped up to help me more than anyone else in this damn town."

"Maybe people would be more willin' to step up if you didn't treat 'em like shit," one of the other men said.

Bingham shot him a dark look, but when he turned back to Hank, he said, "Gates has got a good point. You turned this town against you after Barb died."

Hank remained silent, his entire body tense.

"I claim Carly Moore as kin," Hank said. "You recognize and honor that, and I'll let you take that body and clean up the mess."

Bingham released a harsh laugh. "I ain't your cleanup crew, Chalmers."

"Either agree to my terms or get the hell off my land," Hank said. "And I'll bury that body and his identity with him."

Bingham scrubbed his face. "It's late, old man. I don't feel like dickin' around."

"And neither do I. Either agree to my terms or leave," Hank said. "Those are your options. You have ten seconds to make up your mind."

Several seconds ticked by before Bingham said, "Fine, I'll leave her be, but I want to talk to her."

"No," Hank barked.

"I just want to talk to her, old man," he said in frustration. "You would have done the same durin' your time." Then he shrugged and added, "How about this? We'll have the meetin' in public. Lots of witnesses."

"And what if you don't like what I have to say? Maybe I have some questions of my own," I called out as I got to my feet.

Hank didn't respond, but Bingham released a laugh. "So she speaks after all."

"You know damn good and well that I speak," I snapped. "We've met before."

Hank shot me a quick glance.

"That we have," Bingham said. "Although I've come to realize I was under the wrong impression about your identity."

"And just who did you think I was?" I asked, hoping he'd let slip something I didn't already know.

Bingham was silent for a moment, then laughed again. "You're something else, woman." He shifted his attention to Hank. "Is this part of your agreement? Answerin' her questions?"

"She's in the middle of this, Bingham," Hank said. "She's entitled to ask."

Rubbing his chin, Bingham seemed to consider it then said, "Here's what I'll do. I want ten minutes with the woman—she gets to ask her questions and I'll ask mine. Once the ten minutes are up, I'll honor the terms."

"Shouldn't you address *me* with that part of the deal?" I said. "And how do I know you'll answer my questions?"

"How do I know you'll answer mine?" he retorted.

He had a point.

Hank shot me a long look. "Up to you, girl."

The thought of being interrogated by Bingham for ten minutes scared the shit out of me, but I wanted answers. The real question was whether it would be a waste of time.

"I need a moment to decide," I said.

"Take your time." Sounding amused, he added, "I'll be more generous with my time than your new kin was with his."

I sat back down and turned to the elderly man next to me while keeping the outlaw in my peripheral vision.

"Hank?" I whispered.

"There's pros and cons to this," Hank said under his breath. "The remaining murderers will see you talkin' to 'im, and they might think you're teamin' up with 'im."

"Which is likely what he wants," I said.

He gave me a slight nod. "Exactly. But they might not send a second guy if they think you're under Bingham's protection."

"Or I might draw their wrath."

"That too." A wobbly smile tilted the corners of his mouth, but I could see the exhaustion beyond it. This had been too much for him, though he'd never admit it.

"But we might draw them out," I said. "Next time we'll be ready for them."

He nodded slowly. "Next time we will."

I stood and faced Bingham. "I'll agree to your terms."

He held his hands wide. "Now we're talkin'."

"But I have one more requirement of my own to add."

Bingham laughed in what appeared to be genuine amusement. "Go on."

"You will reimburse Wyatt Drummond for all expenses incurred from his *accident*."

"Now, hold on," Bingham protested.

"And in exchange, I guarantee that I will give you one piece of information the sheriff doesn't know."

"What is it?" he asked.

I dialed up the attitude. "If I told you now, then we wouldn't need an agreement, would we?"

Bingham turned to Hank. "Now I see why you like 'er. She's got backbone."

Hank remained silent.

Bingham's shoulders lifted as he gave me his full attention for five long seconds. Sweat broke out at the base of my spine, and I was sure he was just going to shoot Hank and take me off to get his answers however he saw fit. But then his body relaxed. "Okay. You've piqued my interest. You've got your deal, Ms. Moore, and so do you, Chalmers. Let's hope neither one of you make me regret it."

I was already having regrets.

Chapter
Twenty-Two

Bingham strode up to the dead guy, crouched over, and jerked off his ski mask before letting the head flop back down onto the ground.

"Know 'im?" Hank asked.

Bingham laughed, but it sounded bitter. "You didn't check?"

"Nope. Decided to let you unwrap your present."

Bingham stared up at me. He was closer now and the porch light revealed the features the darkness had hid before. Despite his wry grin, I could see that he was a hard man whose answer to problems typically involved violence.

"Ms. Moore," he said. "Would you like to take a look at him?"

I shot Hank a questioning look and he shrugged.

"I want to see if I've served him before," I said. "I know you've sent men to watch me. I want to see if anyone else has done the same."

Bingham didn't deny sending someone to watch me, not that I expected him to.

I walked past Hank and down the two steps, walking around the body to look down at his face.

"Well?" Bingham asked.

"There's not enough light."

"Gates," Bingham called out, and within seconds, one of his men was shining a flashlight on the man's face.

I froze. I'd seen him all right. He'd been at the bar tonight. Ruth had told me that he and his buddy were Bingham's men. His friend had answered my questions, but this guy had refused to answer me. Had he known that I'd heard him talking with the others in the parking lot?

Had Bingham sent both men to watch me, unaware Cecil was a traitor? Or had the two guys at the bar been working together apart from Bingham? I wasn't sure, but I suspected that if Bingham hadn't known they'd been at the bar tonight, he'd assume the friend was a traitor too. I didn't like the idea of condemning an innocent man.

"He looks familiar," I said. "And I'm sure I've seen him in the bar. Definitely on Monday night."

"Any other times?" he asked.

I looked up at him. "I'll think it over and give you an answer during our Q & A."

I realized we hadn't determined a time or place, but I had no doubt he'd get in touch.

A slow smile spread across his face. This had become a game to him, and he was enjoying every bit of it.

"Is it one of your guys?" Hank asked.

"Yep," Bingham confirmed, then motioned to his men. "Cecil Abrams."

His men surged forward, and the three of them picked up the man—two at his shoulders, the other at his feet—and started to lift him.

"Hold on there," I said, standing to the side. "Part of your job is cleanup, which means you can't be spreading DNA all over Hank's yard. Wrap him up before you carry him off."

"She's right," Hank said. "You clean up the yard. We'll take care of the porch."

"You heard 'em," Bingham said. "Get a tarp. Besides, you don't want to dirty up the back of your truck, Gates."

The men dropped the body with a sick thud, and I recoiled in horror. The guy who had brought over the flashlight walked back to the dented truck. A short while later, he returned with the tarp, and they made quick work of wrapping up the body and stowing it in the back of the truck.

"Now the ground," I said when they opened the truck doors, looking like they were about to load up on their trucks. Even in the dark I could see where Cecil had bled onto the dirt path that led from the drive to the front porch. Cleanup would entail a whole lot more work than just removing the body.

"Excuse me?" Bingham said, sounding incredulous.

"There's blood on the ground. Clean it up." He started to advance toward me, but I lifted my shotgun and pointed it at him. "You agreed to clean up the outside, Mr. Bingham. You're not finished yet."

"What the hell do you expect me to do?"

"Get rid of the blood."

One of Bingham's men strode toward me. "Who the fuck do you think you are?"

Hank pointed his weapon at the man. "You heard 'er. Clean up the blood. There's a couple of shovels in the garage you can use, but don't be takin' any of my buckets. If you've got nothin' to put it in, use a trash bag."

Bingham stared at me for a long second, then said, his face expressionless, "You heard the lady. Clean up the blood."

I lowered my weapon.

The men shot angry, deadly looks in my direction as they took off toward Hank's detached garage, which sat about twenty feet to the left of the house. It took them about a minute to open the overhead door and find a couple of shovels and several trash bags. They had to squeeze in around a car that was parked in the middle of the two-car garage, its hood open.

Gates shone his flashlight beam on the ground and the other two men dug up the dark-stained, hard-packed earth that made up the path leading from the porch toward the gravel drive. The blood-soaked soil went into trash bags.

Bingham watched me the entire time, his narrow gaze studying me with only occasional glances toward his men to assess their progress.

"I'm starting to wonder if it wasn't a case of mistaken identity after all, Ms. Moore."

"Why?" I asked in a sassy tone to cover my fear. "Because I've watched a few episodes of *Law and Order*? Please. I'd be plain stupid to let you leave evidence behind, and I can assure you, Mr. Bingham, that I'm not stupid."

He tilted his head, his eyes lighting up. "No. You most definitely aren't."

"We got it all," one of the men said. "Let's get."

A smile spread across Bingham's face. "Nope. We don't go until Ms. Moore gives us our leave."

I cast a glance at Hank, who gave me a quick nod, telling me it was my decision. Gates panned his flashlight over the dug-up path, and I drifted closer for a better look. The dirt would need to be smoothed over and packed down to escape notice, but we could handle that ourselves. I'd just wanted most of the blood evidence gone. After a quick survey, I looked Bingham in the eye and said, "It's far from thorough, but it will do."

Bingham burst out laughing. When he settled a bit, he tipped an imaginary hat to me. "I'm very much lookin' forward to our tête-à-tête later."

On his signal, he and his men got into their trucks. They backed up in the yard and took off down the mountain.

I stood on the porch and watched them drive away, taking several deep breaths as I tried to settle my nerves.

"You okay?" Hank asked.

I spun around to face him, realizing again that he'd pushed himself way too far. "We need to get you back to bed."

"The hell we do. We ain't done yet."

"I can do it myself, Hank. You can't be scrubbing the porch." I didn't see much blood splatter, but it would be enough to incriminate us.

"No, but I might think of things you wouldn't. The bleach is in the house. We need to clean them shovels before we put 'em away."

I nodded. He was right.

"That was some smooth thinkin', girl," he said. "If I hadn't known better, I would have thought you'd done this before."

I slowly shook my head, starting to tremble. "No. I'm just good at thinking on my feet. That's what made me a good teacher."

"You were a teacher?" he asked, surprised.

Shit. I gave him a weak smile. "When I was training new employees."

He looked me over as though seeing me with new eyes.

He was making me nervous. "If you think I had anything to do with Seth's death, I'll go stay with Ruth and her boyfriend."

"Nah," he said shrewdly. "I know you didn't have nothin' to do with it other than what you told me. And I know you're not here lookin' for my mythical fortune."

"But you don't trust me now?" I finished.

He smiled. "The hell I don't. You had my back and I had yours, which is why I declared you kin."

"I don't understand. Why do you have an agreement with Bingham?"

"Because I used to run the drug business in these parts," he said. "Until I sold it all to Bingham."

My mouth dropped open and I stared at him in shock. I was living with and caring for a man who had poisoned countless people.

"The look on your face right now tells me all I need to know about your supposed involvement in this Georgia drug scheme." He suddenly looked eighty years old, although I suspected he was in his late sixties.

"You said used to. What made you stop?"

"A lot of reasons. It was a different world back then. My main competition was Bart Drummond and his moonshine. I didn't handle any of the bad stuff, usually just pot and uppers and downers. A bit of cocaine, but most people around these parts couldn't afford it. I didn't have the stomach or a cook for meth, and oxy was too hard to acquire. Then my Mary got sick and she begged me to give it up. I'd tried to hide it from her and Barb." He shook his head. "So I sold it all to Bingham. We agreed that I'd burn my weed farm, and he'd leave me and my kin alone. No sellin' 'em drugs. No contactin' 'em for any reason in regards to drugs. When Barb started usin', I went to Bingham and damn near shot his head off his shoulders, but he insisted he hadn't been part of it. Her boyfriend was bringin' in drugs from Georgia."

"And you believed him?"

"He was just as pissed as I was, but he let George be as long as he wasn't dealin' in Drum. And then George started dealin'. So Bingham had him dealt with."

"You told me that a deputy shot him after he started smashing things in town."

A cockeyed grin twisted Hank's mouth. "That's what the report says, but it seems mighty convenient to me. Mind you, it's just a hunch."

But it was probably a good one. "So someone else is tryin' to sell drugs here now?"

"So it seems," he said, his voice weary. "And Bingham is determined to stop them. He denies it, but I know he encouraged Seth to go after that drop."

"The person who was coming in from Atlanta?"

"Yep."

I opened my mouth to ask him more questions, but he spoke before I could. "Wyatt's on an emergency call and I suspect he'll be comin' back soon. We need to have all of this cleaned up before he gets here. We can't be tellin' him what happened here until we know for certain he has our backs."

Emergency call my ear. Someone had wanted him out of the way. I only hope he didn't end up down a ravine this time. In the meantime, we had no way of getting in touch with him.

"I hope Wyatt's all right," I said.

Hank just shrugged. "Seems mighty convenient he got called out just before that boy showed up."

"We both know it was probably a setup," I said.

"Perhaps," he said, scratching his chin, "but it's like I said, blood runs deep. I wouldn't be surprised if Bart still has his claws in him."

"Sometimes a last name is just a name," I responded.

"He never cottoned to his father much," Hank admitted. "Always rebellin'. His daddy gave him that bar to let 'im think he was makin' his own way, but a few years later, something happened, and Wyatt disowned the lot of 'em. Just a few weeks later, he was arrested for DUI and robbery. Half the town thought it was a setup, the other didn't care."

That wasn't the way I'd heard it. Ruth had told me that he'd been disowned after his arrest.

"Are you sure?" I asked. "That he disowned them before his arrest?"

"Damn sure."

That put everything about his situation in a whole new light. "His own father sent him to prison?"

"Who's to say? Although I suspect Bart wouldn't want the family name tarnished, no matter how he feels about the boy. I suspect he's the one who got the robbery charges dropped to B & E—and that the judge gave Wyatt such a stiff sentence in retaliation. People say Bart gave Wyatt the money to buy that service station as some sort of amends, but no one knows for certain. All I know is Wyatt went to prison penniless. He used a damn public defender instead of hirin' an attorney, but then he came back and bought the station with cash."

"I keep hearing about this robbery," I said. "What did he supposedly steal?" Now that I knew Wyatt, if only a little, I had a hard time picturing it. Then again, I hadn't thought Jake capable of any sort of wrongdoing either. I couldn't trust myself, especially since I was attracted to Wyatt.

"The same service station he now owns," Hank said. "It sold gas and snacks back in the day. His girlfriend was with him and was the lone witness. But then she recanted and left town."

"And people think the Drummonds paid her off." Max had all but confirmed the story, but I didn't feel comfortable saying so.

"Yep."

"He seems pretty loyal to you, Hank. Hell, you claimed him as your kin with Bingham. Do you really think he'd turn on you?"

"No, but I've learned it's best to be sure. I've had a lifetime of distrustin' everyone. It's just like breathin'."

"But you seem to trust me," I said, unable to stop myself.

His gaze softened. "You're the first person I've trusted in a very long time."

I stared at him in shock. I vowed to myself that I wouldn't let him down.

He was right about all of it, but I knew one thing for certain. It was time for Wyatt to lay his cards on the table, and if he gave me the answers I was looking for, I'd lay down all of mine, because at this point, I needed all the help I could get.

Chapter
Twenty-Three

By the time Wyatt came back, I'd raked the path and scrubbed the porch and shovels with bleach. I'd even spread some dirt onto the porch and swept it off to make the cleaning less obvious. I was putting the shovels away when the headlights of his tow truck appeared on the road and turned onto Hank's property.

Wyatt didn't waste any time rushing out of his truck. "What happened?"

The panic in his voice sent guilt washing through me. He genuinely cared about our well-being—no one was that good of an actor.

Except I could still hear Jake's voice in my head, saying how much he wanted us to spend the rest of our lives together. Of course, he'd intended for our togetherness to be short-lived.

"We had a break-in," Hank said evenly. He was still sitting on the front porch with the shotgun across his lap.

"Did Henderson show up?" he asked, his eyes wide with concern.

"The intruder wore a mask," Hank said. "I ran 'im off with my shotgun."

Wyatt turned to me. "Carly?"

"He broke in through Seth's bedroom window," I said as I stopped halfway between the porch and Wyatt.

"Jesus," he said, striding toward me. "Are you okay?"

"I'm fine."

"He tackled her to the floor," Hank said, his tone cold. "Threatened to kill her if she didn't take him to the stash."

Fury washed over Wyatt's face. "Did he hurt you?"

If Wyatt was pretending, he was doing a damn fine job of it. That fury had reached his eyes. "A few bumps and bruises, but I'm okay."

Wyatt stood stock-still for several seconds. "I'm goin' to fuckin' kill Dwight Henderson with my goddamn bare hands." He stomped to his truck.

While Dwight was far from my favorite person, he hadn't done us any harm tonight. I couldn't let Wyatt go after the wrong man.

"Hank!" I called out in a panic. "Tell him what happened!"

Wyatt stopped in his tracks. "Was there an intruder or not?"

When we didn't answer, his gaze swept over the front of the house, landing on the disturbed ground in front of the front porch.

"Please, dear God, tell me neither one of you was stupid enough to bury a body on the path to the driveway," he said in a weary tone.

I paused a beat, waiting to see if Hank would answer, and when he didn't, I inched closer to Wyatt. "No," I said. "We didn't bury anyone."

He swiveled his head to look at me from the side. "But somebody's dead."

It wasn't phrased as a question.

"Where'd you go, boy?" Hank asked.

"I got called on a run," Wyatt said, running a hand through his hair and looking like he was about to collapse from exhaustion. "Abandoned car on Highway 25, parked in the middle of a curve. Obviously a dangerous situation or I would have turned it down. I hauled it down to Ewing. You heard me take the call. Why the sudden suspicion?"

"Timing of that call seems suspect," Hank said.

Wyatt's brow shot up in outrage. "You're damn right. That car was planted in the road. Someone knew I was here and lured me away so you two would be little more than sittin' ducks." He waved his hand toward the gun on Hank's lap. "I suspect he paid for *that* mistake."

Hank remained silent, but I'd had enough. Everything in me screamed that he could be trusted, and even if it made me a fool, I was going to listen. "You either trust him or you don't, Hank. Time to decide."

Hank didn't answer.

"Are you shittin' me?" Wyatt shouted. "After everything, you still don't trust me?"

"Did your daddy have his hand in this?" Hank asked, sounding furious. "Are you coverin' up his mess?"

All the fight bled out of Wyatt, and I could see that Hank had gravely hurt him. But I reminded myself that they had plenty of history, years of it, while I'd only been in Drum for a few days.

Wyatt turned to me, his eyes pleading. "What about you? Do you trust me?"

Time for us to put our cards on the table. "How did you know about the person from Georgia?" I asked.

My question had caught him off guard.

"Answer the question, boy," Hank called out.

"I heard rumors," Wyatt said.

287

"Did you find out from Seth?" Hank asked. "And don't forget you swore to tell me the truth."

Wyatt released a bitter laugh. "You don't fully trust me, but you trust me enough to tell you the truth. Do you realize how ridiculous that is?"

"Answer the question," Hank said.

"No," he said, his voice hard. "Seth didn't tell me, and had I guessed what he was up to, I would have handcuffed him to me to keep him from gettin' involved."

"That didn't answer the question, now did it, boy?" Hank asked in a hard voice. "Who told you?"

Wyatt hesitated. "I can't tell you."

I watched the two men carefully, feeling like I was in the middle of an Old West standoff. Wyatt looked imposing with his stiff back and squared shoulders, while Hank's face was set in stubborn determination.

Hank finally said, "Get off my land."

Wyatt's mouth dropped open. "You're fuckin' kiddin' me."

Hank lifted his weapon. "Do I look like I'm kiddin'?"

"Hank!" I shouted as I stepped between them. "Stop!"

"Carly," Wyatt said in a low growl, sliding up behind me. "Go get in my truck."

I glanced over my shoulder at Wyatt, then back at Hank, who had lowered his weapon. "I can't."

"Why the fuck not?"

I turned to face him. "I promised Hank I'd stay and take care of him."

Wyatt lowered his voice so Hank couldn't overhear. "He's kickin' me off his property. I'm not comfortable leavin' you here when I have no idea what really happened tonight." He gently grasped my chin with his hand and turned my cheek to examine my bruises in the beam of his headlights. His eyes turned murderous. "Did Henderson do this to you?"

My heartbeat took off like a jackrabbit. "No," I whispered. "It wasn't Dwight."

"But you know who it was." It wasn't a question.

I lifted my chin and said with more confidence than I felt, "You don't have to worry. Hank took care of him."

Wyatt's eyes widened slightly, and he glanced up at Hank. "Where's the body? Did he ask you to move it?"

I shook my head. "No. He called someone to clean it up."

He was silent for several seconds. "There are only two people in these hills I can think of who'd be capable of such a thing, and Hank Chalmers would sooner cut off his other leg than call my father. Which means he called Bingham. What did Hank offer him? Is he gonna grow pot for him? Word has it that Bingham can't duplicate Hank's quality and people are complainin'."

"No. That's not it."

When I didn't look all that surprised by his question, he said, "But you know about Hank's previous profession."

"He told me a short while ago," I confessed. "But I'd heard some insinuations."

Wyatt cast a glance at the porch then back to me. "You've really worked a spell on the old man." I expected him to be pissed, but he sounded like he was in awe.

"He and Bingham worked out some kind of deal that involves Bingham leaving Hank's kin alone." I stared into Wyatt's eyes. "Wyatt, Hank has claimed us both as kin."

Surprise covered his face. "Yet he's kickin' me off his land."

"Just tell him how you knew about the Atlanta dealer. He just needs to know he can trust you."

"I've never once done anything to harm him," Wyatt spat. "*Never.*"

"You're the one who told me that trust has to be earned," I countered. "Earn it by telling him how you found out."

"I *can't*, Carly," he said, his voice breaking. "I swore I wouldn't tell and my word means something to me."

"Are you working with the sheriff?" I asked. "Or some kind of law enforcement to bring them down?"

He released a hard scoff. "You've watched too many damn movies or TV shows. No, I'm not workin' with law enforcement. They don't give a shit about what I'm doin'. They don't give a shit about anything that goes on up here unless it lines their pockets." He pushed out a breath. "This is between you and me and no one else, do you understand?" He flicked another gaze at Hank. "*No one* else. The old man's not gonna like that you have a secret of mine, and he's liable to kick you out too if he finds out."

"You know I have secrets of my own, Wyatt," I said. "You can trust me."

"I'm workin' to bring down my father, which makes Hank's accusation laughable. But I have people I'm using to do it, and I can't reveal my sources."

"Your father had something to do with the outside drugs coming in?"

"I don't know. I doubt it, but that piece of information about the Atlanta deal came to me with the rest."

Was Carson the source of his intel? Was that why he wanted to talk to me?

"Wyatt," Hank called out. "You've had plenty of time to say your goodbyes. Go!"

Wyatt grabbed my upper arms and looked into my eyes. "Check his blood sugar. When he gets mean, it's often because it's high."

"He wouldn't really shoot you, would he?" I asked.

"Nah," he said softly. "He'll come around in a few days, but that's a few days that you're on your own with him. And who's gonna watch him while you're at work? Who's gonna watch over you while you're sleepin'?"

"No offense, Wyatt," I said, "but you weren't around when this happened. And the guy who broke in knew you wouldn't be."

His expression darkened. "Who knew I was stayin' here?"

"I don't know," I said. "Max. Ruth, although I don't think she knew you were plannin' to sleep over."

"That wouldn't be hard for her to figure out. All she'd have to do is drive by."

I narrowed my eyes at him. "You think Ruth had something to do with this?" I shook my head. "Look, I know you two don't care for each other, but you have to admit that's far-fetched. What would she have to gain?"

"Maybe someone threatened her. Maybe they offered to pay her money. Is she talkin' about makin' any big purchases?"

There was no way I was going to admit she'd been talking about buying a house less than eight hours ago. "You're barkin' up the wrong tree."

"Am I? Because I'm not seein' many trees, Carly, and I suspect this isn't the last guy who's gonna come after you. With me leavin', the only thing standin' between you and them is a one-legged man's shotgun."

"That one-legged man's shotgun saved me once."

"I'm not sure if I'd count on it happenin' again." He glanced at Hank and then back at me. "Do you know who broke in?"

"A guy named Cecil Abrams. One of Bingham's men."

He didn't say anything, and his expression was inscrutable, so I wasn't sure whether he was surprised.

"Does that mean anything to you?" I asked.

"Does it mean anything to you?" he parroted.

I pushed out a defeated sigh. I didn't want to fight with him. I was so sick of fighting, and I wanted Wyatt to be the man he seemed to be.

His expression softened. "You're exhausted. Go inside and get some sleep. I'll pick you up tomorrow for work. You workin' the evening shift?"

"Yeah."

"Call me if you have any trouble. My home and garage numbers are on a paper taped to the side of the fridge." With one final glance back at Hank, he got in his tow truck and drove away.

Hank shook his head as I walked up to the porch. "There's only one reason that boy wouldn't answer your question. His daddy has something to do with this."

"He can't stand his father," I said, wearily climbing the steps. "I don't believe he'd ever turn on you, Hank. I think you're the father he wished he had. Turning him away like that hurt him."

He was silent.

"I'm tired and I know you have to be too. Let's go inside and check your blood sugar before you go back to bed."

"I don't need to check my damn blood sugar," he grumped as he let me help him out of the chair.

I handed him the crutches I'd brought out earlier. "Well, we're gonna check it anyway."

I helped him into his room and onto the bed. A quick check showed his sugar was high, so he gave himself an insulin injection before getting under the covers.

"Carly," he said as I started to walk out of the room.

I stopped and turned back to him.

"I know you never asked to be part of all this, but you're holdin' your own, girl."

That was funny, because I felt like I was drowning.

Chapter
Twenty-Four

There was no way I was sleeping in Seth's room after what had happened, so I grabbed my purse and set it on the floor next to the sofa, placing the gun Max had given me on the coffee table.

My sleep was fitful. I kept having nightmares of Seth's murder and Cecil Abrams breaking into my room.

I finally sank into a deep sleep around six, and I woke up to the smell of coffee. Bright sunlight streamed in through the windows behind me.

Had Wyatt come back?

I sat up and went into the kitchen, shocked to see Hank sitting at the kitchen table. But then I wondered why I was so surprised. Last night he'd killed a man and held his own with a hardened criminal. A man like that wouldn't hesitate to try getting around his house days after a major surgery.

"You shouldn't overdo it," I said, heading straight for the coffee maker.

"Girl, my leg didn't get bad overnight. I was fighting ulcers and whatnot for months and gettin' along with one leg. I just need to get my strength back up, which should happen sooner than later with your cookin'."

"What time is it?" I asked, rubbing my eyes.

"Nine thirty."

"*What?*" Not counting my pity party in Little Rock and Gatlinburg, I hadn't slept so late in years. "How long have *you* been up?"

"A couple of hours."

"I'm sorry." Some caretaker I was turning out to be.

"You needed your sleep," he said.

"And so do you." I opened the fridge and pulled out the creamer as well as the carton of eggs. "Do you want me to change your bandage before or after breakfast?"

"After," he said. "Give me something to look forward to." He was trying to make a joke, but his voice was flat.

"If you think I'm too much trouble, Hank, I can go back to the motel."

"You ain't goin' nowhere, so you hush about that," he said as he picked up his coffee cup. "Those assholes are lookin' for somethin' they think Seth hid. They would've broken in whether you were here or not."

I made him fried eggs and toast, hoping it would be okay for his diabetes. I had no way of knowing. There were no bookstores in Drum and no internet in Hank's house. I was stuck. *We* were stuck.

After picking at my scrambled eggs, I cleaned up the kitchen, then got all the supplies ready to change his dressing. We decided to do it on his bed, but the sheets likely hadn't been changed in a while, judging by the state of his room, so I stripped the bed and stuffed them in the washing machine with the sheets Wyatt had taken from Seth's bed. After I covered the mattress with clean sheets from the closet, I set out several towels to help keep the mattress and new sheet from getting soiled. Hank refused help getting onto the bed, but he looked pretty worn out by the time he laid his head on his pillow.

"I'm gonna try not to hurt you," I said anxiously.

He closed his eyes. "You don't worry about that, girl. You'll do fine."

I'd been counting on Wyatt to help me, and for some stupid reason, tears sprang to my eyes. But I blinked them away, telling myself I was being ridiculous. I had made my agreement with Hank before Wyatt had offered—insisted—on helping out. I could do this.

Hank's incision looked good and there was no sign of infection. The nurse had been much quicker and more efficient, but I was determined to do it right, even though I hated causing him pain. When I finally announced I was done, Hank just nodded and said, "You done good, girl."

I was sweating from exertion and nerves, but I didn't want him to see it. "Why don't you rest for a bit?"

I knew I'd worn him out when he grunted and closed his eyes.

The washing machine had finished, but the dryer didn't work, so I carried the basket outside to hang the sheets on the clothesline I'd seen the day before.

I was hanging the second sheet when I heard a car engine coming up the mountain.

Shit.

I hadn't thought to bring my gun outside, and I was about to run in and get it when I caught sight of the faded red tow truck.

Wyatt.

He parked in front of the house, bold as could be, and got out of his truck and headed straight for me.

"You're playin' with fire," I said.

He stopped in front of me and grinned, his eyes lighting up with mischief. "I'll take my chances."

"What brings you up the mountain?" I asked.

He studied my face, still smiling. "You."

Flutters rippled through my stomach. Turned out a man wanting to defend my honor did funny things to my hormones. But I had to be honest with myself—this went way beyond hormones. I admired the way his strength was tempered by gentleness. The devotion with which he'd thrown himself into mentoring a teenage boy in need of guidance. And I couldn't help but respond to the way he cared for all of the people around him, from Seth to Hank to me.

Wyatt Drummond was a man I could deeply care for, and it scared the crap out of me. I lowered my gaze, suddenly unable to look him in the eye.

Sensing my change in demeanor, his tone softened. "Did you change Hank's dressing?"

"Yeah."

"I'm sorry you had to do it alone." He glanced up at the house. "He doin' okay?"

"I wasn't as gentle or as quick as the nurse," I said. "He's resting."

"I'm sure you did fine," he said softly. Then he lifted my chin so that I was looking into his warm eyes.

An electrical current ran from his hand down to my core, and my mouth parted slightly as I gasped in surprise.

His gaze dropped to my mouth, and he asked in a husky tone, "Did you have any trouble after I left?"

His hand gently cradled my jaw, sending another flutter through my insides.

"No" was all I could seem to get out. Wyatt Drummond was doing strange things to my mental capacity, and all I could think about was whether I'd let him kiss me if he closed the short distance from his mouth to mine.

I took a slow step back, and his hand dropped to his side. I wondered if I'd see aggravation or disappointment on his face, but all I saw was warmth and understanding.

It made me like him even more.

"I've got to finish the laundry." I gestured lamely at the basket of sheets. Then, to remind us both that my situation was temporary, I asked, "Any word on the estimate for my car?"

He grimaced. "We both know it's not worth the trouble. Your best bet is for me to sell it to a junkyard for you. In the meantime, I started workin' on Hank's car last night so you can get to work and back and haul him around if need be. I should have it up and runnin' by tomorrow."

That explained the open hood of the car in the garage last night.

He gave me a soft smile. "I'll go start workin'."

He headed toward the garage, and I heard the sounds of metal clanging as I went inside. Under the guise of cleaning, I searched for any evidence or drugs Seth might have found. Nearly two hours later, I'd come up with a big fat nothing.

I glanced at the clock. It was close to one, so I made sandwiches for lunch. After, I handed one to Hank, who was in his recliner watching a game show.

"I know that boy's out there in my garage," he barked.

"And you're not kicking him off your land?"

He frowned. "He's out there for you, so it don't seem right."

"You mean workin' on your car so we can get around?" I asked.

He glanced up at me with a knowing look. "We both know it's more than that."

He was right. We did.

I took the second sandwich out to the garage. I considered bringing my own to eat with him, but I couldn't do it. Eating together was too familiar, and while my heart seemed ready to make that leap, my head knew it was a bad idea.

Wyatt grinned when he stopped and watched me walk across the yard toward him. When I reached the edge of the garage, he said, "You're feedin' me again."

"Well, you *are* workin' on a car for me to use," I said, putting the plate on a shelf since his hands were dirty. "It's the least I can do." I gestured to the exposed engine. "How's it looking? Think I'll be able to drive it to work?"

A frown creased his forehead. "Hopefully tomorrow. The source who gave me the information about the dealer from Atlanta wants to meet with me in Ewing this afternoon. I plan to pick up a few parts while I'm there."

I suppressed a gasp. "Do you think your source has information about Seth's murderer?"

"I don't know. After last night, I hate to leave you, but I think it's worth going. I don't want to leave you up here without a car, and since I'm your ride, Junior's wife is comin' by to stay with Hank so I can get you back into town. In fact," he said slowly, as though unsure if he should suggest it, "I was wondering if you'd like to come to Ewing with me."

I narrowed my eyes. "How'd you work all that out without a phone?"

Instead of taking offense, he laughed. "I used the radio in my tow truck. Ginger should be here in about a half hour. I was just about to come up to the house and tell you." He grimaced looking pointedly at the sandwich. "I was also gonna ask if you wanted to grab lunch, but you beat me to it."

While the thought of spending the afternoon with him appealed to me far too much, I already had plans. "I appreciate the offer, but can I take a rain check? Every time I feed Hank, I feel like I'm killing him with food. I really want to see if there are any diabetic cookbooks in the library."

"Yeah," he said softly. "Good idea."

Something lurched in my stomach. Should I tell him my other reason for going? I hesitated, although I wasn't sure why. Maybe it was because I was still worried he'd betray me, or it could be the opposite—maybe I knew it would twine us even closer together.

By the time Ginger showed up, I was ready to go. I gave her a few instructions on how to care for Hank and then gathered my bag. At the last minute I grabbed the gun Max had given me from Seth's room, where I'd stowed it in a nightstand drawer, and tucked it back into my purse. I could get in serious trouble for carrying a gun without a concealed carry permit, but it seemed worth the risk.

Wyatt was waiting for me at the bottom of the steps. Appreciation filled his eyes when he saw me. I'd taken a quick shower and blow-dried my hair, adding a bit of a wave to the short ends. I'd gone to the trouble of applying makeup, not enough to look done up, but enough so that I didn't look so washed out and tired. I'd tucked my work shirt into my purse and was wearing a white eyelet peasant-style shirt with my jeans, a pair of black ankle boots, and a gray cardigan since my freshly washed jacket was hanging on the clothesline along with my other pair of jeans.

"You look beautiful," he said, and then his eyes widened slightly in surprise as though he hadn't meant to say it out loud.

"Thanks," I said, descending the steps, suddenly feeling unbalanced.

He walked alongside me as we made our way to the truck, and to my surprise, he opened the passenger door for me. My body was humming with anticipation as he came around and slid behind the wheel. When he turned over the key, he snuck a glance at me before looking back at the windshield.

"I must have looked pretty rough before," I teased.

Wyatt shook his head. "No. You were beautiful before too." He pulled onto the road and headed down the mountain. "I just never told you."

We rode in silence, my longing fighting with reason. I'd waited my whole life to feel something like this with a man. Why did he have to live in this godforsaken town?

I knew it didn't matter, that we couldn't have any sort of future together, what with our dual vendettas against our fathers—his need to face his, my need to flee mine. But I couldn't stop myself from trying to learn more about him.

"How did you end up in prison, Wyatt?" I blurted out.

"As you already know," he said without any sign of defensiveness, "I was charged with a DUI and breaking and entering."

"But there were other charges at first. Robbery. I heard you broke into the garage you now own. Is any of that true?"

He dared to sneak a quick glance at me. "Yeah. I broke into the garage, but I didn't steal anything that wasn't rightfully mine. And I *was* driving while drunk. I deserved the conviction. I could have killed someone."

"Is that why you wouldn't allow your parents to hire an attorney?"

He snorted. "No, I'd already told my father I didn't want anythin' to do with him or his money, and that included hirin' me an attorney."

"What were you trying to get back that was yours?"

He was silent for a moment, as if considering how much he wanted to share. I started to think he was done talking when he said, "A baseball. My grandfather had given it to me when I was a kid." He shot me a sideways grin. "It was signed by Joe DiMaggio. I loved that stupid thing."

A baseball? It obviously had sentimental meaning if he'd gotten it from his grandfather. "How did it end up in the garage?"

"My maternal grandfather and my dad didn't get along, but that old man loved me, which pissed my father off to no end. So when I told my father I wanted nothin' to do with him, he sold the baseball to Earl Cartwright out of spite. I tried to buy it back, but Earl refused to part with it. One night I was pissed and drunk—never a good combination—and I decided to get it out of the display case in Earl's garage."

"So you got it back?" I asked.

He shook his head with a wry look. "No. The sheriff took it as evidence. It went missing. My father paid Earl enough to get him to drop the robbery charges, then paid my girlfriend to leave town." He tilted his head toward me. "He thought she wasn't good enough for me."

"Was she?" I asked with a hint of a smile.

"This was one of those rare instances when he was right. Turns out she was more interested in the Drummond money than the Drummond's eldest son."

"I'm sorry," I said. "I faced the same thing. Turns out most men were more interested in the fact that I was the Blakely Oil heiress than they were in me."

"Including the guy you left at the altar?" he asked.

"Nooo…" I said, drawing out the word. "I didn't technically leave him at the altar. I left him the night before the wedding. And while I'm sure Jake was interested in my father's oil money, he was much more drawn to my father's illegal business ventures."

His brow shot up. "Like corporate espionage?"

I released a short laugh. "It's a hell of a lot worse than that. Think drugs and arms smuggling."

"Shit," he said, his shock evident. "Is that why he wants you back? Because you know too much?"

"No, although I'm sure he's probably concerned about that too."

He gave me a worried look. "So why does he want you?"

Did I risk telling him? Hadn't I already risked enough? What was this admission compared to everything else?

Mistaking my hesitation, he said, "I'm not going to turn you in, Carly. I hope you know that by now."

I turned to him in surprise. "That hadn't even crossed my mind."

He smiled, his face lighting up. "Progress."

"Progress," I admitted, suddenly feeling self-conscious. Admitting I was so dispensable to my father was humiliating. "How much do you want to know?"

"As much as you're willing to share. I'll guard your secrets, Carly. I swear."

Call me a fool, but I believed him. "Okay. I'll tell you everything."

Chapter Twenty-Five

I think I need to start with my mother's death," I said, shifting my gaze to stare out the windshield. It hurt too much to look at him.

To my surprise, he reached across the seat and took my hand, twining our fingers together. "Take your time."

His touch meant more than it should. Feeling like this was dangerous. Yet the warmth and strength of his hand gave me the courage to continue. "My mother was killed in a car accident when I was nine. Up until a year or so before she died, I thought my life was perfect. I knew we had money, but I didn't truly understand it. I went to a private school where *everyone* had money."

"I knew," Wyatt said softly. "I knew right away. Max and I went to public school, and the contrast between what we had and what our friends had was startling."

I hadn't thought about that. "I suspect that was even harder, realizing everything you had while your friends struggled."

He shrugged. "It is what it is. Go on."

"I'm fairly certain my mother was happy. That's how I remember it anyway. She and my father were trying to get pregnant. They kept talking about my future baby brother or sister. My father loved me. Doted on me. He couldn't wait to have another baby. And then, suddenly, they started fighting. I was too young to truly understand what was happening, but now that I'm older, and after I heard my father talking to Jake…" I paused. "My father found out that I'm not his biological child. My mother had an affair."

"How did he find out?" Wyatt asked.

I shook my head. "I don't know. The logical guess is that they did fertility testing and my father found out he was sterile. It would explain why he never remarried and tried to have more kids. In any case, they both took it as gospel, so it must be true."

"So what happened?"

"My mother was upset, and I didn't understand what was going on. I only knew my father quit coming home most nights. Then my mother got in that accident, and I was left alone." I shifted in my seat to look at him. "Only it turns out it wasn't an accident. My father had her killed."

He squeezed my hand. "God, Carly. I'm sorry."

I didn't respond. I didn't see the point. "Hired help raised me until my father thought I was too old for a nanny. After that, I was alone in our mansion until I left for college, but through it all, I had Jake."

"Your former fiancé?" he asked in surprise.

"One and the same. He was my best friend growing up, but now I'm pretty sure my father used him to keep tabs on me. He couldn't be bothered to watch me himself." I released a short laugh. "I didn't understand why my father didn't love me anymore, so I decided I must be unlovable."

"Carly."

I couldn't bring myself to look at him. "When I left for school, I swore I was never going back. That I was leaving forever. I went out east and got a college degree and a master's in elementary education. But my father had left his mark on me, and I never really let myself get close to anyone. So when Jake called me and begged me to come back to Dallas, I went. Mostly because I was lonely, and I'd never really put down roots anywhere else."

"You started datin' him?" he asked, his voice tight.

"No," I said, then took a second to gather my thoughts. "No, I got a job at my old private school and fell in love with a new batch of students every year. It felt safe. I knew they were leaving me, so it made it easier to get close to them." I shook my head. "That sounds pathetic."

"No. Believe it or not, I can relate. My father manipulated everyone in this town, including my friends. I never trusted anyone."

"What about Max?" I asked, glancing at him. "Did you trust him?"

"Max was the only one I *could* trust. Until I broke away from my father." He sat up straighter. "You said men wanted you for your inheritance, so there must have been men in your life."

"I dated," I admitted. "I had a few semiserious relationships, but they all ended the same way. With the guy falling all over himself to meet my father. I'd just ended the last one—a guy I was *sure* was different—until I found out he wasn't. So I did what I always did and cried on Jake's shoulder. He was between his many girlfriends, and we went out and got drunk, and the next thing I knew he proposed."

"You weren't even datin'?"

"We hadn't even kissed at that point."

"But you said yes?"

I sighed, feeling like a fool. "We were friends and I *really* wanted to have a family someday. I figured I knew what I was getting with Jake. I could trust him." Releasing a bitter laugh, I said, "Boy was I wrong." When he didn't respond, I added, "Jake convinced me that the best component of a relationship was friendship. That we would eventually fall in love and we'd grow old together as best friends. That we'd raise our kids in a stable environment, and not the way we'd been raised."

When he didn't comment, I said, "You must think I'm an idiot."

"No," he said. "Quite the opposite. So why did you run? What happened?"

"The rehearsal dinner was at my father's house, and after the meal, Jake and my father wandered upstairs. I wondered what was taking them so long, so I went to find them." I waited for the tears to come, but my eyes remained remarkably dry. "They were in my father's upstairs study, smoking cigars and discussing the timeline of my upcoming accident. My father suggested that it should happen a few months after the wedding—not too soon for people to get suspicious, but not long enough for Jake to lose his nerve. To his credit, Jake said he thought it should be later." My throat tightened. "At least until I'd had a baby or two to preserve the family lineage. Otherwise, my father's partners might protest."

"What the fuck, Carly?" he asked, pulling his hand from mine and gripping the steering wheel so tightly it made a screeching sound. His outrage rose with every word. "Why would they kill you? Why not have the bastard divorce you? Or better yet, not marry you at all. Just hand it over to the fucker, since it sounds like you never wanted the money anyway?"

"I've since found out that my father's part of an international crime syndicate called the Hardshaw Group. Three men run it, all successful businessmen in their own right. They made some archaic rule that their positions can only be handed down to blood. If the inheriting biological child dies, then the spouse can take over. And since he must have realized that I didn't have the stomach for it, he needed a son-in-law he could trust. He'd been grooming Jake for years, and Jake was just biding his time until I was weak enough to marry someone I didn't love. I suspect he paid a few of the jerks I'd dated to make sure I was primed and desperate enough to accept his proposal."

He was silent for a long stretch before he said in a calmer tone, "So you overheard them then ran?"

"Yeah. I went to a friend Jake didn't know about and stayed with him for the weekend while I tried to figure out what to do. Austin and I both decided the best thing I could do was run. He gave me his mother's old car, and I took off toward Arkansas, where my car promptly died outside of a town called Henryetta. I was fortunate that two women found me and took me in. Rose gave me a job and let me stay at her house. The last month I took care of her dying sister."

"Jesus, Carly. I feel like an ass over the way I treated you with Hank. You're more qualified to take care of him than I am."

I shook my head. "No. Violet was dying from leukemia. There weren't any wounds to take care of, and she spent most of her last days sleeping." Tears streaked down my cheeks. "I only knew her two months, but her death ripped my heart out."

"Is that why you left?" he asked.

I wiped the tears from my face. "No. I found out that someone from Hardshaw had discovered I was there. So I left, because I don't have any evidence implicating my father or Jake, and Hardshaw's too big and powerful for one person to fight. I can't get justice for my mother or for me, but I can get justice for Seth."

"You don't have to find justice for Seth alone. I loved that boy. I want to make his killers pay for his death as much or more than you do." Silence lingered between us for a moment. Then he said, "You know more about his murder than you've let on."

It was time to tell him.

"I do," I admitted.

He shot me a glance.

"You've suspected," I said. "Don't look so surprised."

"I'm surprised you're tellin' me is all. Hank knows what you saw. That's why you went to see him in the hospital."

"Seth asked me to give him a message and warned me not to tell the sheriff. I was hoping Hank would know who to turn to for help."

"He didn't suggest me?" he asked, his voice tight.

"No, but I think part of it was to protect you."

"But most of it was because he doesn't trust me."

We both knew he was right.

"What about you?" he asked. "Do you trust me?"

"I'm about to tell you what I saw. I think that's answer enough." And I did. I told him about waking up and seeing the three men. About setting off my car alarm and watching, helpless, as that man shot Seth and then took off with the others in the red truck. About running out and finding Seth bleeding to death. Listening to Seth's last words. Sending Max to find the gun and key fob only to learn they were missing. But I held back the numbers on Seth's hand, because it might make him change his mind about going to Ewing. If his source knew something, I wasn't going to give Wyatt a reason to cancel.

He was quiet for nearly a minute, and I could see he was processing everything.

"Somebody knows you're lyin'. They have the proof with your gun and your key fob."

"Max swears a deputy couldn't have gotten it. Do you think *he* took them?" I didn't think so, but Wyatt had known his brother far longer.

"No. Max is too protective of you to have set you up. He's not lyin'.""

Relief rushed through me, I wanted to able to trust Max.

I gave Wyatt a tight smile. "When you came into the tavern and accused me of doing something, I wondered if you'd found them."

His jaw tightened. "I've been an utter ass to you. I'm sorry."

"No," I said. "I like that you're so protective of them."

"I'm protective of the people I care about Carly." Something in his words warmed my blood...and other parts.

We were closing in on Drum as I turned sideways in my seat to face him. "I am too."

He slowed down and gave me a long, searching look. "I know."

He pulled into a parking spot across the street from the library and put the truck in park. Tucking his leg at an angle on the seat, he turned to face me completely. "I don't feel good about leavin' you. I'm worried Bingham might try to snatch you and question you about what you know."

I realized I hadn't filled him in on that part. "He won't. Unless he's not a man of his word."

His body stiffened. "What did Hank do?"

"It was my doing," I said. "It seemed the safest way to get him to let me be."

"What arrangement did you make?"

"We're meeting in public for ten minutes, and we get to ask each other questions."

His eyes nearly popped out of his head. "You want to ask Bingham questions? Have you lost your mind? Do you plan to tell him everything?"

"No. Hank said it's never best to show your hand right off the bat, and in this instance, I think he's right. I plan to tell Bingham as little as possible and let him sort the rest out."

"Todd Bingham's no fool. You can't string him along, Carly."

"I don't plan to. And I'm counting on the public place to keep me safe."

He grimaced. "Maybe it will. Maybe it won't. When and where are you meetin'?"

"I don't know." And it worried me more than I wanted to let on.

"All the more reason for me to stay close. Maybe Ewing's a bad idea."

"No, if there's even the slightest chance your source knows something, you need to go," I said. "And I have another purpose for going to the library—I'm hoping to get onto a computer to do some internet sleuthing."

He frowned, looking like he was at war with himself. Finally, he said, "Don't use the computer at the library. Go to the garage and use mine. In fact, when you finish at the library, call Junior and have him walk you to the garage and then the tavern. I'll give you a ride back to Hank's after you finish your shift. The old man will have to suck it up because I'm stayin'. I'm not leavin' you alone tonight. If someone breaks in, I plan to be there to kick his ass to kingdom come."

I smiled up at him.

"What?" he asked, his brow furrowed.

"Nothing," I said, feeling like a fool. The last thing I should do was indulge in my feelings for him, or encourage any feelings he might have for me.

I released my seatbelt and started to reach for the door handle.

"Carly."

I turned back to face him, then sucked in a breath when I saw the longing in his eyes. Every nerve ending in my body pinged.

His hand lifted to my cheek as he lowered his mouth to mine in a surprising gentle kiss. When he lifted his head, he smiled. "I've been wantin' to do that since I saw you sittin' on that rock at the overlook."

Before I could respond, he kissed me again, this time with a hunger that matched my own. Needing more of him, I lifted my hand to the back of his neck, pressing him closer and tilting my head to give him better access.

He groaned and my body reacted with a primal urge I'd never felt with another man. And *that* was what brought me to my senses.

I pulled back, my chest heaving, and I took some satisfaction in the fact that Wyatt was in the same state.

"I can't," I said, sliding back toward the door to get some distance.

"I'm sorry," he said. "I told myself I wouldn't kiss you, but you're…" His voice trailed off.

"I'm not sorry you kissed me," I said. "And obviously I kissed you back. But…" How did I explain this without insulting him and destroying the bridge of trust we'd just spanned? "I trust you to keep me safe, Wyatt. And I trust you to help find Seth's murderer. But after what happened with Jake, I'm not sure I can trust any man with my heart." Despite everything that had transpired between us since meeting a few days ago, I knew Wyatt was a good man, and he deserved more than what I could give him. I had so little to offer.

And here I was, keeping secrets from him still, having withheld Seth's numbers from him. But I'd tell him when he came back.

He gave me a sad smile. "We'll take it slow. Give me time."

I just smiled and scooted out of the car. We both knew time was a luxury I didn't have. As soon as I found some closure for Hank and some justice for Seth, I had to leave town.

Suddenly, I wasn't so eager to go.

Chapter
Twenty-Six

W hen I looked back at Wyatt from the door of the library, he was still sitting there in his truck, keeping watch. I gave him a little wave and a smile, and he smiled back and took off toward Ewing.

The library was smaller than I'd imagined, and a quick glance told me there were more DVDs than books. The DVDs occupied four rows of shelves along the left side of the space, while three computer stations were situated along the right wall, currently in use by an older man, an even older woman, and a man in his twenties. The librarian sat at a desk at the wall opposite the front door, and she was on her own computer. Books lined the wall behind her, and the room opened past the computer stations, revealing an alcove full of books. In the middle of the book alcove was a small table with two beat-up elementary school chairs.

The middle-aged librarian greeted me with a warm smile.

"I'm looking for diabetic cookbooks," I said, "but I don't have a library card."

"I'm Carnita," she said, her eyes bright. "Welcome to the Drum Library. You can't check out any books, but you're welcome to look at whatever you'd like." She stood and walked around the desk. "I take it you're here for Hank?"

I nodded, unsure if it was a good thing she knew who I was when I hadn't introduced myself, but she seemed pleased. "I've been trying to push information on that man for years. Let's hope you're more successful."

She led me to a small section of cookbooks and pulled one out. "We don't have many, but this is a good one."

"Thanks, Carnita," I said. "I'll take a look." She headed back to her desk while I carried the book back to the table and took a small notebook out of my purse, taking notes. I'd been working for about fifteen minutes when I felt someone brush by me then take a seat on the opposite side of the table.

My heart kick-started when I realized it was Bingham.

He smiled, but it didn't reach his eyes. "This public enough for you?"

I didn't answer.

He removed his phone from his coat pocket and opened the screen. Once he had his clock app open, he set the timer for ten minutes.

"I believe we agreed on ten minutes?" he asked with a quirked brow, setting the phone down between us without starting the timer. I suspected he was a good decade and a half older than me, but it wasn't obvious from his appearance—until you looked in his eyes. His eyes bore the weight of all the hard living he'd done. They were hard and dark, and I could tell they'd seen things that would likely give me nightmares. And he'd been the cause of many of them.

"That's right," I said, hoping I sounded assertive and not as terrified as I felt. "But do you think it's smart having this conversation in a library where everyone can hear us?"

He gestured to the area behind me. "There's no one here. Just you and me."

I turned around, and sure enough, Carnita and the people who had been using the computers were nowhere to be seen.

When I spun back to face him, he was grinning. "I'm not sure what you've heard about me, but I'm not as scary as everyone claims."

I gave him a sideways glance, trying to pretend I wasn't afraid of him. "I suspect you're an intelligent man. A stupid man wouldn't be in the position you're in now."

He grinned. "I'll take that as a compliment."

"It was meant as one." I took a breath. "An intelligent man would read the person he was interviewing and adjust his attitude to put them at ease…or to intimidate them. Whichever the situation required."

He scooted his chair back and crossed his legs, which were too long to comfortably fit under the small table. He wasn't a huge man, but the chairs were on the dainty side, making him look like he'd stepped onto the set of an *Alice in Wonderland* production. "And what does this situation call for?"

I leaned back in my chair as well. "I'm not some hardened criminal, so you'll try to appeal to my reasonable side. If that doesn't work, you'll pull out the intimidation, but you would prefer to start with the soft approach."

He laughed. "You see that in an episode of *Law and Order?*"

"No. That's how I'd do it."

He laughed again. "You sure you're not that drug runner from Atlanta?"

I gestured to his phone. "Shouldn't that be running now?"

His eyes lit up with amusement, and he reached for the phone, pressing the start button. "How'd you end up movin' in with Hank Chalmers?"

"I went to visit him in the hospital and found out that he wouldn't be able to come home unless someone brought him back to Drum. I needed a place to stay, so we worked out a barter."

"Why'd you go see him?"

"I held his grandson's hand while he died. I thought Hank might like to meet the person who'd comforted Seth in his last moments." I figured his next questions would be about those last moments, so I was surprised when he didn't address it.

"Seems like Hank's pretty taken with you for only knowin' you a couple of days."

I shrugged and quoted Shakespeare. "'Misery acquaints a man with strange bedfellows.'"

His eyes narrowed. "Only you're not sleepin' with him."

I groaned in disgust. "What is everyone's fascination with me sleepin' with Hank? He's old enough to be my father and crotchety enough to be my grandfather."

"No, you're hookin' up with Wyatt Drummond."

I forced myself to shake my head. "You heard wrong."

"That wasn't you kissin' the man outside the library?" he asked with a grin. He gestured to his phone. "I've got a photo if you'd like to see it."

My chest tightened. I was certain a man like Bingham did everything for a reason, which meant he had a reason for mentioning Wyatt. But the bigger concern was that he or one of his cronies had been stalking me.

"You've spent thirty seconds discussing your take on my personal life. Is that really how you want to use your time?"

His smile fell and his face became expressionless except for the hard glint in his eyes. "I'm just tryin' to figure you out."

"There's nothing to figure out. You want to talk about the night Seth died, so I suggest we get right to it, because I'm holding you to the ten minutes."

"Why don't you tell me what you saw?"

"I'm sure you've heard the story by now."

"That you woke up and found him dyin'? I call bullshit."

"So what do you *think* I saw?"

"You saw him get killed. For all I know, you're the one who took the drugs."

"I thought we'd already confirmed that I'm not a drug dealer from Georgia," I said. "It was a coincidence that my car broke down the same night the dealer was supposed to come to Drum."

"The dealer was supposed to stay at the Alpine Inn, and you were there too. You're the only stranger who rented a room that night."

"What about on the weekend?" I asked. "Seems Max doesn't get much traffic. Someone could have rented a room, hidden the stash in it, then notified the buyers a day or two later."

"Wouldn't be smart to leave that much product unsupervised," Bingham said. "Especially since Max sometimes rents those rooms at an hourly rate."

Gross. "So you're suggesting the person never showed?" I asked.

"Seems to me," he said slowly, "that the real dealer wouldn't make as much fuss as you did when you came to town. Then again, what do I know?" He winked and shot me a wry grin.

Did he think I was the dealer after all? "If the dealer never showed, then why were Cecil and his friends searching the rooms? Why was Seth there?"

"Because I told him I expected a drug deal to go down there. I already suspected there were traitors in my midst, and I didn't want to clue them in. So I told the boy I'd make it worth his while if he went as my eyes and ears."

"You asked a teenage boy to watch hardened criminals in the middle of a transaction?" I asked, outraged.

He shrugged. "The boy wasn't as innocent as you might think. He'd done a few things that could have gotten him into trouble."

Something about the way he said it caught my attention. "You threatened to expose him."

He scoffed. "I didn't need to threaten him with anything. He agreed to be my eyes and ears, but I warned him not to interfere. I can't help thinkin' he tried to apprehend them."

"You put him in the position to be killed," I said, my anger rising. "This is your fault."

"I caught him spyin' on me. I had a choice—tell him what he wanted to know or let him go and lose face. Third option was beatin' the shit out of him." He leaned closer and lowered his voice. "Most people would find this hard to believe, but I don't cotton to beatin' up teenage boys who are set on avengin' their mother's death."

"Well, aren't *you* the nice guy."

His attitude shifted, from defensive to sly as he narrowed his eyes. "Let's back up to something else. You said they were searchin' rooms. What makes you say that?"

Oh. Shit.

"Why else would they be busting down doors?" I asked, thinking quickly. "Cecil showed up at Hank's looking for the stash. Stands to reason that's what they were doing at the motel."

"So you're just speculatin'?" he asked.

"Of course. Isn't that what most people do when they only have a few pieces of information? They take what they know and try to make it fit."

He scanned me up and down, although his perusal felt more calculating than it did lustful. "Yeah," he finally said. "That's exactly what they do." He paused. "You keep usin' *they* when you talk about the people who did this. As in more than one," he said. "I find that peculiar."

319

"Why? It's like Hank said, Cecil talked about looking for the stash for his buddies. Stands to reason there are more of them."

"Cecil could have done this on his own. Just because his buddies wanted a piece of the stash doesn't mean they were involved in the murder." He tilted his head toward me. "Got anything else to volunteer?" When I didn't say anything, he asked, "Which hand did you hold while the boy was dyin'?"

"Does it matter?"

"It seems to matter to *you* since you're not willin' to tell me. Shouldn't be too hard to figure out."

I knew where he was headed with this question, and I had no idea how to thwart his agenda other than to play dumb. "Well, when you put it that way, I guess I was on his left side."

"So you held his left hand?"

"Yes."

He gave me a long look. "You didn't notice anything on his hand?" he pressed.

My pulse escalated. He knew about the numbers. Did he also know what they meant?

I shook my head, hoping my directness would sell my story. "Should I have?"

He frowned. "You promised me a piece of information that you claimed the sheriff's office didn't have."

"All in good time," I said. "This is supposed to be a question and answer session, not an interrogation."

A smirk lit up his eyes. "I prefer the word interview."

"Call it what you like, it's still the same thing." I narrowed my eyes. Then in a risky and perhaps foolish move, I decided to goad him. "I've heard that Bart Drummond runs this town."

A fire flashed in his eyes and then quickly faded to indifference. So he was a man who could control his temper.

"The Drummonds are history in this town. They may have run it in the past, but I'm in charge now."

"Does Bart Drummond know that?"

The left corner of his mouth lifted and a playfulness danced in his eyes. "Where'd you come from, girl?"

"I'm not a girl. I'm a woman who happened to be passing through and got stuck in a nightmare. I intend on finding my way out, so answer my question. Does Bart know you're running it?"

"He's deluded himself into thinking he's in charge," he smirked.

"So *you're* in charge?"

His grin spread. "That's right."

"And someone's trying to take over your turf." I paused, then added, "Or take it back."

He chuckled. "You think Bart Drummond's trying to take over my drug business?"

"I don't know," I said. "But if he wants the town back and you're in charge, then it stands to reason he needs to knock you off your throne."

He studied me again, more intensely than before. "So you have a theory?"

"No," I said. "Just tryin' to make the pieces fit."

Uncrossing his legs, he leaned forward. "Bart Drummond is as crooked as it gets, but he'd never lower himself into the gutter of drugs."

I shrugged. "You know this town better than me, but it's obvious that you have dissension in your ranks. Cecil Abrams was one of your own."

He was silent for a moment, then leaned back again, his face inscrutable. "And what about Dwight Henderson?"

Had he heard about my run-in with Dwight? "I don't follow."

His brow lifted. "Do you think *he* was one of the murderers?"

"And how would I know that?"

"We've established there was more than one," he said, crossing his arms. "And we know one of my men was involved. We've deduced that someone is trying to horn in on my business. What do you know about Dwight?"

"I know he worked at Mobley's funeral home until he was fired yesterday."

"Wonder why he was so pissed to have lost his job?" Bingham asked with a sly grin.

"No," I said slowly, "but I have a feeling you do."

"Guess where Mobley gets his caskets?"

Dread pooled in my gut. "Atlanta."

He sat up and pointed a finger at me. "I knew you were a smart woman."

"So the drugs didn't come into Drum at all?"

"The drugs didn't come on Monday night. The dealer got scared off." The pleased look on his face clued me in on who'd run them off. "But the plan was to send the drug shipments with the caskets. The motel meeting was supposed to confirm the details…and according to my source, bring a few samples."

My heart sank. "Seth was there waiting for his proof to bring back to you. He died for nothing."

"He didn't die for nothin'. He flushed out two of the interlopers, and a traitor to boot."

There were multiple things wrong with his statement, the greatest of which was his acceptance of Seth's death as collateral damage. But very high up on that list was the fact that I would have recognized Dwight's voice if he'd been in that parking lot. Could he have been the driver?

"Do you have any idea how many people are involved in this project?" I asked.

He laughed. "Project? I like that." He shook his head in amusement, but his smile quickly faded. "No, but I suspect you can help fill in some of the blanks."

I tried to keep my breath even and my body still so I didn't give away my fear. "Hypothetically speaking," I said slowly, "let's say I do know more than I've been lettin' on. What guarantee do I have that it's enough to placate you?"

"I guess you don't," he said. "It's a high-risk game for all of us."

"So let's say I *did* see more, why wouldn't I have told the sheriff?"

"That is a mighty fine question indeed," he said. "By the time I left the bar that night, I knew you weren't the dealer. You were too inept. Too soft." His gaze lowered to my chest, and then he glanced back up with a grin. "But if you were who you claimed to be, you'd have no reason to lie to the sheriff, and I know you did. Which means the boy warned you that they were crooked."

It was on my lips to agree with him. To tell him he'd guessed correctly. So why didn't I just tell him everything and be done with it?

Because I ran the risk of signing their death warrant. I suspected Bingham was his own judge, jury, and executioner.

He shifted in his seat, a knowing grin lighting up his face. "You know, the Alpine Inn is fairly close to your boyfriend's garage."

Panic swamped my thoughts, addling my senses. I quickly pulled myself together.

He knew.

"What are you talking about?" I asked, trying to sound stumped.

"A car alarm went off the night of Seth's murder."

"And how do you know that?"

"There were other people there that night," Bingham said. "People who didn't see things but heard them. Loud voices. A car alarm, then gunshots." He leaned forward. "See, that's the important part. The car alarm went off *before* the gunshots. Why do you suppose that was?"

Sweat broke out at the nape of my neck. "So you think someone saw something and set off the alarm?"

Confidence lit up his eyes. "I can understand your hesitation." He held his hands out at his sides. "You're holding cards I want. Cards I need to play my hand. You're worried what I'll do once I get 'em, but you ain't got nothin' to be worried about. I only go after my enemies." His face changed, and I could see he was about to whip out intimidation tactics, just as I'd predicted.

He leaned in, within arm's reach of me, and quirked a brow. "Are you my enemy, Carly Moore?"

Fear was a cold lump in my chest. "I'm no one's enemy."

"See, that's not true. People standing in my way are my enemy, and you, Carly Moore are standing in my way."

I glanced at his phone surprised it hadn't gone to sleep. The timer was forty-three seconds from going off. "I promised you information the sheriff didn't have." By admitting this, I was letting him know I was aware of so much more, but with my person-of-interest status, the sheriff's department was my greatest threat at the moment. Bingham was a very close second. Maybe I could take care of both at the same time by sending him after a deputy. "You were right about why I didn't tell the sheriff's department everything."

His smile was full of evil. "*Now* we're gettin' somewhere."

"Seth said it was a sheriff's deputy who pulled the trigger."

His eyes widened. "Is that so?"

"Didn't expect that?"

He cocked his head and pursed his lips as though weighing his decision to answer. "No," he finally said. "I didn't."

Then I told a lie. "He said three men confronted him in the parking lot, and a fourth man drove them away."

His eyes narrowed. "What else did he share?"

"He wanted me to tell Hank that he was sorry."

He gave a slight nod. "What else?"

The timer went off, and an annoyed look crossed his face. I stood. "Looks like our time is done."

He stood too. "Is it?"

"I don't have anything else to share with you, Bingham."

"Maybe you don't want to share it, but you know more. That car alarm that went off before the boy was shot?" He paused. "That car was yours. I know that for a fact, and no one was at the garage at the time, which means *you* set it off."

My heartbeat pulsed in my head.

He leaned closer. "Dwight Henderson crossed me. You don't want you or your new friends to end up like him." He took a step back and smiled. "I'll give you some time to think about it."

Then he walked past me and out of the library.

Chapter
Twenty-Seven

What had happened to Dwight Henderson?

I closed my notebook and grabbed my purse, realizing I'd never once thought about using my gun. Then again, he hadn't given me reason to, but the threat for the future was clear. What if I told him everything I knew and it wasn't enough to appease him?

What if I'd handled this all wrong?

I shot out the front door and headed down the sidewalk toward the bar instead of Wyatt's garage, because I needed to see my friends with my own eyes to make sure they were safe. But I caught something out of the corner of my eye, and I noticed Jerry standing next to the edge of Watson's Café. When he saw me, he ducked his head and took off toward the Laundromat, in the opposite direction of the tavern and motel.

Was Jerry spying on me for Bingham? Even if there wasn't a photo as he'd claimed, *someone* had reported seeing me with Wyatt. Bingham had said people had heard things in the motel parking lot. Had he meant Jerry?

I hustled to the tavern and burst through the door, worried the actual murderers would nab me off the street and make sure

I took anything I might know to my grave. All the more reason to be open with Bingham, right?

But it felt so wrong.

"Carly," Max said in surprise. "What are you doin' here already? Your shift doesn't start for a couple of hours."

I took a look around the room and saw there were only two occupied tables—an older couple and a man who looked to be in his forties.

Ruth appeared at the entrance to the back. She paused when she saw me and hurried forward. "From the look on your face, you've heard the news."

"What news?"

"Then you don't know?"

"What happened?"

A peek at Max confirmed that he knew what she was talking about. He walked around to the front of the bar and shot a glance at the customers. "We should go in the back."

"Is Hank okay?" I asked in a near panic. "Oh, my God. *Is it Wyatt?*"

Ruth's nose scrunched with her confusion. "Wyatt?"

Max gently took my arm and guided me to the back, next to the food counter. "Detective Daniels was in here earlier, askin' questions about what happened last night." He paused and held my gaze. "Carly, Dwight Henderson was murdered."

I felt myself start to sway.

Bingham had killed Dwight Henderson, and he'd *bragged* about it.

"Whoa there." Max slipped an arm around my back to keep me upright.

"What happened?"

"Nobody seems to know," Max said. "We only know they found his body by the dump outside of town."

"Detective Daniels thinks I did it?" I whispered.

327

"He didn't say that," Ruth said reassuringly. "But he was askin' a lot of questions about what happened here and what happened at the funeral home."

"You didn't see him last night after I dropped you off, did you?" Max asked. "He didn't drop by and threaten you?"

I nearly laughed. "No. He didn't."

But Cecil Abrams had, and no matter how much we'd cleaned, it was inevitable we'd left some sort of DNA evidence behind.

Which Bingham was fully aware of.

He'd intentionally put me in a tight bind so he would have control of me.

"Who brought you into town?" Ruth asked with a frown.

I ran a hand over my hair. I needed to think. "Wyatt. He had to run down to Ewing, so he dropped me off at the library. That's where I've been for the last hour or so."

"What were you doin' at the library?" Max asked as though it was the silliest thing he'd ever heard. "The waiting list for the computers is days long."

"I was looking at diabetic cookbooks."

"Why did you think something happened to Wyatt?" Ruth asked, hanging on to the Wyatt issue like a dog with a bone.

"Uh…" I couldn't tell them Bingham had already run him off the road once. "Nothin' feels safe right now, and the only other people I have a vested interest in are standing next to me." I flashed a smile at Tiny through the pass-through above the food counter so he knew I was including him.

He smiled back. "Don't worry, Little Bit. You'll be okay."

Was he referring to my situation with the sheriff or the overall danger? I hoped to God he was right. I could use a break.

"You're shakin' like a leaf," Max said, worry in his voice. "Do you want to go rest in my apartment upstairs? You can watch TV or take a nap."

"Actually," I said. "I was going to go to Wyatt's garage to use his computer." Then, so he didn't get suspicious, I added, "To look up more recipes. The library only had a few cookbooks and I suspect I'll find some on Pinterest."

"Just use the computer in my office," Max said. "I'm not plannin' on goin' in there, and that way we know you're safe. I don't like the idea of you walkin' down there by yourself."

"Thanks," I said gratefully, then gave him a hug. Truth be told, I didn't like the thought either, and it seemed foolish to call Junior to have him escort me.

Max grinned. "The password to get into the computer is taped to the wall."

"That doesn't seem very safe," I said.

Ruth snorted. "That's what I've been tellin' him."

Max headed back to the dining room, but Ruth stayed and gave me a scrutinizing once-over. "You've got a thing for Wyatt Drummond."

"Why do you say that?" I asked, but my cheeks flushed.

She pushed out a huge sigh. "Girl. That man doesn't get attached to *anyone* or *anything*. You need to steer clear or you're destined for heartache."

That wasn't true. Wyatt had gotten close to Seth, something she clearly knew given she was the one who'd told me. I was about to confront her with it, but she sighed, muttering that women were fools when it came to love, and headed back to the dining room too.

"Don't you listen to her," Tiny said, leaning his elbow on the window ledge. "Wyatt Drummond's a good man."

Relief flooded through me. "Then why does she seem to hate him?"

I couldn't help wondering if she knew something I didn't. She definitely had more history with him.

"That's her story to tell, not mine, but I *will* say that her judgment of him is clouded because of it."

I nodded.

"Have you eaten yet?"

"I had a turkey sandwich earlier."

"Pfft! You go get settled in Max's office. I'll send Bitty in with the lunch special. Homemade mac and cheese. My special recipe."

Tears stung my eyes. "Thanks, Tiny."

He gave me a sharp nod. "We take care of our own."

There it was again. That feeling of being included. Of being protected and cared for. Of being part of something larger than myself.

My heart gave me a little nudge.

What if I didn't leave? What if I stayed like I had in Arkansas?

But that was plain insanity. I was a person of interest in two murders, and a powerful, criminal madman was threatening me. Yet I was smart enough to know that I'd lucked into this position of belonging. All those years I'd spent on the East Coast had been long and lonely, and if I left Drum, I suspected I'd only find more of the same.

I shook my head. This was premature. I needed to get myself out of danger before I considered staying.

But if I intended to stay, I'd have to change my tactics in how I handled Bingham.

I'd figure that out later.

Heading into the small office, I pulled out the chair and promptly banged it into the wall as I made room to squeeze my legs into the desk's kneehole. The room couldn't be more than six or seven feet wide and just about as deep. I strongly suspected it was a repurposed closet.

The computer login info was where Max had said it would be, and Ruth was right. He needed to be more careful with it, especially since he had a spreadsheet open for the tavern's expenses and income. I minimized the screen, then opened a browser. After I logged into my VPN, which showed my location as Minnesota, I went to the eyecam website and found the login section. If the numbers on Seth's hand were the password, I'd still need a username. Whoever else had the numbers may have tried to log in too. Only they likely didn't know what service he'd used.

Bitty appeared in the doorway with a bowl and some silverware.

"I'm not a waitress," she said in a tone that let me know she considered my position beneath hers.

"I appreciate you bringing my food, Bitty," I said, meaning it. "I would have been happy to come get it."

I took her glare to mean I hadn't appeased her. Sighing, I picked up the bowl and took a bite of the creamy, cheesy noodles. Tiny was right. I really needed comfort food right now.

Eyeing the phone on Max's desk, I considered calling Hank and asking him if he could guess Seth's username, but I doubted he would know. I should have told Wyatt about the numbers when I'd had the chance. He might have known something.

That thought reminded me that Junior was likely waiting for my call at the garage. I picked up the receiver and dialed his number.

"Hi, Junior," I said after he answered. "This is Carly." I explained that I was in Max's office and wouldn't need his escort.

"Wyatt's about to have a minor stroke, lookin' for you," he said. "I'm sure you've heard the news about Dwight Henderson by now. A sheriff's deputy came by asking about you and Dwight."

"I did hear," I said. "They came to the garage?"

"Wyatt's scared they're gonna try to pin it on you."

I suspected he had reason to be scared. "Is he back yet?"

"No, he's still in Ewing, but I think he's on his way back. I'll tell him where he can find you. Stay put."

"Trust me, I'm not going anywhere."

Since I had no idea how to get into Seth's account, I decided to do a search for Wyatt's father. Everyone kept insisting that Bart would never dirty himself with drugs, but I suspected the same would be said of my father.

When I typed in Bart's name, the first thing to come up was Drummond Lumber, which had closed ten years ago. The Drummond family had owned the logging company for nearly a century, but they'd been forced to close it due to federal logging restrictions. The town had lost nearly one hundred jobs.

I tried to imagine my father's reaction if the oil company his father had founded were to go bankrupt. It would be a massive understatement to say he wouldn't take it well.

The other reports were about Bart Drummond's fight to stop the feds from moving the Balder Mountain trailhead, and then the subsequent decline of Drum.

On the second page, there was a post about Wyatt's arrest for robbery, breaking and entering, and his DUI. I typed Wyatt Drummond into the search bar and a whole page of posts popped up—the news report I'd already seen, along with several different versions, including one that featured an interview with the young woman who had been arrested with him—Heather Stone. She claimed to be innocent of all wrongdoing and worried that Bart Drummond would pin the robbery on her. The other posts were about Wyatt's hearing and bail—set at thirty thousand dollars. A few more about the robbery dropped charges, and finally one about his trial and conviction for a DUI and breaking and entering. He was sentenced to three years in prison and given a five-thousand-dollar fine. The article stated that the punishment was extremely unusual since Wyatt hadn't been involved in any kind of accident, the owner had declined to press charges, and it was his first offense, but he'd likely only serve two years with good behavior. Bart Drummond had refused comment.

I typed in Heather Stone next, and very little came back. A few posts about Wyatt's arrest that listed her name, the post where she'd confessed her fear at being railroaded, and one about her refusal to testify.

I typed in Todd Bingham next, surprised at how few results came up. Bingham might be the reigning king of the town, but he'd apparently stayed clean in the eyes of the law.

Dwight Henderson was next. There was more about him—including the domestic violence arrest a year ago and several robbery and possession charges, all dropped or pled down to lesser charges that involved a few months of jail time. Nothing about his murder yet.

Next, I searched for Barb Chalmers. Her overdose was front and center, along with her boyfriend's vandalism spree and murder by a sheriff's deputy—Timothy Spigot. The post showed photos of Barb, her boyfriend George Davis, and Deputy Spigot. (Something about him looked familiar, although I was certain I hadn't seen him in the tavern. Had he been at the crime scene?) There was an obituary notice for Barb, as well as an obituary for Mary Chalmers, Hank's wife.

I considered searching for Jerry, but I didn't have his last name. An uneasy feeling washed over me when I thought about him, quickly followed by disappointment. I'd really liked Jerry. But then I reminded myself I didn't have proof that he'd been spying on me.

"Carly?"

I'd been so absorbed in my work that I hadn't heard anyone approach. My stomach fluttered when I saw Wyatt leaning against the doorframe.

"Hi," I said softly.

He entered the office and sat on the corner of the desk, worry in his eyes. "Has Daniels come by to talk to you?"

"No." I hesitated, then said, "I'd bet good money that Bingham killed him. He told me to be careful or I'd end up like Henderson."

His jaw tightened and fury filled his eyes. "Bingham threatened you? When? *Here?*"

"No," I said. "The library."

He got to his feet, looking like he was about to rush out the door and hunt Bingham down.

I jumped up and grabbed his arm to keep him in place. "He dropped by to get his ten minutes in a public place." I glanced at the clock on the wall. I had less than ten minutes now before I had to report for my shift. "There's something I didn't tell you about the night Seth died." When he didn't react, I added, "He told me that he found evidence."

His eyes flew wide. "*What?* Why didn't you tell me before?" Then he shook his head. "No. It doesn't matter. You need to trust me at your own pace."

"I was worried if I told you, you might not meet your source in Ewing. Did you find out anything that will help?"

Pursing his lips, he shook his head. "He never showed."

"Does that mean anything? Is your source reliable?"

"I'm not sure what it means."

"There's something I held back from you. I want to tell you now."

"In the scheme of things, it doesn't matter *when* you tell me. I'm just relieved you trust me."

Did he really mean it? Jake had told me things like that during our engagement, saying that we'd learn to love each other, that we could set our own pace, and praising and thanking me with every step closer to a real relationship, especially the physical side. What if Wyatt was doing the same now?

Tears filled my eyes.

"Hey," he said reassuringly as he cupped my face. "I'm not mad, okay? I'm grateful."

I nodded and looked down. "Seth showed me a string of numbers written on the palm of his hand. There was a digital video camera in that motel room, so I can't help but think the numbers are the password or PIN to access the footage. What else could it be?"

He grimaced. "That doesn't do us much good since we don't know where the footage ended up."

"And that's presuming the camera had internet access."

"Max's wifi reaches to the motel. He likely hooked up to it."

"I think I know where to find the footage," I said. "I was searching through the clothes on Seth's floor, and I found a slip of paper in the pocket of a pair of his pants with the web address for a video cam site. All we need is the login name. Any ideas what it could be?"

He frowned. "Maybe. But I really don't want to look at it here. I'd rather use the computer in the garage."

"I'm not waiting," I said. "I've logged into my VPN, and we'll be sure to clear the search history." Something I had neglected to do with his computer.

His face wavered with indecision. "Just give me the code and I'll look it up at my garage."

Was he really just being careful, or did he intend to look at the footage without me? For one awful moment, I wondered if he'd been pumping me for information all along. But something deep inside of me rejected the notion. Even though I'd learned to question my own instincts, I truly believed I could trust this man. Even so, I had promised Seth I'd guard his secrets. I wasn't going to hand them off to someone else.

"No," I said slowly. "I'm not letting you do it without me."

Disappointment filled Wyatt's eyes. "You don't trust me."

"It's not that. Seth gave the code to *me. I* have to be the one to use it."

"You don't trust me," he repeated, more firmly.

"Shelve your stupid pride, Wyatt Drummond," I snapped. "I made that boy a promise, and I aim to keep it. *Me.* I'm not passing the buck. Now what's the username?"

He watched me for several seconds before he said, "Sit down and go to the website."

I plopped back into the chair and quickly pulled up the page. When the sign-in screen appeared, I glanced up at Wyatt.

"SDChalmers03@gmail.com," he said.

"His email address?" I asked. Of course it was.

"Not his main one. Most people don't know about this one. It stands to reason that's what he'd use."

I entered the email, said a quick prayer, and plugged in the code. I held my breath as the site decided whether to give me access.

The screen changed, and a page popped up with several thumbnails of videos.

Wyatt leaned over me, studying the screen. "You did it," he said in awe.

I looked over my shoulder at him. "*We* did it."

He grinned, but any sense of celebration quickly faded as we turned our attention back to the page. Reaching around me, Wyatt put his hand over mine on the mouse and clicked on the last video.

My stomach knotted as the video began to play. The image was bad due to poor lighting, but it was clear enough that we could tell it had been taken in a motel room. Based on the floor plan of the room I'd been assigned, the camera was propped on the bathroom counter, along the wall opposite the door. A few seconds in, the door burst open and two men rushed in. They searched the room, then began to toss things around, obviously looking for something. One of the men opened a closet door and jerked a figure out of his hiding place.

"That's Seth, isn't it?" I asked, feeling nauseated.

"Yeah," he said in a tight voice. "I think so."

One of the men moved toward the camera before he moved out of view, giving us a clear view of his face.

"Do you know him?" I asked, my voice shaking.

"No," he said. "I don't. But he looks familiar."

"He's a deputy sheriff," I said. "Timothy Spigot. I saw his photo while I was looking for information on the internet. He was involved in the shooting death of Barb's boyfriend."

"Shit," Wyatt bit out.

"We can take this to the state police," I said. "With what I witnessed and this video, we can go above the sheriff's department."

He nodded. "Yeah. You're right. Let me call my attorney and get his advice about how to proceed, but we might not be able to go to the state police until tomorrow."

"Do you have cloud storage?" I asked. "The file is too big to email, and I really don't want to download it to Max's computer."

He hesitated. "Yeah, but I rarely use it. I hope I remember how to access it." He directed me to his account, and after three attempts at the password, we got in and I started the download.

"Okay," I said once the download was complete. I shut down the page and logged out of the VPN. Next I cleaned out the search history so no one would be able to see what I'd been doing.

"The funeral's tomorrow," he said softly. "Goin' to the state police will likely take all day."

"Are you saying we can't go to the state police because of the funeral?" I demanded, my temper rising as I swung around to face him. "Isn't getting justice for Seth more important than laying him to rest?"

"Do you really want to leave Hank all alone?" he asked. "Because I'm not lettin' *you* do this by yourself."

He was right. We needed to be here for Hank, but surely we could at least send them the video in advance. I could give my interview after the funeral, or on Saturday. Why was he acting so hesitant?

Perhaps he'd realized what was just now dawning on me. If I went to the state police, my picture might be published or circulated. I could be found.

Either way, I had to do it. I had to get justice for Seth.

"Hey," he said, "I'm not the enemy here, Carly. I want to nail the bastards who did this as much as you do, okay?"

Tears stung my eyes. He was right, and truth be told, he had more emotional investment in this situation than I did.

I glanced up at the clock on the wall. "I've got to go to work. Are you going out to relieve Ginger with Hank?"

His forehead wrinkled. "I don't want to leave with you upset with me. I don't want to leave you alone at all."

"I won't be alone. I'll have Max, and Ruth, and Tiny."

Wyatt still looked worried, but he nodded.

I grabbed my shirt out of my purse and stood.

"I'll be back to pick you up at midnight," he said. He started to reach for me, then stopped.

I smiled up at him. "Okay."

I was tempted to kiss him, but there were too many uncertainties right now. I needed to put my time and energy into making Seth's murderers pay.

I left the room, with Wyatt on my heels, and nearly collided with Jerry on my way to the bathroom. When he saw me, he hightailed it into the dining room.

"Is there a problem?" Wyatt asked when he saw my reaction.

"No," I said, because I had no real proof of anything. I didn't have as much as a hunch he was doing anything wrong... he just seemed to be everywhere I was in town. "We'll talk about it tonight."

Worry filled his eyes, and he nodded. "If you need me, call me at Hank's. I'll come straightaway."

"Thanks." I went into the restroom and changed in a matter of seconds, then emerged from the bathroom to see Bitty coming around the corner from the office with my dirty dishes. She shot me a glare as she headed to the kitchen.

"I was going to bring them back," I called after her, but she ignored me.

I still had to figure out how to win her over, but I had bigger fish to fry. I needed to make it through my shift without getting arrested. Or murdered.

Chapter
Twenty-Eight

The dinner shift was busy, and stayed that way well past eight and into the much less popular, but still well-attended, Thursday Night Football. The Cowboys were playing the Broncos, and the sides were evenly divided in the room.

The crowd was mostly some of the first group of patrons from Monday, but around nine, Bingham and a couple of his cronies showed up. Bingham's gaze searched me out straightaway, and he gave me a knowing smile that didn't reach his eyes.

My heart leapt into my rib cage. He was here for his answers.

Bingham sat at a table by the windows in Ruth's section—away from the crowd huddled in front of the TV. When she went to take his order, he loudly insisted over the hum of the crowd that he wanted to be waited on by the new girl.

I was taking another customer's order for beer and wings, but I cast a glance at a flummoxed Ruth, who gave me a shrug.

Max wasn't as nonchalant. "Carly," he called out. "Can I see you for a moment?"

I glanced back at Bingham before I slipped behind the bar. He looked pretty pleased with himself. It was becoming increasingly clear that Bingham wasn't a fly-under-the-radar kind of guy, despite his relative lack of footprint on the internet.

"You do *not* have to wait on him," Max said when I reached him, his jaw set. "In fact, it's probably better if you don't."

"He's here to see me, Max," I said. "If we get this over with now, maybe he'll leave."

He wrapped a hand around his still sheathed knife handle. "I could force him to leave."

Bingham wasn't a guy to be tangled with, and I couldn't risk Max or Tiny getting hurt or killed on my account. "He'd just track me down later."

"Wyatt can handle him," Max said, although it looked like it pained him to admit it.

"I'd just be putting off the inevitable." And risking the lives of the people I'd begun to care about. I gave Max a reassuring smile. "I can do this."

"Do I need to remind you about Dwight?"

The crowd roared at the TV, half of the men groaning while the others cheered.

"Dwight was an impulsive hothead," I said, leaning closer so he could hear me. "Bingham loves control too much to do anything in here."

Max leveled his gaze on me. "And how do you know Bingham's temperament? He wasn't exactly in control on Monday night." His eyes narrowed. "You've had a run-in with him outside of here, haven't you?"

"I'm okay, Max."

"You don't have to go over there, Carly," Max pleaded. "I've got Carson workin' on it."

My mouth dropped open. "What?"

Max leaned into my ear. "I told you I had an ace up my sleeve. My father still has pull in the county."

Although I knew Max wanted to help, I wouldn't be surprised if his father was partially behind my person-of-interest status. "While I appreciate the offer, I still need to talk to him."

Before I could change my mind, I strode over to Bingham's table.

He was as cocky as the only rooster in a henhouse as I approached him. He saw this exercise in intimidation as a win.

"Have a seat, Carly Moore," he said, gesturing to the empty chair at the table.

"We're having this conversation here?" I asked, slightly incredulous.

The crowd released a string of curses and cheers.

"That's what happens when you meet in a public place. You have *witnesses*," he said, cocking an eyebrow.

I wanted to argue but decided not to waste my breath. I sat in the open chair directly across from him. Gesturing toward his men, both of whom I recognized from Monday night, I said in a firm voice, "I want them to leave the table."

Bingham gave me a cold stare. "We don't have any secrets."

"So fill them in later. You don't see me bringin' my friends over to hold my damn hand," I taunted. It might be a stupid move, but I could tell he was using his men's presence as an intimidation tactic.

Bingham looked at me for what felt like ten minutes but was probably only ten seconds. Finally, he flicked his hand. "Go watch the game."

One of the men got up and walked away without complaint, but the other guy gave me a look that suggested he'd shoot me on the spot if he could get away with it.

"Wilson," Bingham snapped, and the man got up, throwing his chair back several inches in a fit of temper before he stomped off.

I worried Max or Tiny would rush over to my defense, but Bingham had positioned my chair so that my back was to the bar, which I was certain was intentional.

"I've been doin' some investigatin'," Bingham said with a satisfied smirk. "I think I know who the other two guys might be."

I couldn't hide my surprise.

The crowd roared again as he pulled out his phone and tapped his photo app. A crisp image filled the screen. A rough-looking man was sitting on a dirt bike, wearing a white shirt covered in splotches of mud. "Does he look familiar?"

"I didn't see the men in the parking lot, Bingham," I said, sounding as exhausted as I suddenly felt.

His eyes turned cruel as his gaze pinned on me. "The time for lyin' is *done*," he snarled. "Your life just might depend on it."

I swallowed down my fear and waited for him to continue.

Bingham swiped his screen, pulling up a new photo. "What about him?"

He held up the screen for my perusal.

The image was of a man in camo with a rifle slung over his shoulder, holding up the head of a deer carcass by the antlers.

That was Deputy Timothy Spigot. And suddenly I knew where I'd seen him before, aside from the video and the news article.

Bingham's eyes lit up. "He's one of them."

I lifted my gaze to fully meet his. "I didn't see his face in the parking lot. I meant what I said, I didn't see any of their faces."

Anger distorted his features, and it was clear that he was about to chew me out.

I placed a hand on the table and leaned closer. "If you lose your temper," I said in a no-nonsense tone, "Max will kick you out in a heartbeat, so I suggest you rein it in. Now."

His face reddened. "I'm gonna need you to cut the shit, *Ms. Moore*. Did you see this man outside your motel room or not?"

"For the last time, I'm telling you that I didn't see any of their faces." Then, before he could erupt, I said, "But I *heard* them."

Bingham went still and several long seconds passed before he finally said in a much calmer voice, "But you recognize the last man?"

I nodded, licking my bottom lip. Was this the right thing to do? Could I hold Bingham off for one more day so I could share my information with the state police?

But the cold hard truth was, I was unlikely to be alive tomorrow unless I appeased Todd Bingham, and the time for stringing him along was done.

I nodded. "I saw him the morning of the shooting. He was at the hospital in Greeneville. He was getting on the elevator on Hank's floor while I was getting off."

Bingham held up the phone again. "This man? You're certain?"

Tears stung my eyes. "Yes."

I knew the full weight of my admission, and it was heavy on my soul.

His grin was the thoroughly pleased look of an asshole who was used to getting everything he wanted. I'd seen it on my father's face more times than I could count. Bingham wasn't just pleased I'd caved—he was getting off on my tears too. He'd broken me, and my emotions were feeding his sick need to control everything and everyone.

That thought straightened my backbone. I was done kowtowing to men like my father. Men like Todd Bingham.

Grow a fucking spine, Carly Moore.

And in that moment, I let Caroline Blakely go. What was left of her was flung into the universe, and Charlene Moore took charge.

"I might have seen him in that elevator, but that's hardly proof of his involvement," I scoffed, leaning forward as I eyed him with disdain. There was no way I was letting him know about the videos. "He *is* a sheriff's deputy. He could have been there on official sheriff business."

Surprise filled his eyes as he took in my change in countenance. He shook his head. "He was off duty Tuesday morning."

"Just because he was off duty doesn't mean he was one of the murderers," I said.

He released a bitter laugh. "Spoken like an innocent."

"Turn him in," I said. "Let the law take care of him."

He laughed again, this time with more mirth. "Turn him in to the same snake pit he crawled out of? Are you insane?"

"So turn him over to the state police. Let them sort it out."

He shifted in his seat and stared at me with cold, ruthless eyes. "Do you have any idea what can of worms would be opened if I did that?" He snorted. "No. This is a Drum problem, and it needs to be taken care of in Drum." Tilting his head to the side, he studied me as if I were a conundrum he wasn't sure how to handle. "So you're claimin' you heard them but didn't see their faces?" He leaned forward until he was halfway across the table, his face only a couple of feet from mine. I could smell tobacco on his breath. "You're telling me that you didn't look out the window?" A grin cracked his lips. "You expect me to believe that? You seem like a curious kind of gal."

"The lighting in the parking lot sucks," I said, my pulse pounding in my head. "Their faces were covered in shadows. But I know their voices. Cecil was definitely one of them. I recognized his voice straightaway when he broke into Seth's room."

Bingham studied me for a moment. "So you're sayin' you'd recognize their voices if you heard them again?"

I didn't answer, but he seemed pleased as punch. He sent off a quick text, then laid his phone facedown on the table.

I sat back and crossed my legs, giving him a hard look of my own. "I have something you want, and you expect me to just hand it over after you set me up for Dwight Henderson's murder?"

He laughed. "I didn't set you up for Henderson's murder."

"Then why does Detective Daniels have a hard-on to link me to these murders?"

He flicked a gaze to the bar behind me, then landed on my face. "Why do *you* think?"

"Bart Drummond."

He grinned again, but it didn't reach his eyes. "Rumor has it he's working on a multi-million-dollar project to revive the town. A resort and spa."

"And two murders aren't good for potential business," I said, stating what I'd already guessed. "Better to pin it on the outsider, otherwise the town looks unsafe."

Maybe they were the ones who'd gotten ahold of my gun and keys too, through someone who'd been near the scene.

I only hoped that Max hadn't been involved in that.

He winked. "You sure you've only been in this town for a few days?"

I pushed out a breath, wondering if I was about to work out a deal with the devil. "I need help getting Bart Drummond off my back."

He let out a belly laugh. "Not my problem."

"It's your problem when I hold information you want."

He leaned forward again. "Tell you what. I'll help get the monkey off your back if you tell me the numbers written on Seth's hand."

From the way Bingham had acted earlier, I'd believed he already had them. "If you don't have the numbers, how'd you find out about them?"

"Henderson."

"He told you before you killed him."

He pressed his hands to his chest. "*I* didn't kill him, but I *did* interrogate 'im." He cast a lingering glance at his two men before turning back to me. "Wilson's got a taste for violence. He got carried away, and the man died before I could get everything I needed." He shrugged, yet the look in his eyes told me he wasn't happy with his lieutenant. But surely this was good news for me. If Dwight had been beaten to death, it had to be obvious that I wasn't the killer.

"Seth told me he had evidence, but he never said what," I confessed. "And while I *did* see something written on his hand, I was too busy freaking out and trying to save his life to pay attention." Then, hoping to convince him I didn't remember, I added, "But I intentionally looked for them when I took Hank to the funeral home, and someone had burned them off."

He scowled. "That was Henderson's doin'." He was lost in thought for a few seconds, then said, "Do you remember any of them?"

"There had to be eight or ten of them," I said. "I think it started with a 673, but I don't remember the rest." It was a huge risk lying to him, but there was no way I was telling him that code. That video was the only way to expose the corrupt sheriff's deputy. "I have no idea what they stand for. A bank account number maybe?"

A grin played on his lips. He knew what they stood for, and thankfully he seemed to accept my supposed ignorance.

The front door opened and a man walked in. He stopped at the entrance, scanning the room until his gaze landed on Bingham. He sauntered over but hesitated when he saw me.

It was the guy in the first photo Bingham had shown me.

"Have a seat, Thomas," Bingham said good-naturedly.

Thomas put his hand on the back of the chair to my left and kept it there for a moment, as if deciding whether he wanted to follow orders. Ultimately, he sat.

Bingham leaned forward and directed his attention to his man. "What's the latest word on the sheriff's investigation into Henderson?"

The guy scrubbed his face, his hand shaking slightly. "Uh... The detective in charge of Chalmers' murder was assigned to Henderson's case too."

It was him. He was the second guy. The triumphant look in Bingham's eyes when he saw my reaction was confirmation that he knew it too.

Thomas cast a quick glance at me. "He seems determined to pin it on her, but Sheriff Fletcher ain't buyin' it." He huddled in, lowering his voice. "Should we be talkin' about this in front of her?"

"Why not?" Bingham asked with a shrug. "She won't be in the position to tell anyone." An evil grin played on his lips.

Did that mean he planned on killing me after all?

Somehow—call it intuition—I suspected he didn't. He was playing Thomas like a fiddle and I was the bow.

"So who does the good sheriff like for Henderson's murder?" Bingham asked.

Thomas gestured to Bingham. "They think you beat 'im for information."

"Is that so?" Bingham asked with a knowing grin. "Looks like you're in the clear, Ms. Moore."

"Not necessarily," I countered. "They won't let it rest until they arrest someone, and *if* you're responsible, it's not like you'll be turning yourself in."

Bingham looked pleased I hadn't admitted that I knew he was responsible. What was he up to?

"And Chalmers' murder?" Bingham asked Thomas. "What's the word on that?"

"They can't find any evidence to pin it on her."

"The bullet casings at the scene?" Bingham asked.

"They weren't the same caliber of bullets that killed the boy." He leaned closer, looking worried.

"What aren't you telling me?" Bingham asked, his voice turning hard.

I was prepared for him to say they were from another gun—my gun—but he surprised me. "They were the same caliber that killed George Davis." He paused and licked his lip as though debating whether to continue. His back straightened and a resolve filled his eyes. "Fired from the same gun."

"Barb Chalmers' boyfriend?" I blurted out in shock.

"One and the same," Bingham said, and I could see the wheels in his head spinning as he tried to make this puzzle piece fit.

But I didn't need to take any time. "Deputy Spigot killed George Davis."

He'd killed George, although not because he was bashing downtown Drum. He'd killed him to keep him quiet. To cover up his own involvement in the drug enterprise.

Had someone picked up the casings at George Davis's murder scene and planted them at Seth's? Or did they have access to Deputy Spigot's gun? One of Bingham's men? Was it the person who'd taken my gun and key fob?

Thomas tried to sit still, but nervous energy rolled off him.

"Someone planted those casings," Bingham said. He pinned Thomas with a hard gaze. "Any idea who might have done that?"

A sheen of sweat broke out on Thomas's forehead. "Some of the casings were missing from the scene of Davis's murder. No one ever knew what happened to them."

The quirk of Bingham's brow suggested this wasn't new information. He was prodding Thomas to release it for my benefit…and likely to make his newly revealed traitor squirm.

It was working.

"I bet Spigot's shittin' his pants," Bingham said with a grin. He was loving every minute of this.

My horror grew, and it took everything in me to stay in my seat, knowing what Bingham had in store for the man next to me.

"Yeah," Thomas conceded.

Bingham nodded. "That'll be all."

Thomas got up and shot toward the front door.

"So?" Bingham asked with a satisfied grin. "Still worried about your imminent arrest?"

"That doesn't clear me," I said.

"But it seems highly unlikely a woman who had never been to Drum before would have the casings from the gun of a Hensen County sheriff's deputy." A frown crossed his face. "And as loath as I am to admit it, Bart Drummond didn't play a part in this." He tilted his head toward me. "He doesn't have Detective Daniels in his pocket." A grin spread across his face.

I felt like an idiot. "You do."

He'd used Daniels to pressure me to talk. And he'd pretended he was connected to Bart Drummond to make me feel helpless.

His grin spread and he looked ready to spring up from his seat. "Me, own a sheriff's deputy?" He laughed. "That, my dear, would be illegal." His smile faded, but he didn't look as intimidating as before. There was a hint of kindness in his gaze that caught me by surprise. "You have my word that you're safe from the sheriff's department."

"And you'll take care of the others?" I felt nauseated.

He snorted. "Thomas is already halfway out of the county."

"What?"

He leaned forward until our faces were about a foot apart. "Too many dead bodies poppin' up begins to look suspicious. I'll let him run. Spigot too. And trust me, they'll run."

"Why do I have trouble thinking you'll just let them go? Seems like you'd want to make an example of them."

He shrugged. "Sometimes you need to know when to cut your losses." His eyes took on an almost wistful look. "And sometimes you need to know when to bide your time."

He stood and extended his hand to me.

I slowly rose, not trusting him, but I took his hand anyway.

He had a firm grasp on my hand as he shook. "Ms. Moore. It's been a pleasure doin' business with you."

Then he winked as he released my hand and strode out the door, his two men hot on his heels.

Bingham had insinuated this was over, but how would he feel when I released Seth's videos to the state police? Because justice may have been served in his eyes, but I had to disagree.

Chapter
Twenty-Nine

I headed back to the bar, where Max and Ruth stood staring at me, but just before I made it, Wyatt burst through the back door like his pants were on fire. He bolted to me and grabbed my upper arms, scanning me up and down for signs of injury.

"I'm fine," I said as I jerked free. "Really Max?" I asked in a withering tone. "You called Wyatt?"

He didn't look apologetic. "I didn't know if we'd need backup."

"I handled it on my own. *I'm fine.*" I knew none of this was his fault, but I was still shaken up. It was time to come clean with some of what I knew. "Bingham knows who murdered Seth," I said, my adrenaline crashing. "Thomas—the guy who came in and left—was one of them. Cecil Purdy was another. Deputy Spigot pulled the trigger, and it looks like Dwight Henderson probably drove the getaway truck."

Max's eyes about bugged out of his head. "Bingham told you all of that?"

I nodded. "Yeah. I helped him puzzle it out."

I still felt sick over that.

"What about the bullet casings they found on the ground?" Max asked.

"They came from Deputy Spigot's gun. The one that killed George Davis."

"Barb's boyfriend?" Wyatt asked in surprise.

I nodded.

"Spigot was stupid enough to leave behind bullet casings tying him to Seth's murder?" Max asked in disgust.

I didn't correct him and tell him it was a different gun. I probably shouldn't have told them so much, but I was so sick of secrets and lies.

"What about Daniels?" Max asked. "He's still after you."

"Bingham said he'd take care of it."

"And how's that?" Wyatt asked skeptically.

I gave him a knowing look, and his lips pursed as understanding filled his eyes.

"So it's over?" Ruth asked.

"Yeah," I said, even though I still had to turn the videos over to the state police. "It's over."

We were silent for a long moment, all of us feeling the gravity of the situation.

"Carly," Max said in a tone that brooked no refusal. "Go home."

My mouth dropped open in my dismay. "You're firing me?"

"What?" he said. "No! I just think it would be better to go home and get some rest. Stay with Hank tomorrow, and I'll see you at the funeral. You can work tomorrow night."

I nodded and tears stung my eyes. "I'm sorry I was such a bitch about calling Wyatt. You were just looking out for me, and I bit your head off."

"Hey," Max said with a smile. "We're good. I know you're not really mad at me. You're just upset over all of it."

"Thank you, Max. For everything," I said as I gave him a hug.

"I meant what I said the other night," he whispered in my ear. "You're one of us. I hope you'll stick around." Then he gave me a tight smile and headed out to the tables to slap hands with his customers.

Ruth had hung back, watching us, but I reached for her and gave her a hug too. "Thank you."

"I would have fought the bastard if he'd tried to take you out of here," she said.

I laughed. "I know, and you have no idea how much I appreciate that."

"Don't forget the clothes I left you for the funeral, on top of the lockers."

I smiled, so grateful to have found these people. On top of that lookout, I'd mused to myself that lightning couldn't strike twice, but it had.

I headed to the back, but not before I noticed Jerry at a table in the corner, watching me with open interest. Ignoring him, I grabbed my things out of my locker. Wyatt was waiting in the hallway to the back door, a grave expression on his face.

"I would have thought you'd look happier now that we've identified the killers," I said as he ushered me out the door.

He was silent as he led me to his tow truck, opening the passenger door and shutting me in. When he got behind the wheel, he still didn't say anything.

"You're scaring me, Wyatt."

That shook him from his stupor. Turning to me, he grabbed my hand and cradled it between both of his. "I'm sorry. I never want you to be afraid of me."

"I'm not afraid of you," I said. "But it's obvious that something's wrong."

He stared into my eyes, clearly wrestling with something.

"Just tell me."

"Someone deleted the videos."

My mouth dropped open, and it took me a moment to speak. "But we were the only ones who knew how to get into the site."

"After I left you, I went to the shop and helped Junior with a car. Ginger told me that she and Hank were good, so I logged in to the website in my office to look at the other videos. I planned to see if Seth had anything else before I called my attorney, but they were gone."

"What about the one we downloaded to your cloud?"

He grimaced. "It's corrupt. I'm sorry."

I slowly shook my head, my eyes burning. "No."

"We need to figure out who else had access."

I continued shaking my head. Now Seth wouldn't get justice at all.

I'd failed him.

"Carly. Who could have done this?" he asked, snapping me out of my shock. If I'd had even a niggling suspicion that he might have done it himself, his tone would have convinced me otherwise. "Bingham?"

"No. Bingham didn't know the numbers. He knew *of* them from Dwight, but he didn't get the full code."

"Did you tell him the numbers?"

"No," I said, not taking offense. "I told him I didn't remember but I thought they started with a 673."

"You're sure he wasn't playin' you?"

"I watched him play Thomas, and while he's skilled at it, in this instance, I think we can clear him as a suspect."

"What about Max?" Wyatt asked.

My eyes widened. "You think Max would betray me?" When he didn't answer, some of my outrage deflated. "Your father."

"He has deputies on his payroll. He wouldn't want to risk that getting out."

"It couldn't be Max. He didn't even know about the numbers. The only people I discussed them with are Hank, Bingham, and you." I paused. "But Dwight Henderson had them. He burned them off Seth's hand."

"And he could have given them to anyone."

"But he was killed sometime between last night and noon today. Don't you think it's a big coincidence that whoever accessed Seth's page did it after we did? Why not earlier?"

Wyatt's body tensed. "You think they got the information from Max's computer?"

"I don't see how," I insisted. "I logged out of everything. I cleaned the history. There was no trace of any of it."

"An expert could have accessed it," Wyatt said. "Someone who knew what they were doin'. Does Max still leave his office unlocked?"

"Yeah," I said, "but it doesn't seem likely. How many people in this town have that kind of skill?" A new thought hit me. "Jerry."

His eyes went wide with surprise. "Jerry Nelson? You think he's a computer expert?" he asked in disbelief.

I'd never heard his last name before. "The guy who lives in Max's motel?"

"That's him. Jerry couldn't hurt a fly."

"That's what I had thought too, but I feel like he's been watching me. Since the shooting, he's always around. He's at the tavern while I'm working, and I saw him across the street when I left the library. Plus, Bingham knew I'd kissed you in the truck. What if Jerry has been following me for him?"

"That doesn't explain the numbers and the website," Wyatt said.

"What if Jerry's reporting to someone else?" I asked.

His lips pursed. "Jerry would be the last person on any suspect list for any crime, but I'm not going to dismiss this. I think we need to do more digging."

"Thanks."

"Who else?"

Movement in the side mirror caught my attention, and I caught sight of Bitty hurrying out the back door toward the street. A red pickup truck was parked on the side of the street, its headlights on and a white cloud billowing from the exhaust pipe. Bitty was leaning into the open window on the passenger side.

My heart skipped a beat. The truck had a long scratch on the back side panel. It was the getaway truck from Seth's murder.

A loud pop filled the air and Wyatt threw himself on top of me.

The squeal of tires filled my ears as I scrambled to push Wyatt off me. "That's the truck!"

"Stay down," he grunted, wrapping himself around me.

I strained against him and got free. "Wyatt. I'm fine!"

But the prostrate body on the sidewalk revealed that Bitty wasn't.

And the truck was long gone.

Chapter Thirty

I was thankful Detective Daniels hadn't been assigned to Bitty's murder, although I had to wonder why not. I wasn't an expert, but two murders within less than a hundred feet from one another in four days? Even I knew her murder was somehow related to Seth's. Not that I was sharing that information with the sheriff's deputies.

Wyatt and I gave our statements, and then Detective Marta White interviewed Tiny, Max, and Ruth to see if Bitty had any enemies.

"She wasn't the friendliest woman in the world," Tiny admitted. "But she didn't have anyone who hated her enough to kill her."

The detective nodded. "She havin' any money trouble?"

Tiny released a scoff. "Who doesn't around these parts?"

Max closed the tavern early, and we all sat around a table waiting for Detective White to give us permission to go home.

"Who do you think did it?" Ruth asked Max and Tiny.

Max shook his head and took a long pull of his whiskey. "Haven't got a clue."

But I was starting to come up with my own conclusion. One I wasn't comfortable sharing with anyone except Wyatt.

We left an hour later, and I didn't waste any time telling Wyatt my theory as soon as he started driving me toward Hank's.

"What if it was Bitty?" I asked. "What if she got the website and login info?"

"How would Bitty get that?" he asked in disbelief. "I doubt she knew much about usin' a computer let alone how to find a deleted history."

"What if she didn't need the history? She brought me lunch in Max's office. I'm pretty sure I was on the video cam website, Wyatt."

He inhaled sharply. "But she'd still need the username."

"You told me the email address out loud. She could have heard it. I said the numbers out loud too." How could I have been so careless?

"And she gave the information to one of the murderers," he said. "Maybe she thought she was meetin' him to get her reward, but instead of money, she got a bullet to her head."

Sadly, I suspected he was right.

"Shit." He shot me a glance. "Someone's tyin' up loose ends."

My stomach dropped.

He hit the brakes and pulled to the side of the road, making a screeching U-turn before heading back to Drum.

"What are you doing?" I asked, starting to panic.

"Gettin' you the hell out of this town." He hit the gas and started to speed.

"Wyatt, slow down. We can't risk getting pulled over."

"I'm not slowing down until we're out of this county," he said, his hands tight on the steering wheel.

But he did adjust his speed as we passed through Drum. I cast a glance at the motel as we slowly pulled past it. The crime scene tape was gone, and so was the old station wagon.

"Who owns that old station wagon that's always there?" I asked, my voice tight. "I've never seen it gone."

"It's Jerry's."

"Where's Jerry?" I asked in a panic. "What if someone kills him next?"

"We can't worry about Jerry right now," Wyatt said, reaching over and snagging my hand. "You are my main concern. Once I know you're safe, I'll find him."

"What about Hank? Who's going to take care of him tonight?"

"He's fine on his own. After Max called and said Bingham had you cornered, he practically kicked me out the door with his remaining foot." He gave me a reassuring smile. "Hank will be fine. That man knows how to take care of himself."

We'd made it through to the other side of Drum, and Wyatt increased his speed but kept to the speed limit on the winding road. As we approached the turnoff to Ewing, red flashing lights appeared behind us.

I turned in my seat, trying to see into the windshield of the pursuing car, but the glare of the headlights made it impossible. "What are you going to do?"

"I'm not speeding," Wyatt said. "They have no reason to pull me over."

My stomach churned. "So you're not pulling over?"

"No."

Wyatt was a convicted felon. What kind of trouble could he get into if he didn't obey an officer of the law?

I started to cry.

He grabbed my hand and squeezed. "Don't worry. I'm gonna make sure you're safe."

"I'm more worried about *you*."

He shot me a grin. "I knew you liked me," he said, repeating what I'd told him when I was saving him from the truck.

"Wyatt."

He eyed the rearview mirror.

Desperate for a solution that wouldn't end in his arrest, I said, "If we pull over and Deputy Spigot gets out of the car, we'll take off before he reaches your door. Or we can call ahead somewhere and tell them we're worried for our safety. That way we can prove we had just cause to not pull over."

He frowned but gave it a couple of seconds of consideration. Moments later, he made a hard right onto the county road toward Ewing and picked up his radio. It shocked the hell out of me when I heard him say, "Drummond Ranch. Do you copy?"

"You're calling your father?"

He cast a glance at the sheriff car that was still trailing us. "Other than Bingham, he's the only one powerful enough to help us, and I'd rather not be askin' any favors from Bingham."

"The devil you know," I said, my heart sinking. This was all my fault.

"Drummond Ranch," Wyatt said, more insistently. "This is Wyatt Drummond needing emergency assistance. Copy?"

"Wyatt?" Carson's voice crackled over the radio. "Where are you?"

"On Highway 25, heading toward Ewing. I have a deputy with lights following us, and I don't think it's legit. I have Carly with me, and I suspect Seth Chalmers' murderers are tyin' up loose ends."

"I'm coming back from Ewing," Carson said, "I have a few men with me. Pull into the parking lot for Balder Mountain

Trailhead, and I'll meet you there in five minutes with reinforcements."

"Roger," Wyatt said, but he didn't look reassured.

"Do you trust him?"

"While there's no love lost between me and my father, my mother is a different story." He cast me a quick glance. "She's why I came back. She's sick. Cancer."

A lump formed in my throat. "Wyatt. I'm sorry."

He gave a quick shake of his head. "I'm only tellin' you because Carson has a soft spot for her. He won't let anything happen to me. It would kill her if something happened to me."

"Then we'll do as he says and meet him there."

He nodded. "Okay."

The sheriff's car still followed us, but it wasn't gaining on us. The driver didn't seem too worried about the possibility of losing us.

"What if the sheriff car's legit?" I asked.

"I don't see how," Wyatt said. "I didn't do anything wrong." He made the turnoff for the trailhead, then pulled into the lot and parked the truck sideways in front of the trail. "Come on," he said, unfastening his seatbelt while I did the same. "We're sittin' ducks here. We'll hide in the trees until Carson shows up."

I fumbled with the door handle, then practically fell out, remembering to grab my purse at the last minute. Wyatt took my hand and pulled me into the darkness. The path was smooth at the entrance, but less than ten feet in, my boot hit a stone and I nearly face-planted. Wyatt caught me just before I hit, but my ankle screamed with pain.

The sheriff car pulled to a halt, and a few seconds later a man called out, "Wyatt! It's Marco! Max's friend!"

Wyatt froze as though weighing his options. He positioned us behind a tree, pressing my belly into the trunk while his body completely covered mine from behind.

"Why were you tryin' to pull me over?" he yelled back.

"Detective White is worried about Carly. She thinks someone is going to try to kill her. I'm supposed to bring her to the sheriff's station until the state troopers arrive."

"Why is she involving the state troopers?" Wyatt shouted back.

"Because we've tied Deputy Spigot to Seth Chalmers' murder with the bullet casings found in the parking lot. She thinks the department needs outside supervision."

Wyatt was silent for a moment. "This is your call," he whispered.

"You believe him?"

He pushed out a heavy sigh. "I don't trust anyone as far as you're concerned."

"What if we ask him to escort us to the nearest state troopers' headquarters?" I glanced over my shoulder at him. "He could have tried to run us off the road, but he didn't. He kept his distance."

"But that doesn't explain why he didn't call me on the radio. Everyone in town knows my call sign."

He had a point.

Wyatt spun me around so that I was facing him, pressing my back to the tree.

"I'm not sure the best way to handle this," he admitted. "I just know I can't let anyone hurt you."

"Wyatt…" My voice broke.

"I've been waiting my entire life for someone like you, Charlene Moore," he said with a chuckle, but his voice broke, and it wasn't lost on me that he'd used my alias. "I don't want to risk losin' you now." He paused for a moment. "If you still want to leave when this nightmare is over—and if you're open to it—I'll go with you. We'll find a way to take down your father so you'll be safe."

His mouth lowered to mine as his hand skimmed my neck. Tears streamed down my cheeks, and I kissed him back with everything I had.

"Let's go with my plan," I said, pulling away slightly. "Do you know where the nearest state trooper headquarters is?"

"Knoxville. That's two hours away."

"Then we better get movin'," I said with a forced smile.

He let that settle for a second, then called out, "Okay. We're comin' out, Marco, but we're going to the Highway Patrol headquarters in Knoxville ourselves."

"That's fine," Marco called out. "But I still plan on givin' you an escort to keep Carly safe."

Wyatt took my hand and led me back to the path. My ankle still hurt, and I limped slightly, but at least I could put weight on it. We'd just started down the path when I heard a truck engine approaching.

"That's bound to be Carson," Wyatt said as we continued heading out. "I'll let him know the plan."

But just as we reached the opening of the trailhead, two gunshots rang out, and Wyatt hauled me back into the trees.

Chapter
Thirty-One

Wyatt ran deeper into the woods, but the tree canopy was so thick I struggled to see the path. My burner phone didn't have a flashlight, but I wouldn't have risked using one anyway. The path was littered with rocks of various sizes, which tumbled as we climbed, revealing our position.

"You're safe now, Carly," Carson called out. "You can come on out."

Beams of light speared the darkness, so I pulled Wyatt off the path into the trees. We crouched in front of a small opening in the leaves that gave us a bird's-eye view of the parking lot.

At the trailhead, Wyatt's tow truck had obscured our view of the deputy's SUV, but I could now see it parked at the back end of the tow truck. Ten feet to the side of the sheriff's vehicle was the beat-up old pickup truck that I'd now seen at two murders.

"Carson was the driver, not Dwight," I whispered. "Carson killed Bitty. That's the truck."

"You're certain?" When I shot him a dirty look, he lifted a hand. "Sorry. I had to ask."

Carson stood next to the tow truck and was looking inside the window. A rifle hung from his right hand.

"We're in deep shit, aren't we?" I whispered.

"We're definitely at a disadvantage without a gun," he conceded.

"I have one." I opened my purse and pulled it out. "But there are only four bullets." Foolishly, I'd left the box of ammunition at Hank's.

Wyatt frowned as he reached for it.

"Are you allowed to hold a gun?" I asked. "Isn't it against the law for you because of your felony?"

He took the gun from me and checked the clip. "I'll do whatever is needed to keep you safe, but in this case, *you're* keepin' the gun. I'm going to lead him deeper into the woods, and you're going to hide in the trees until he passes you. Once he's out of sight, run to the truck and go get help." He handed the gun back to me, and I tucked it in the waistband of my jeans at my back.

I clutched his arm. "I'm not leaving you here, Wyatt."

"It's *you* he wants, not me. I'll be fine."

I didn't buy that for a second. "Wyatt."

"Look, Carly. You're not used to hiking, and you're definitely not wearing the right footwear." He glanced down at my ankle boots. "Carson's an experienced hiker, and if we try to run together, he *will* catch up with us. This is the best plan. Take the gun and the tow truck and head back to Drum. Go to Max. He'll help."

I could see the wisdom of his plan, but it seemed like the chickenshit way to go. Even though I didn't stand much of a chance of protecting him against a murderer, it felt like I'd be relinquishing all control of the situation if I just left.

"Carly," he begged in a whisper. "*Please.* I'll be okay. I know this trail like the back of my hand."

"Okay," I said, mostly because I knew I would slow him down and this way he might have a chance. "I'll go to Max."

He gave me a soft kiss.

"Promise me you'll be careful," I said. "Because I need you too."

He grinned against my lips. "Nothin's keepin' me from you, Carly Moore. Now do what we discussed, okay? Take off and get Max."

He pressed the keys into my hand and headed toward the trail.

"What happened to the deputy?" Wyatt shouted down to Carson once he was back on the path and heading up the incline.

Carson was squatted next to the tow truck, looking underneath, but at the sound of Wyatt's voice, he stood and turned to face the trail entrance. "You were right about the police being crooked. I got some information that he intended to hurt Carly," Carson said as he started for the trail, his rifle now slung over his shoulder. "I had to protect her."

"I'm sure Max will appreciate it," Wyatt called out as he climbed the rocky trail, making a lot more noise than he had before. "He and Tiny have grown quite attached to her."

"Seems like both Drummond boys have."

Wyatt was right about Carson being experienced. He was advancing up the trail at a much faster pace than I had with Wyatt.

"Why don't you come on down?" Carson said good-naturedly. "You've got nothing to be worried about now."

"Seems like a good night for stargazing," Wyatt called down. "I used to bring girls up here all the time when I was growin' up. Hate to be rude, Carson, but you're killing the mood."

Carson laughed. He was about to pass my position on the trail, and I realized why Wyatt was keeping him talking—we would both know Carson's location, and Carson wouldn't think we were purposefully hiding.

"I have to say that I've never brought a woman up here," Carson said. "Maybe you could show me the best spot."

They were silent for several seconds, but I could hear Carson's footsteps on the rocky part of the trail. Which meant he'd be able to hear me too.

They were both moving at a fast clip, and Wyatt had a good lead. Still, Wyatt wouldn't have any way of defending himself if Carson caught up with him. He didn't have a gun.

"There's a good spot up here," Wyatt shouted. "You can check it out, but Carly and I will have to find another one."

"That's not very hospitable," Carson said, and I realized he was about twenty feet above me.

Time to move.

My heart was pounding with fear, equal parts for me and for Wyatt. I didn't feel right about leaving him, but I told myself it was the best way to get him help.

Holding on to the trees, I descended down the side of the trail, trying to keep the sound to a minimum.

"Have you got a girlfriend, Carson?" Wyatt asked, his voice echoing. He was starting to sound winded. He must be in a clearing, which meant he wouldn't have much cover. "In all these years, I've known you to have dated only a handful of women."

I had been descending at a slow pace, but once I hit a dirt path, I fled at a faster clip. My eyes had adjusted to the dim light, so I could better see the terrain.

"Why isn't Carly joinin' this chat?" Carson asked, his words coming in pants. "Seems a bit rude of us not to include her."

"Well, now," Wyatt said in a drawl. "Carly's more of an indoors kind of girl and she's not used to hikin', so she's conservin' her breath."

"Still," Carson said, his voice faint. "I'd just as soon hear from her."

I hurried now, because Carson had clearly figured out our plan. Hopefully he thought I'd stayed hidden in the trees.

It took me several more minutes to make it to the trail entrance, but once I did, I realized what Carson had been up to while he was squatting next to the truck. The tires on the passenger side were completely flat. There was no way I was driving anywhere.

Hurrying around the front of the truck, I found Marco lying on the asphalt parking lot, completely still.

"Marco!" I whisper-shouted as I dropped down next to him.

He released a low groan and I nearly cried with relief. His left thigh was bloody, and he was bleeding from the abdomen.

"I need to call for help," I whispered. "How do I use the radio in your car?"

"Button..." he said, then released a loud cry of pain.

"Shh!" I whispered, feeling like a first-class bitch, but I suspected Carson was on his way down, and if he thought Marco was still alive, he wouldn't hesitate to put another bullet in him.

Dashing for the driver's door of the sheriff vehicle, I formulated a new plan. I'd get Marco into his SUV, then take him to the sheriff station in Ewing. Surely there were *some* good deputies in the county.

But as soon as I got into the driver's seat, I realized my plan wasn't going to work. The keys weren't in the ignition, and the radio's mic cord had been cut.

I ran to Carson's truck, and I wasn't surprised when I found it locked. I had no doubt Carson had taken both sets of keys.

We were in big trouble.

The county road was fairly close, but we were miles from either town, and I hadn't seen any other traffic when Wyatt and I had driven out of Drum.

Tears burned my eyes, but I stood up and forced myself to square my shoulders. Charlene Moore wasn't going down without a fight.

I hurried back to Marco and squatted next to him, feeling terrible that I hadn't bothered to assess his wounds.

"Did you call for help?" he whispered.

"He cut the radio mic," I said. "Do you have the keys? They aren't in the ignition."

His head barely moved with a shake. "Left… them…in…"

"I know this is against the rules, but can I borrow your gun? I only have four bullets and I'm not the best shot when stressed." I vowed to book some time at the firing range first chance I got.

"He…took…"

"He took it." Tears filled my eyes again. Things kept going from bad to worse.

"Carly!" Carson called out from the trail, and I knew he was close.

"I'm going to move you, Marco," I said. "I'm scared he's going to shoot you again, so I want to put you in the backseat of your car. It's not perfect, but…"

"No. Go hide," he whispered.

I would, but not yet. Marco wouldn't have gotten shot if he hadn't tried to help me. I wasn't leaving him here as a sitting duck.

"This might hurt." Grabbing his legs at his ankles, I started dragging him across the pavement.

He released a loud groan. Not only was I possibly making things worse, I'd just pointed a big neon sign at him that said, *Marco's still alive*. Still, I'd started this and couldn't stop now.

I opened the back door of Marco's SUV. Slipping my arms under his armpits, I hauled him to the door and propped him up against the back tire, not an easy feat considering he probably weighed nearly twice what I did. I was trying to figure out how I was going to get him up to the backseat when I heard Carson say, "Carly, come on now. No need to hide from me."

He hadn't reached the entrance to the trail, but he was close.

"Do you have any other weapons?" I whispered.

"In…the back. But it's locked."

Carson had the keys.

"I've only got four bullets, Marco." My voice broke.

He looked up at me and a smile tugged at his lips. "I guess you'd better make 'em count."

I nodded and then crept to the front of the SUV and peered around the edge. Carson was standing at the entrance to the trail, his gaze scanning the area. His rifle was slung over his shoulder.

"Max sent me to fetch you, girl," he said as he strode toward the tow truck. "Come on out. Let's talk."

I knew better than to take his bait. He wanted me to tell him where I was so he could shoot me.

How did I get us out of this?

Carson was waiting for an opening to kill me. I knew I could do the same to him. I could save myself, Marco, and Wyatt, who was still somewhere up the mountain and likely to put himself in danger to keep me safe. But I couldn't bring myself to kill Carson in cold blood—then I wouldn't be any better than him and the men who'd killed Seth. Yet I couldn't figure out any other way to end this.

"Carson!" Wyatt shouted from somewhere up the trail. "Let her go!"

Carson spun around to face him.

"Take the shot," Marco said.

"I can't," I whispered. But Wyatt was unarmed, and Carson had a rifle. Could I afford *not* to? Wouldn't that be akin to letting him kill Wyatt?

I pulled the gun out from my waistband and stood up. "Carson. It's me you want. I need your word you'll let everyone else go."

"Carly, no!" Wyatt shouted from up the trail.

Carson tugged the rifle off his shoulder and aimed it into the trees.

"No!" I shouted, pointing my handgun at Carson. "It's me you want. Leave him alone!"

"I can take care of you both," he said, and a shot went off, the boom echoing around us.

I squeezed the trigger, aiming for Carson, but he remained standing. I could only hope his shot had missed too.

"Carly!" Wyatt shouted, sounding panicked.

Carson spun around and pointed his rifle at me, then fired off two shots, but I'd ducked behind the SUV as soon as I saw him turning.

"That's five," Marco said with a grimace.

"What?" I asked, shaking my head. I slid toward Marco at the back of the SUV.

"He has ten shots. He's used five." When I gave him a blank look, he said, "I know his gun. The cartridge holds ten rounds."

"If it was a new one," I said. And I only had three shots left. I couldn't waste another.

Peering around the back of the car, I spotted Carson standing halfway between the tow truck and the woods, seemingly torn about which direction to take.

"Where'd you get the gun, Carly?" he said into the air.

"Don't answer," Marco whispered. "Try again."

"I can't kill him in cold blood, Marco," I whispered back.

"It's not cold blood when he's actively tryin' to shoot you first," he said.

He was right. If he had the chance, he'd kill all three of us. I couldn't let that happen. I had to make the remaining three shots count.

Leaning around the back of the deputy's SUV, I lifted my gun to aim at Carson, but he was gone.

Panic gripped me and I held my handgun up to my chest, the muzzle pointed away from me and up to the sky. I needed to be prepared to shoot, but I had to be sure Wyatt wasn't in the line of fire.

"Shit," Marco muttered under his breath, and I turned to see Carson walking around the front of the tow truck, grinning as he strode toward us, his rifle butt tucked under his armpit, the barrel aimed at Marco. I realized I was concealed in shadow and Marco was easy pickings. Without hesitation, I lifted my gun and pointed it at Carson's chest and pulled the trigger.

Carson grunted, then released a chuckle. "I didn't think you had it in you, Carly."

How could he still be talking and advancing toward us? He'd sounded like he was in pain, but he was still moving.

Marco was stretching his hand toward me in desperation, and I knew he wanted the gun. There was no denying he was a better shot, but there wasn't time.

"I'll go with you," I called out. "Unlock your truck and I'll go with you."

"I don't want to take you with me," Carson said, his voice tight. "I want you *dead*."

"Leave her alone, Carson," someone said from behind me. My brain recognized the voice and struggled to understand how its owner had gotten here—until I adjusted my position slightly and caught sight of the station wagon parked at the opening of the parking lot.

"Leave her alone, Carson," Jerry repeated in a trembling voice, holding up a handgun with a hand as shaky as mine felt. He stood at the end of Carson's pickup, and he looked out of breath.

Carson released a short laugh and turned his attention to Jerry. "What are you doin' here, old man? Go home."

"You leave her alone. Carly's a nice girl," Jerry said.

"Don't make me sorry I didn't finish beatin' your ass last year," Carson sneered, aiming his gun at Jerry. "You worthless piece of shit."

Anger erupted in my chest, and I stood, pointing the gun at Carson's chest. "Don't you call him that!"

Carson swung his attention to me, grinning like a fool. "There you are."

He slowly lifted his gun and Jerry pulled his trigger, the shot reverberating in the cold night air. Carson remained standing, unfazed. "When was the last time you went to the firing range, old man?"

Jerry's next round whizzed past its mark too, and Carson whipped back to shoot him.

I pulled my trigger, this time hitting Carson in the arm.

Crying out, he wheeled back to face me, and I fired another shot, hitting him dead center in his chest again.

I was out of bullets, but I'd just made a direct hit. Surely this was over.

But Carson hunched over, as though catching his breath, then stood, his face contorted in pain.

"Bulletproof vest," Marco muttered.

Dammit. I'd just wasted three of my four shots, and even though his left arm was bleeding, I doubted it was going to stop him from killing us all.

"Leave her alone!" Jerry shouted, moving closer. "I'm not gonna let you hurt anyone else!"

"I think I've heard enough," Carson said with a grunt. He was spinning around to make a run for Jerry, when something flew out of the air and struck Carson in the side of the head. Both the object and Carson fell to the pavement, and I realized it was a baseball-sized rock.

Wyatt burst out from around the front of the tow truck and sprinted for Carson, who lay moaning on his side. Wyatt picked up the rifle, tugging it from Carson's loose grasp, and pointed it at the dazed man. "You're not goin' anywhere."

Jerry closed in, pointing his gun at Carson's face, his hand shaking so badly I wasn't sure if he'd hit his target even at the four-foot range. "You're gonna pay for what you did. You're gonna pay for bringin' that poison to Drum. You're the one who killed that boy and his mother. You didn't pull the trigger, but you're still responsible. Just like you killed George when he said he was gonna turn you in."

Sirens wailed in the distance and Carson pushed to a sitting position, blood running down the side of his head.

"Don't do it, Jerry," Wyatt said. "You think this is what you want, but it'll eat you up inside. Let the justice system do its job."

Carson released a laugh. "You think I'll stay in jail? I work for Bart Drummond."

"Who will turn on you in a heartbeat," Wyatt said with a sneer. "You're about to bring disgrace to the Drummond name, and he will cut you off with a chainsaw. Didn't you learn anything after what he did to me?"

The sirens were closer, and Wyatt was still holding Carson's gun, so I walked over and reached for it, tugging slightly. Wyatt glanced at me, his eyes intense with fear and anger, but he must have known what I was doing because he released his grasp, letting me take the weapon. We both knew we couldn't risk him getting in trouble for holding a gun, even if it was to protect all of us. Marco would back me up and confirm that it belonged to Carson.

Flashing lights appeared at the entrance to the parking lot and three sheriff cars pulled in.

"It's over, Carson," Wyatt announced with barely restrained rage. "And you're about to go away for a very long time."

"We'll see about that."

Carson launched forward, tackling Jerry to the ground, and wrestled for his gun.

I tried to point the rifle at Carson's head, but they were rolling around too much for me to get a clear shot.

The sheriff SUVs came to a screeching halt, and deputies poured out of the vehicles, surrounding us.

"Freeze! Everyone put your hands up!" a deputy shouted.

I dropped the gun and threw my hands up, but Carson and Jerry were still tangled up and thrashing around.

A gunshot went off in their heap and both men went still.

"Jerry!" I cried out.

The deputies rushed at the two men and rolled Carson onto his back. The handgun clattered to the pavement. The blank look in Carson's eyes, along with the bloody hole under his chin, made it clear he was dead.

Beside me, Wyatt still had his hands raised high, but as I turned my gaze on him, he lowered his arms and scooped me into his embrace, holding me so tightly I could barely breathe.

"Whoa! Whoa!" Marco shouted at the deputies who had trained their guns at us. "Don't shoot! They're with me!"

Wyatt tilted my head back and looked deep into my eyes. "I thought he was gonna shoot you. I thought I was gonna lose you before we could even see where this thing between us might go."

"I'm fine. You're fine," I said with a soft smile. "We'll be okay."

He nodded, his jaw tight, like he couldn't quite believe it was true.

"I think we both deserve a little happiness, don't you?" I whispered with tears in my eyes. "I'd like to find my happiness with you."

His eyes turned glassy and he nodded. "I want to find it with you too."

Chapter Thirty-Two

The sun shone brightly for Seth's graveside service, warming the nearly two hundred people who had come to pay their respects.

Thankfully Hank and Wyatt had mended fences between them, as Hank really needed friends right now. And not just for moral support. He'd insisted on standing for the short service, so Wyatt and I stood at his sides, helping him to stay upright.

Wyatt made his way to the front and said a few words about Seth. How hardworking and driven he'd been. How loyal he was to friends and family. How he'd wanted to go to college to become a lawyer, not because he wanted to leave Drum, but because he wanted to return to his home and fight for justice. How Seth had inspired everyone around him to become a better person. Wyatt included.

"Seth Chalmers' life was cut way too short," Wyatt finished, his voice tight. "But his memory will live on."

The minister said a prayer, and then Hank picked up a pile of dirt and threw it on the casket in the grave. Wyatt and I did the same. We stood beside Hank as the townspeople offered their condolences.

Hank made it through about fifty people before his endurance gave out, and then Wyatt helped him into his wheelchair.

After we got Hank settled, we gave Hank some space and stepped several feet to his right. Wyatt wrapped an arm around my back and tugged me tightly to him.

I glanced up at him and smiled. My chest warmed when he smiled back.

Max, Ruth, and Tiny came through the line together, telling Hank how sorry they were for his loss. He told them he'd heard about Bitty and offered them the same.

When they reached us, Max stared at his brother for several long seconds before he turned to me. "Now that the danger's over, I'm hopin' you'll stay. Drum's not usually this excitin'."

I smiled. "I was going to wait until tonight to tell you all, but yes. I'm staying."

Ruth beamed and Tiny looked happy enough to burst. Seeing their reaction reassured me that I'd made the right decision. I'd lived most of my life alone, and now that I'd gotten another taste of real friendship, I wasn't so willing to walk away. I needed people to care about—and people to care about me. Living with Rose had taught me that, and while I'd left Arkansas hoping I could return, I realized this was where I belonged—among people who had my back. And in a town lost in time, with only five security cameras. A feature Wyatt had been quick to point out.

"No CCTV," he'd said. "No facial recognition software. Drum, Tennessee, is the last place your father would look for you, and he won't find you if you're completely off the grid."

I'd already decided to stay, but that was like the cherry on top.

Max gave me a hug. "I'm glad you're stayin'. After Carson…"

The investigation was ongoing, but the general consensus with the sheriff department was that Carson had gotten tired of taking orders from Bart Drummond. He'd been the mastermind behind the new drug trade to Drum, bringing the more deadly drugs from Atlanta, even arranging for Dwight's job at the mortuary. He'd hoped to run Bart into bankruptcy, and eventually kill Bingham and take over his territory. I had been cleared of any wrongdoing.

It sounded like a great theory, but part of me couldn't help wondering if Bart knew more than he'd let on.

I told Detective White about Seth's video account and gave her the login information. She told me that she'd turn it over to the state troopers, but she suspected there wasn't anything they could do to recall the deleted footage. Wyatt had sent her the corrupted video file we'd saved, and she said her team would try to recover it, but they weren't hopeful.

"But I'm not lettin' this go," she'd said. "I know there's more corruption in this department, and I plan to root it out."

I suspected she'd have to dig deep.

But now, Max was taking ownership of Carson's wrongdoing, *again*, and I wasn't going to let that stand. "It's not your fault," I assured him, for what was likely the tenth time. "You had no way of knowing." I kissed his cheek. "I'm so grateful for you, Max. Please don't let this get between us."

He kissed me back, his kiss lingering on my cheek for several seconds. When he pulled back, he gave Wyatt a long look and stepped back.

Jerry was hovering behind them, his eyes darting everywhere. He was uncomfortable, and I knew part of the reason he'd come with Max and the others was to see me.

Jerry had admitted to witnessing the murder. He'd recognized Deputy Spigot and had hidden in his room in terror until after I'd gone into the tavern with Max. Then he'd snuck out and planted the bullet casings he'd picked up at George's murder scene, dropping them by the street to implicate Deputy Spigot. Out of guilt, he walked over to Seth to apologize to his body, only to discover my gun and key fob. Worried the sheriff's department would try to pin the murder on me, he'd taken and hidden them, too ashamed to tell me he had them. He'd felt guilty for having watched me as I tried to save Seth, having been too afraid to do the same, though he made it clear he'd taken my gun and key fob in hopes of somehow protecting me from Bingham as well as Spigot and his accomplices.

"Hey, Jerry," I said with a warm smile. I walked toward him and gave him a hug. He was stiff, but he loosened a tiny bit before I released him. "I'll never be able to thank you for saving me."

He wouldn't meet my gaze. "I didn't save you. I was a coward."

"That's not true," I insisted. "You kept Carson from pulling that trigger. If you hadn't shown up, I'd be dead right now. And Marco too."

"They said he's gonna make a full recovery," he whispered.

"That's what I heard too."

"It was teamwork," Wyatt said, sidling up behind me. He placed a hand on my shoulder and squeezed. "Carly kept him from shooting me. You kept Carson from shooting her."

"And Wyatt kept Carson from shooting you," I said. "He's right. Teamwork. We couldn't have done it without you."

His chin slowly rose until his fearful blue eyes met mine. Confronting Carson had helped him to regain some of his pride and confidence, but it would take some time for him to recapture the rest. His guilt wasn't helping. I vowed to help him assuage it, even if it took years.

The group said their goodbyes, then headed to Ruth's car.

I glanced up at Wyatt, but he was staring after his brother with a sad look in his eyes.

"You okay?" I asked softly. I knew he and Max had been close when they were kids. Maybe they could find their way to each other again.

He glanced down at me and his hand squeezed my hip. "Better than okay."

But the contentment in his eyes shuttered as he shifted his attention to something to my side.

An older man and woman were speaking to Hank, but the older gentleman's eyes were on Wyatt.

Wyatt's back stiffened.

The older man had an arrogant air, with a sharpness in his eyes that let me know nothing got by him. His head full of white hair might have given him the appearance of an elderly man if it were not for the fact that he was in great physical shape, with broad shoulders and a trim waist, flaunted by the cut of his expensive suit. I didn't need an introduction to know who he and the woman with him were. Bart and Emily Drummond.

The couple moved toward us, and Wyatt reached out and pulled his mother into a hug. Bart and Wyatt might have been estranged, but Wyatt and his mother weren't. She had kind blue eyes but also the weary look of a woman used to getting beaten down. I suspected Emily's cancer diagnosis wasn't the only thing keeping Wyatt in Drum. It was his overall concern for her.

"You must be Carly," she said in a soft lilt. "I'm Emily Drummond."

"It's so nice to meet you, ma'am." I took her offered hand and shook it, careful not to squeeze too tightly. She looked like she could easily break.

"Carly," she continued, "this is Bart, Wyatt's father."

I turned to face him with a cooler reception. He took my hand and shook with a firm grasp, and I got the message—I'm much stronger than you, and I can and will crush you.

I refrained from offering a greeting. Anything I said would be a lie.

"So you're the woman who seems to have captured my son's heart and attention," he said in an icy tone.

Wyatt's arm dropped from my back. He stepped toward his father, just inches in front of me, but it was enough to get his message across. There was a whole lot of body language going on.

"Terrible business about my man Carson," Bart said, pressing his lips together and shaking his head. "Terrible business. We've offered the sheriff's department our full cooperation to suss this out, but I can assure you that Drummond Properties had nothin' to do with this messy business. In fact, I plan on offerin' money to Hank and all the other families affected by Carson's actions."

Wyatt's eyes narrowed, and he leaned closer to his father, lowering his voice. "You're tellin' me you had no idea what your right-hand man was doin' in your town?"

A muscle in the corner of Bart's left eye began to twitch. "That's right."

Wyatt smiled, but it didn't reach his eyes. "You must really be slippin', old man."

"Wyatt," his mother admonished quietly.

Wyatt's gaze softened as he glanced in her direction, but his eyes were hard as iron when he addressed his father. "I don't buy it for a second, and neither do the state troopers. So I'd lay low if I were you."

"Layin' low has never been my strong suit," Bart said, smoothing his silk tie.

"Then I can only hope it will be your downfall," Wyatt said.

Bart gave him one last look, then marched off toward the cars, leaving Emily to follow.

I wrapped my hand around Wyatt's arm as we watched them walk away.

"You sure you want to stay here?" I asked.

He lowered his gaze, searching my face. "You changed your mind?"

"He won't make it easy for us."

"Live and let live, Carly," he said.

I didn't believe him for a second. "We'll take care of your father first," I said quietly. "Then we'll take care of mine."

He stared deep into my eyes. "Deal."

I stole a glance at Bart Drummond, who stood at the crest of the hill, looking down at us.

A grin twisted his lips as our eyes locked, and in that moment, I wondered if I should have left town after all.

But it was a fleeting thought, quickly dismissed. Bart Drummond was a formidable man, but I was done backing down from powerful men.

I was just getting started.

***

Her Scream in the Silence